Stephen McCranie's

SPACE BOY

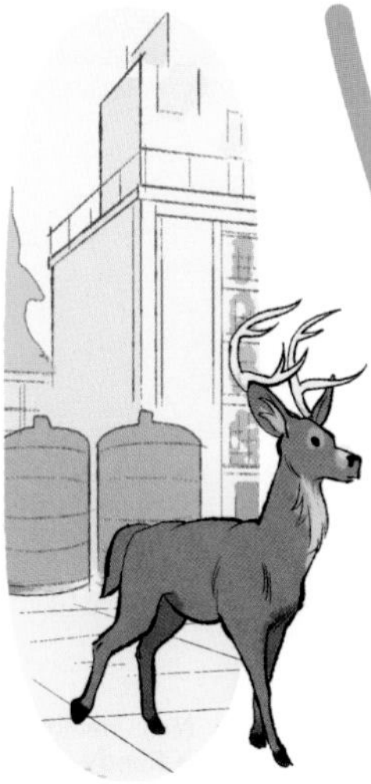

VOLUME 5

Written and illustrated by
STEPHEN McCRANIE

DARK HORSE BOOKS

President and Publisher **Mike Richardson**
Editor **Shantel LaRocque**
Assistant Editor **Brett Israel**
Designer **Anita Magaña**
Digital Art Technician **Allyson Haller**

STEPHEN McCRANIE'S SPACE BOY VOLUME 5

This book collects *Space Boy* episodes 61–75, previously published online at WebToons.com.

Published by Dark Horse Books
A division of Dark Horse Comics LLC
10956 SE Main Street | Milwaukie, OR 97222
StephenMcCranie.com | DarkHorse.com

To find a comics shop in your area,
visit comicshoplocator.com

First edition: October 2019
ISBN 978-1-50671-399-1
10 9 8 7 6 5 4 3 2 1
Printed in China

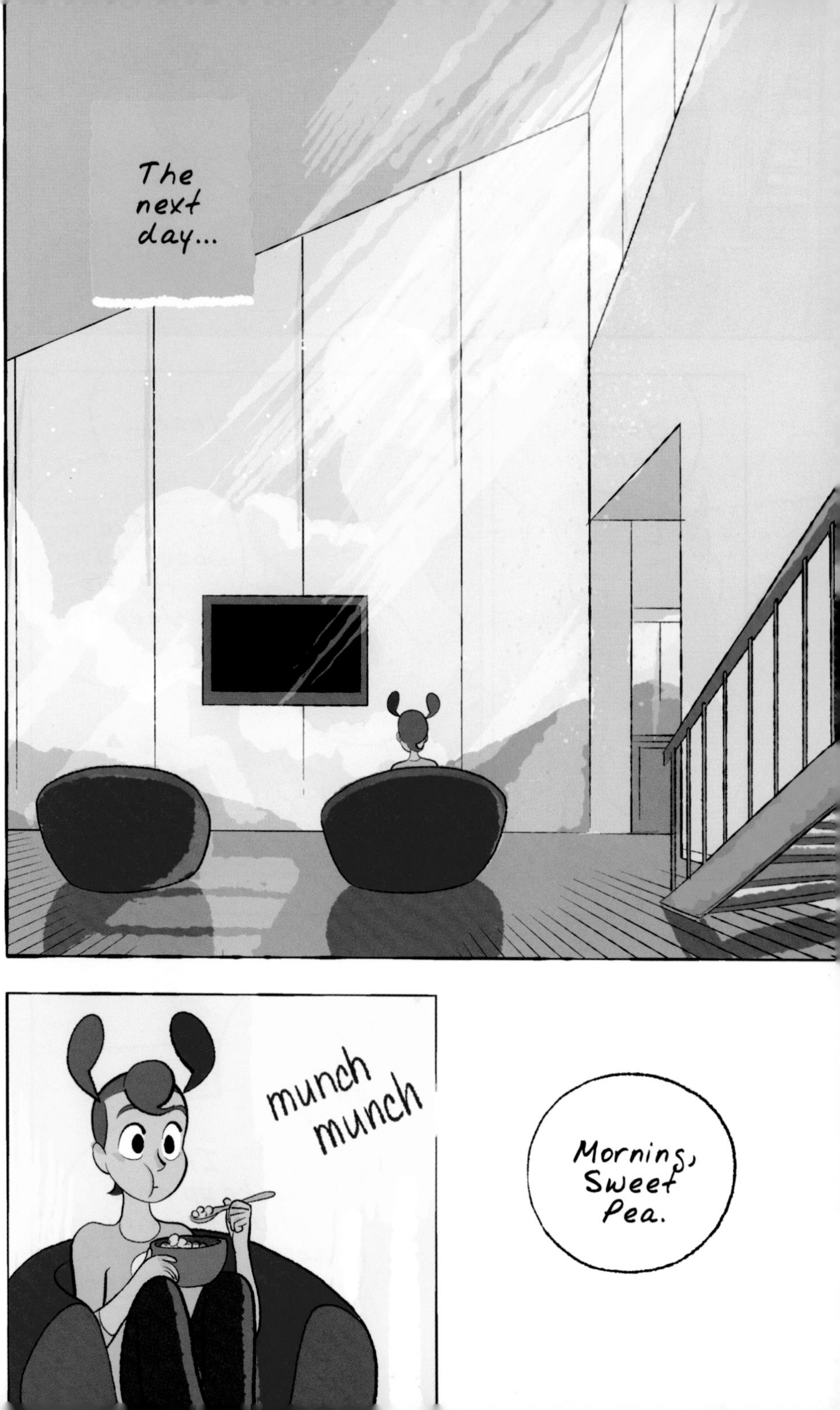
The next day...
munch munch
Mornins, Sweet Pea.

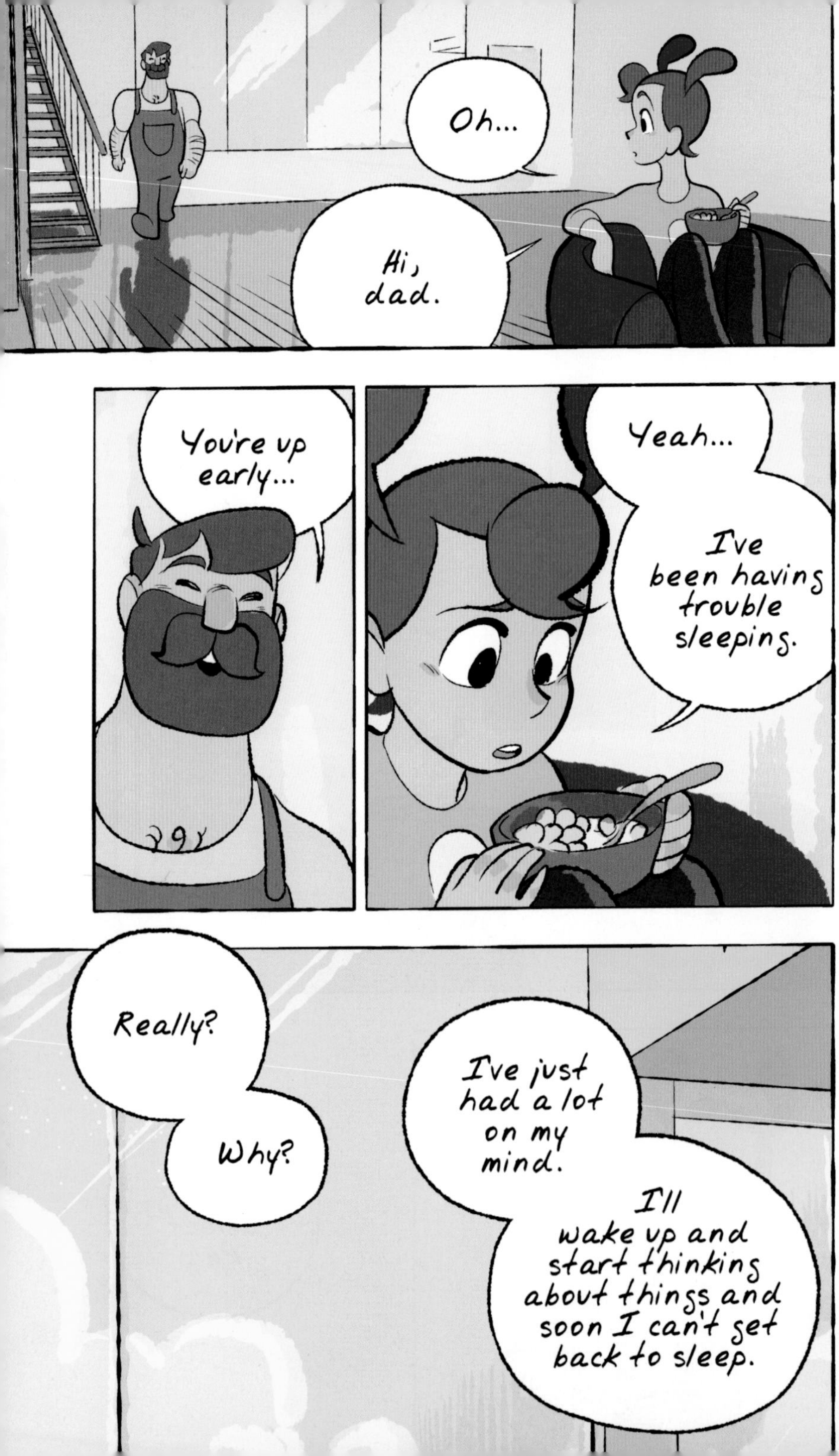
Oh...
Hi, dad.
You're up early...
Yeah...
I've been having trouble sleeping.
Really?
Why?
I've just had a lot on my mind.
I'll wake up and start thinking about things and soon I can't get back to sleep.

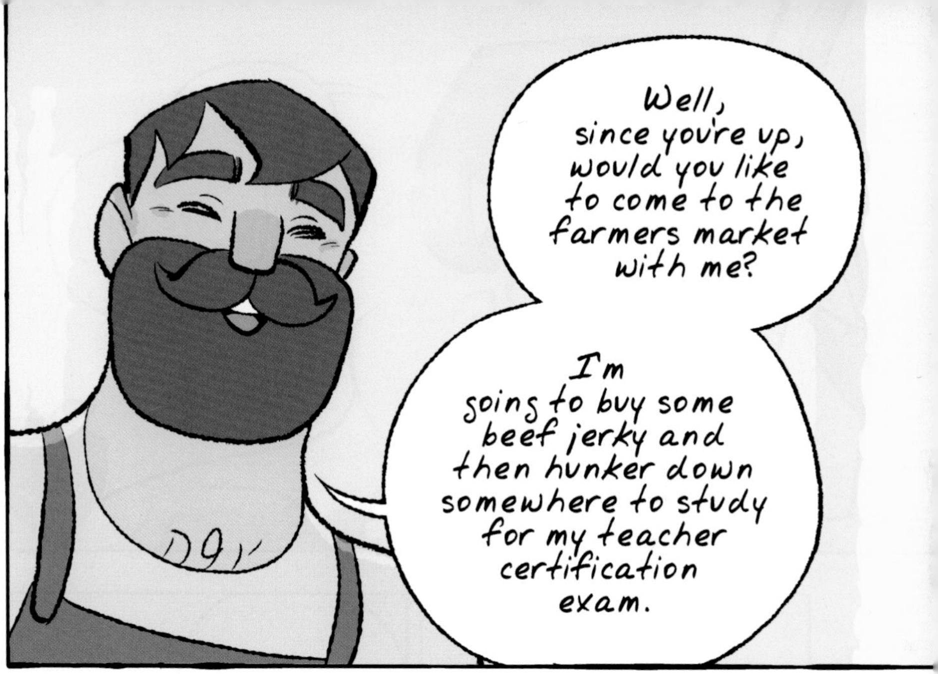
Well, since you're up, would you like to come to the farmers market with me?
I'm going to buy some beef jerky and then hunker down somewhere to study for my teacher certification exam.

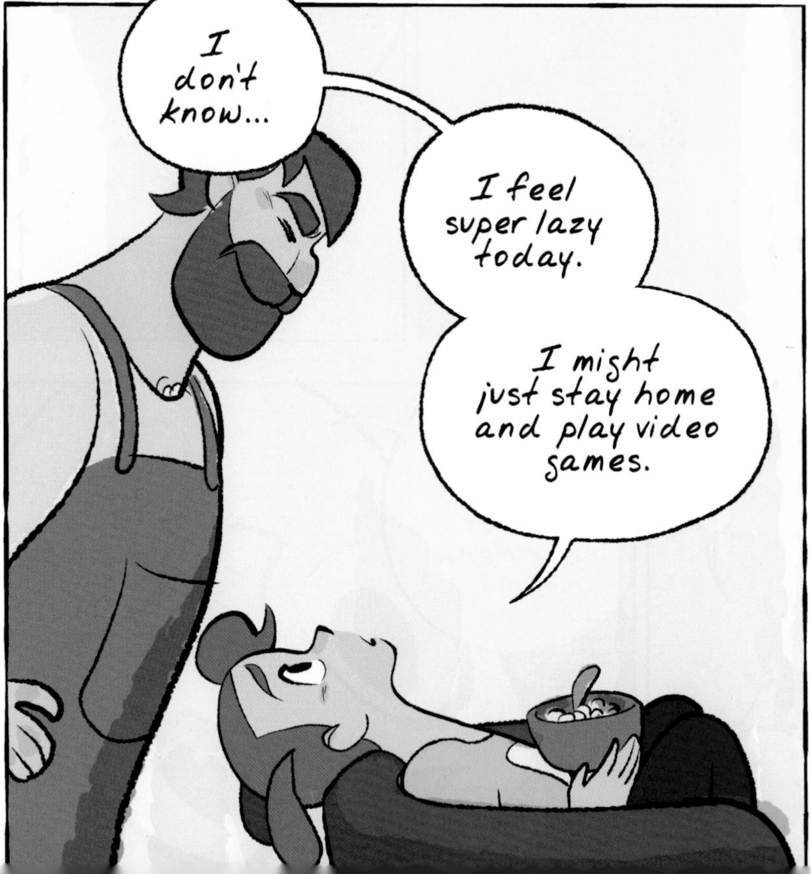
I don't know...
I feel super lazy today.
I might just stay home and play video games.

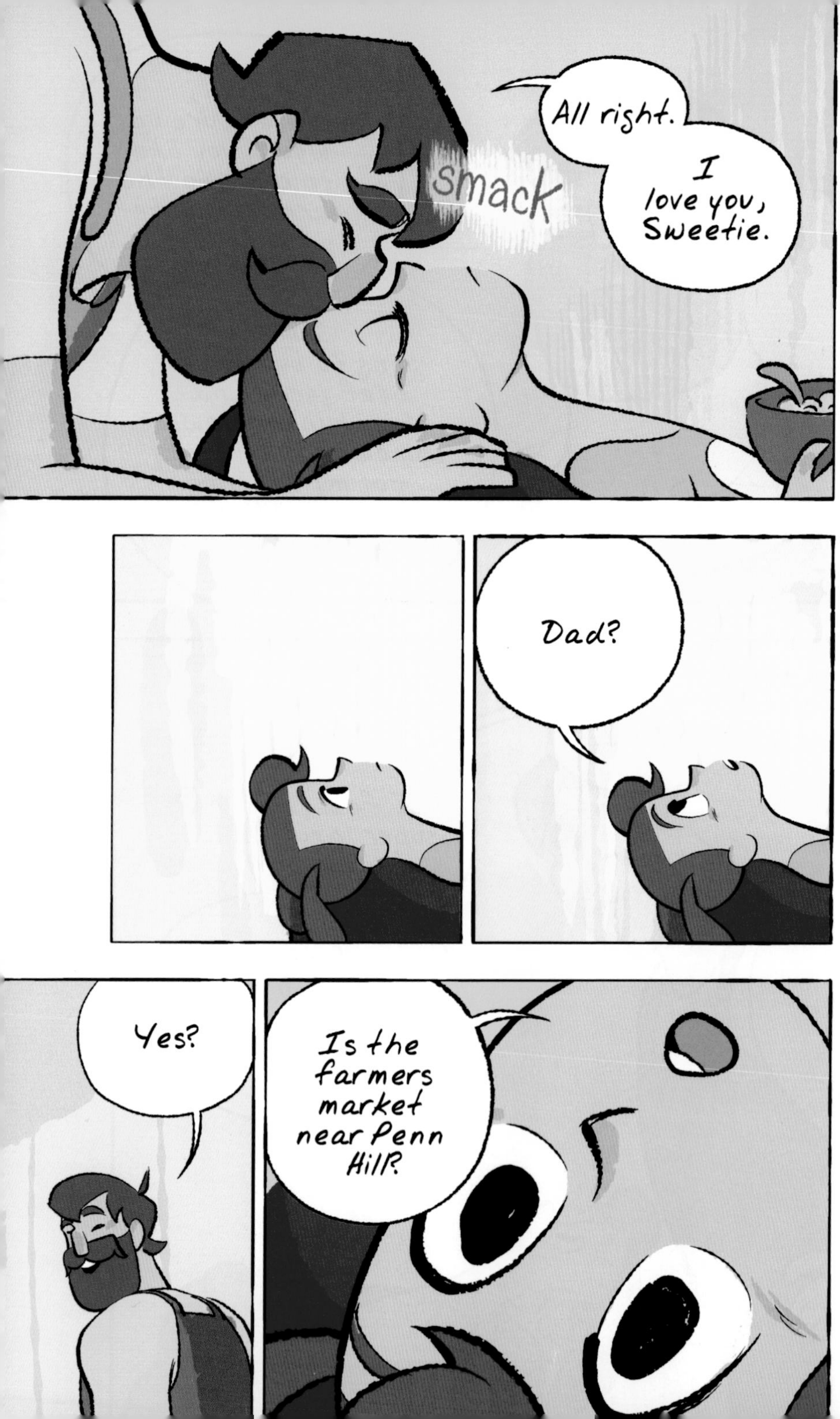
All right.
I love you, Sweetie.
smack
Dad?
Yes?
Is the farmers market near Penn Hill?

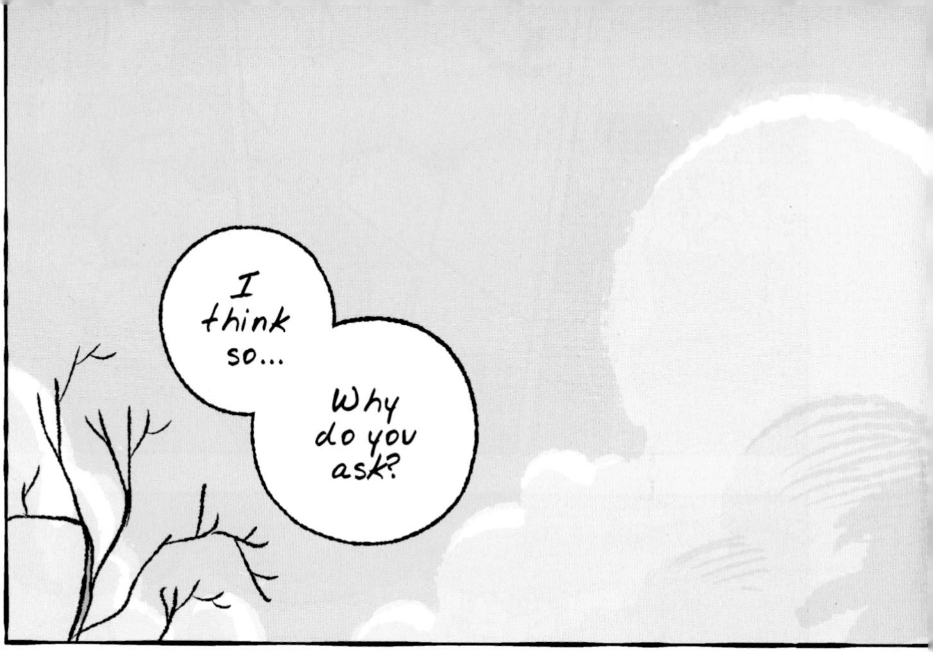
I think so...
Why do you ask?

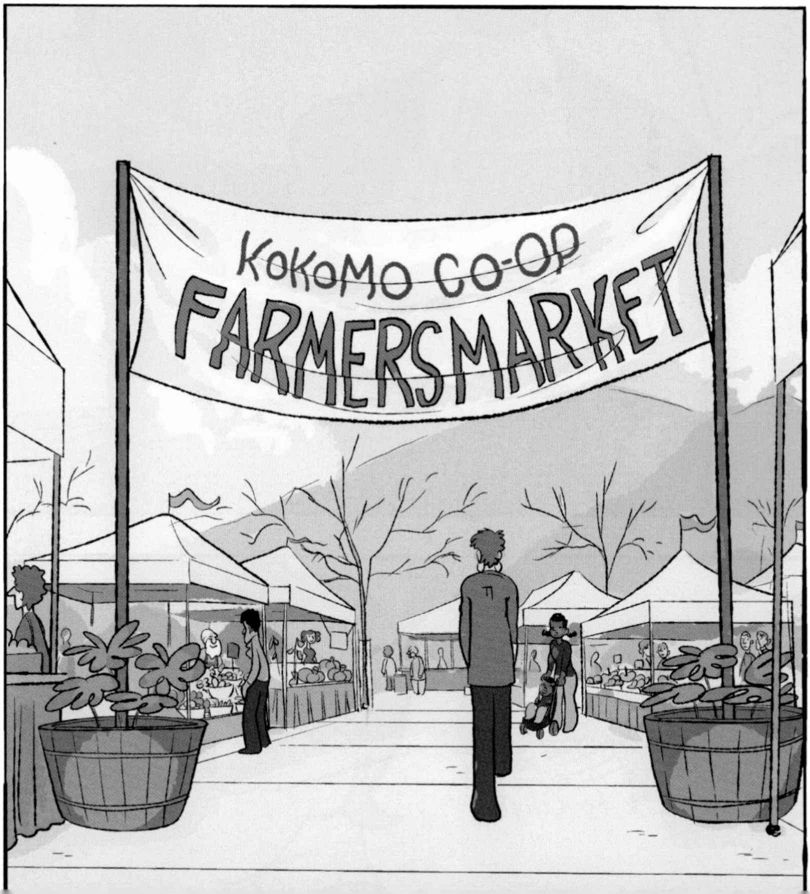
KOKOMO CO-OP
FARMERSMARKET

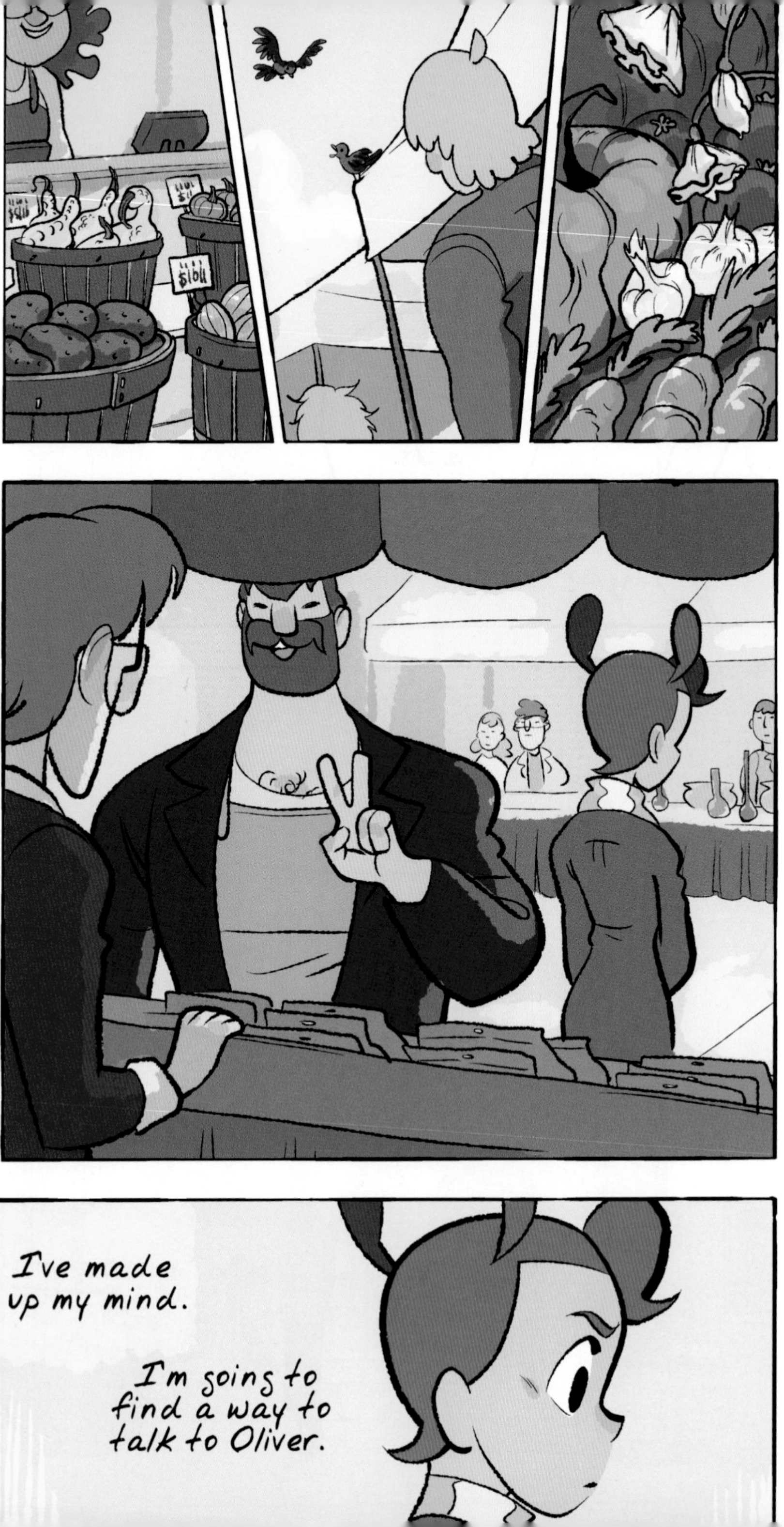
I've made up my mind.
I'm going to find a way to talk to Oliver.

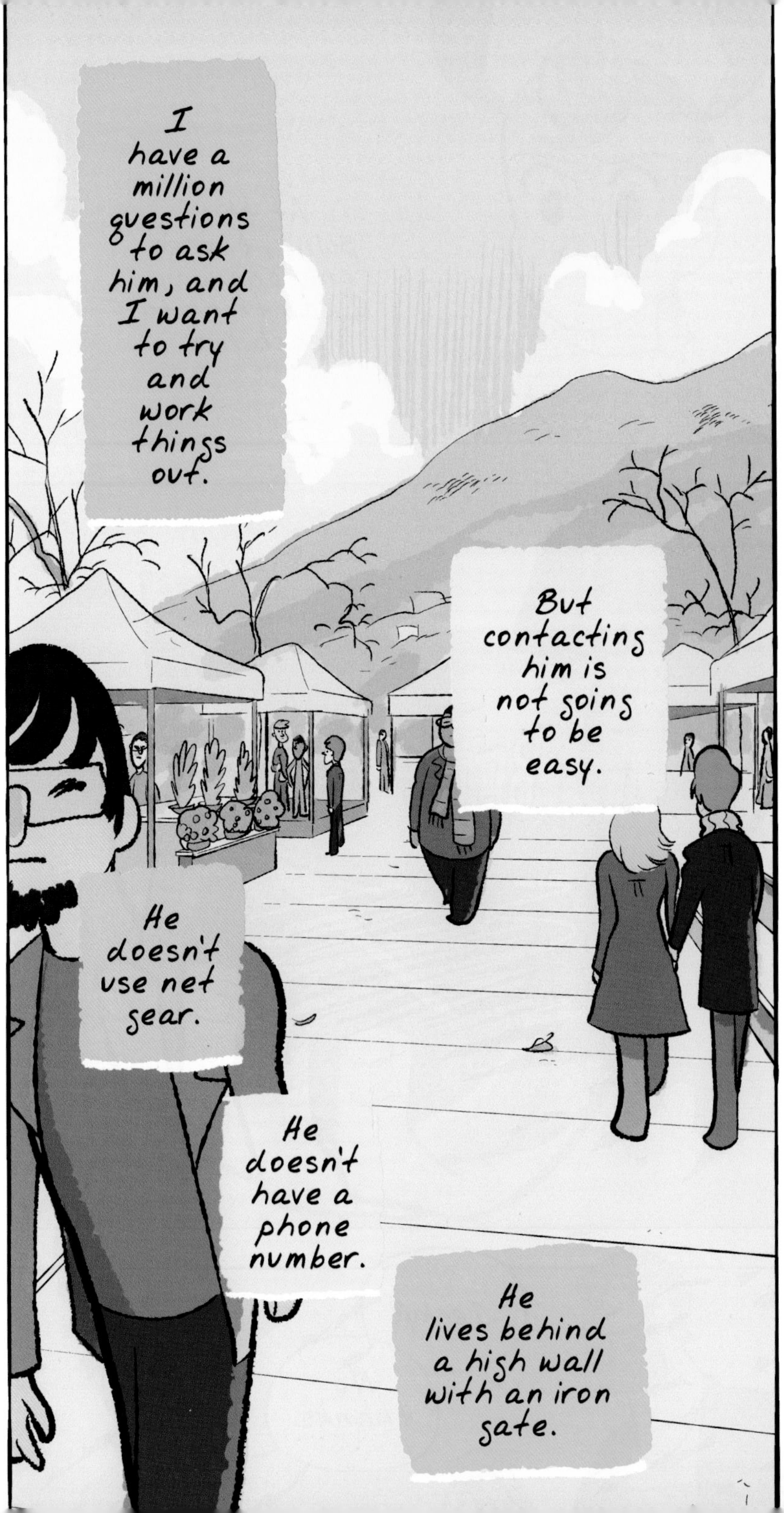
I have a million questions to ask him, and I want to try and work things out.
But contacting him is not going to be easy.
He doesn't use net gear.
He doesn't have a phone number.
He lives behind a high wall with an iron gate.

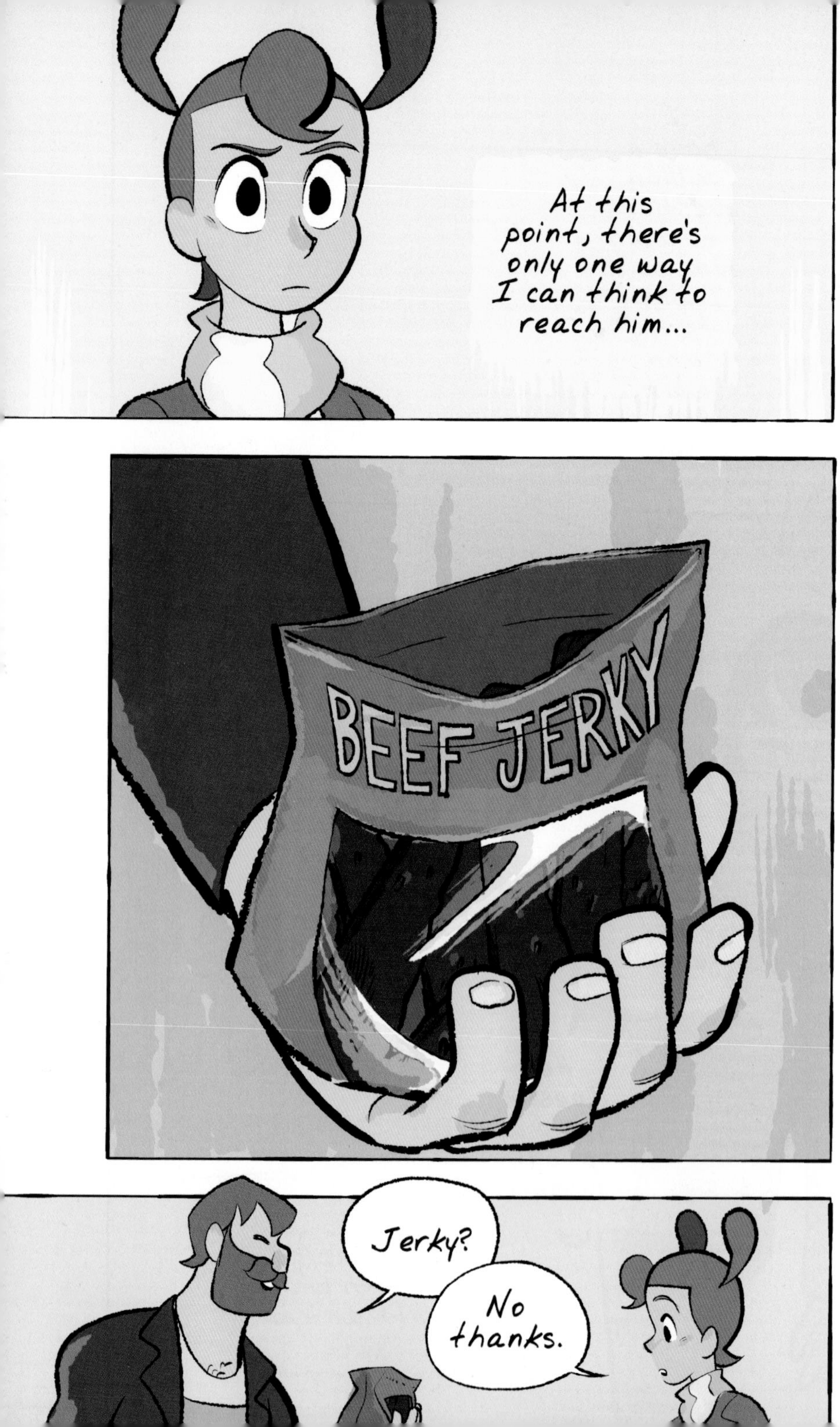
At this point, there's only one way I can think to reach him...
BEEF JERKY
Jerky?
No thanks.

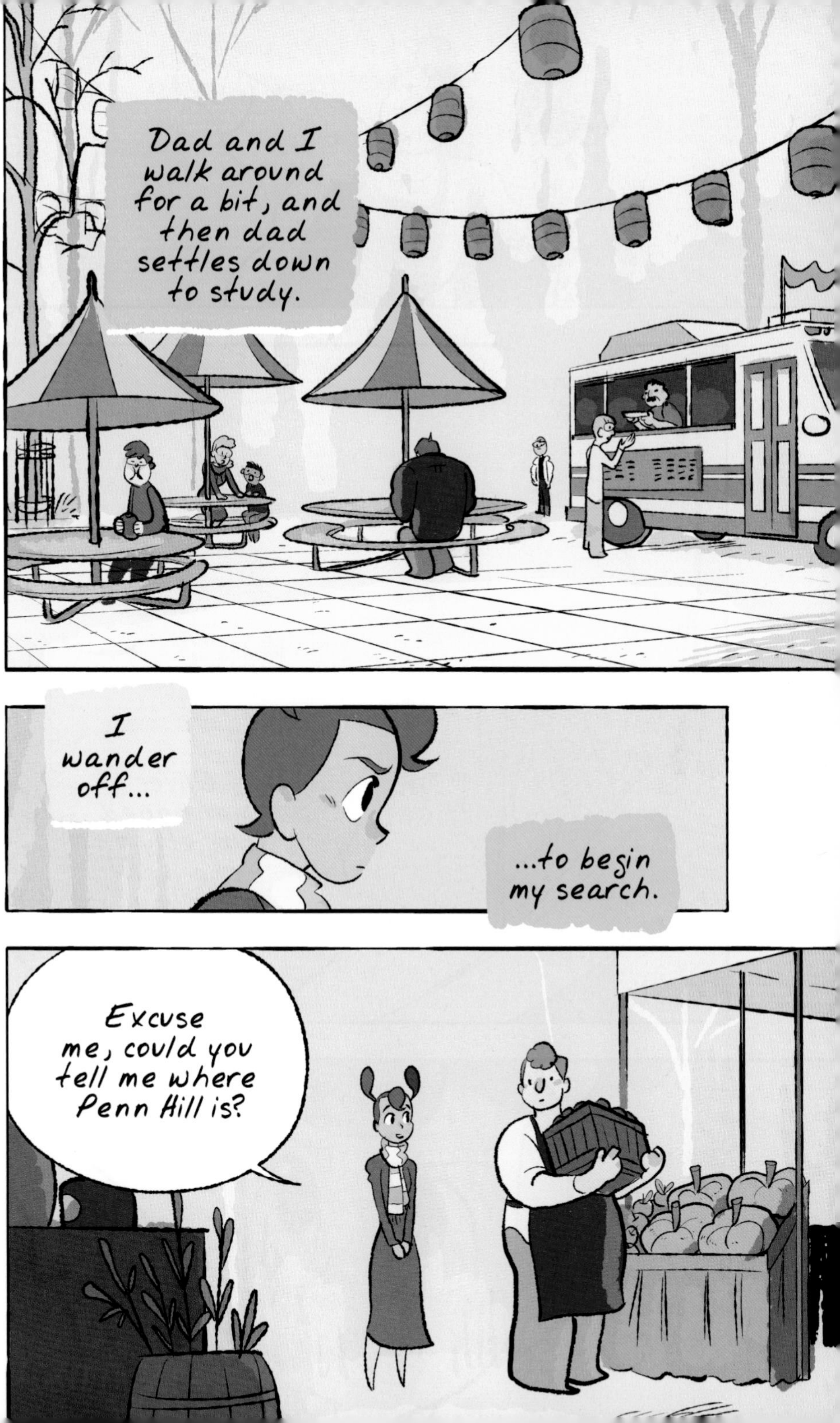

Dad and I walk around for a bit, and then dad settles down to study.
I wander off...
...to begin my search.
Excuse me, could you tell me where Penn Hill is?

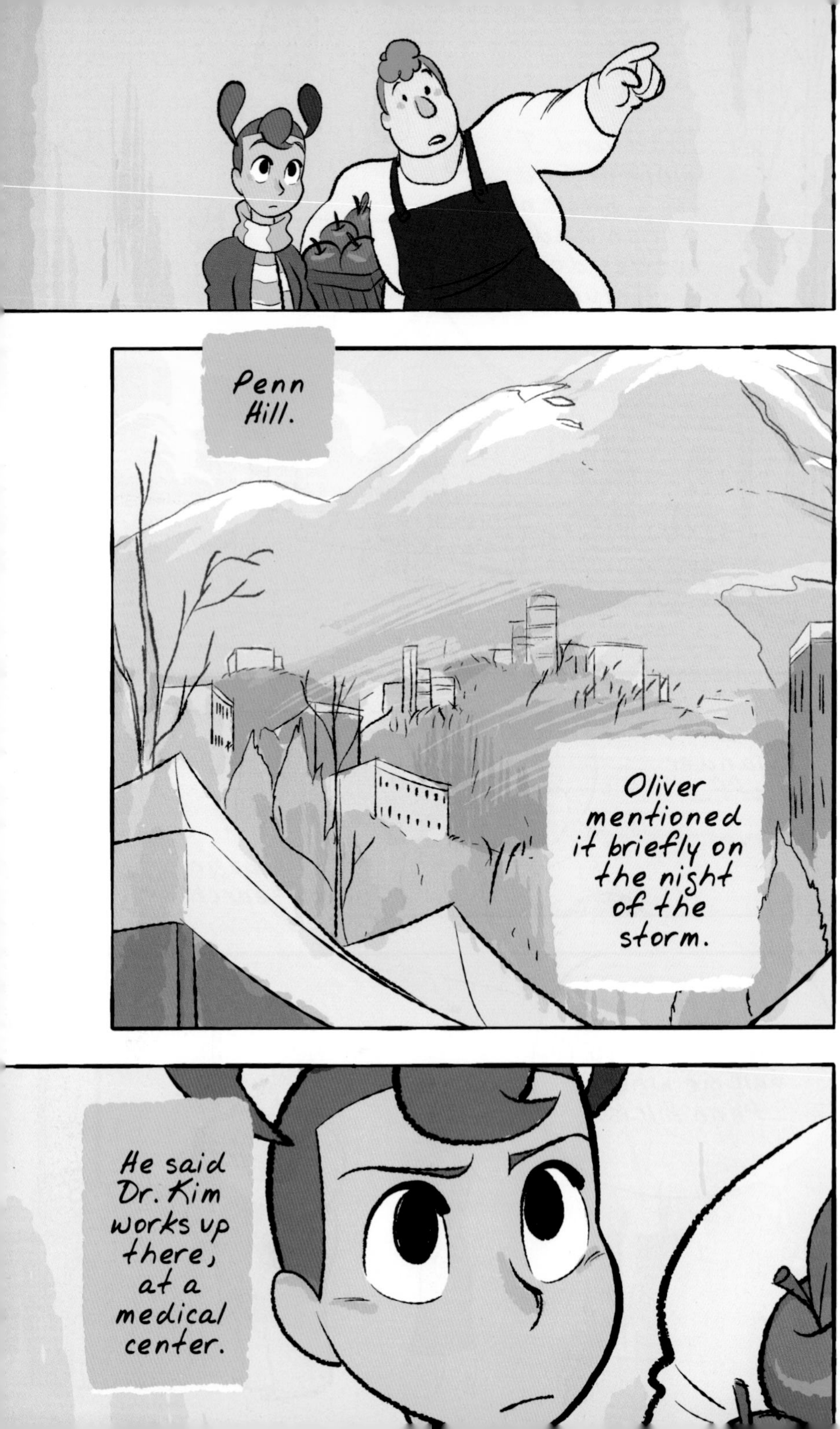
Penn Hill.
Oliver mentioned it briefly on the night of the storm.
He said Dr. Kim works up there, at a medical center.

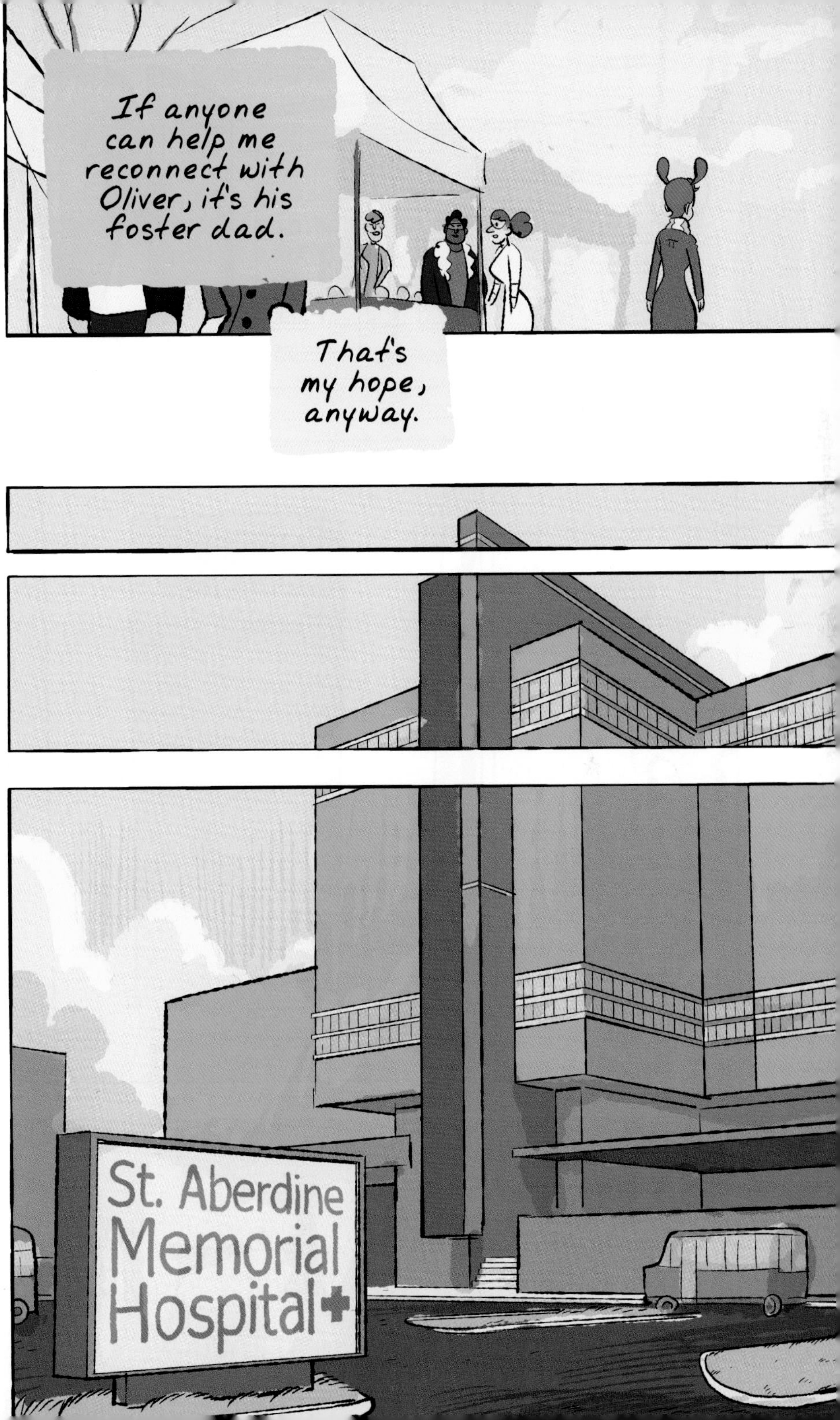
If anyone can help me reconnect with Oliver, it's his foster dad.
That's my hope, anyway.
St. Aberdine Memorial Hospital

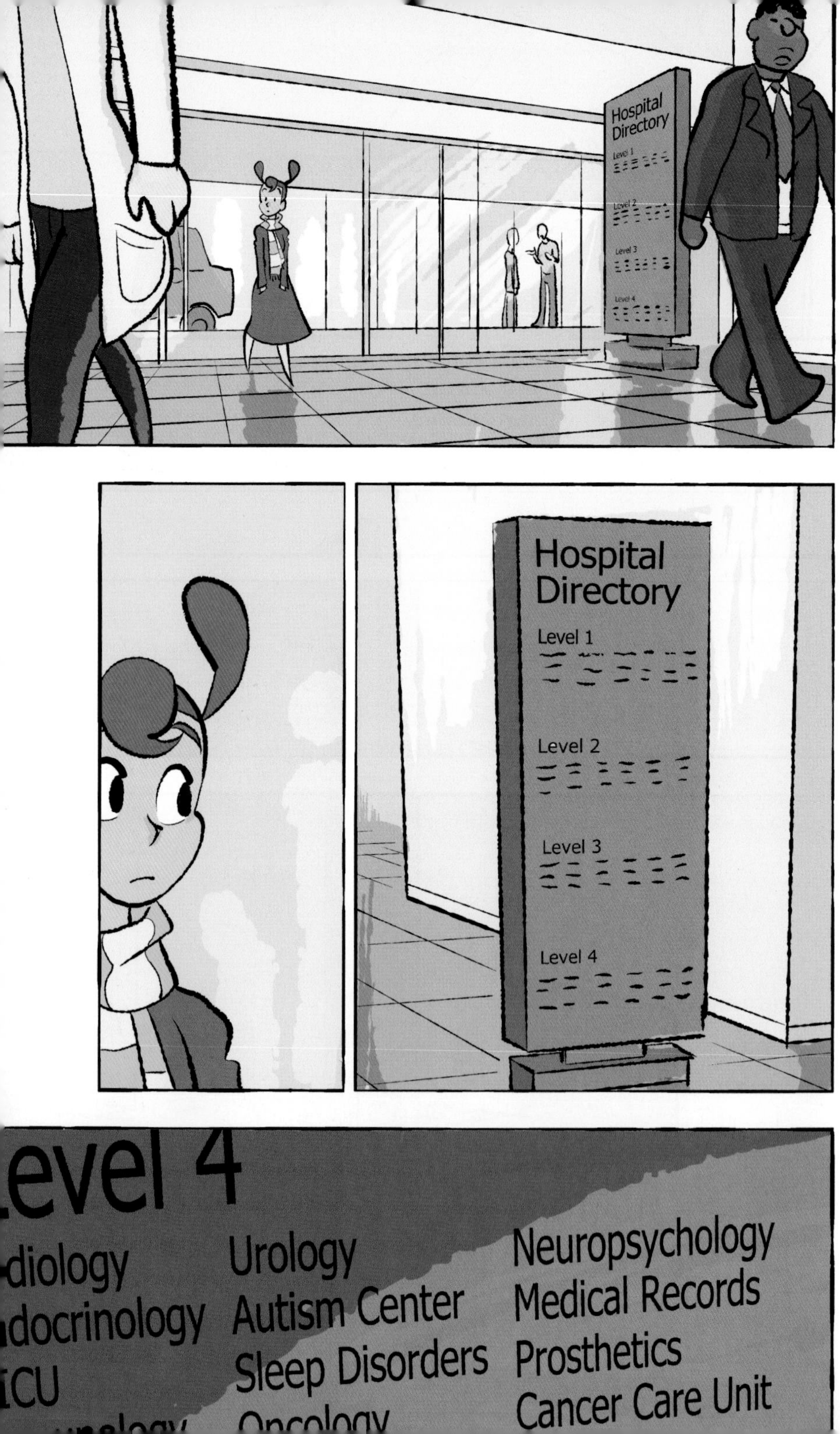

Hospital Directory
Level 1
Level 2
Level 3
Level 4
Hospital Directory
Level 1
Level 2
Level 3
Level 4
Urology
Autism Center
Sleep Disorders
ICU
Neuropsychology
Medical Records
Prosthetics
Cancer Care Unit

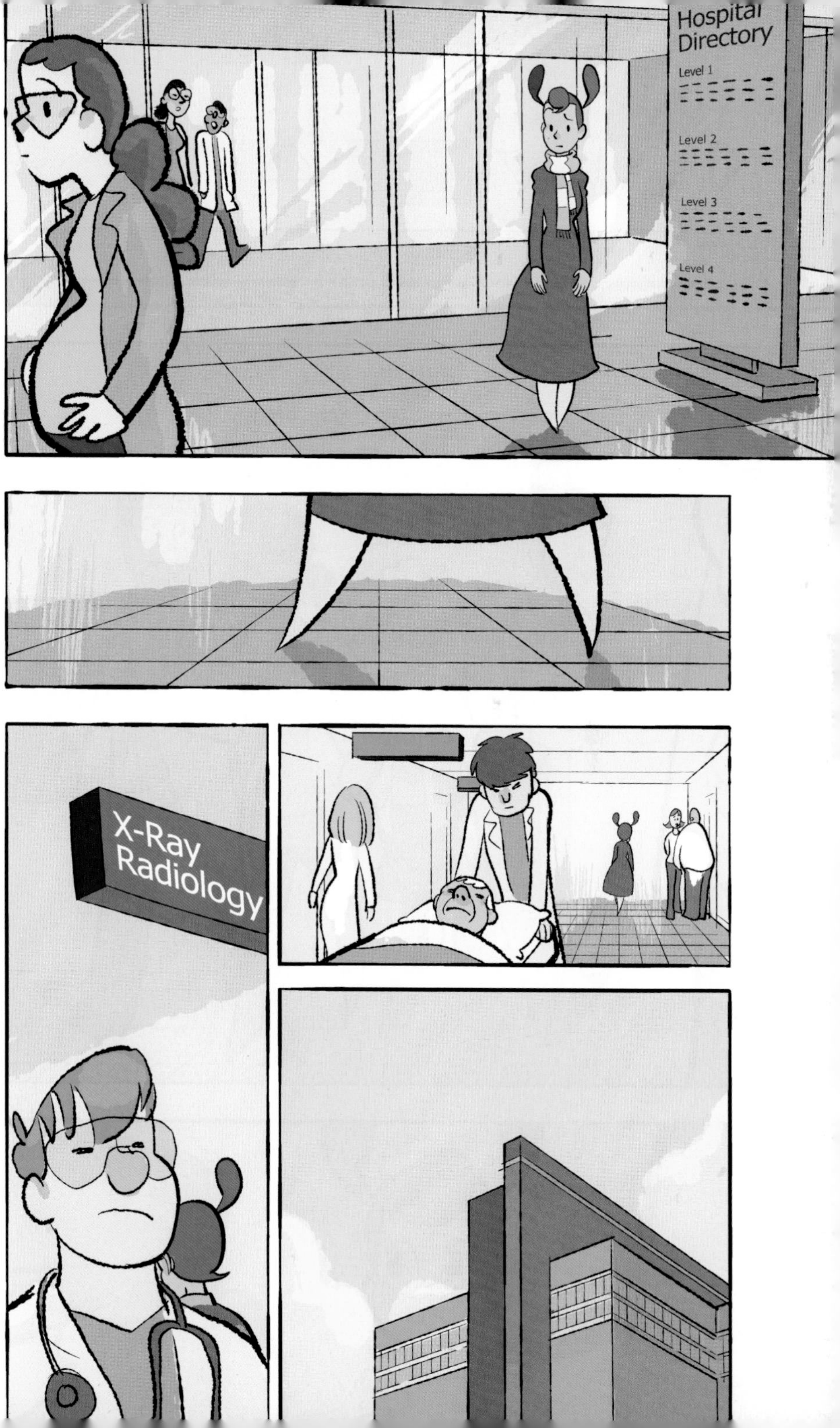
Hospital Directory
Level 1
Level 2
Level 3
Level 4
X-Ray Radiology

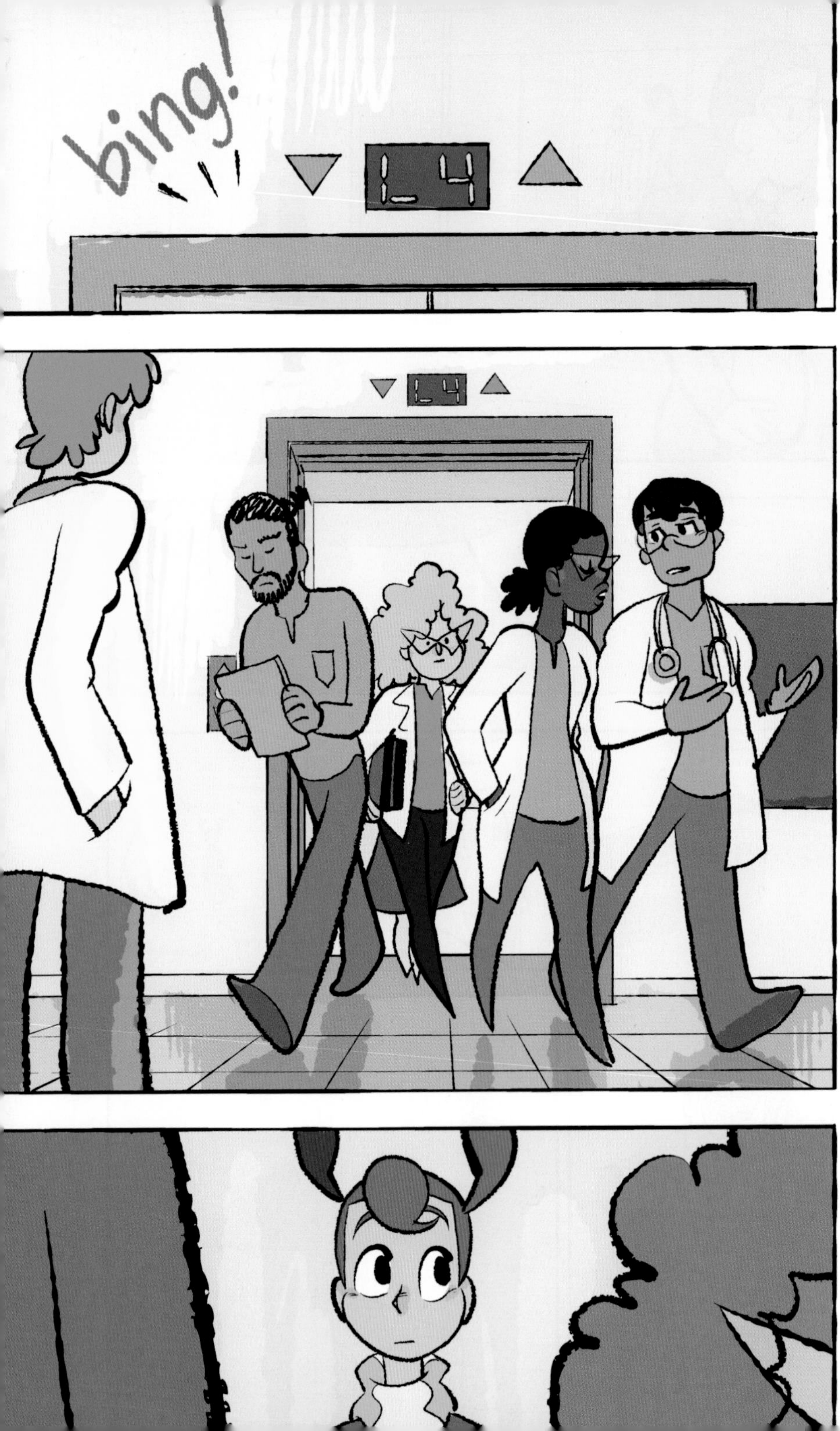
bing!

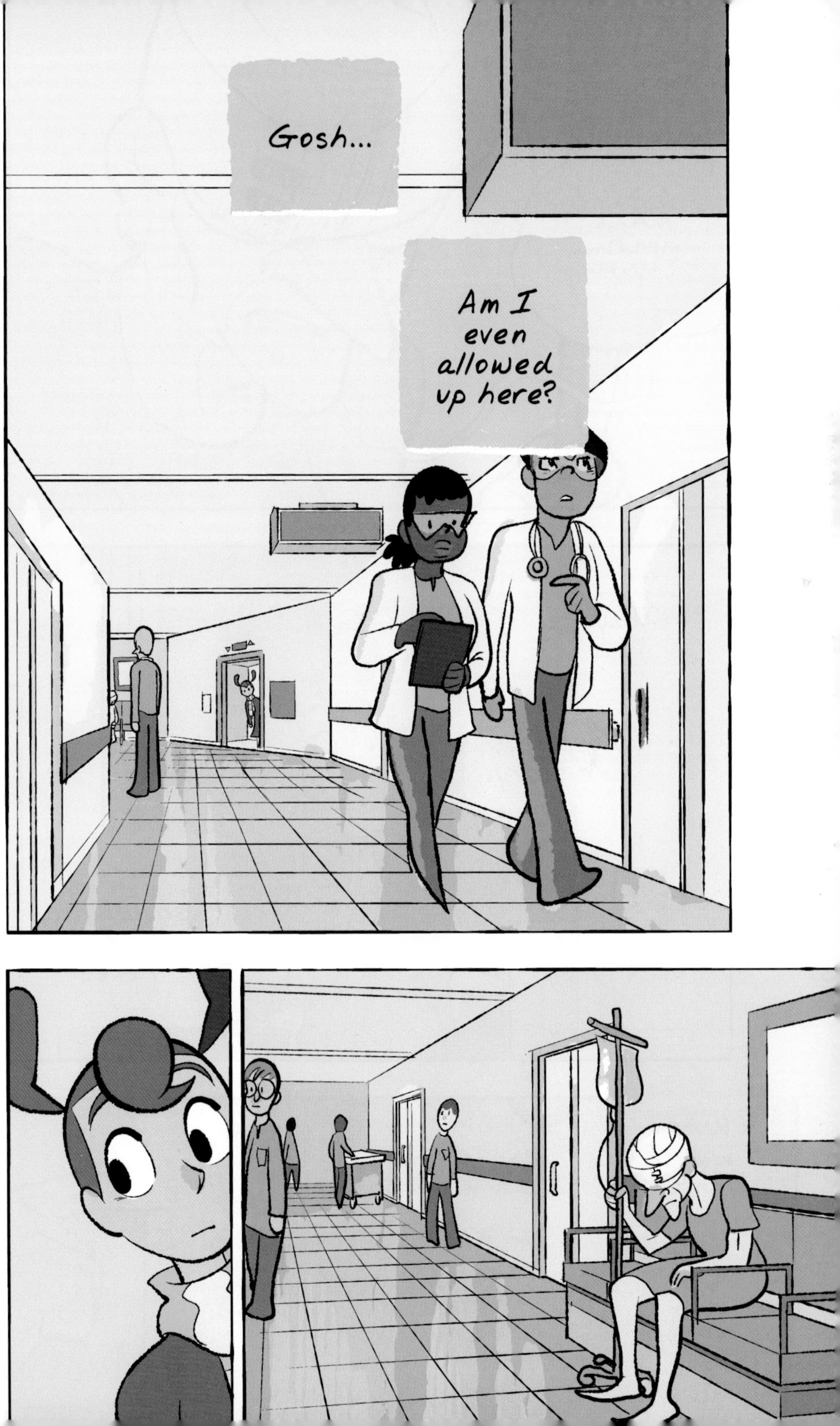
Gosh...
Am I even allowed up here?

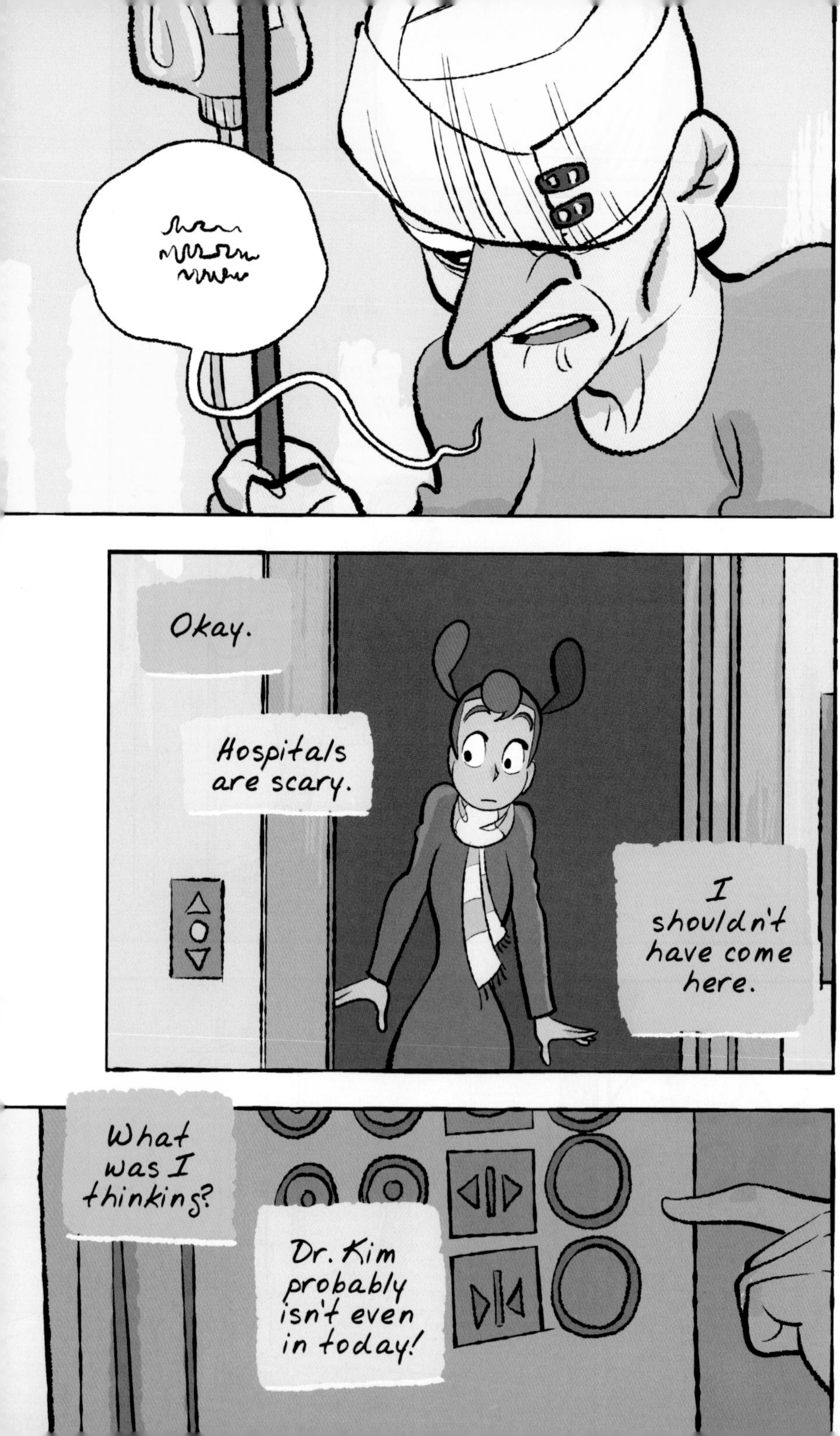
Okay.
Hospitals are scary.
I shouldn't have come here.
What was I thinking?
Dr. Kim probably isn't even in today!

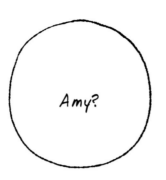

Amy?

What are you doing here?

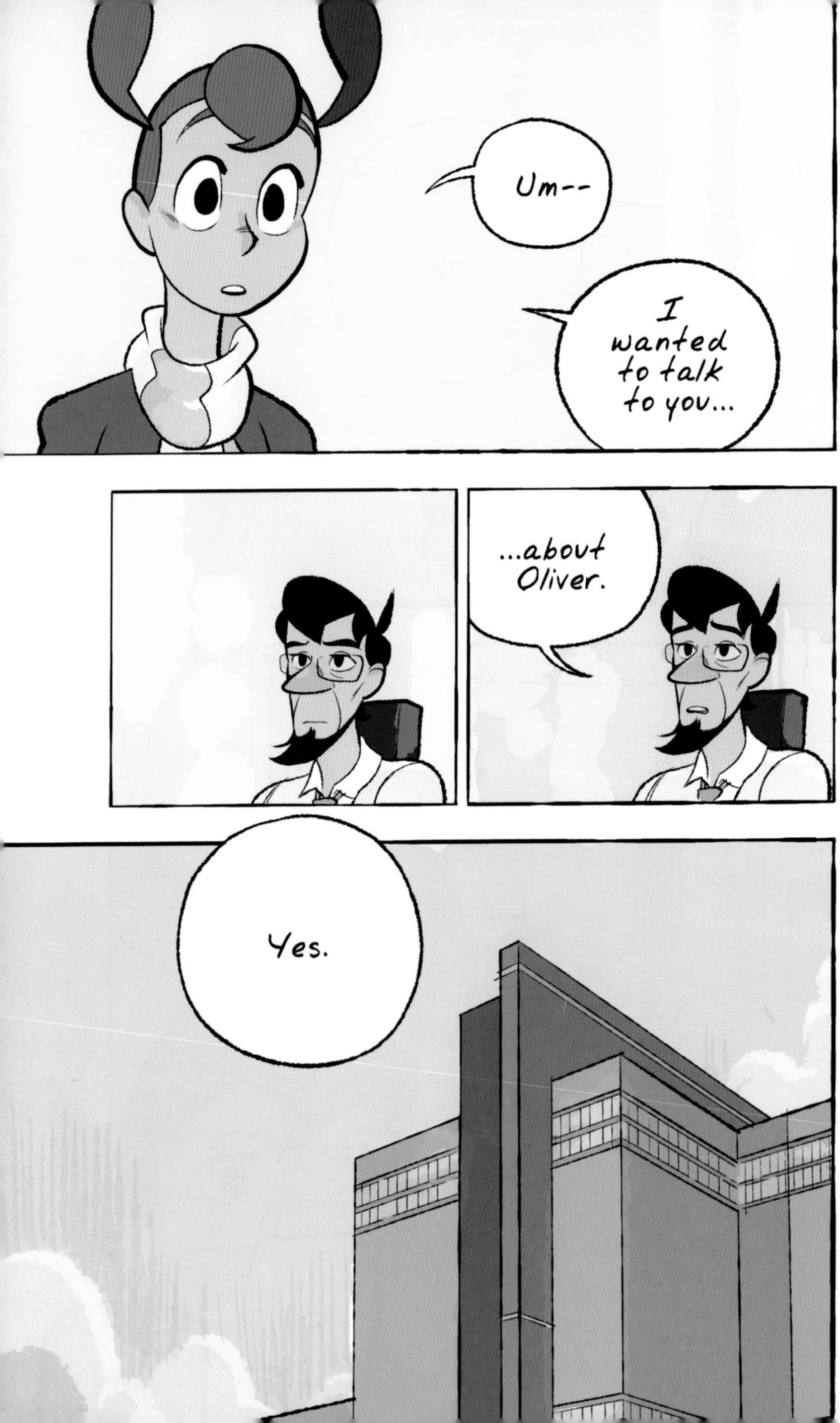
Um--
I wanted to talk to you...
...about Oliver.
Yes.

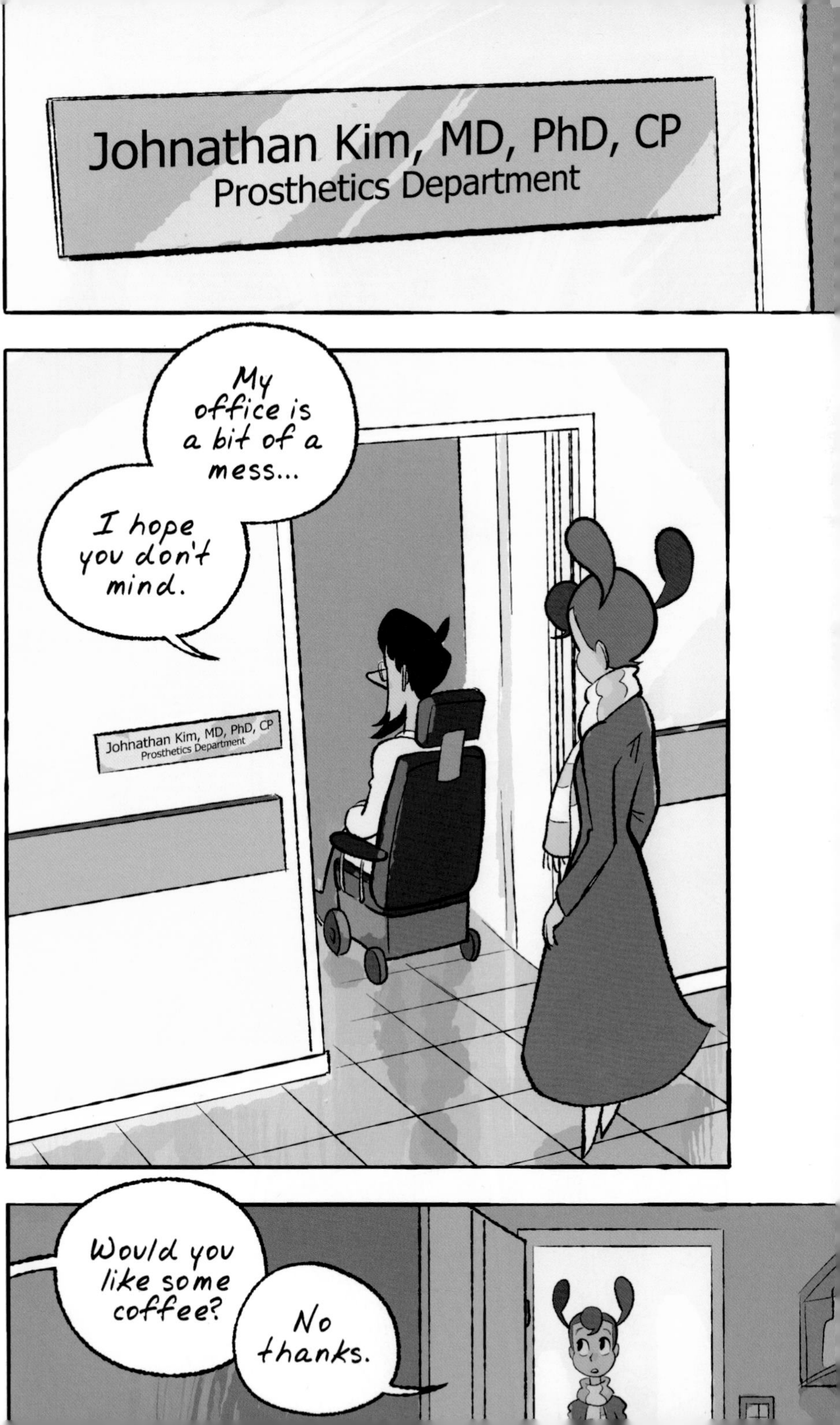
Johnathan Kim, MD, PhD, CP
Prosthetics Department
My office is a bit of a mess...
I hope you don't mind.
Johnathan Kim, MD, PhD, CP
Prosthetics Department
Would you like some coffee?
No thanks.

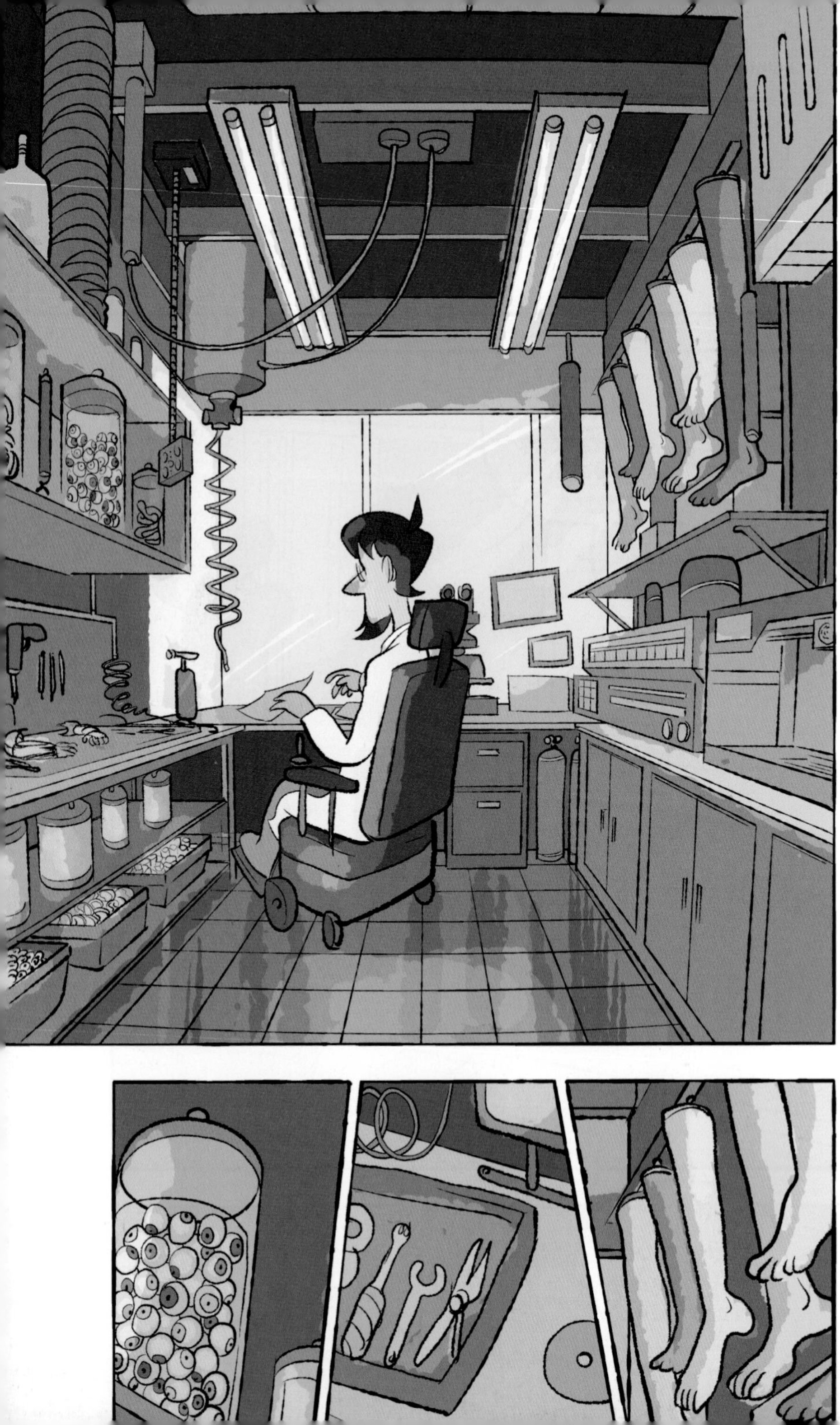

Wow...

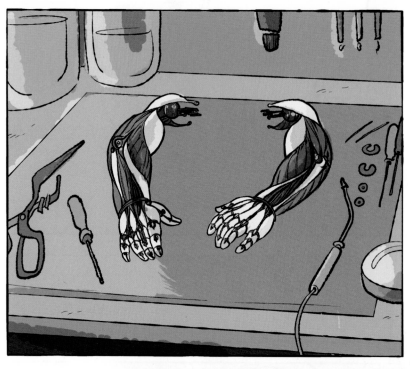

Did you make these little arms?

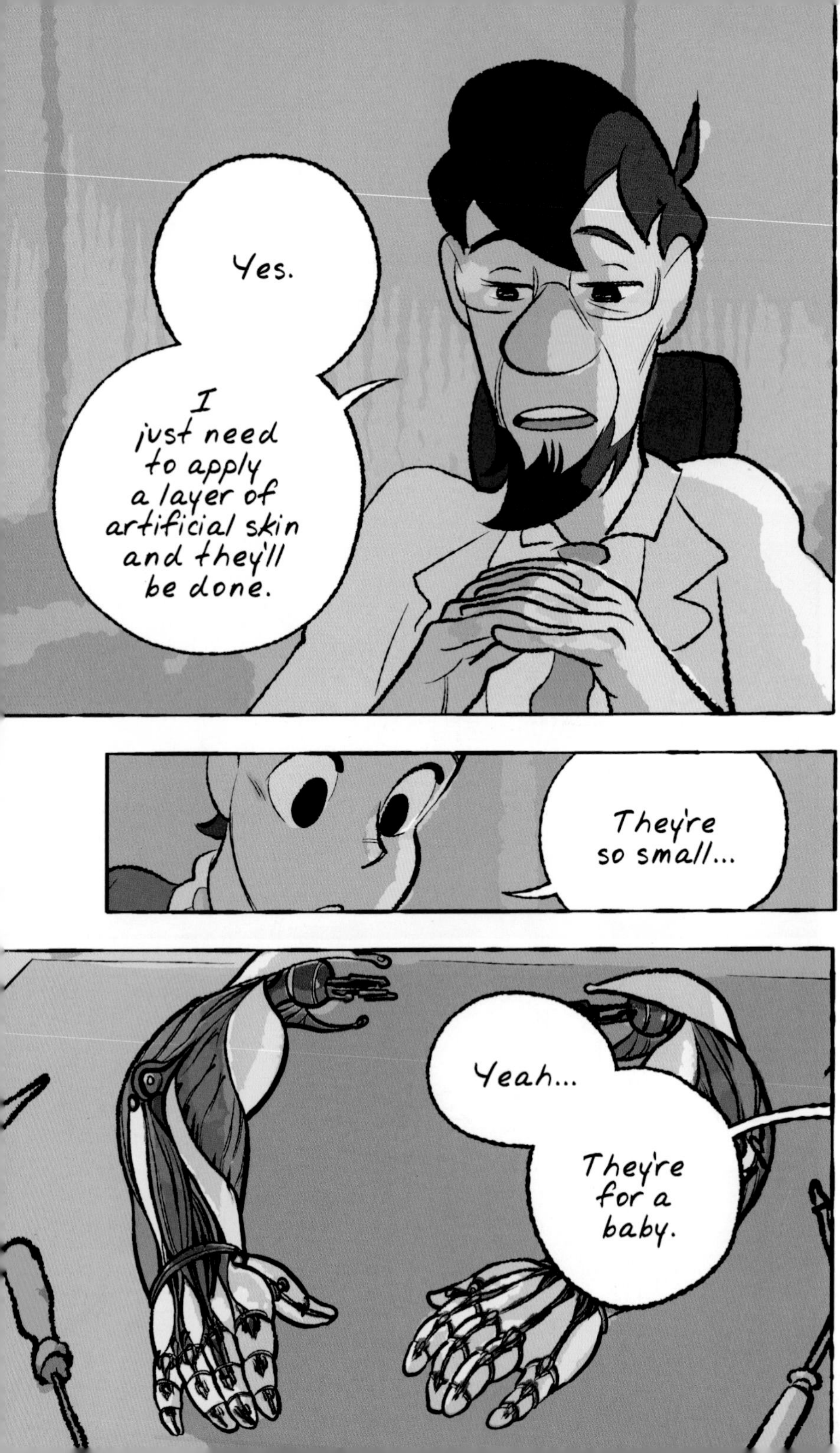
Yes.
I just need to apply a layer of artificial skin and they'll be done.
They're so small...
Yeah...
They're for a baby.

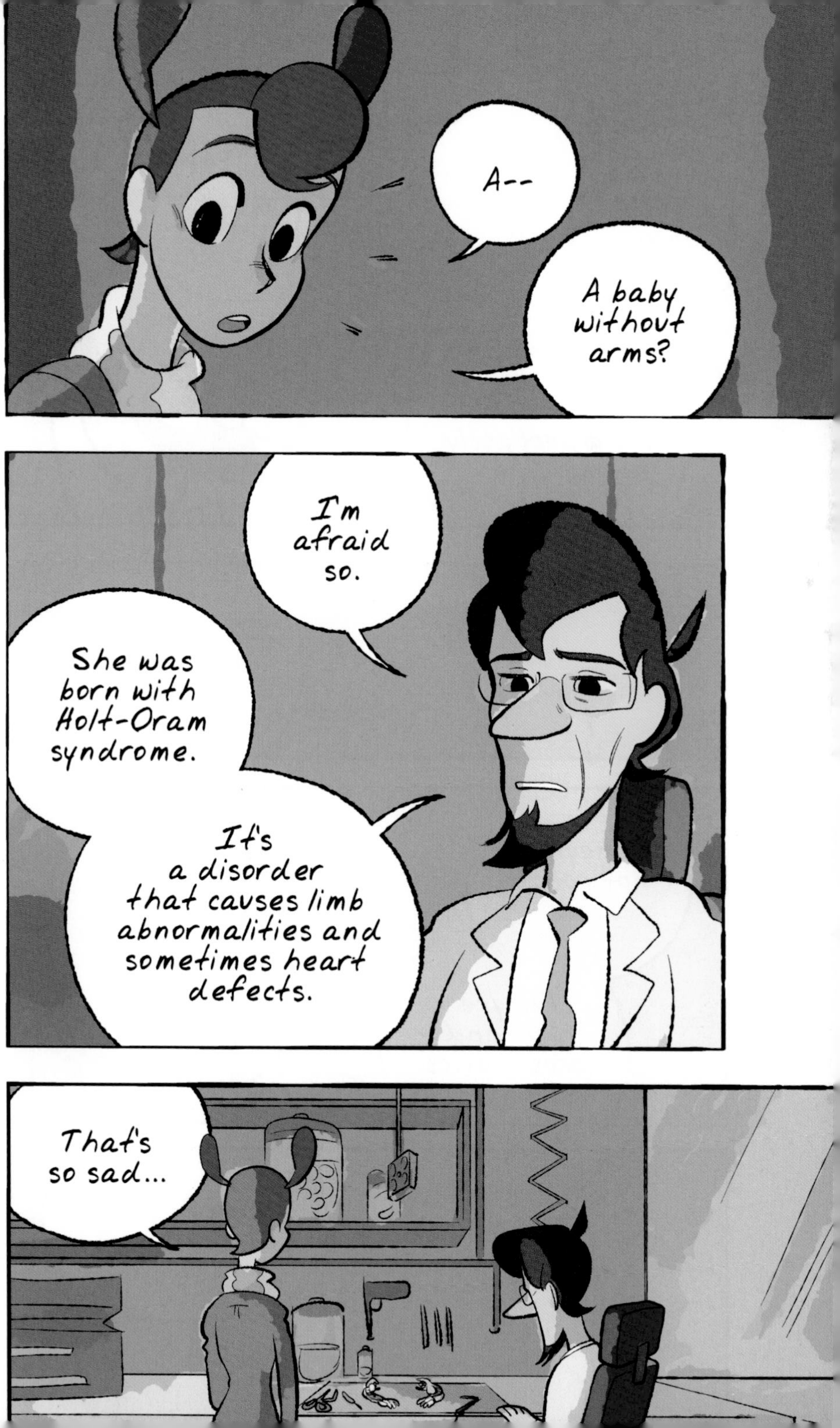
A--
A baby without arms?
I'm afraid so.
She was born with Holt-Oram syndrome.
It's a disorder that causes limb abnormalities and sometimes heart defects.
That's so sad...

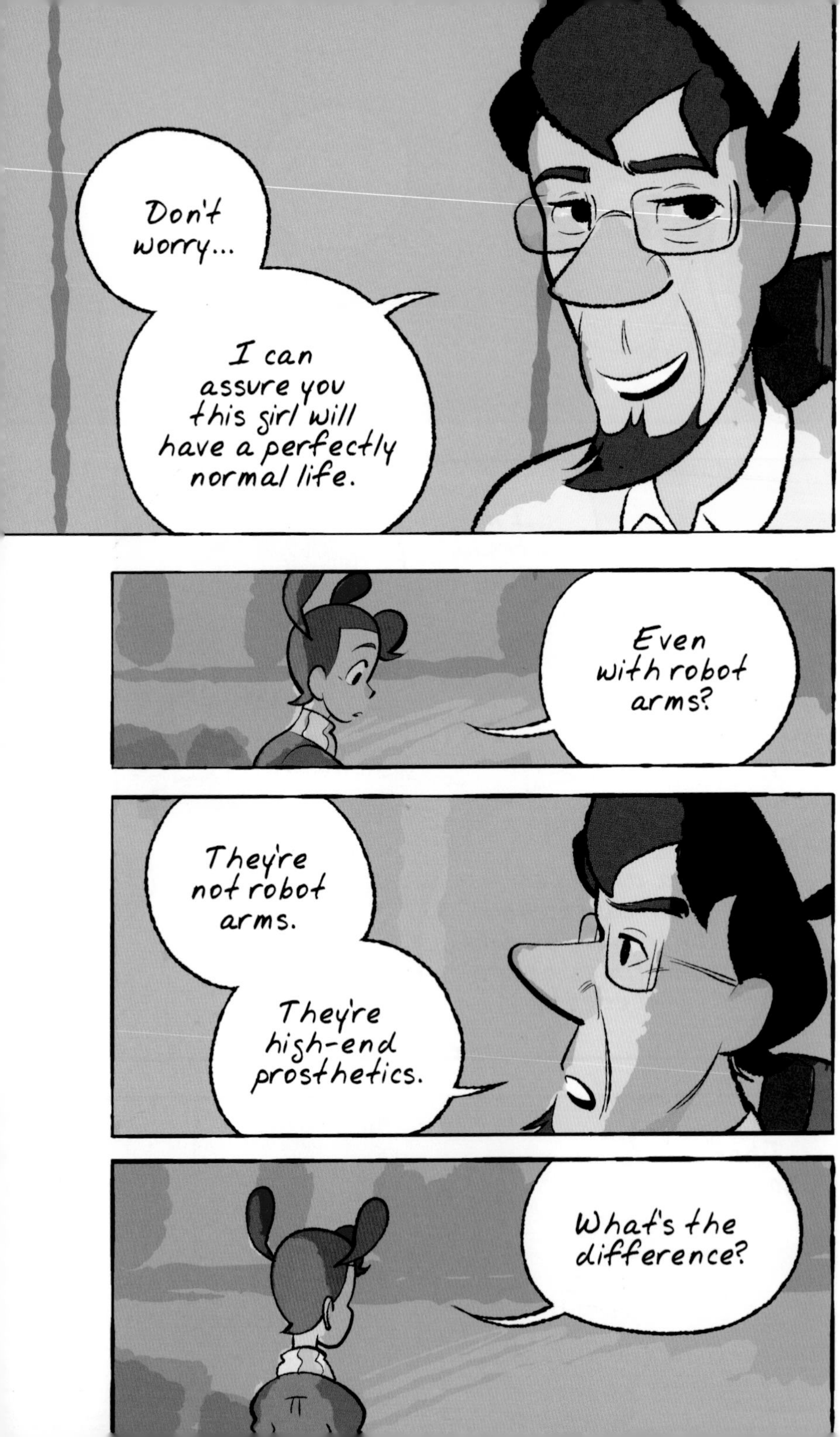
Don't worry...
I can assure you this girl will have a perfectly normal life.
Even with robot arms?
They're not robot arms.
They're high-end prosthetics.
What's the difference?

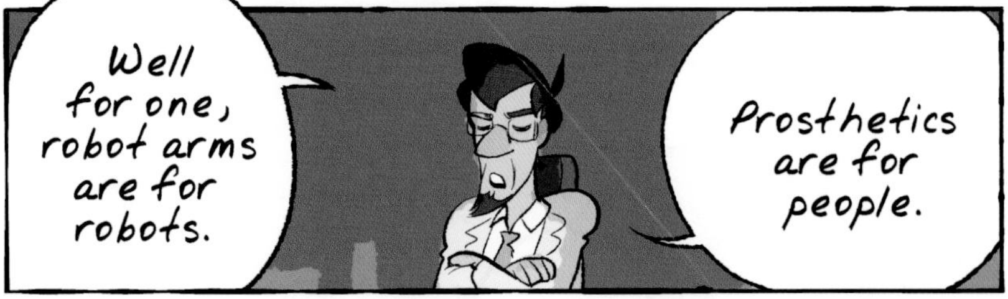
Well for one, robot arms are for robots.
Prosthetics are for people.

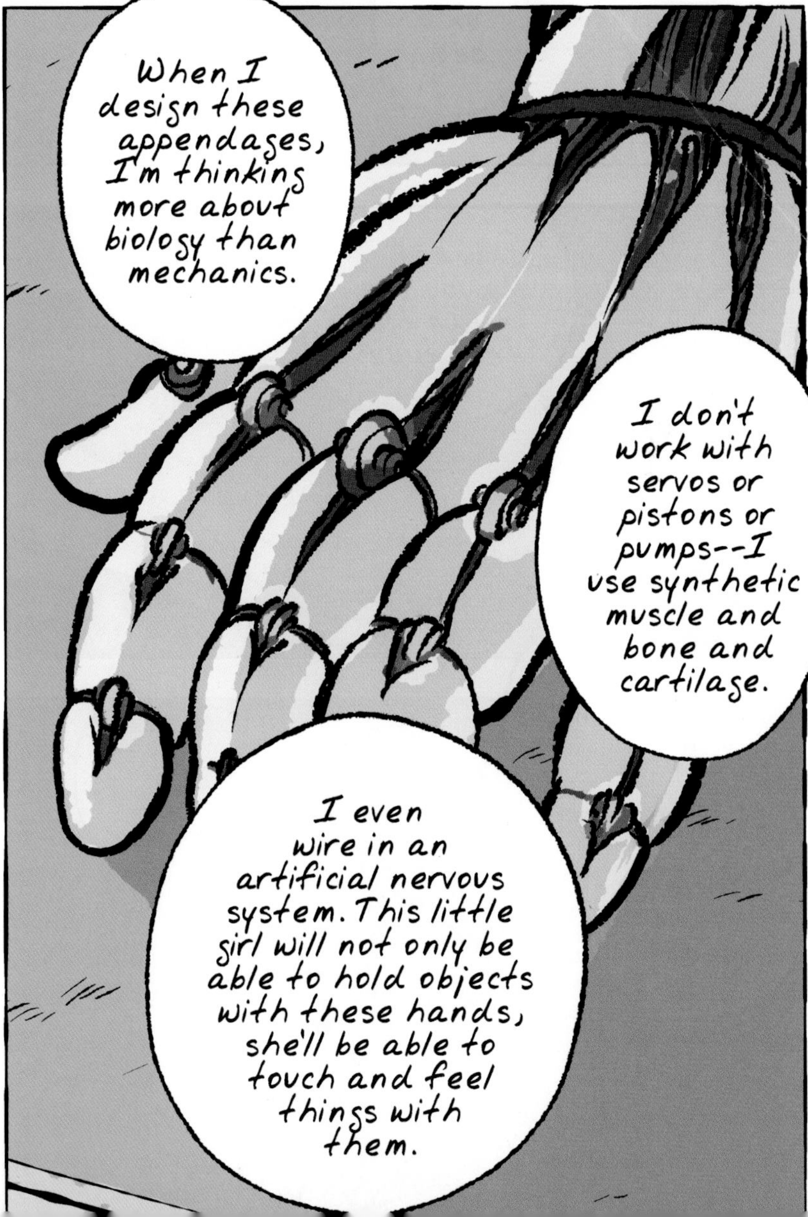
When I design these appendages, I'm thinking more about biology than mechanics.
I don't work with servos or pistons or pumps--I use synthetic muscle and bone and cartilage.
I even wire in an artificial nervous system. This little girl will not only be able to hold objects with these hands, she'll be able to touch and feel things with them.

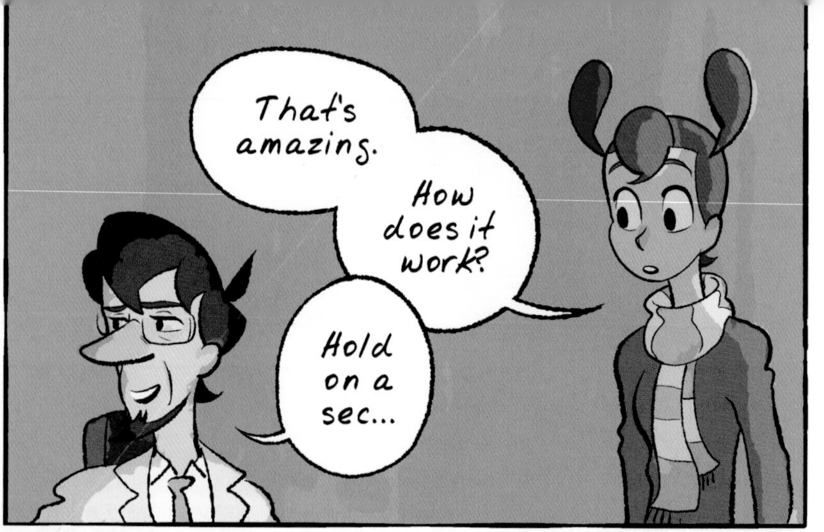
That's amazing.
How does it work?
Hold on a sec...

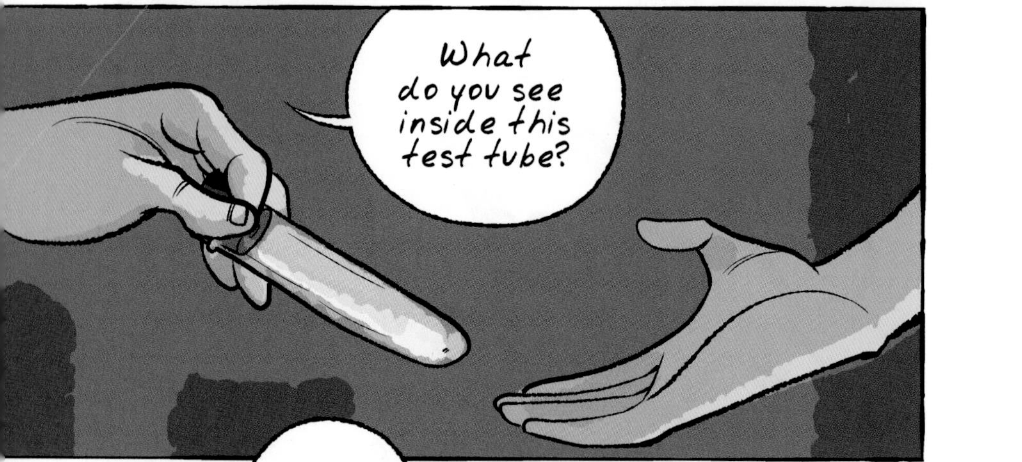
What do you see inside this test tube?

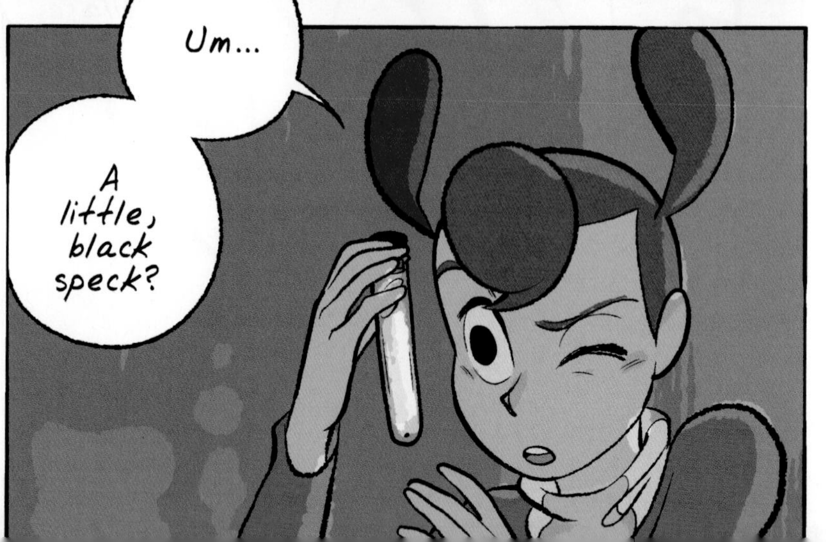
Um...
A little, black speck?

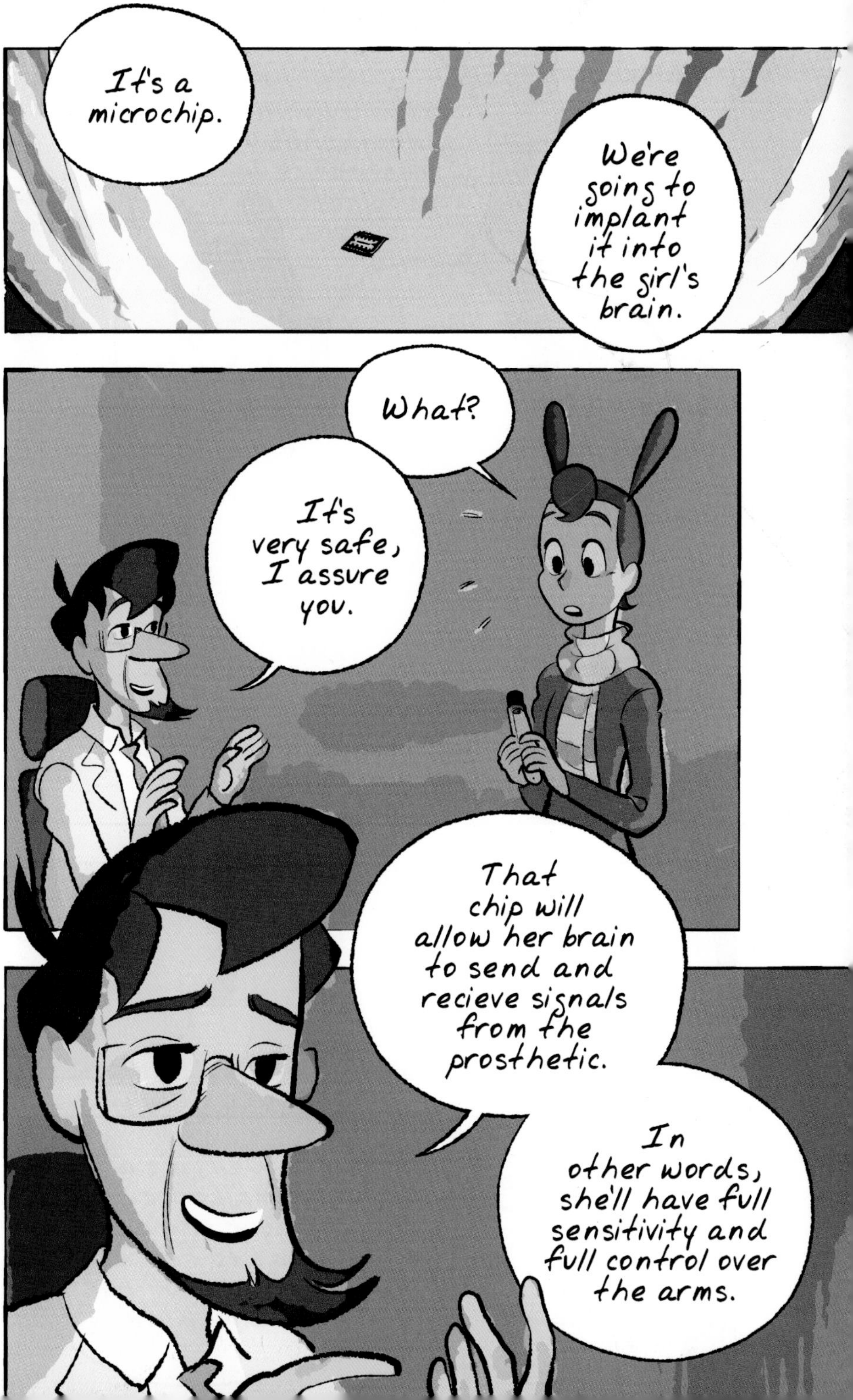
It's a microchip.
We're going to implant it into the girl's brain.
What?
It's very safe, I assure you.
That chip will allow her brain to send and recieve signals from the prosthetic.
In other words, she'll have full sensitivity and full control over the arms.

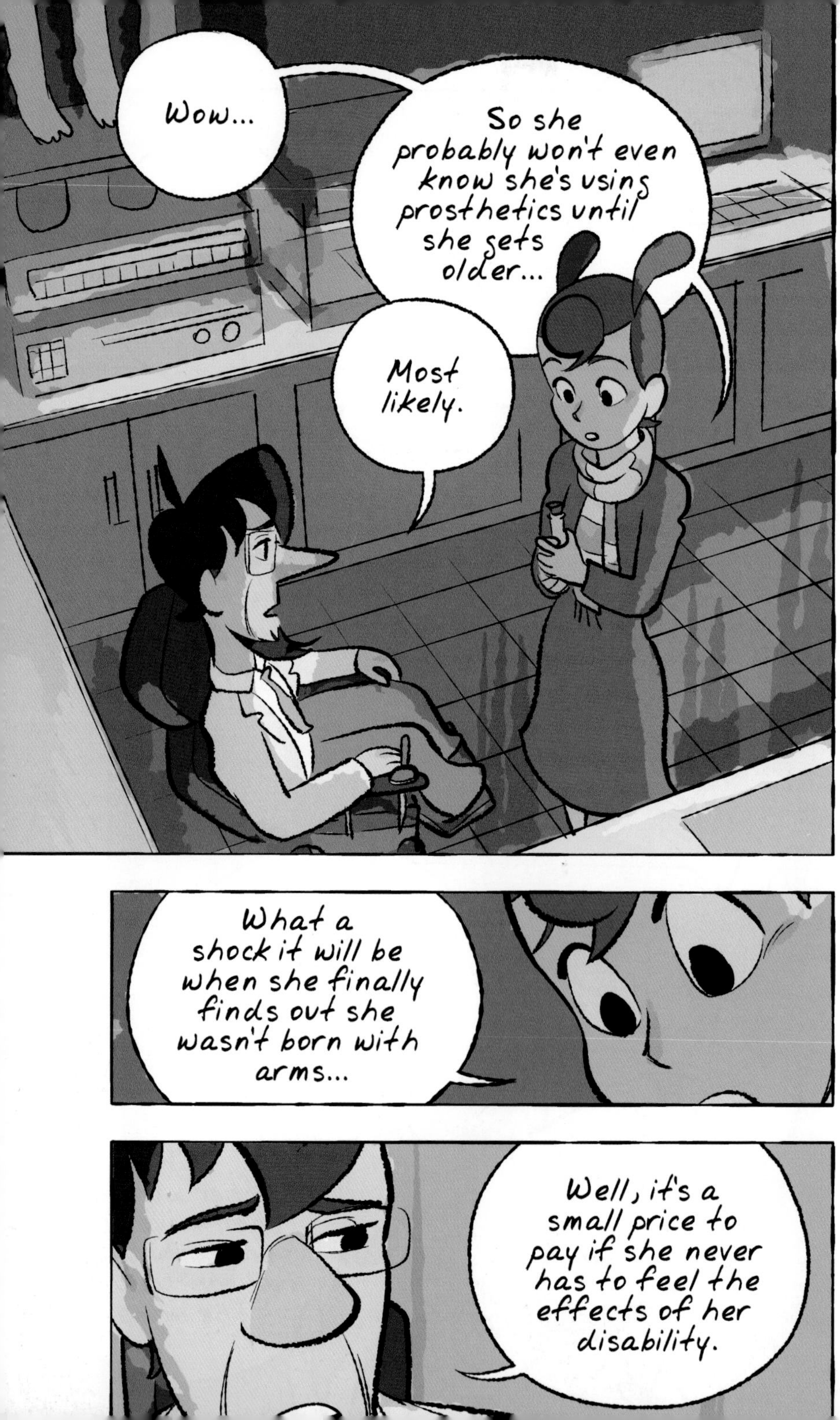
Wow...
So she probably won't even know she's using prosthetics until she gets older...
Most likely.
What a shock it will be when she finally finds out she wasn't born with arms...
Well, it's a small price to pay if she never has to feel the effects of her disability.

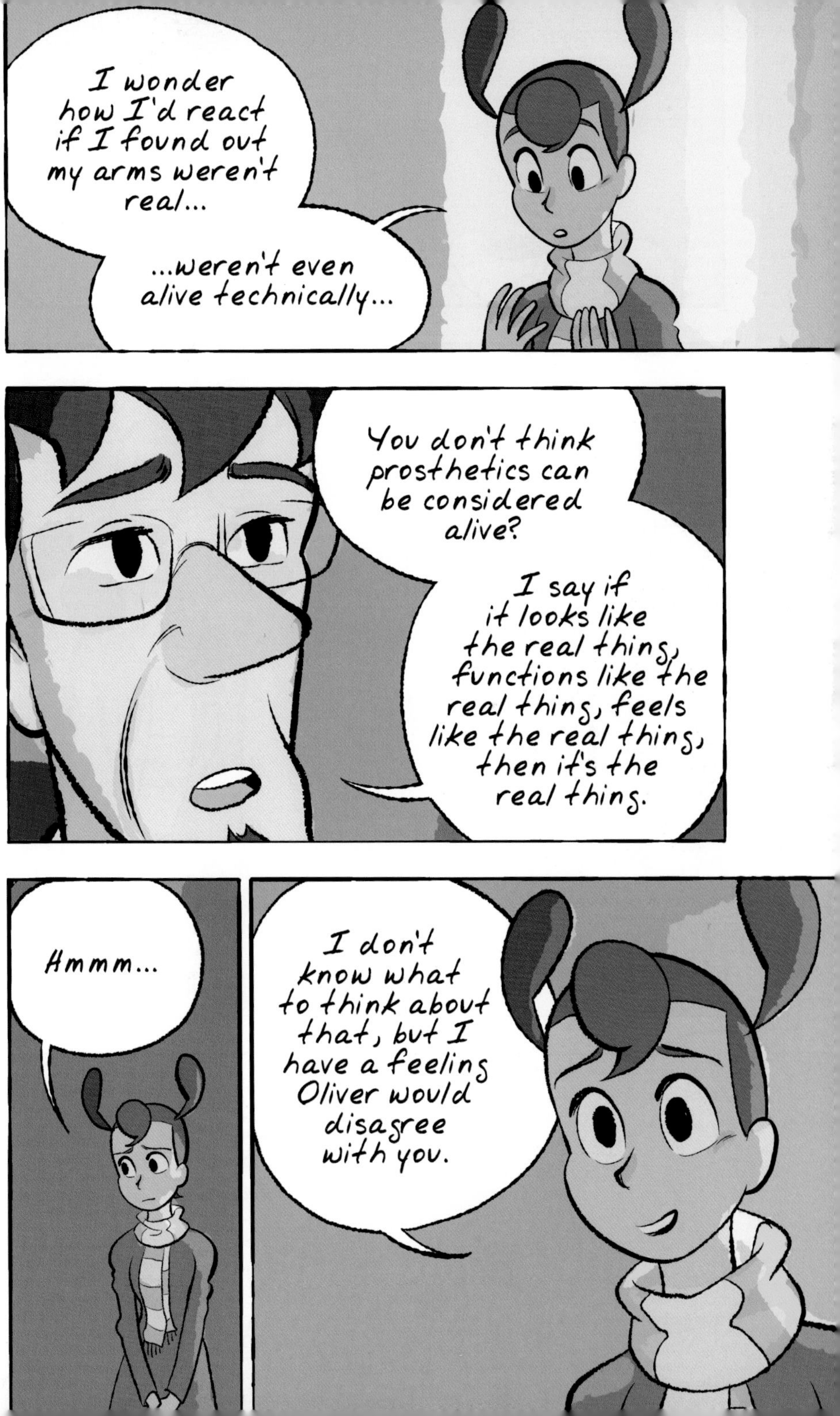
I wonder how I'd react if I found out my arms weren't real...
...weren't even alive technically...
You don't think prosthetics can be considered alive?
I say if it looks like the real thing, functions like the real thing, feels like the real thing, then it's the real thing.
Hmmm...
I don't know what to think about that, but I have a feeling Oliver would disagree with you.

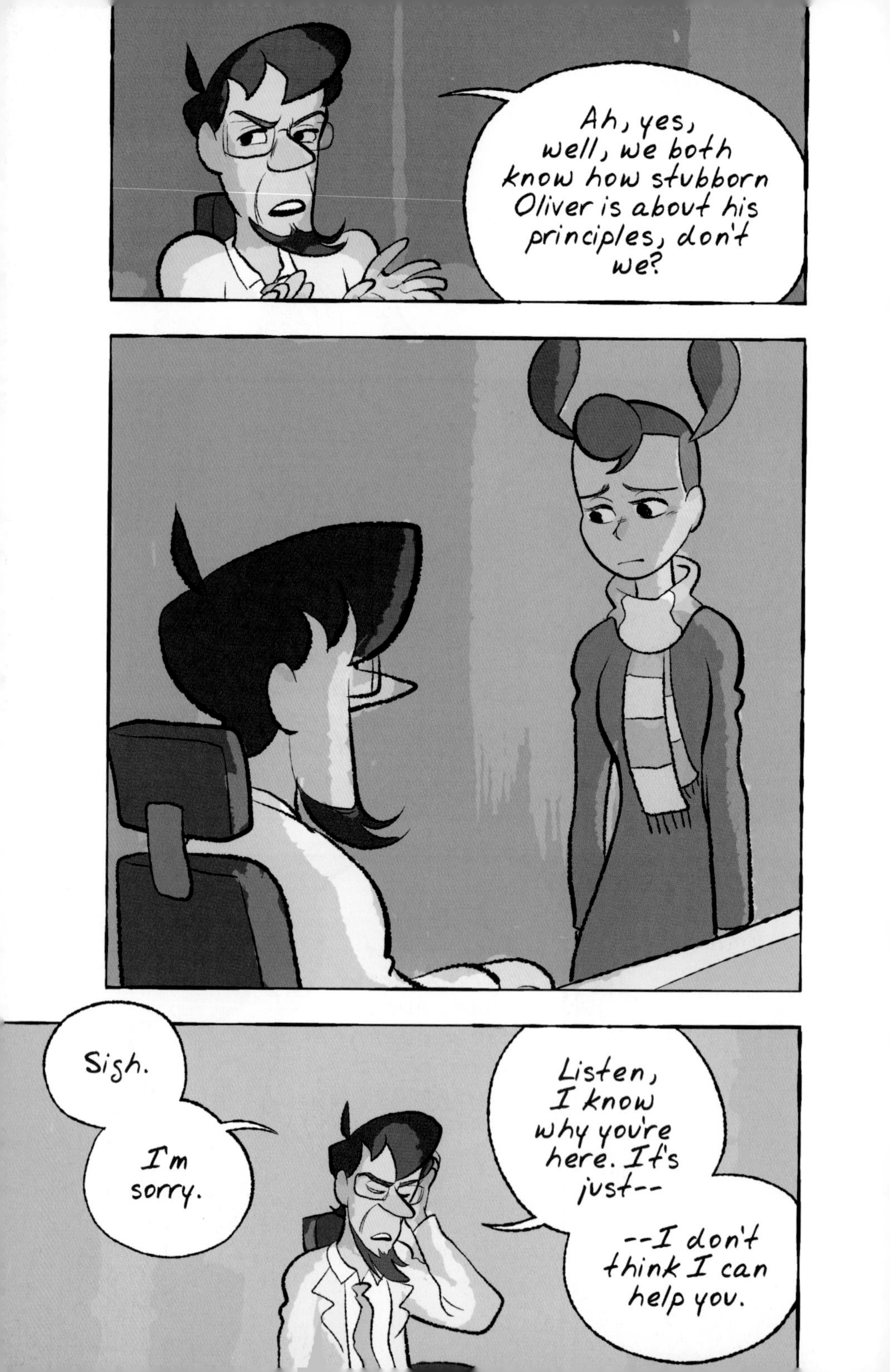
Ah, yes, well, we both know how stubborn Oliver is about his principles, don't we?
Sigh.
I'm sorry.
Listen, I know why you're here. It's just--
--I don't think I can help you.

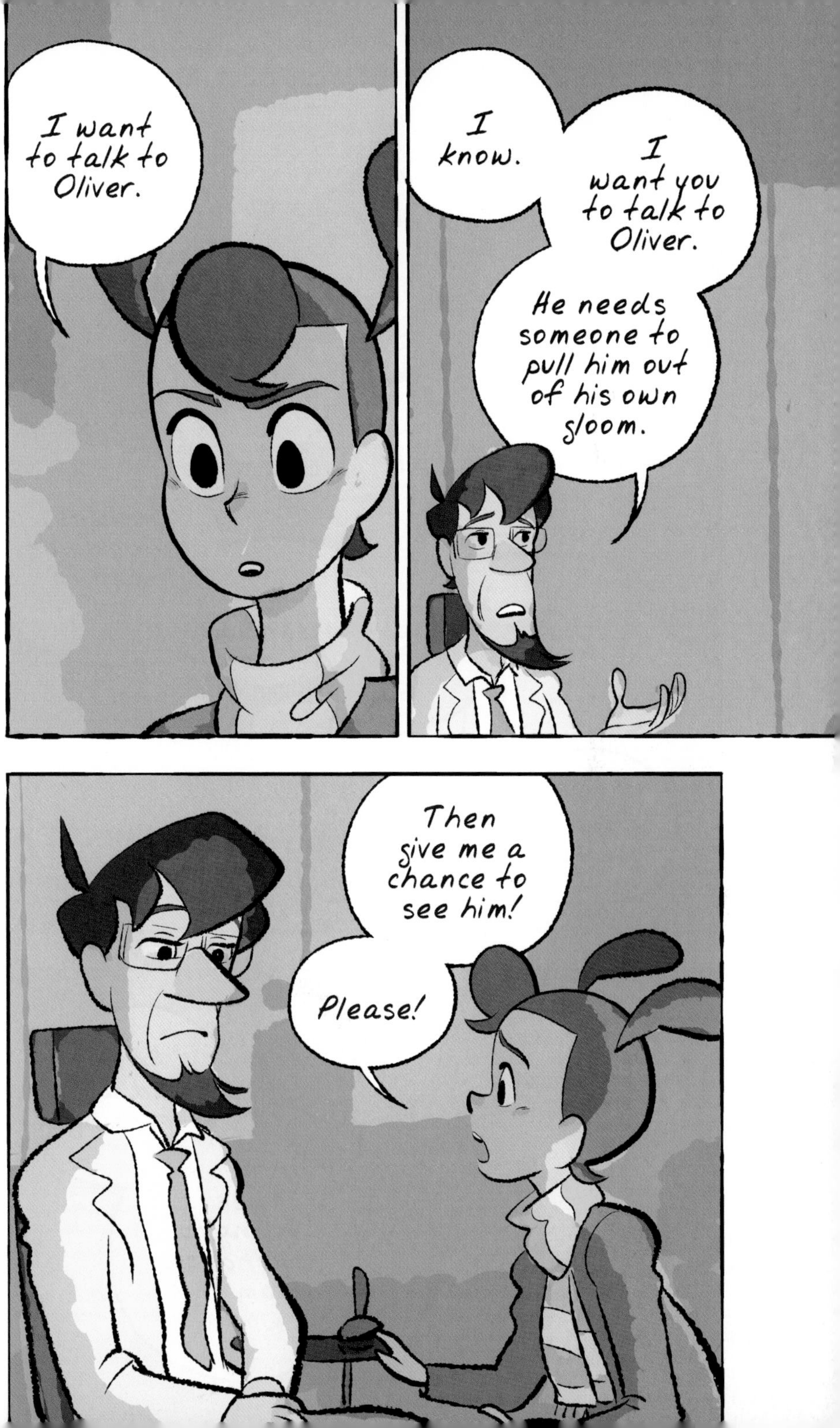

I want to talk to Oliver.
I know.
I want you to talk to Oliver.
He needs someone to pull him out of his own gloom.
Then give me a chance to see him!
Please!

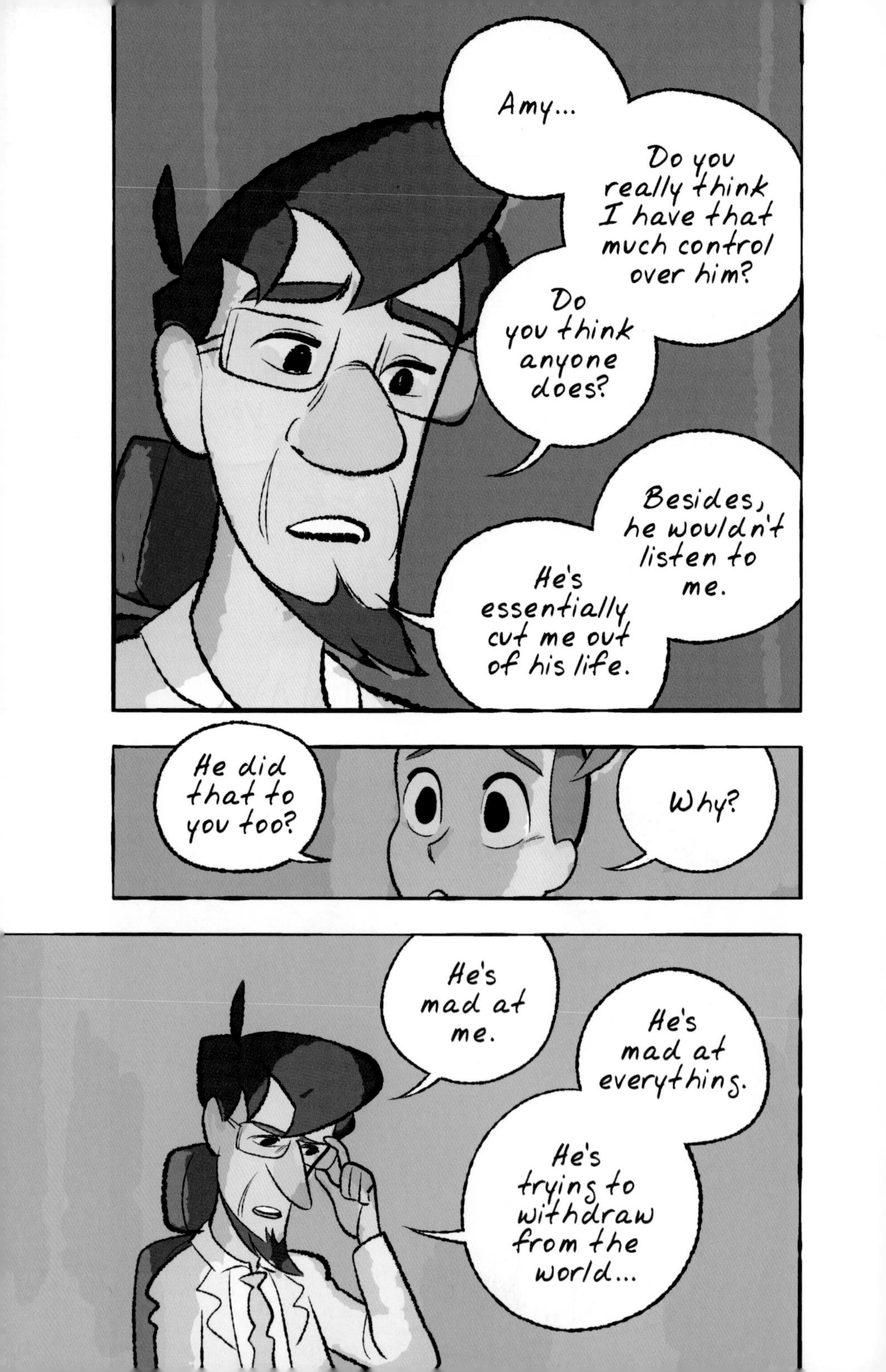
Amy...
Do you really think I have that much control over him?
Do you think anyone does?
Besides, he wouldn't listen to me.
He's essentially cut me out of his life.
He did that to you too?
Why?
He's mad at me.
He's mad at everything.
He's trying to withdraw from the world...

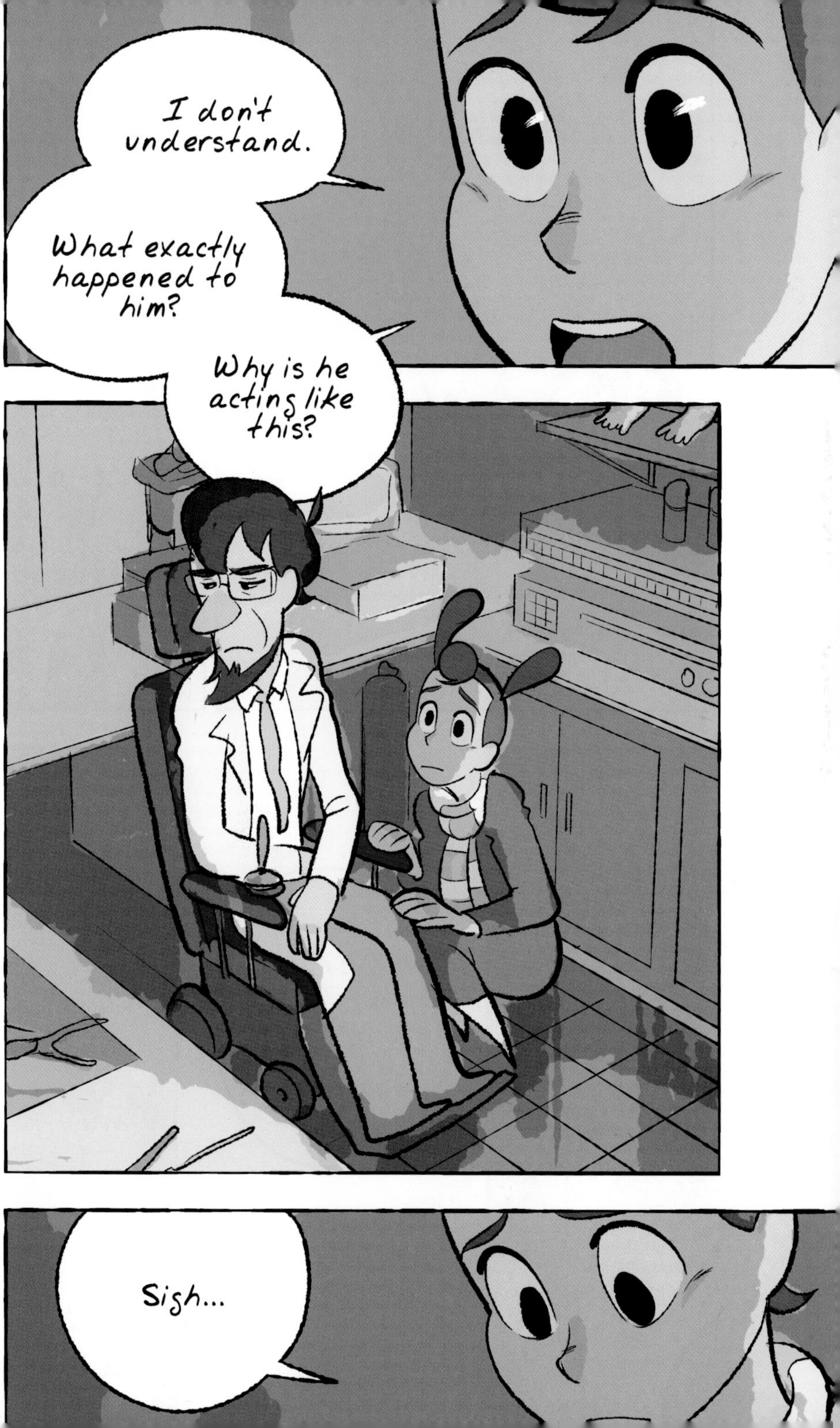
I don't understand.
What exactly happened to him?
Why is he acting like this?
Sigh...

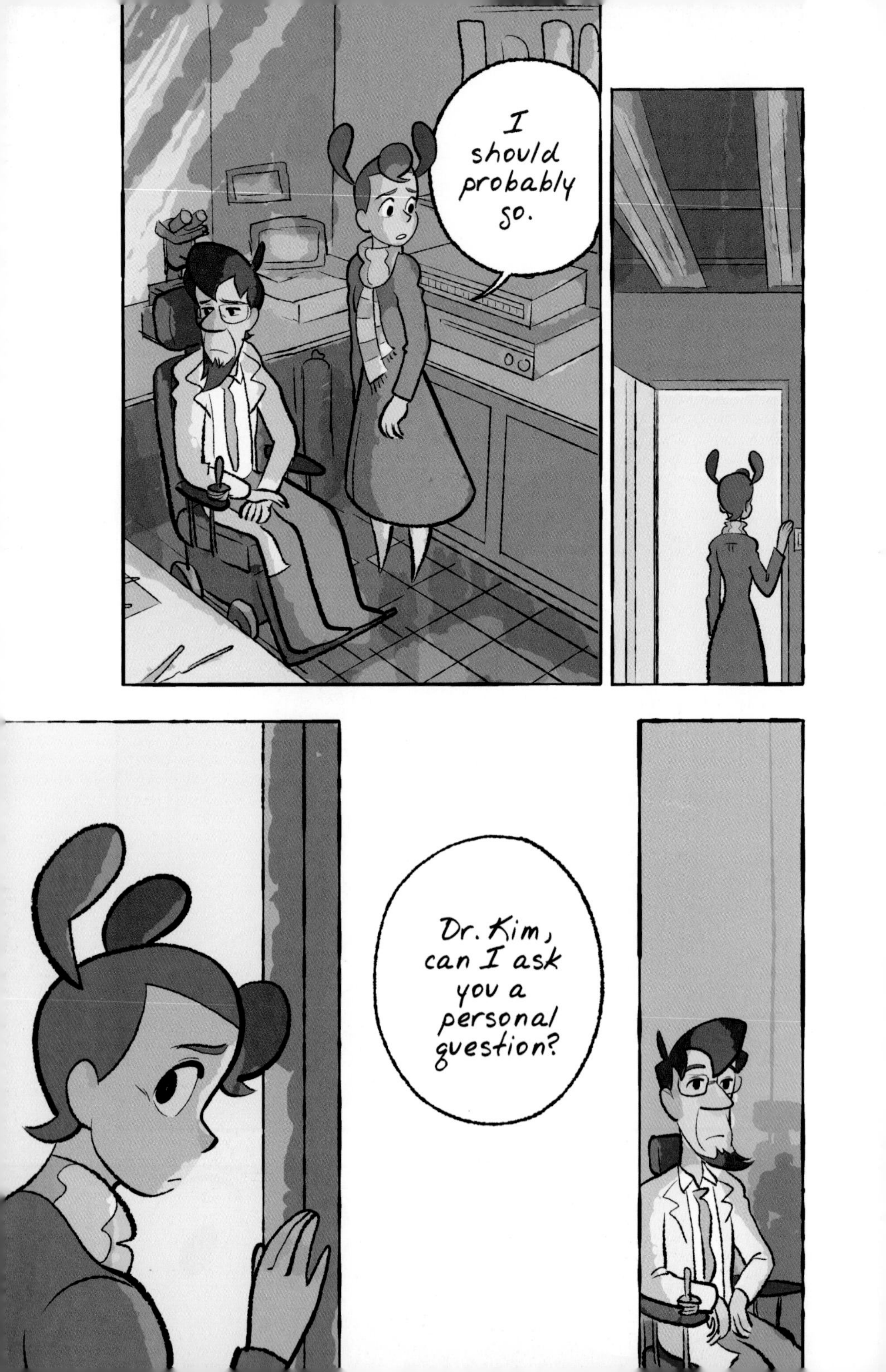
I should probably go.
Dr. Kim, can I ask you a personal question?

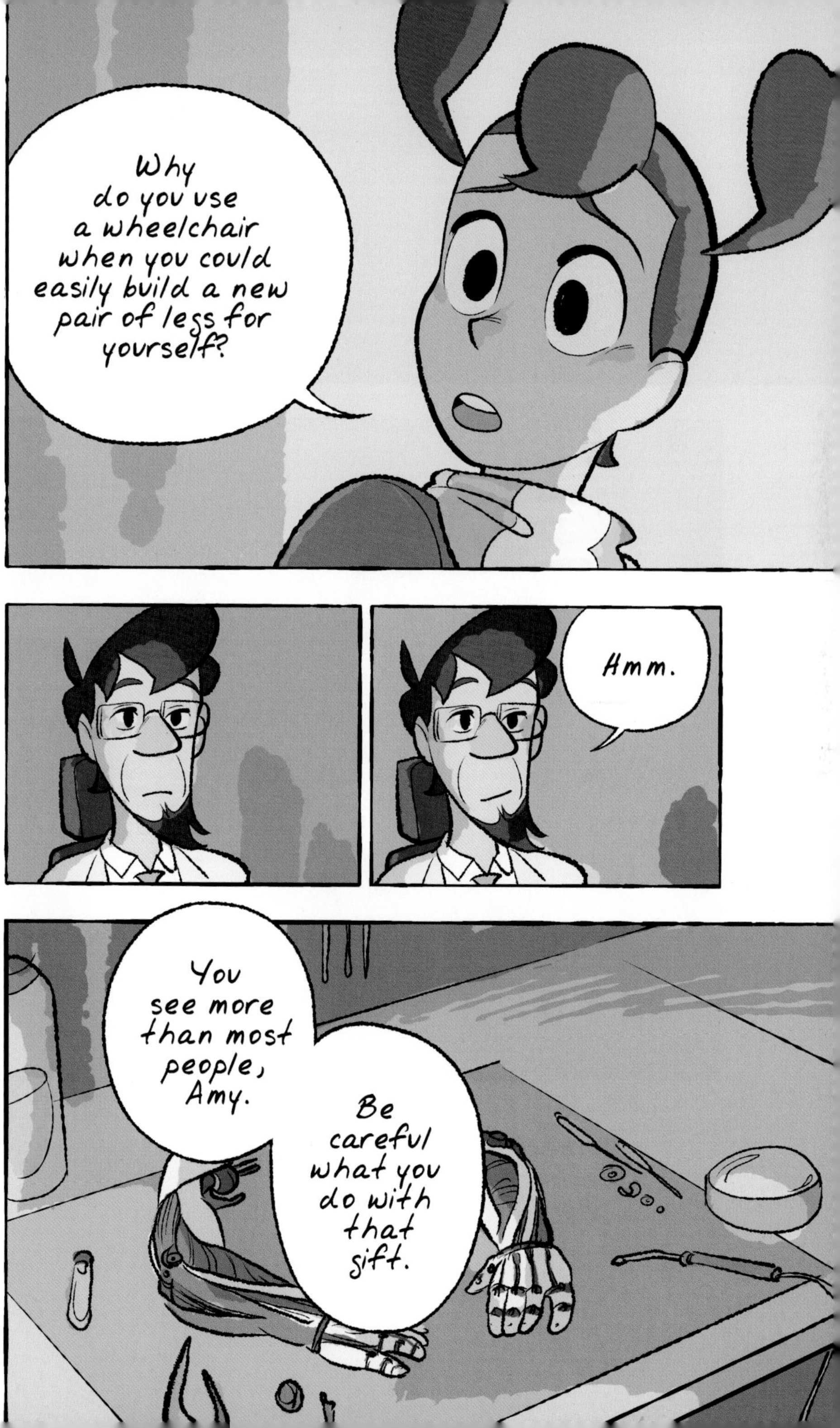
Why do you use a wheelchair when you could easily build a new pair of legs for yourself?
Hmm.
You see more than most people, Amy.
Be careful what you do with that gift.

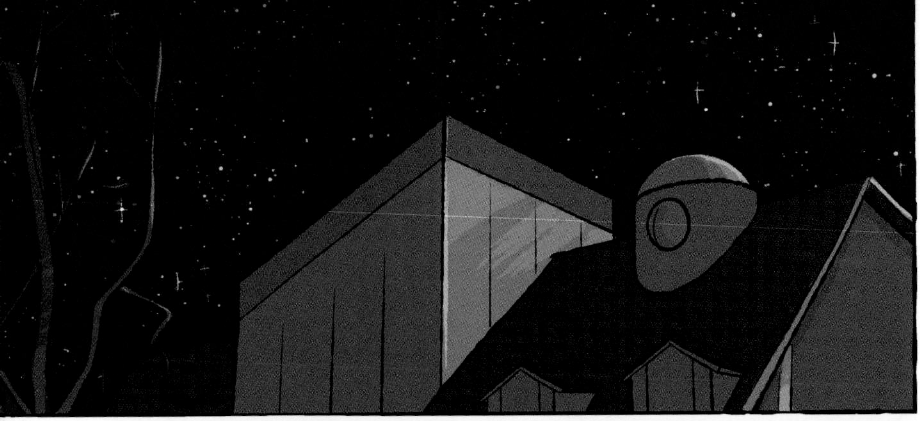

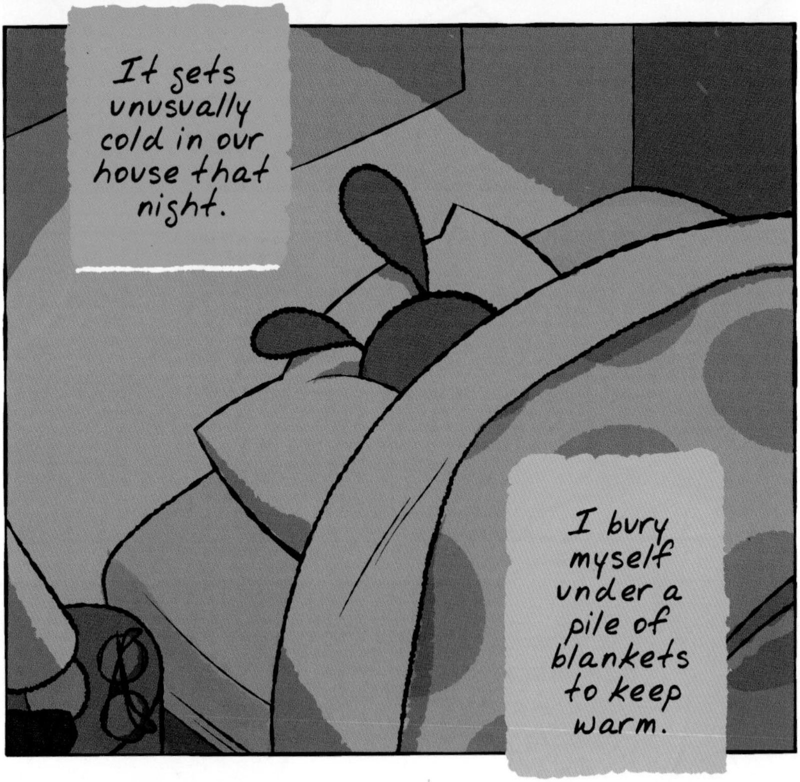
It gets unusually cold in our house that night.
I bury myself under a pile of blankets to keep warm.

Winter is definitely here...

I wonder when it will snow?

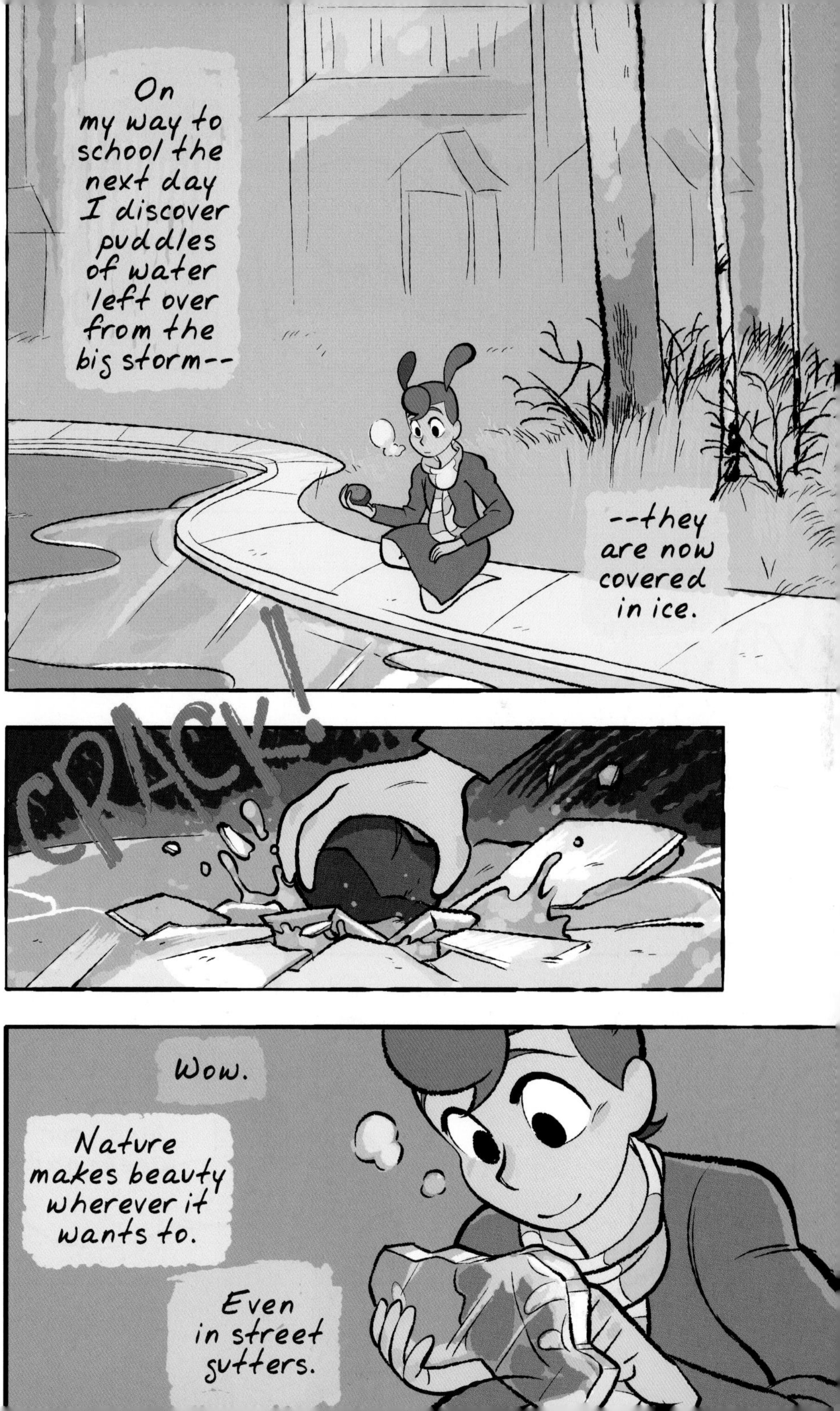
On my way to school the next day I discover puddles of water left over from the big storm--
--they are now covered in ice.
CRACK!
Wow.
Nature makes beauty wherever it wants to.
Even in street gutters.

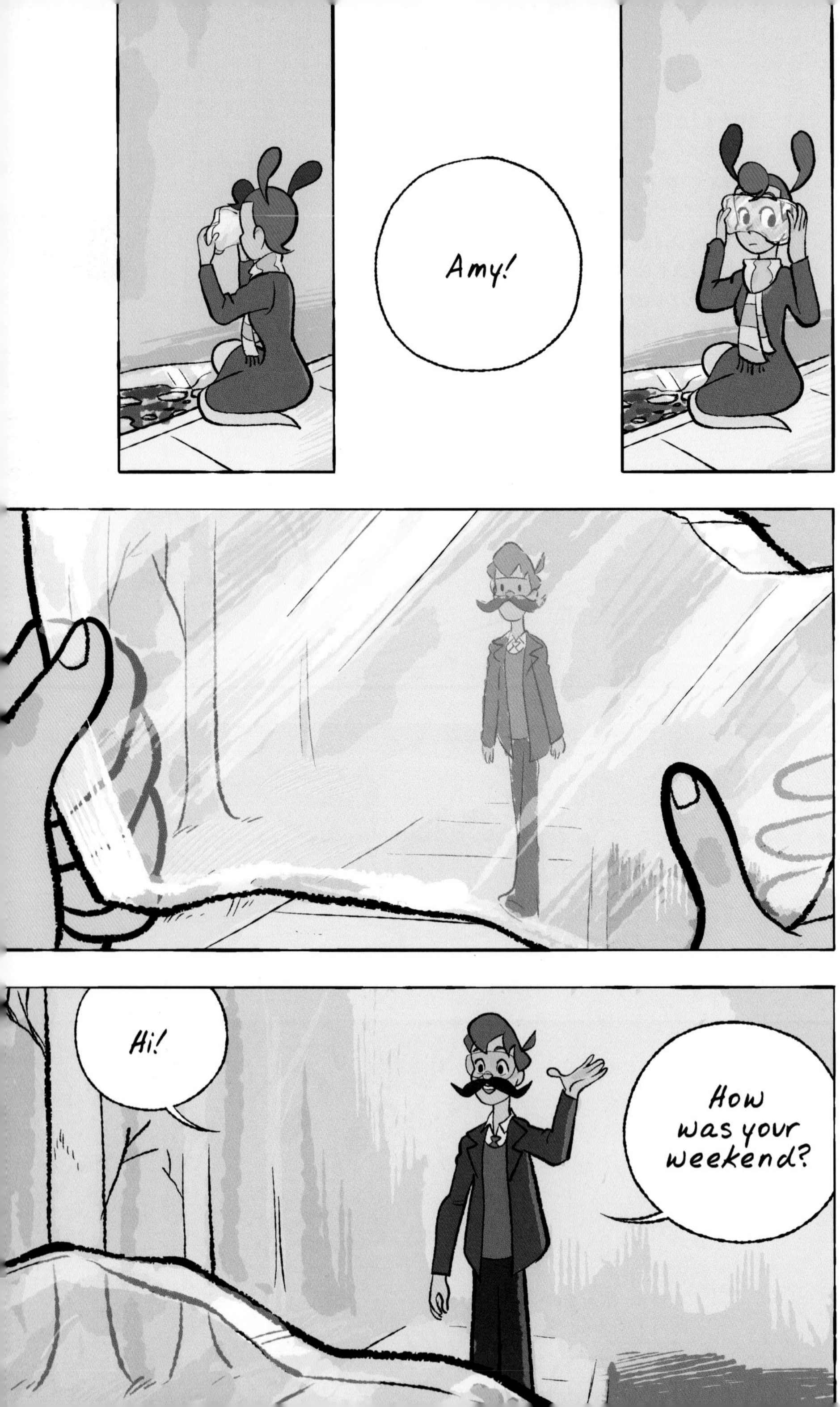
Amy!
Hi!
How was your weekend?

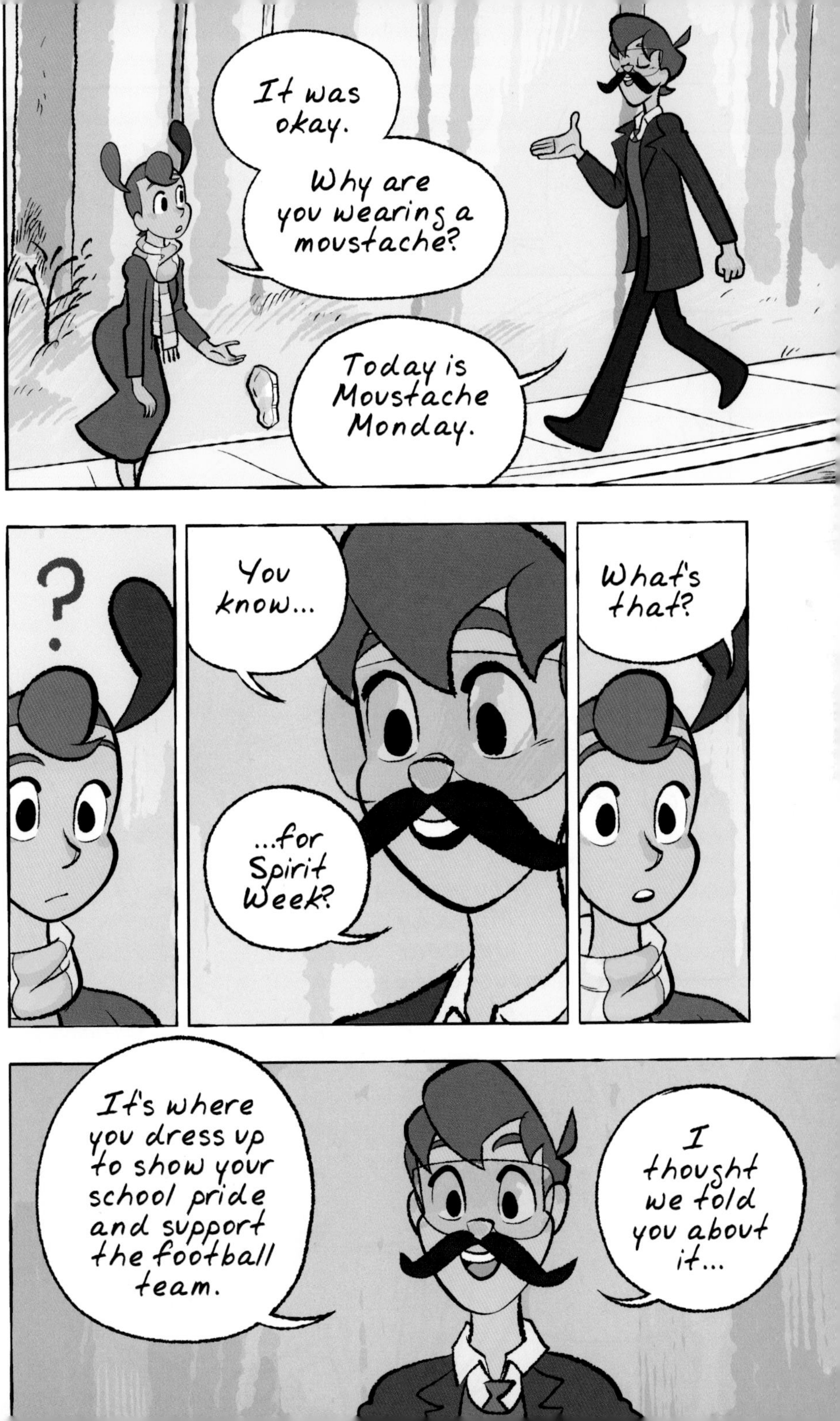
It was okay.
Why are you wearing a moustache?
Today is Moustache Monday.
?
You know...
...for Spirit Week?
What's that?
It's where you dress up to show your school pride and support the football team.
I thought we told you about it...

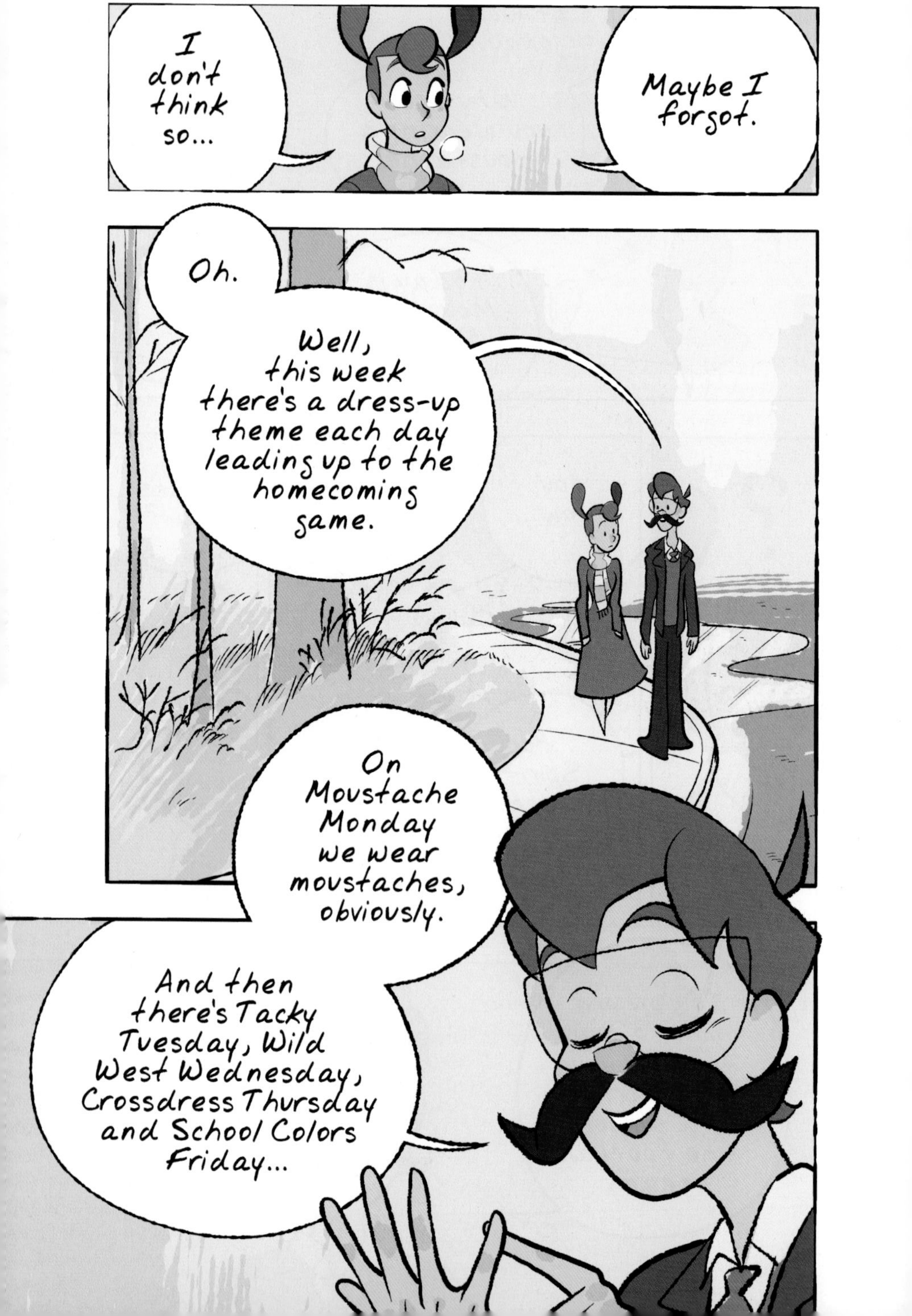
I don't think so...
Maybe I forgot.
Oh.
Well, this week there's a dress-up theme each day leading up to the homecoming game.
On Moustache Monday we wear moustaches, obviously.
And then there's Tacky Tuesday, Wild West Wednesday, Crossdress Thursday and School Colors Friday...

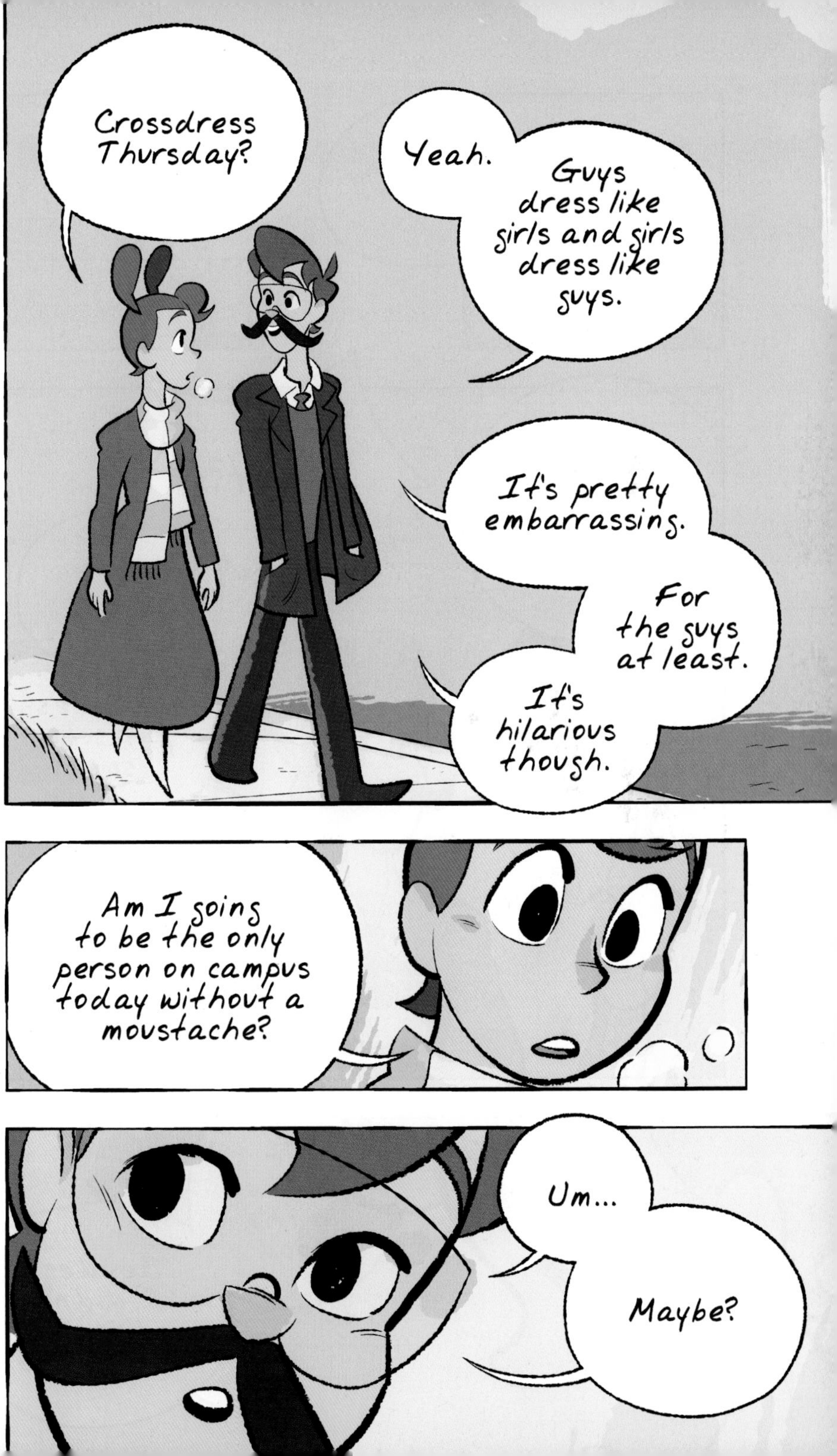

Crossdress Thursday?
Yeah.
Guys dress like girls and girls dress like guys.
It's pretty embarrassing.
For the guys at least.
It's hilarious though.
Am I going to be the only person on campus today without a moustache?
Um...
Maybe?

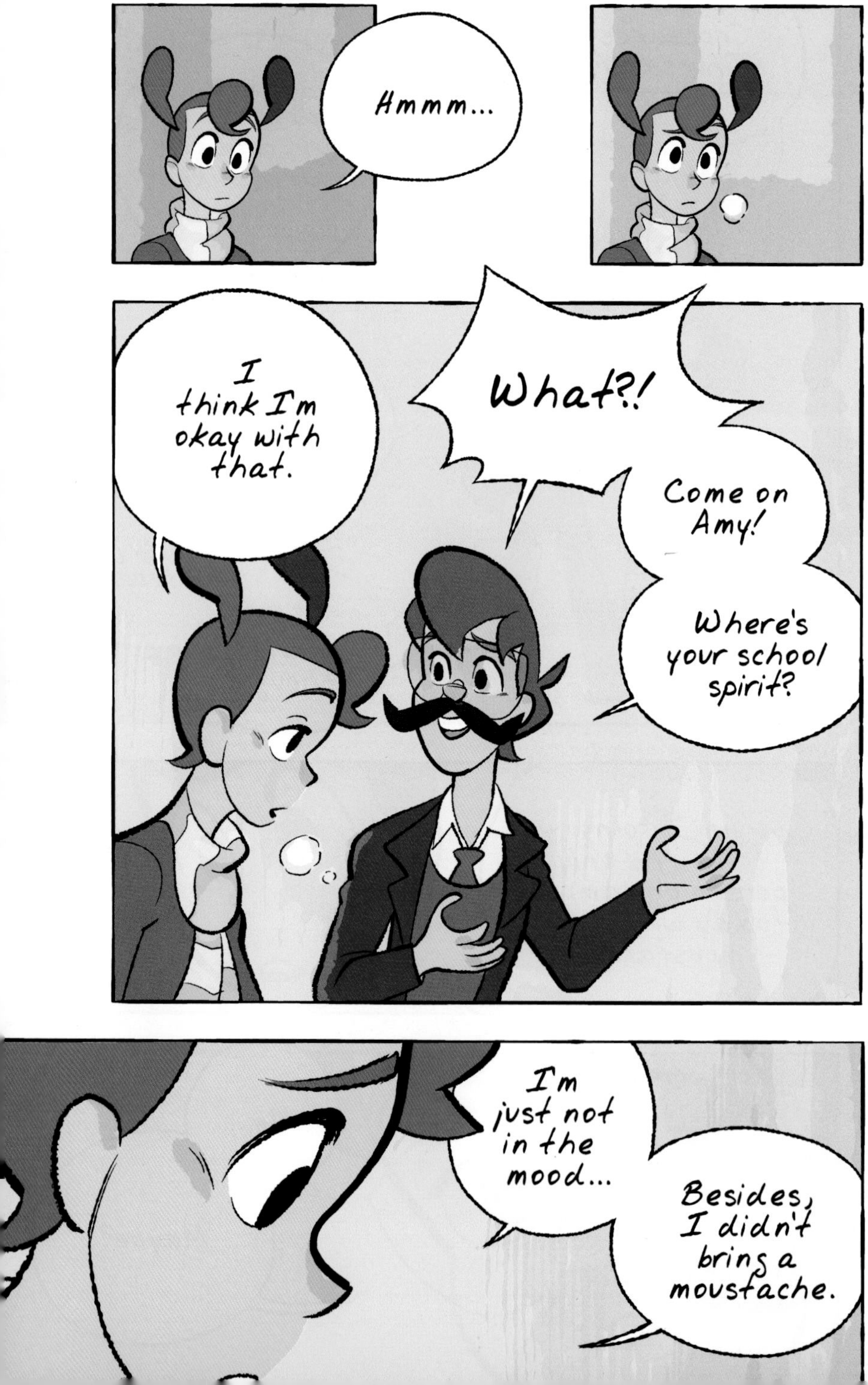
Hmmm...
I think I'm okay with that.
What?!
Come on Amy!
Where's your school spirit?
I'm just not in the mood...
Besides, I didn't bring a moustache.

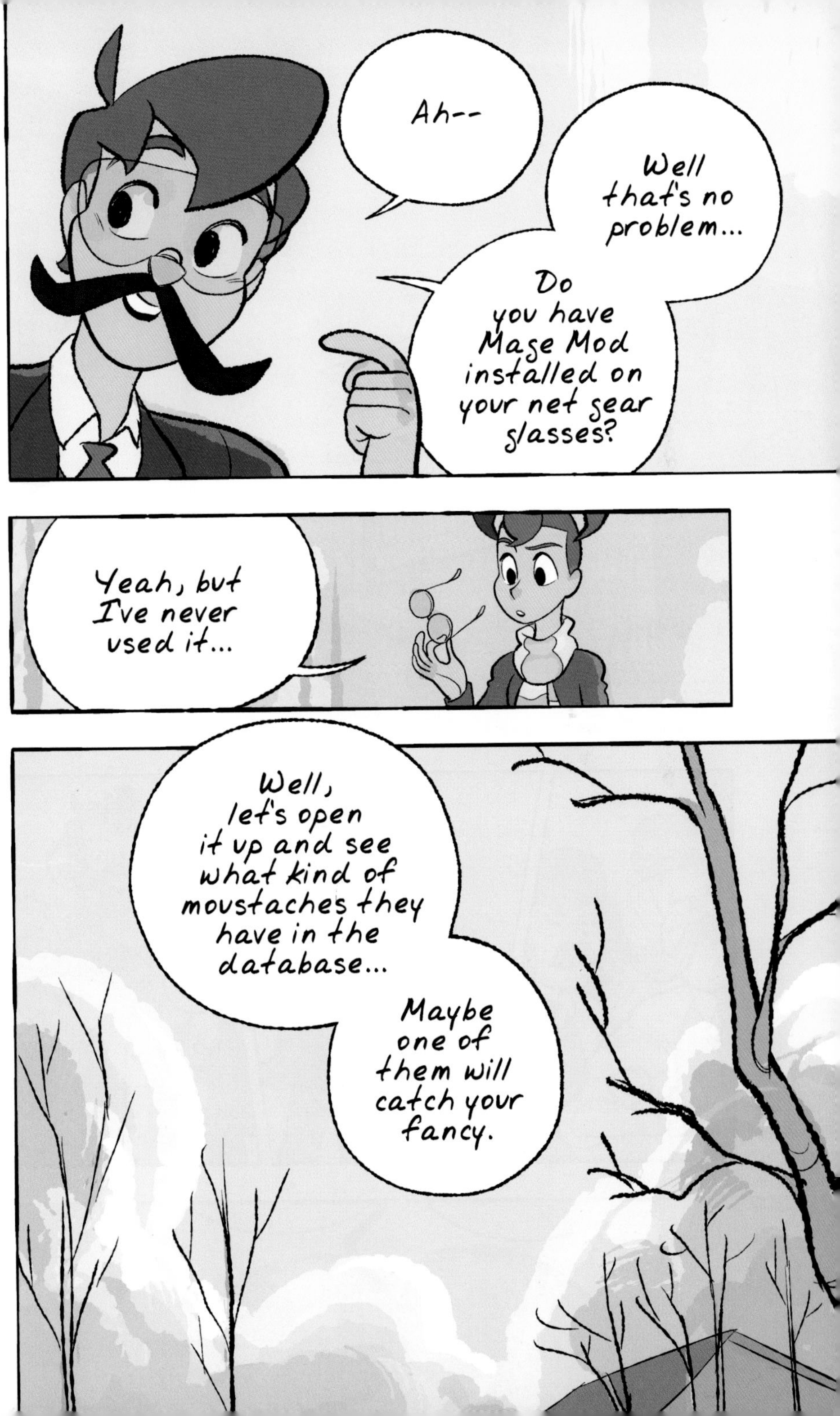
Ah--
Well that's no problem...
Do you have Mage Mod installed on your net gear glasses?
Yeah, but I've never used it...
Well, let's open it up and see what kind of moustaches they have in the database...
Maybe one of them will catch your fancy.

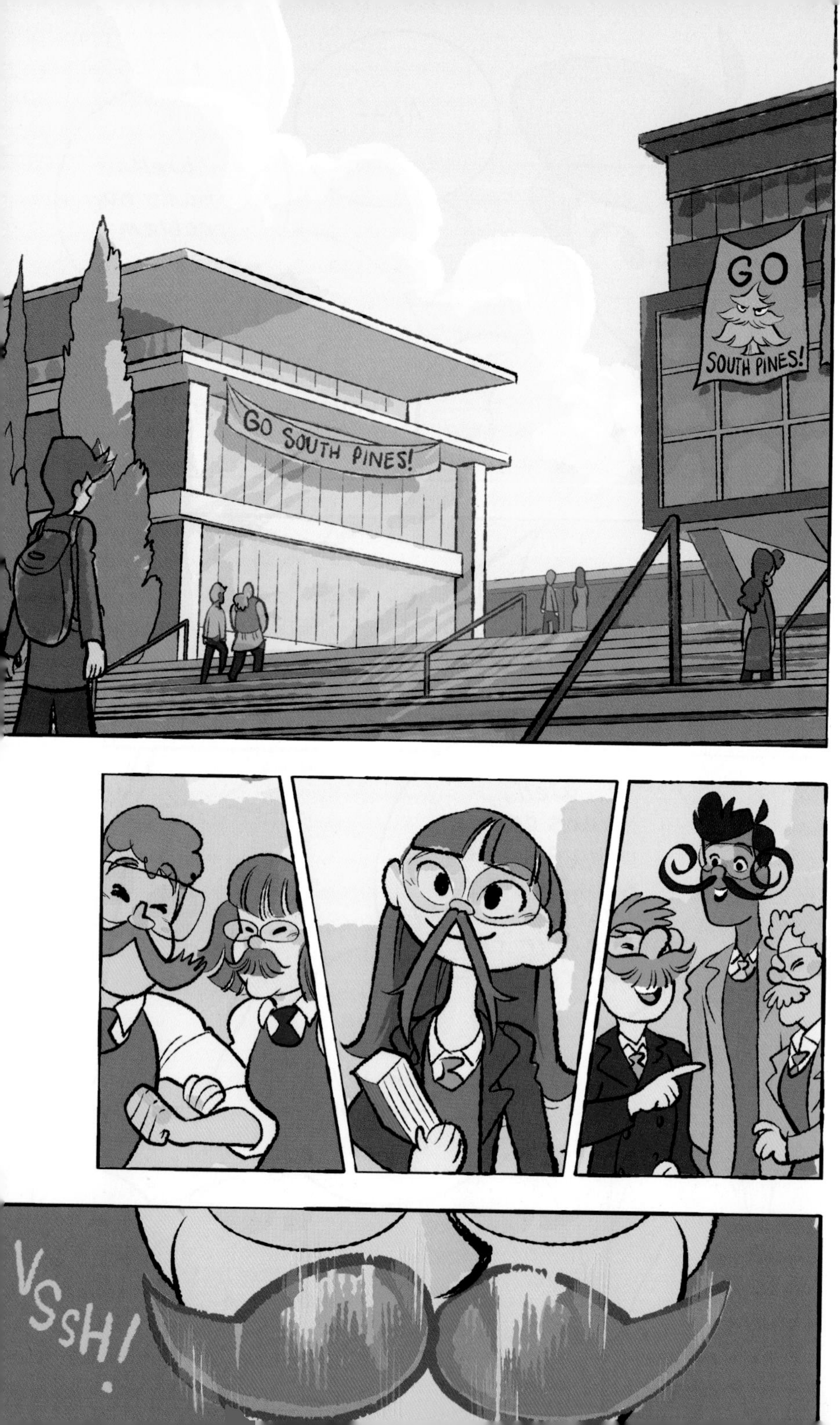
GO SOUTH PINES!
GO
SOUTH PINES!
VSSH!

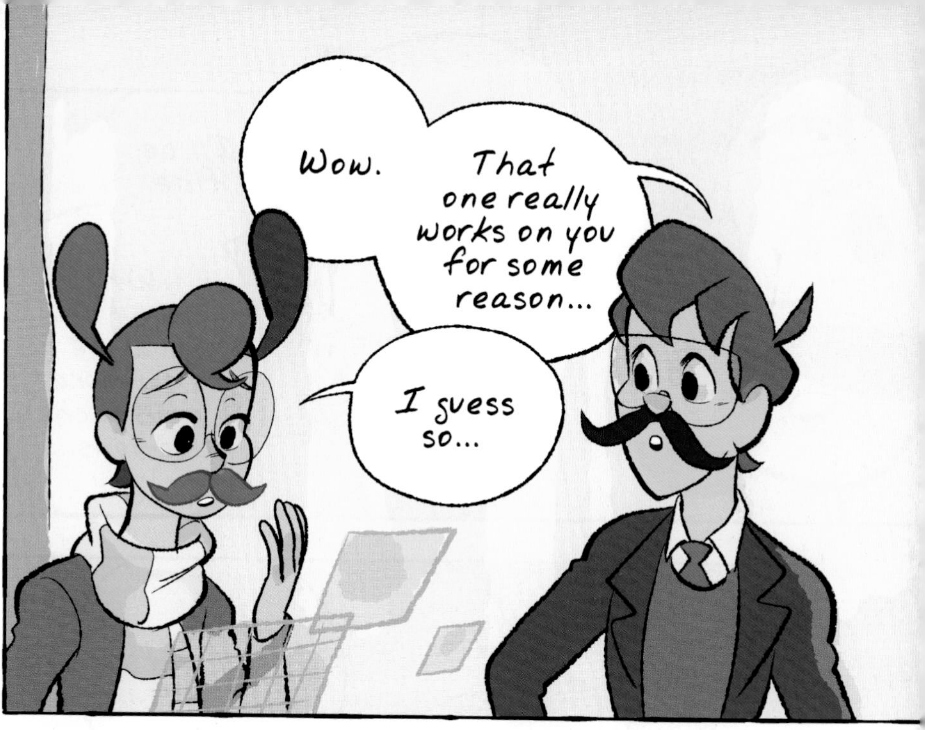
Wow.
That one really works on you for some reason...
I guess so...

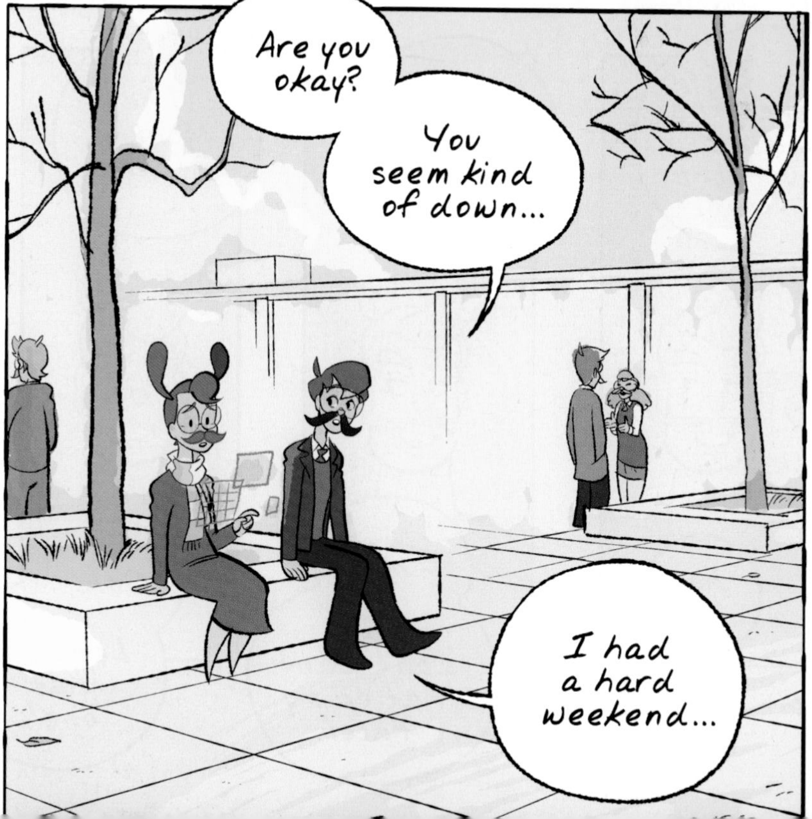
Are you okay?
You seem kind of down...
I had a hard weekend...

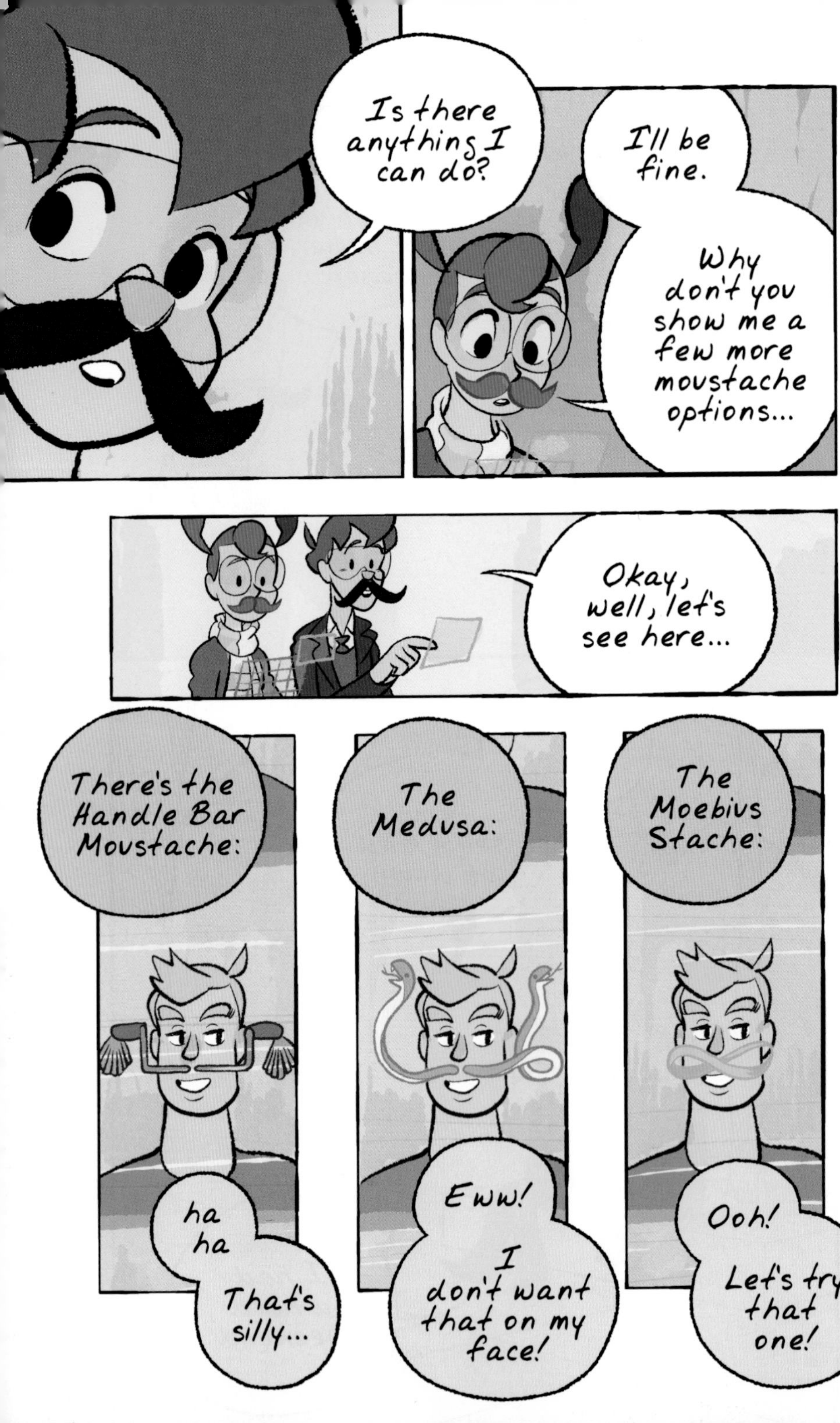
Is there anything I can do?
I'll be fine.
Why don't you show me a few more moustache options...
Okay, well, let's see here...
There's the Handle Bar Moustache:
ha ha
That's silly...
The Medusa:
Eww!
I don't want that on my face!
The Moebius Stache:
Ooh!
Let's try that one!

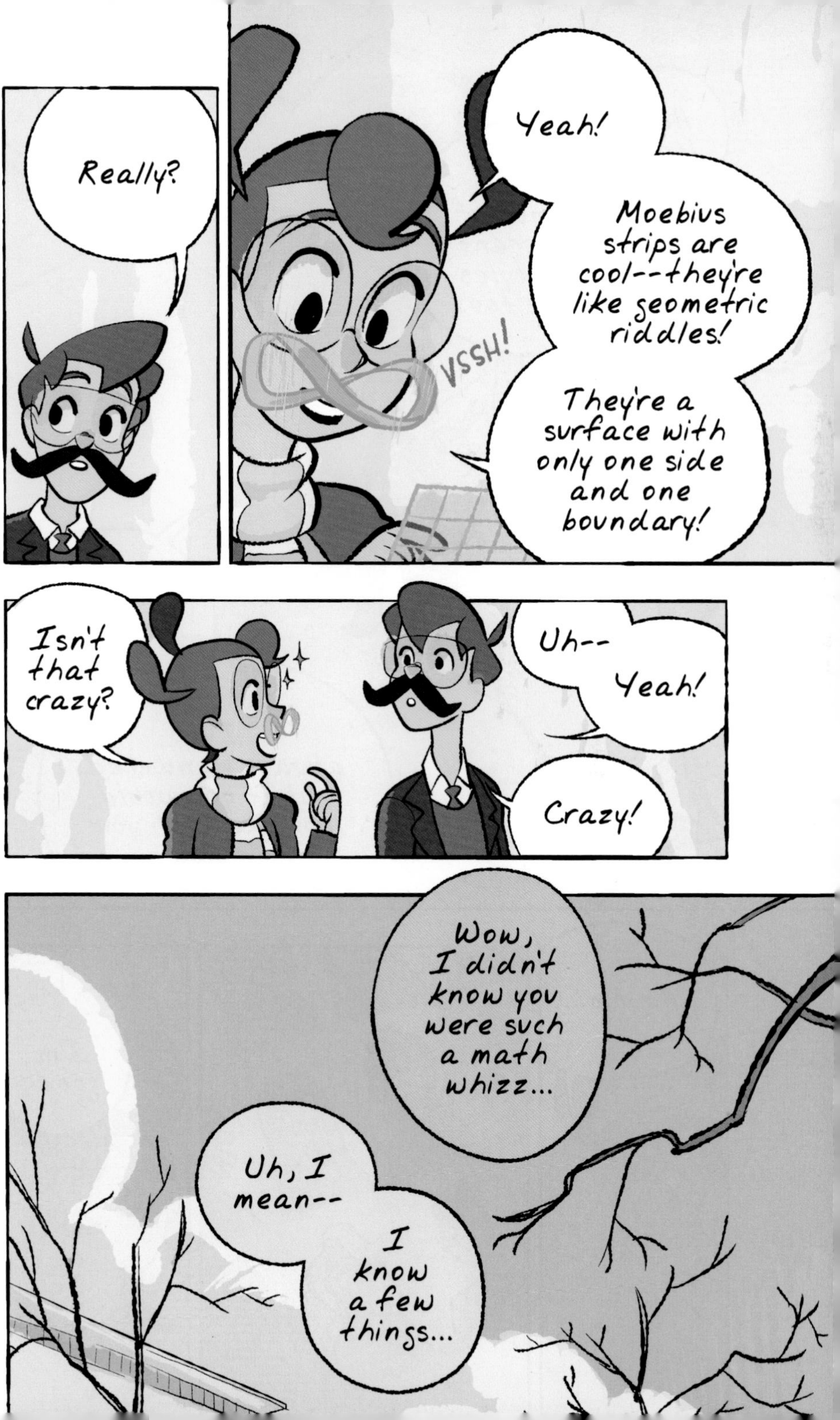
Really?
Yeah!
Moebius strips are cool--they're like geometric riddles!
VSSH!
They're a surface with only one side and one boundary!
Isn't that crazy?
Uh--
Yeah!
Crazy!
Wow, I didn't know you were such a math whizz...
Uh, I mean--
I know a few things...

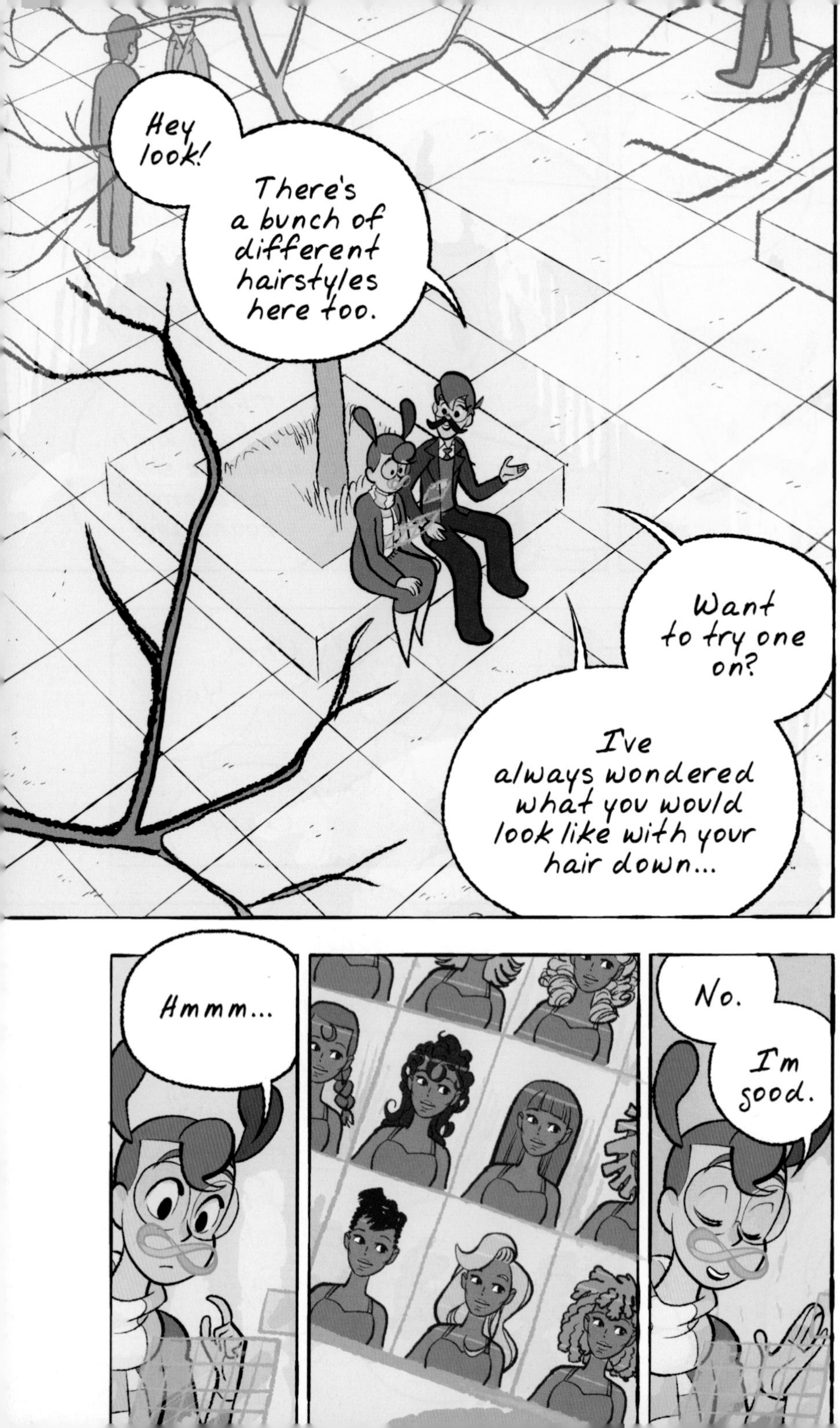
Hey look!
There's a bunch of different hairstyles here too.
Want to try one on?
I've always wondered what you would look like with your hair down...
Hmmm...
No.
I'm good.

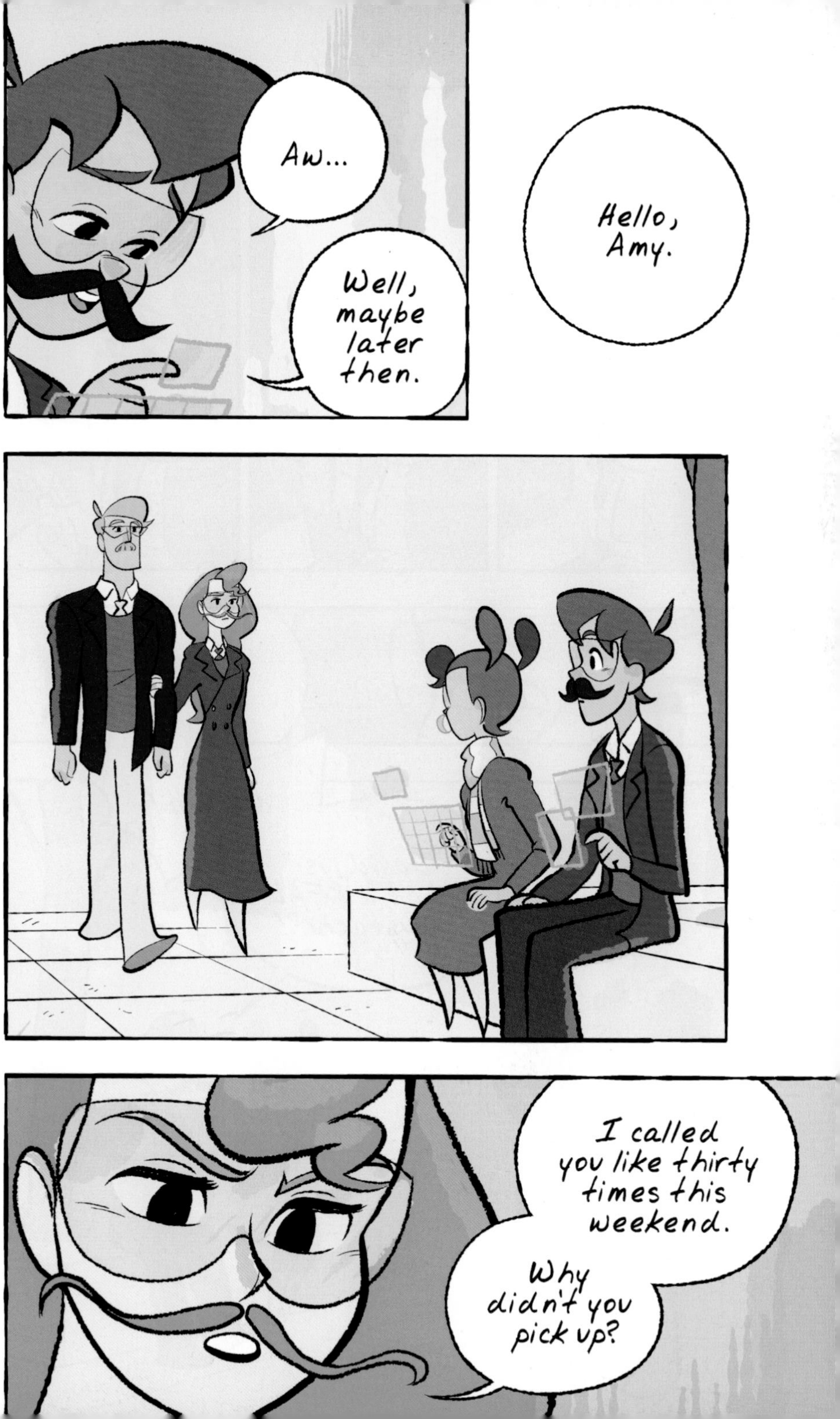
Aw...
Well, maybe later then.
Hello, Amy.
I called you like thirty times this weekend.
Why didn't you pick up?

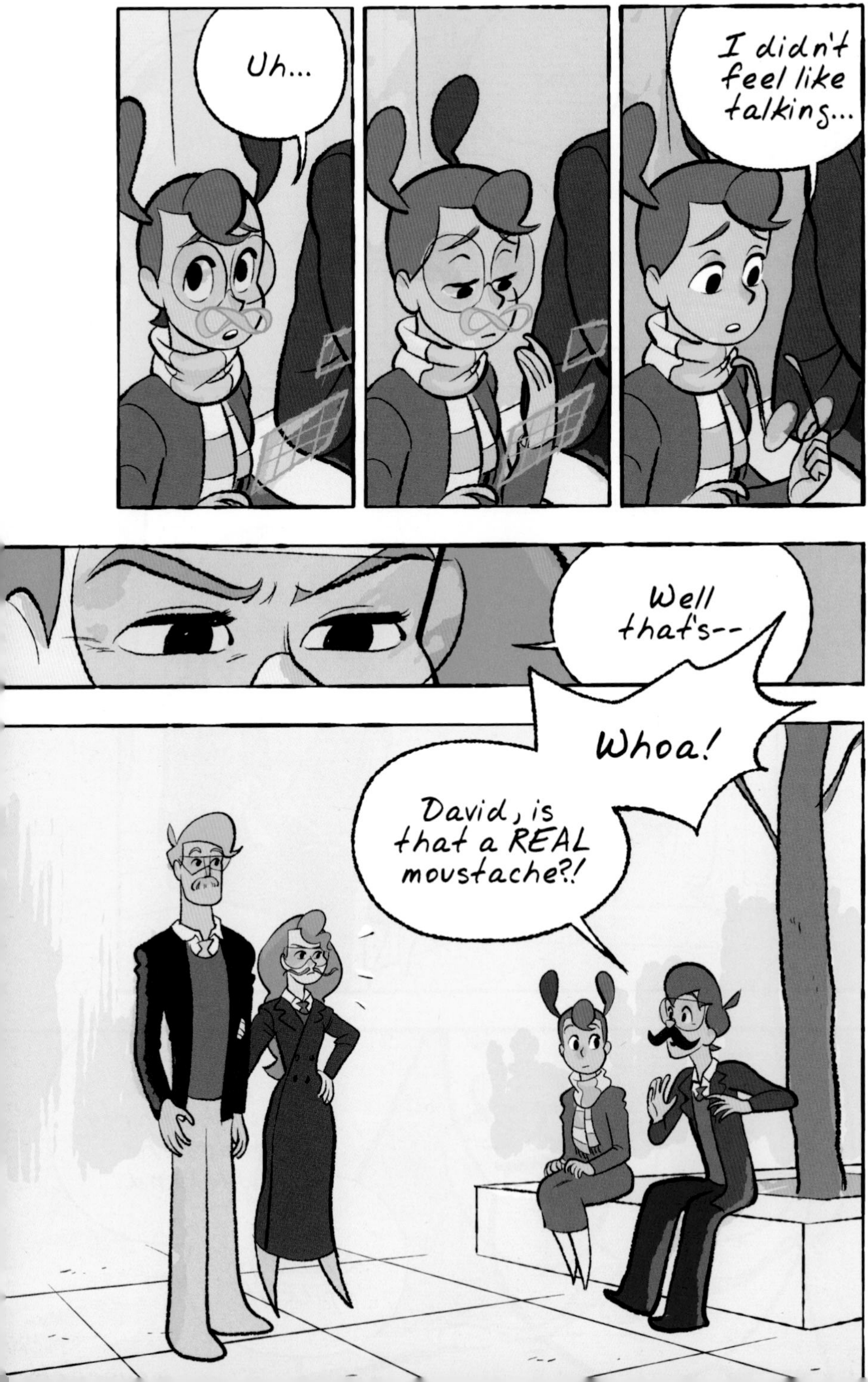
Uh...
I didn't feel like talking...
Well that's--
Whoa!
David, is that a REAL moustache?!

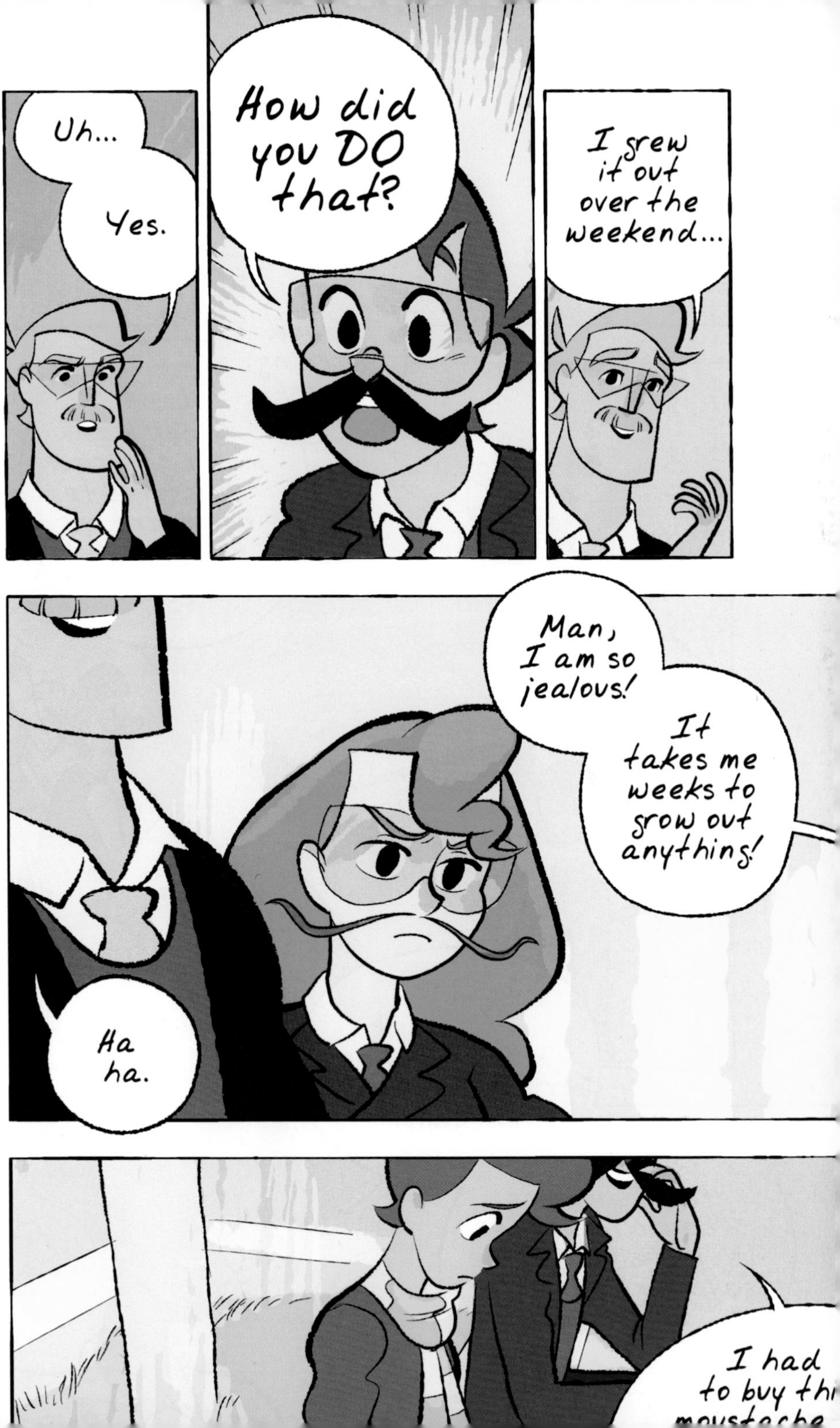

Uh...
Yes.
How did you DO that?
I grew it out over the weekend...
Man, I am so jealous!
It takes me weeks to grow out anything!
Ha ha.
I had to buy thi

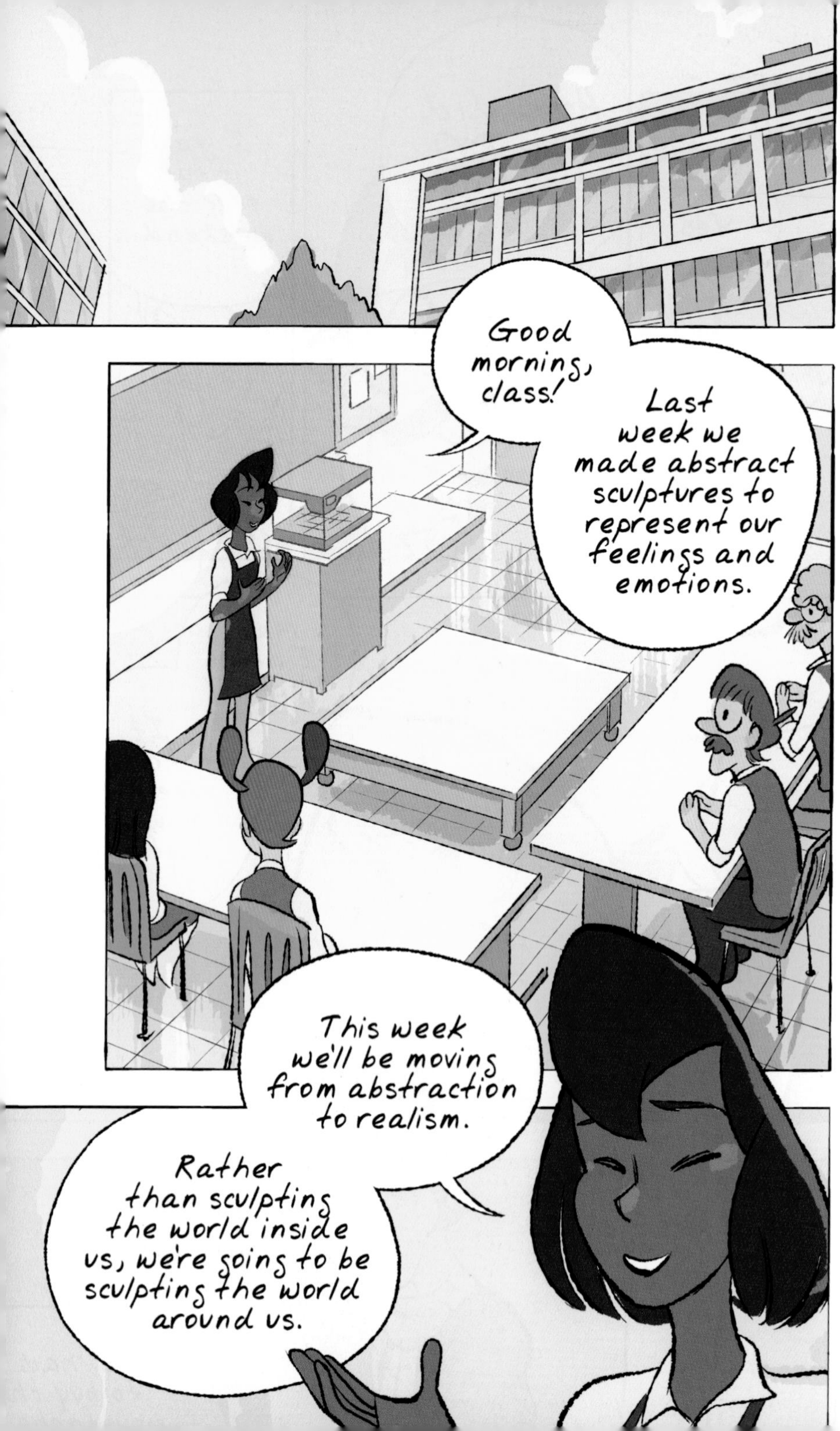
Good morning, class!
Last week we made abstract sculptures to represent our feelings and emotions.
This week we'll be moving from abstraction to realism.
Rather than sculpting the world inside us, we're going to be sculpting the world around us.

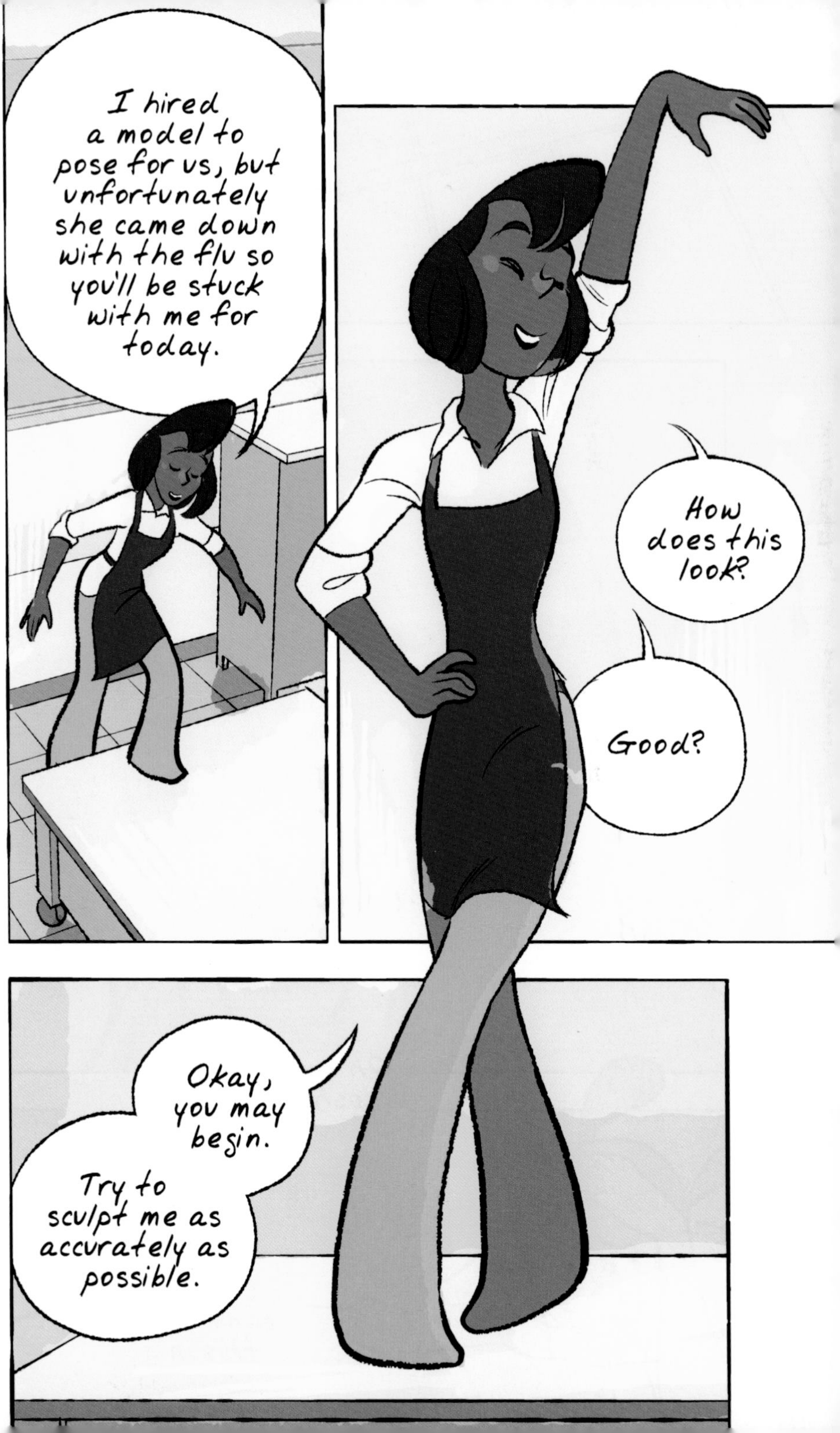
I hired a model to pose for us, but unfortunately she came down with the flu so you'll be stuck with me for today.
How does this look?
Good?
Okay, you may begin.
Try to sculpt me as accurately as possible.

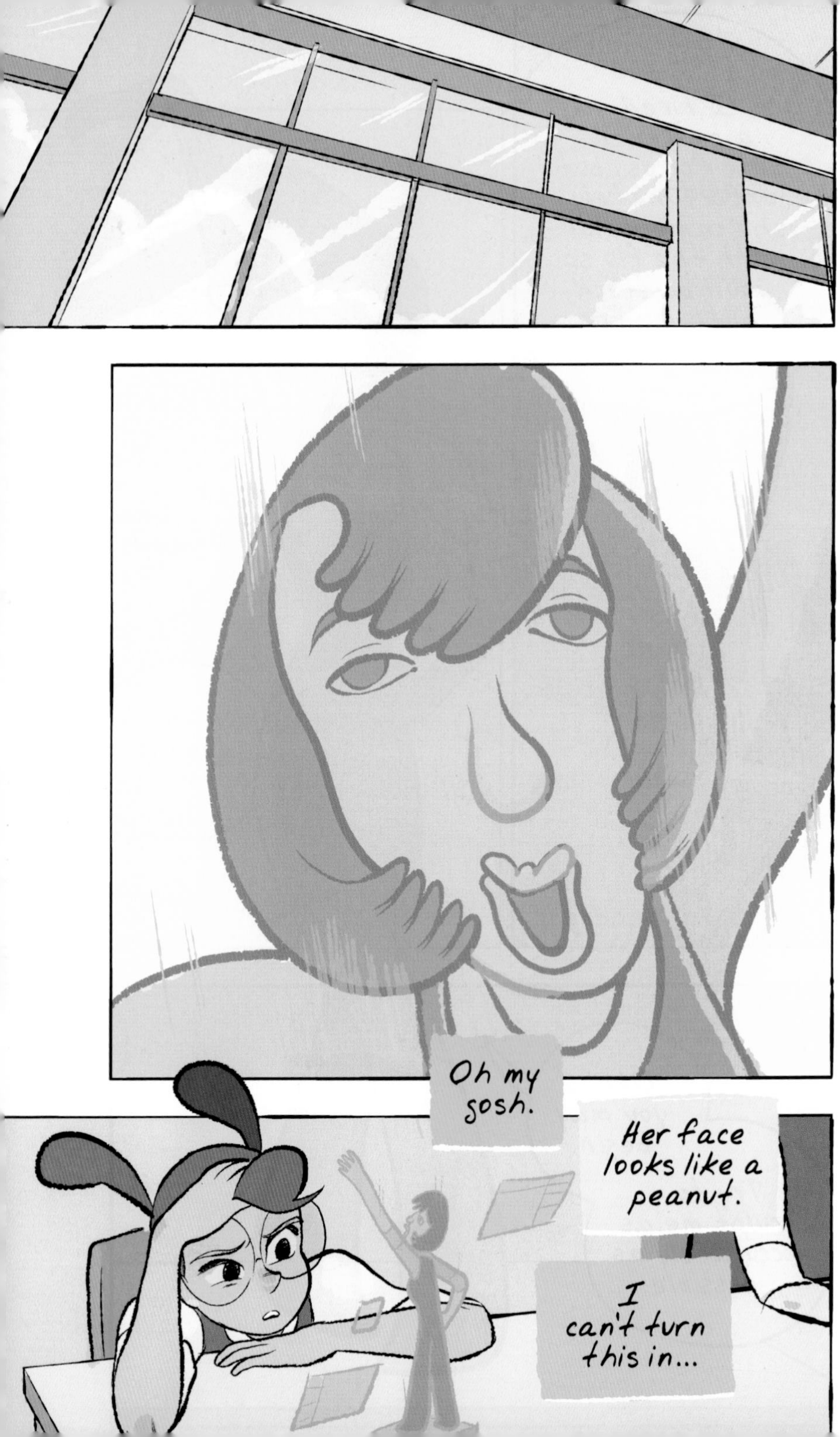
Oh my gosh.
Her face looks like a peanut.
I can't turn this in...

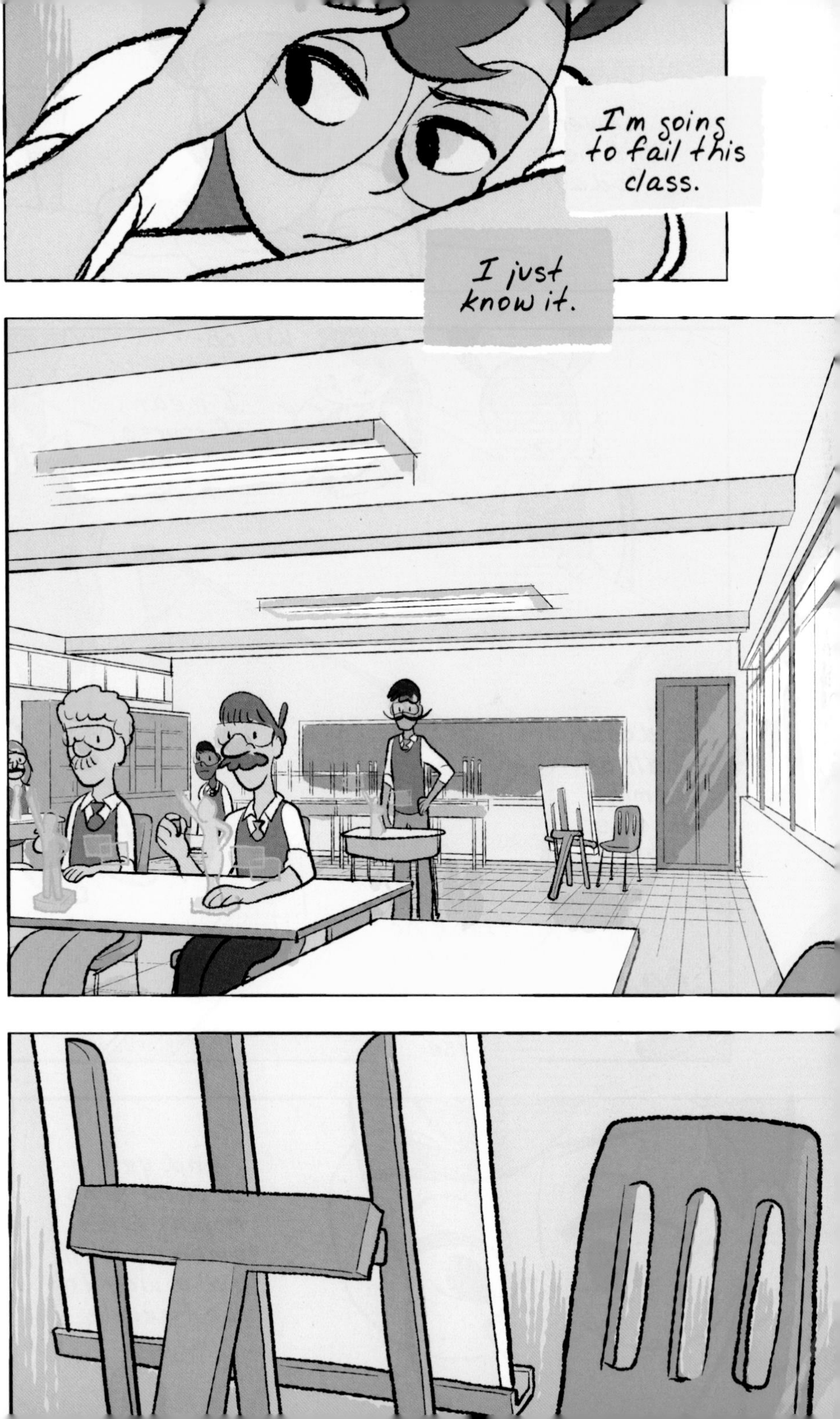
I'm going to fail this class.
I just know it.

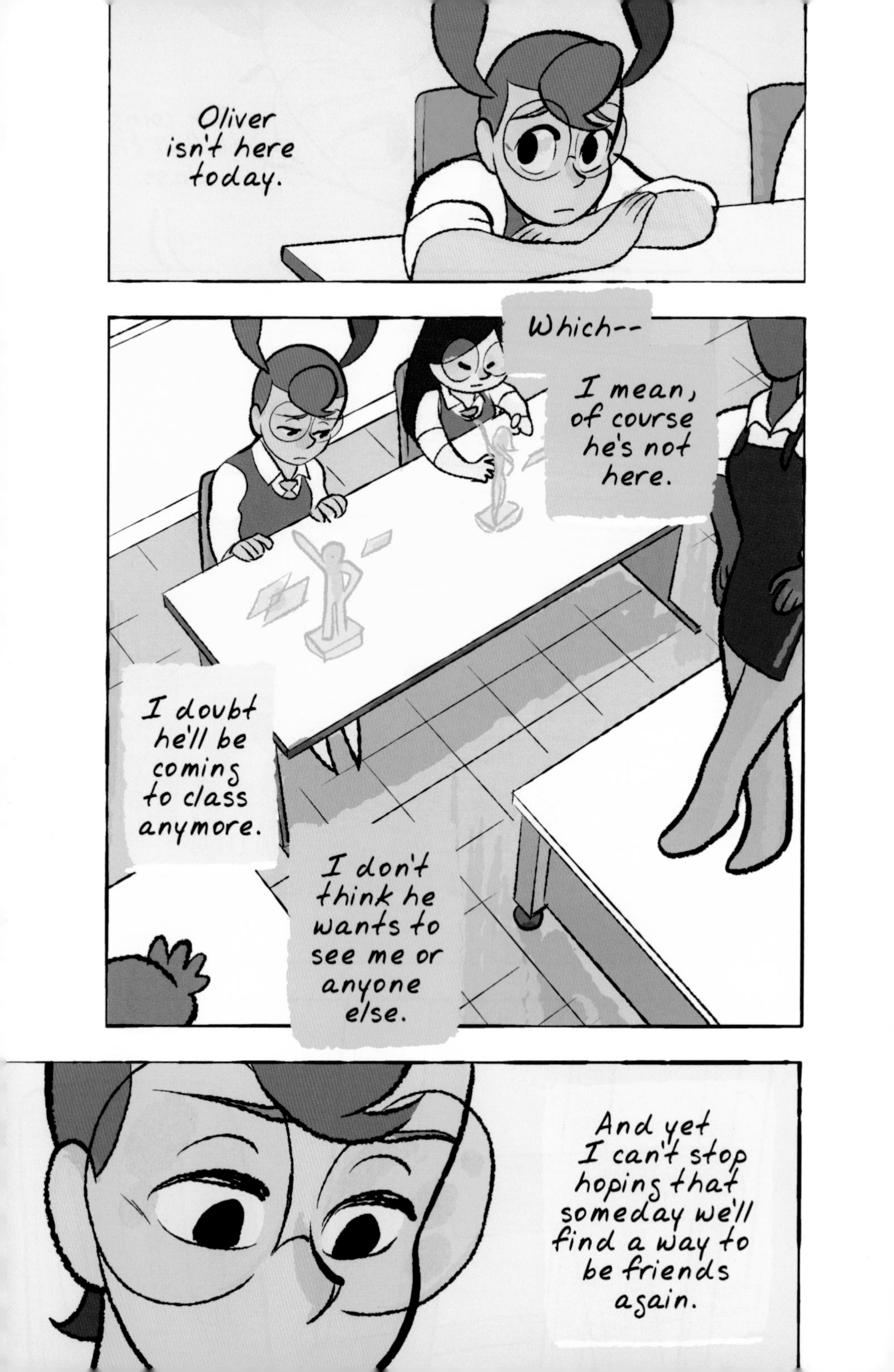
Oliver isn't here today.
Which--
I mean, of course he's not here.
I doubt he'll be coming to class anymore.
I don't think he wants to see me or anyone else.
And yet I can't stop hoping that someday we'll find a way to be friends again.

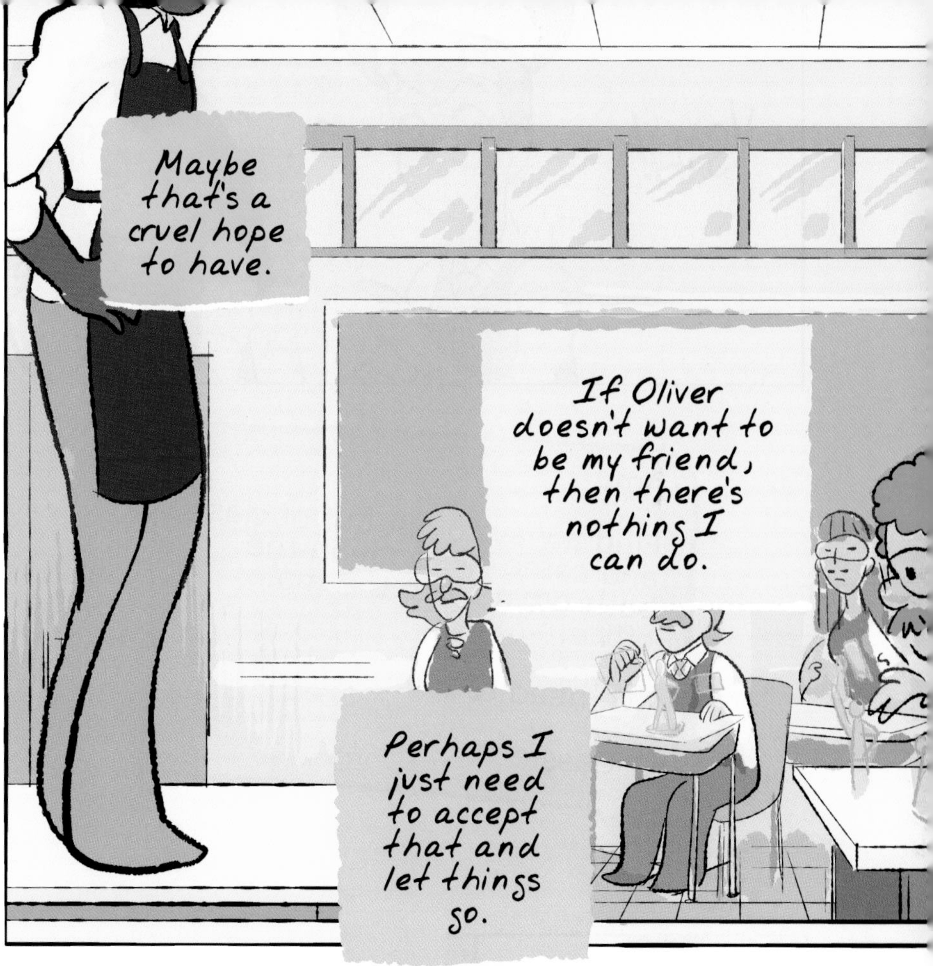
Maybe that's a cruel hope to have.
If Oliver doesn't want to be my friend, then there's nothing I can do.
Perhaps I just need to accept that and let things go.

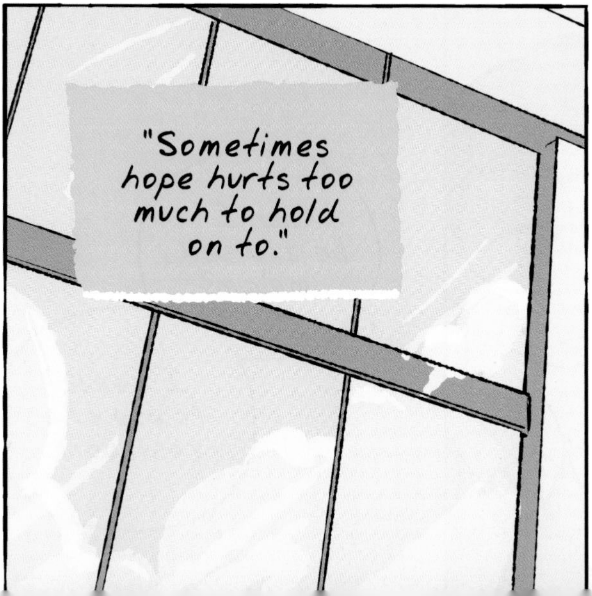
"Sometimes hope hurts too much to hold on to."

Oliver told me that once.

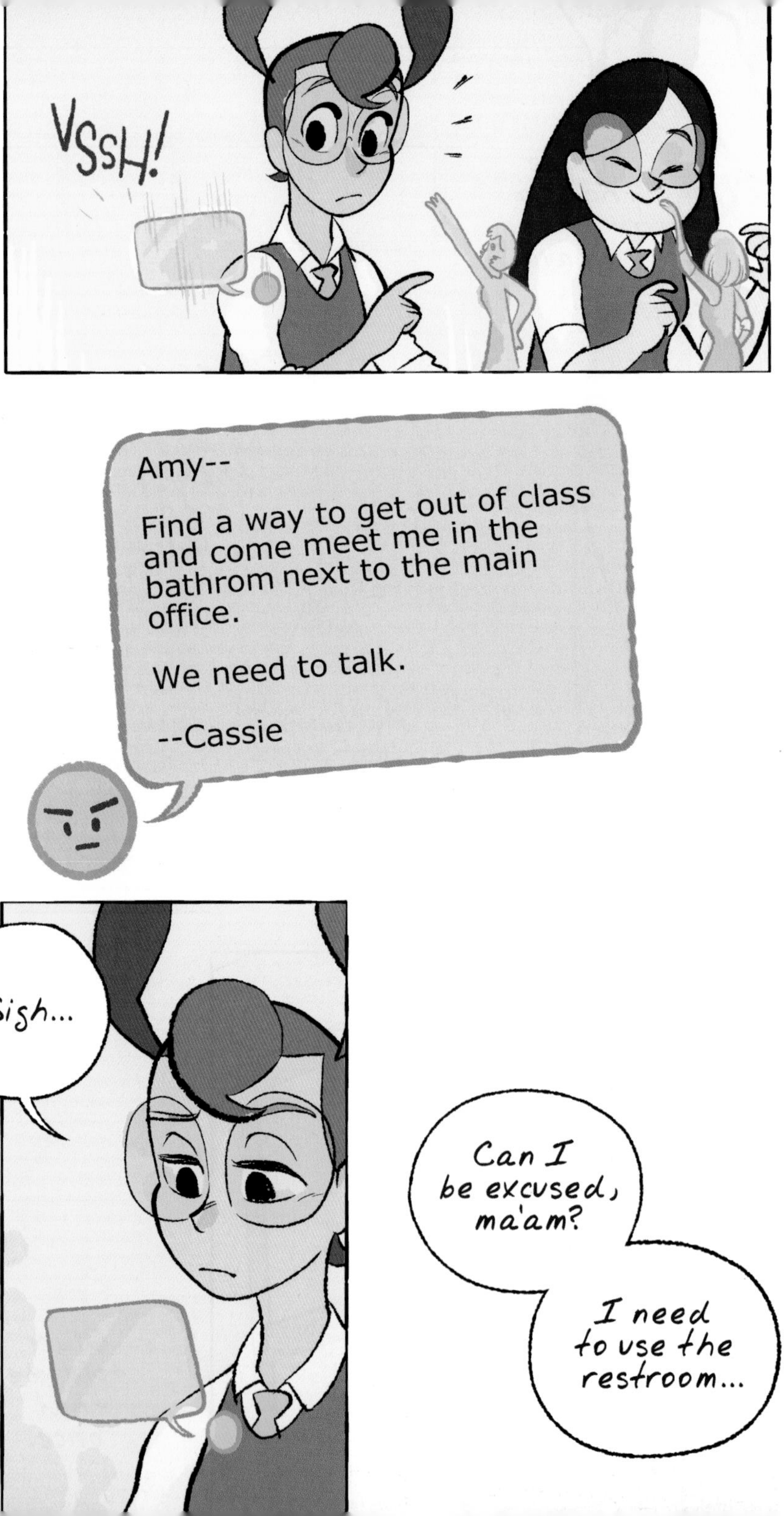
VSSH!
Amy--
Find a way to get out of class and come meet me in the bathrom next to the main office.
We need to talk.
--Cassie
Sigh...
Can I be excused, ma'am?
I need to use the restroom...

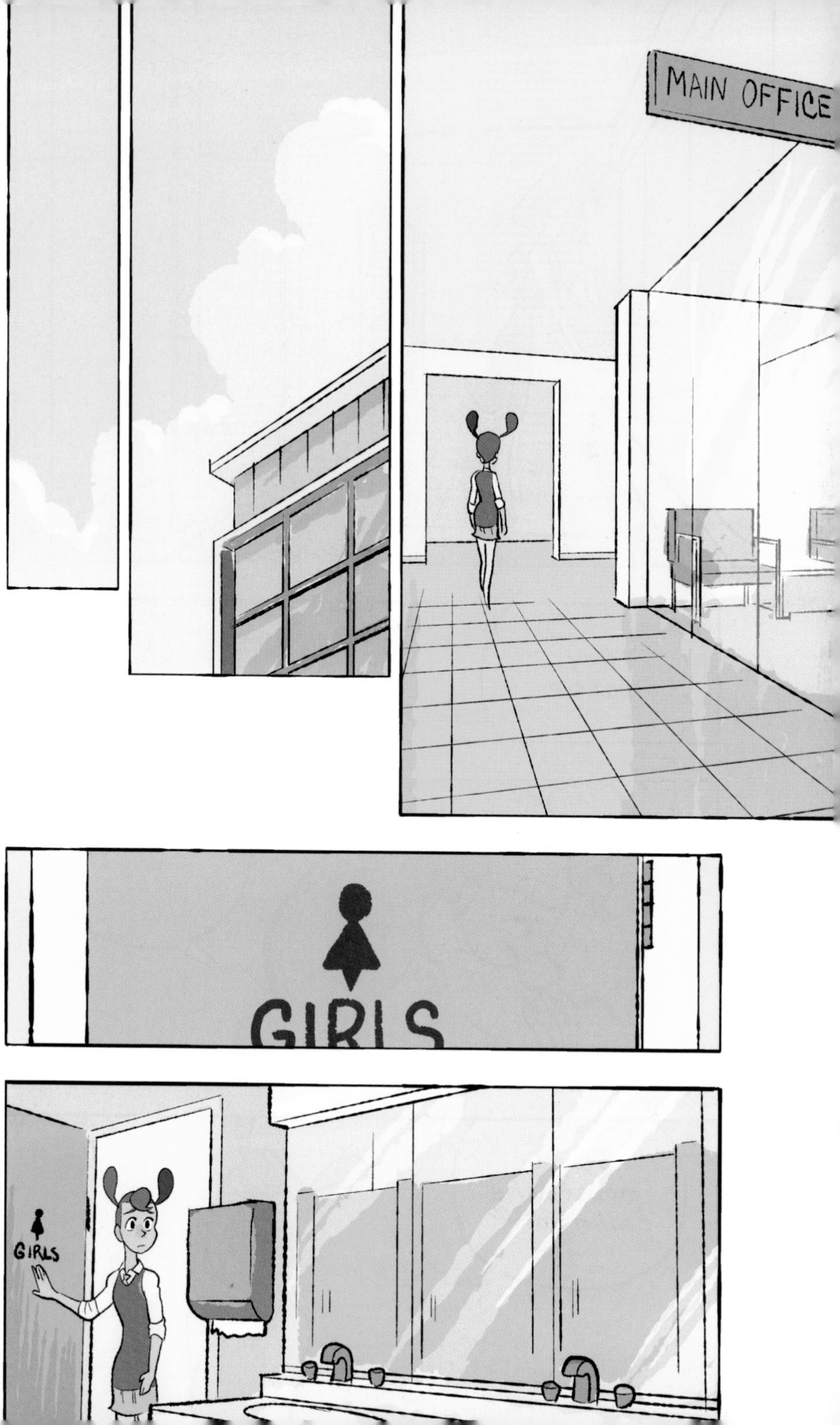
MAIN OFFICE
GIRLS
GIRLS

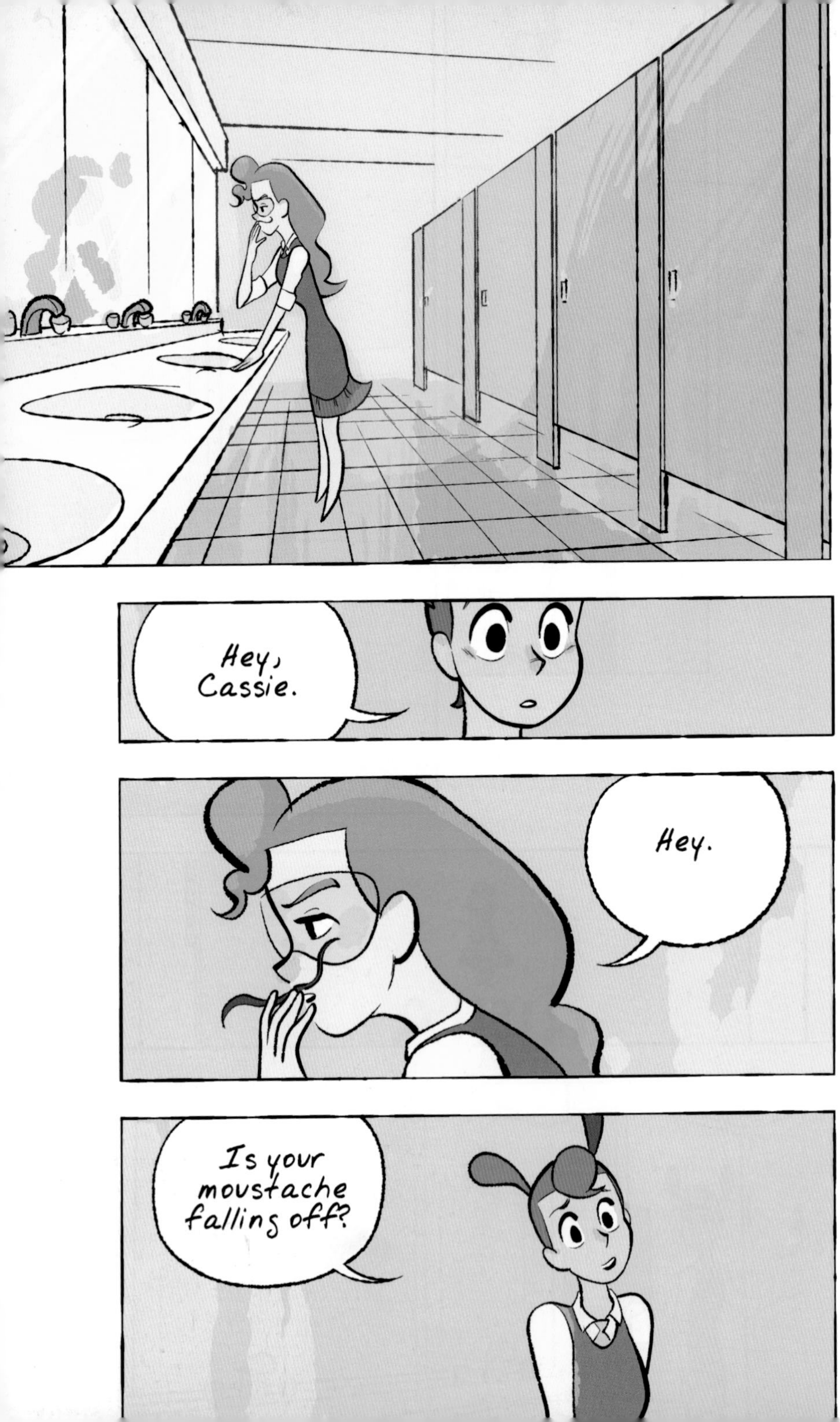
Hey, Cassie.
Hey.
Is your moustache falling off?

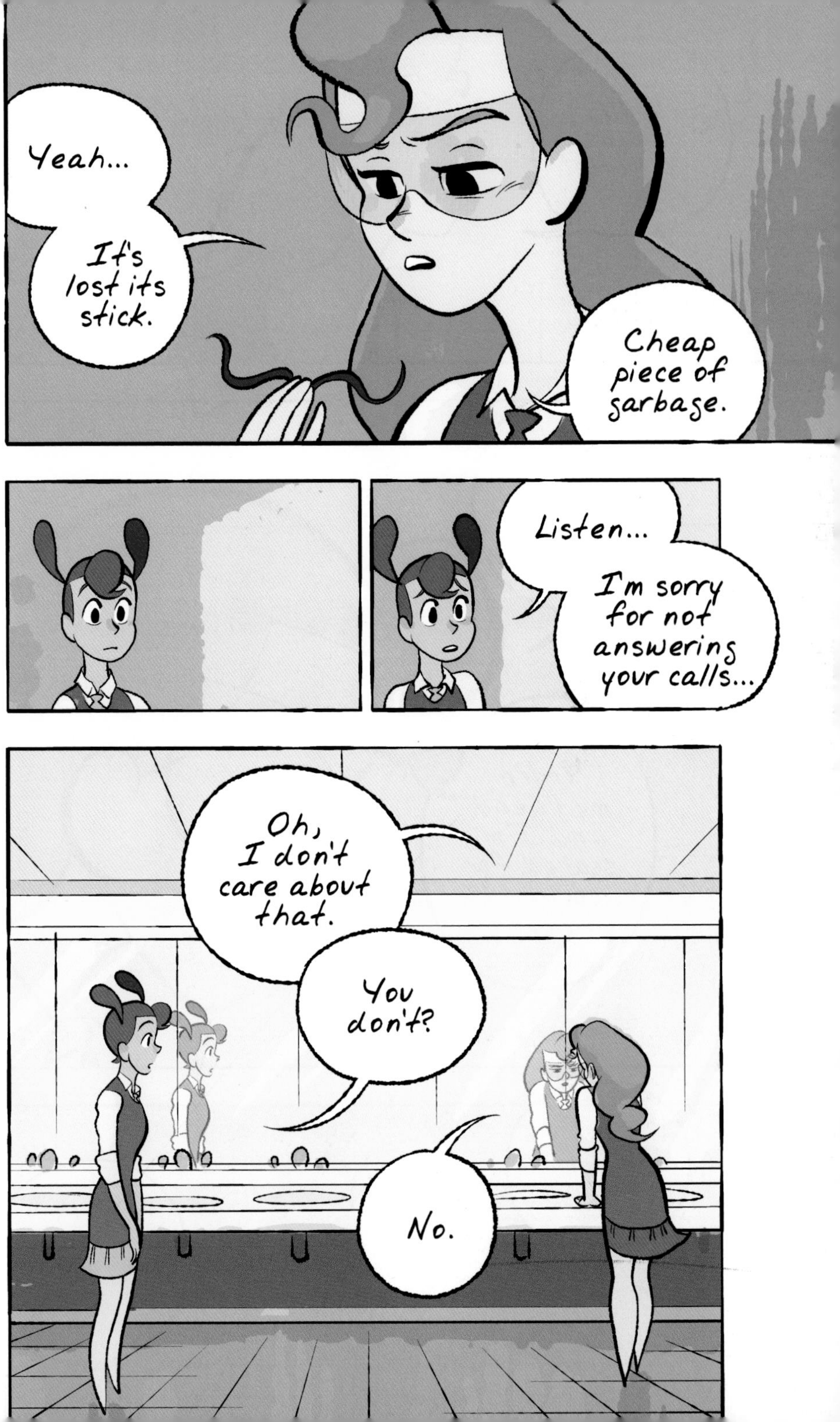
Yeah...
It's lost its stick.
Cheap piece of garbage.
Listen...
I'm sorry for not answering your calls...
Oh, I don't care about that.
You don't?
No.

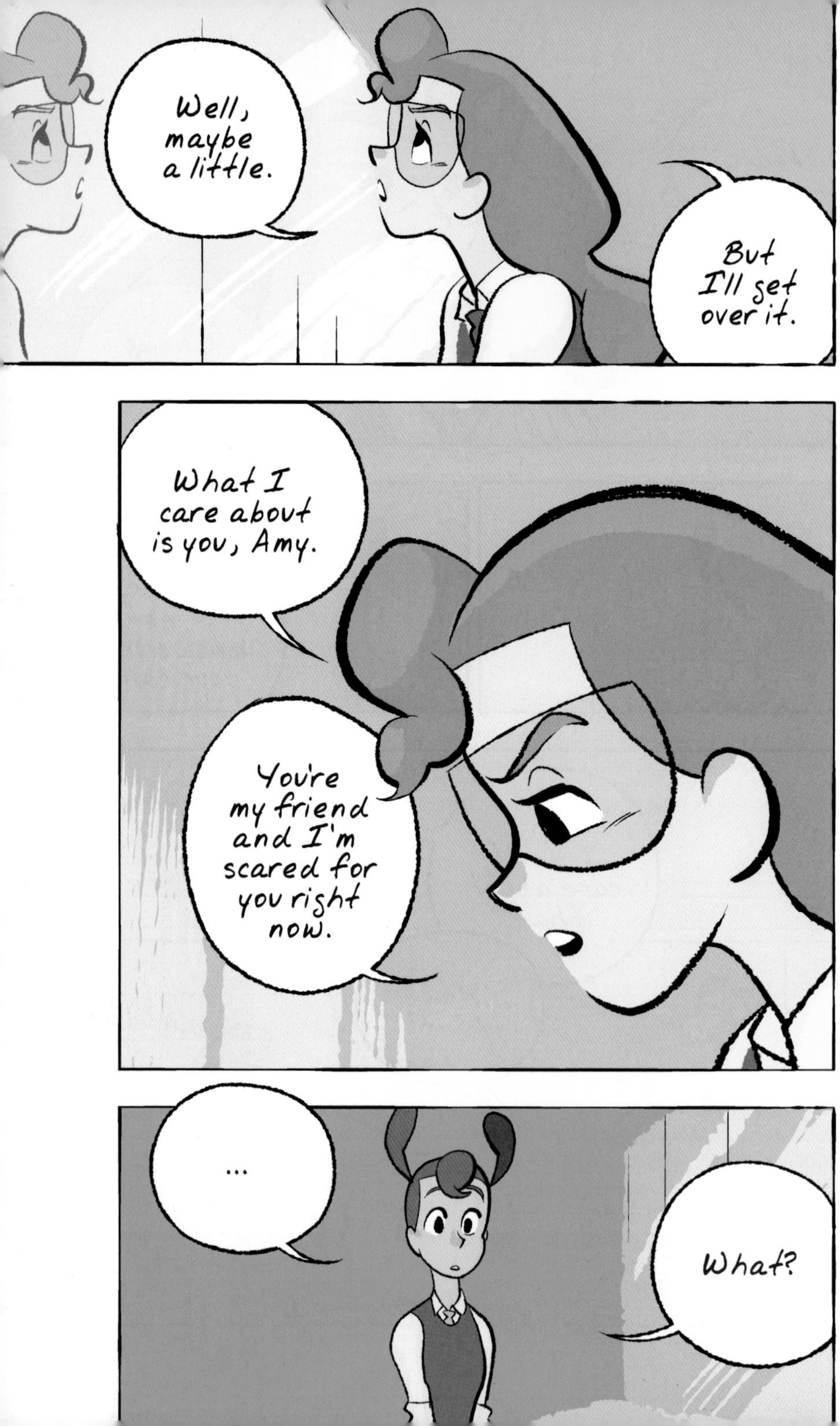
Well, maybe a little.
But I'll get over it.
What I care about is you, Amy.
You're my friend and I'm scared for you right now.
...
What?

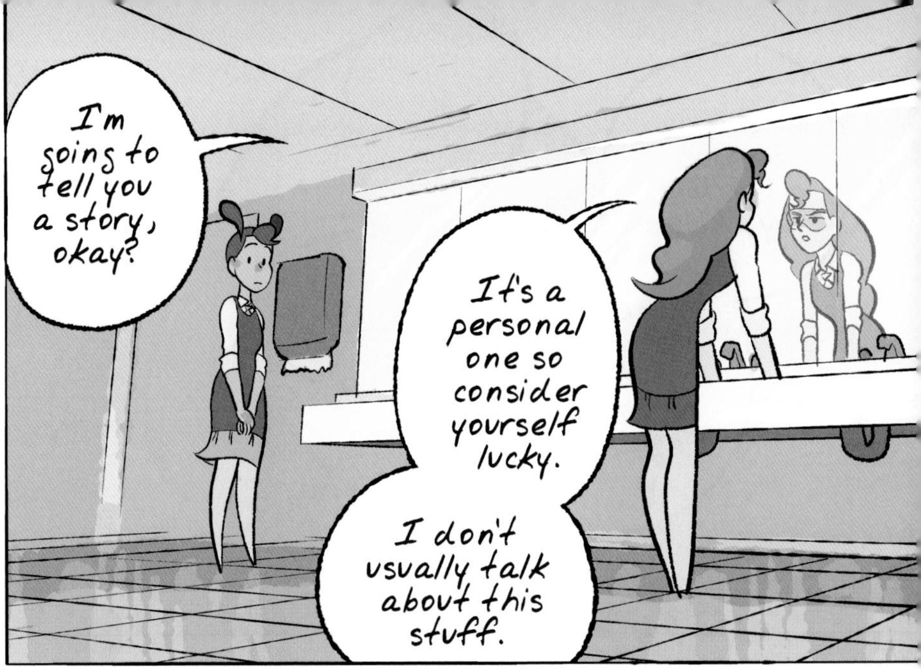
I'm going to tell you a story, okay?
It's a personal one so consider yourself lucky.
I don't usually talk about this stuff.

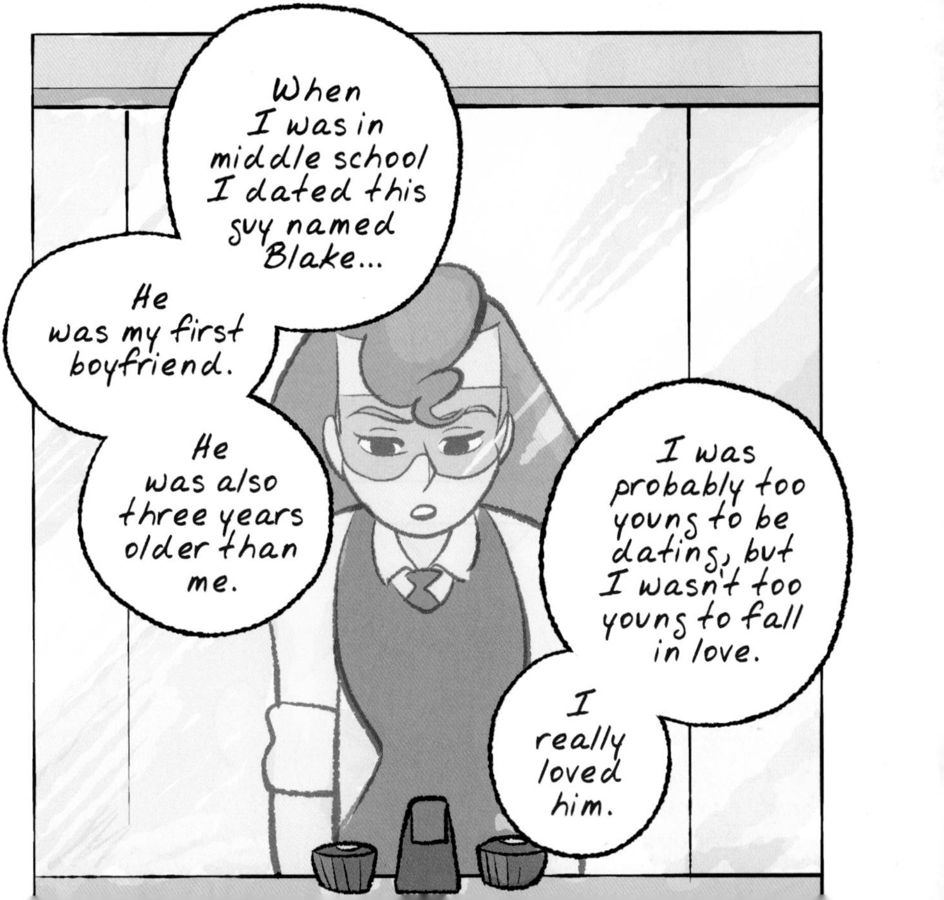
When I was in middle school I dated this guy named Blake...
He was my first boyfriend.
He was also three years older than me.
I was probably too young to be dating, but I wasn't too young to fall in love.
I really loved him.

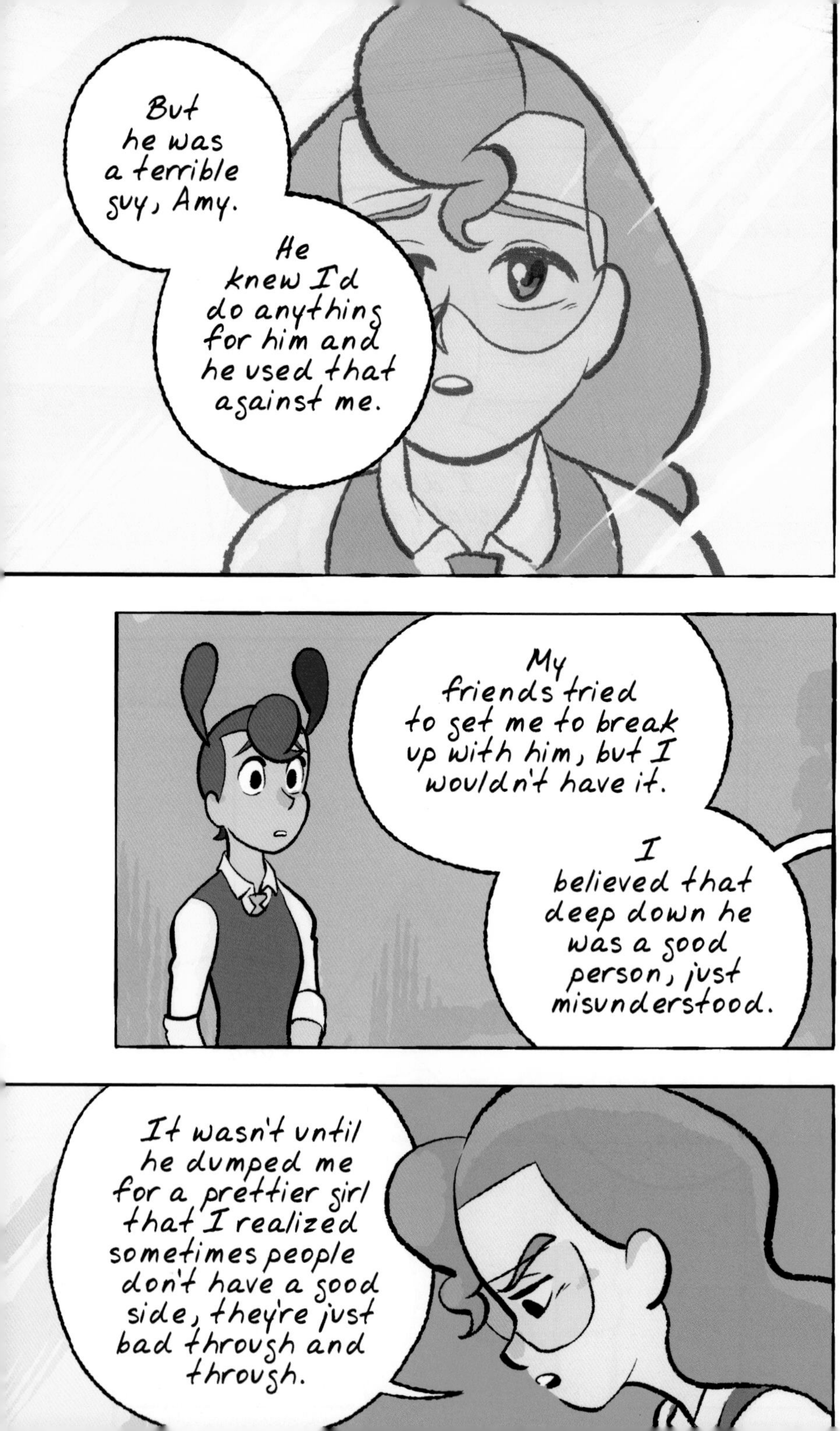
But he was a terrible guy, Amy.
He knew I'd do anything for him and he used that against me.
My friends tried to get me to break up with him, but I wouldn't have it.
I believed that deep down he was a good person, just misunderstood.
It wasn't until he dumped me for a prettier girl that I realized sometimes people don't have a good side, they're just bad through and through.

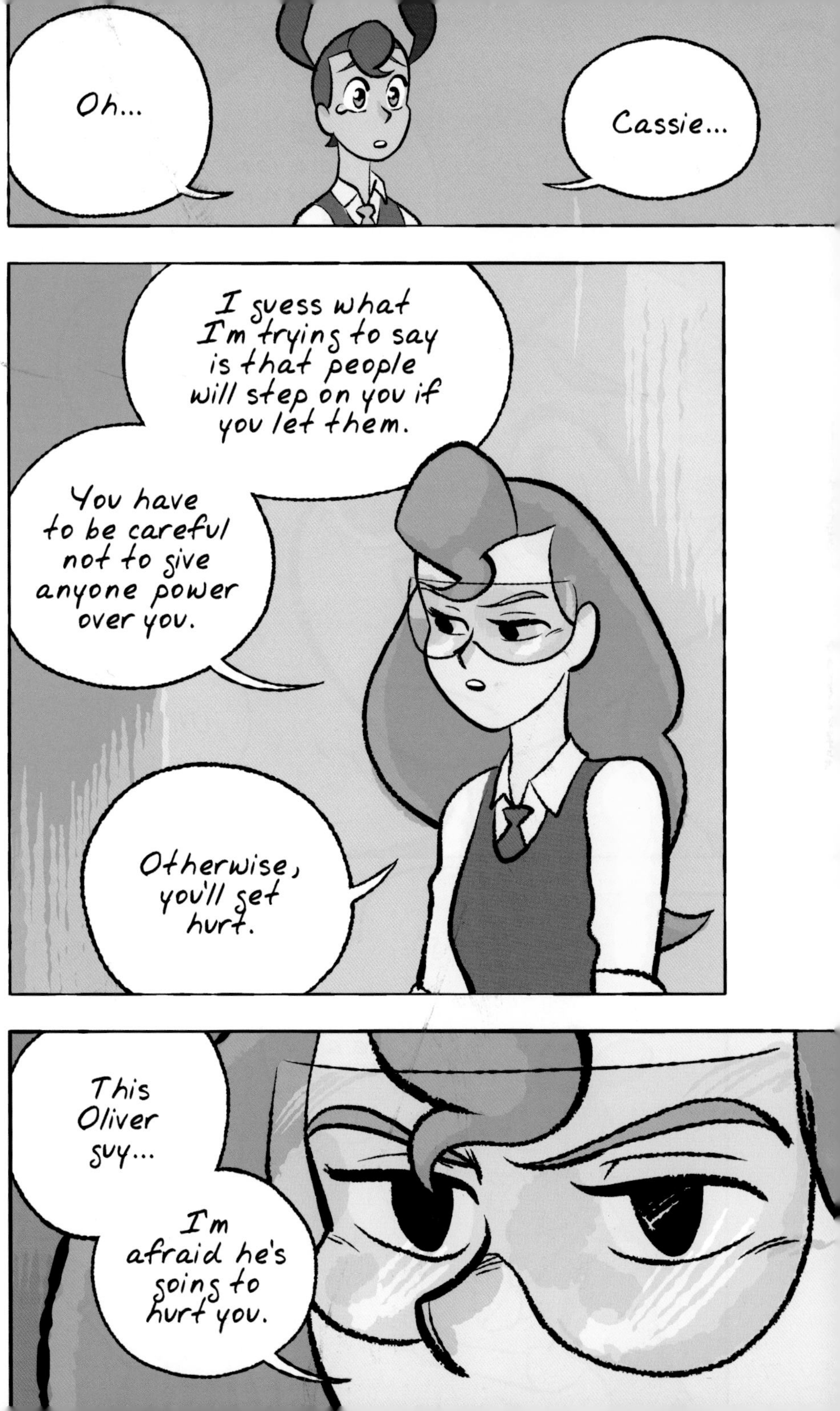
Oh...
Cassie...
I guess what I'm trying to say is that people will step on you if you let them.
You have to be careful not to give anyone power over you.
Otherwise, you'll get hurt.
This Oliver guy...
I'm afraid he's going to hurt you.

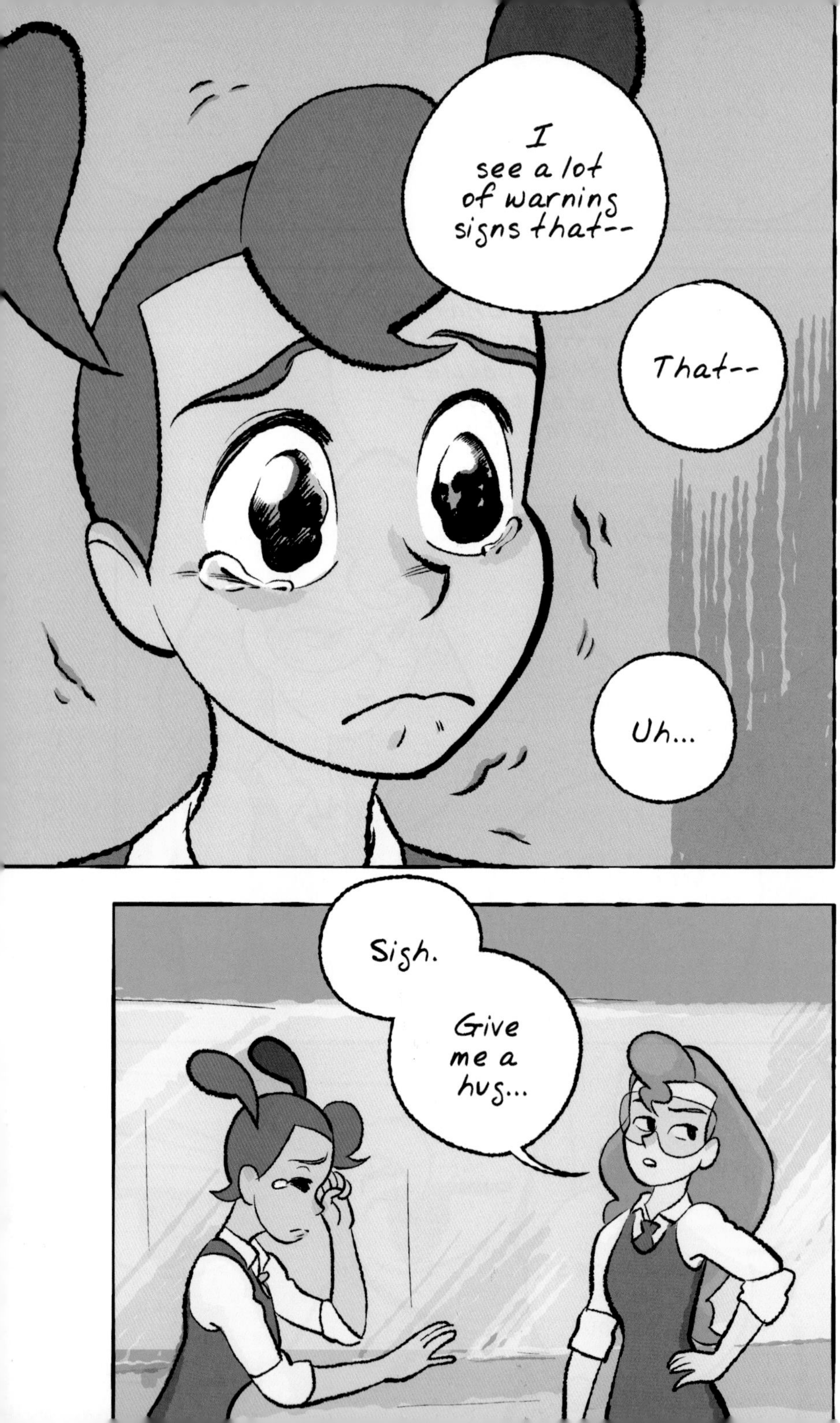
I see a lot of warnings signs that--
That--
Uh...
Sigh.
Give me a hug...

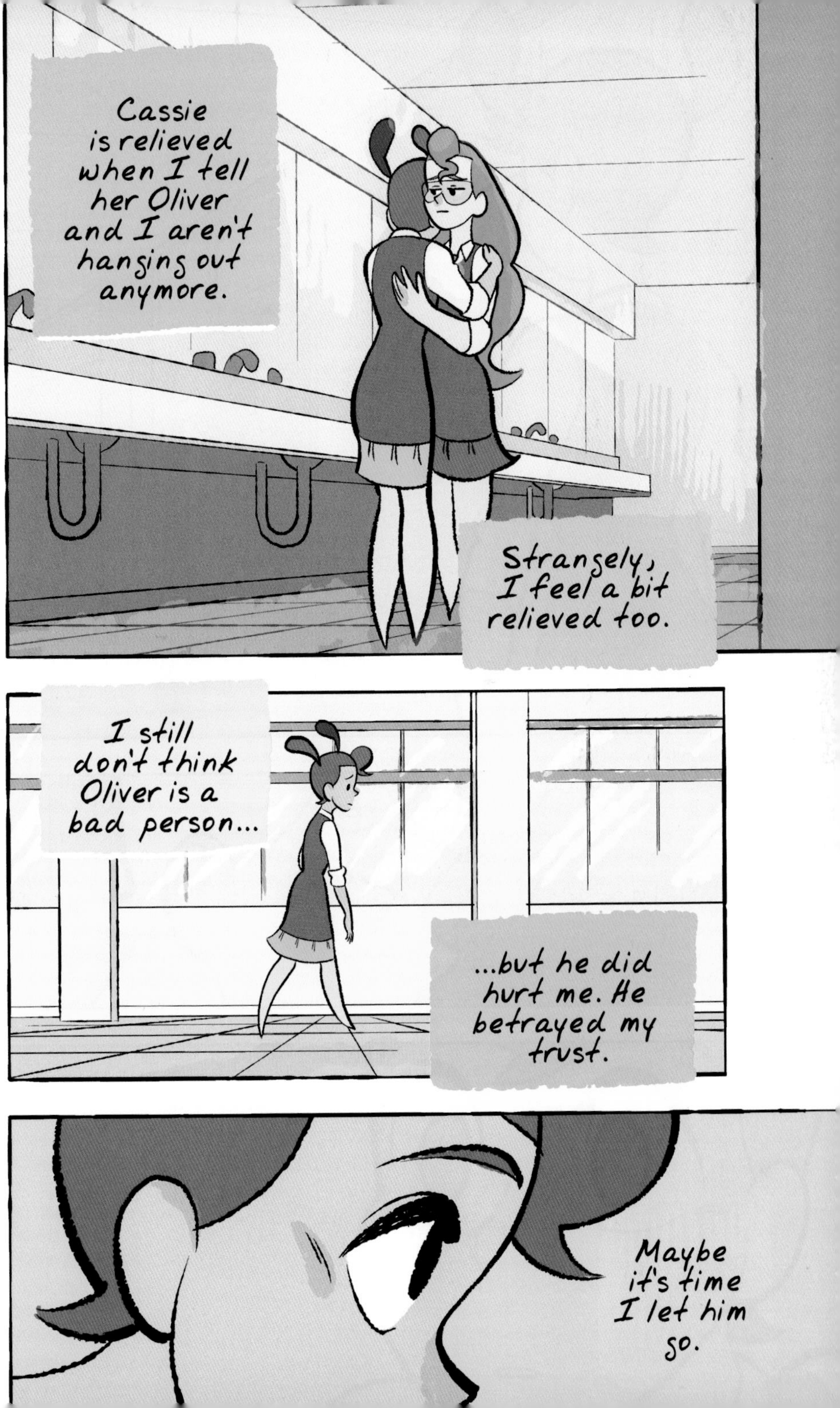
Cassie is relieved when I tell her Oliver and I aren't hanging out anymore.
Strangely, I feel a bit relieved too.
I still don't think Oliver is a bad person...
...but he did hurt me. He betrayed my trust.
Maybe it's time I let him go.

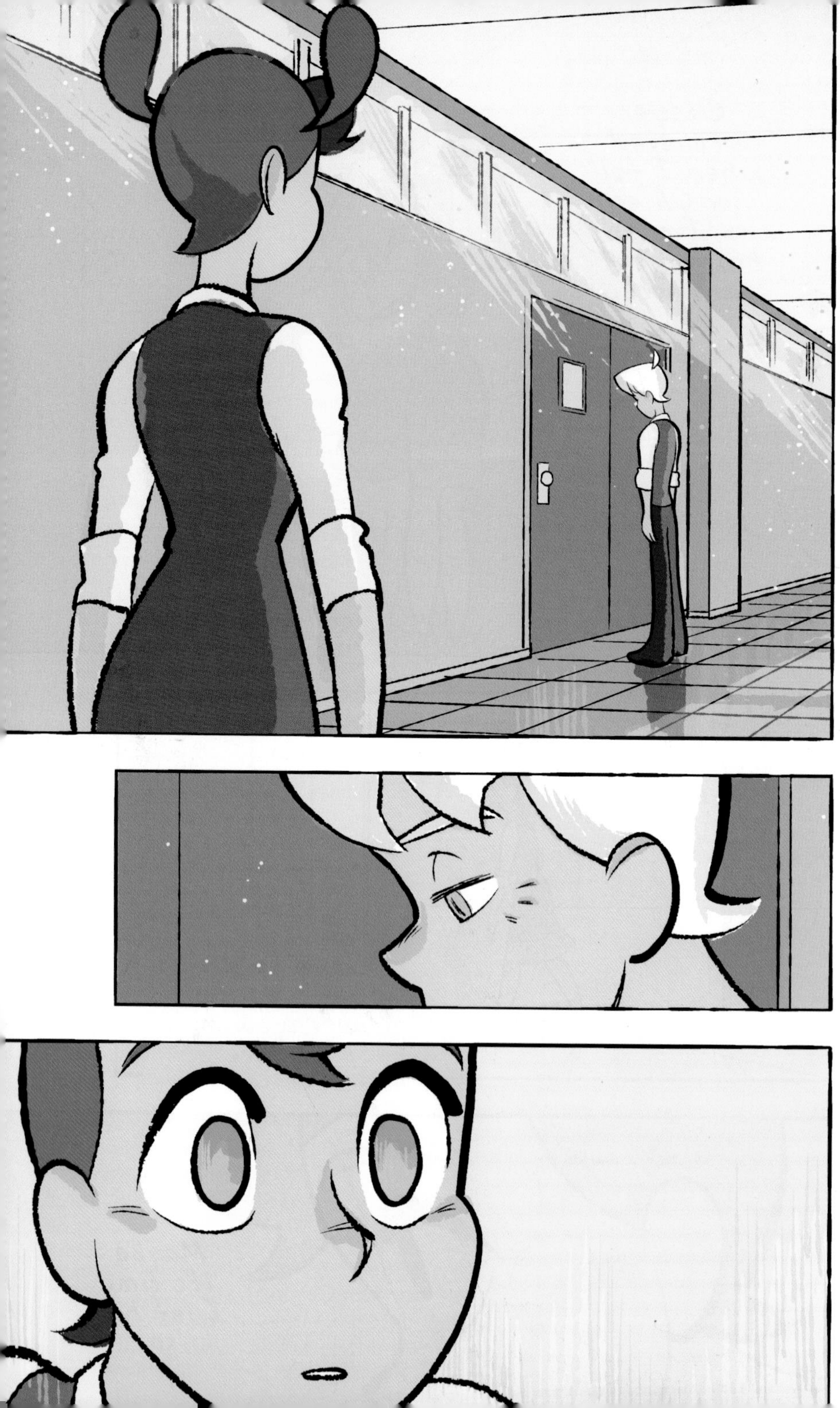

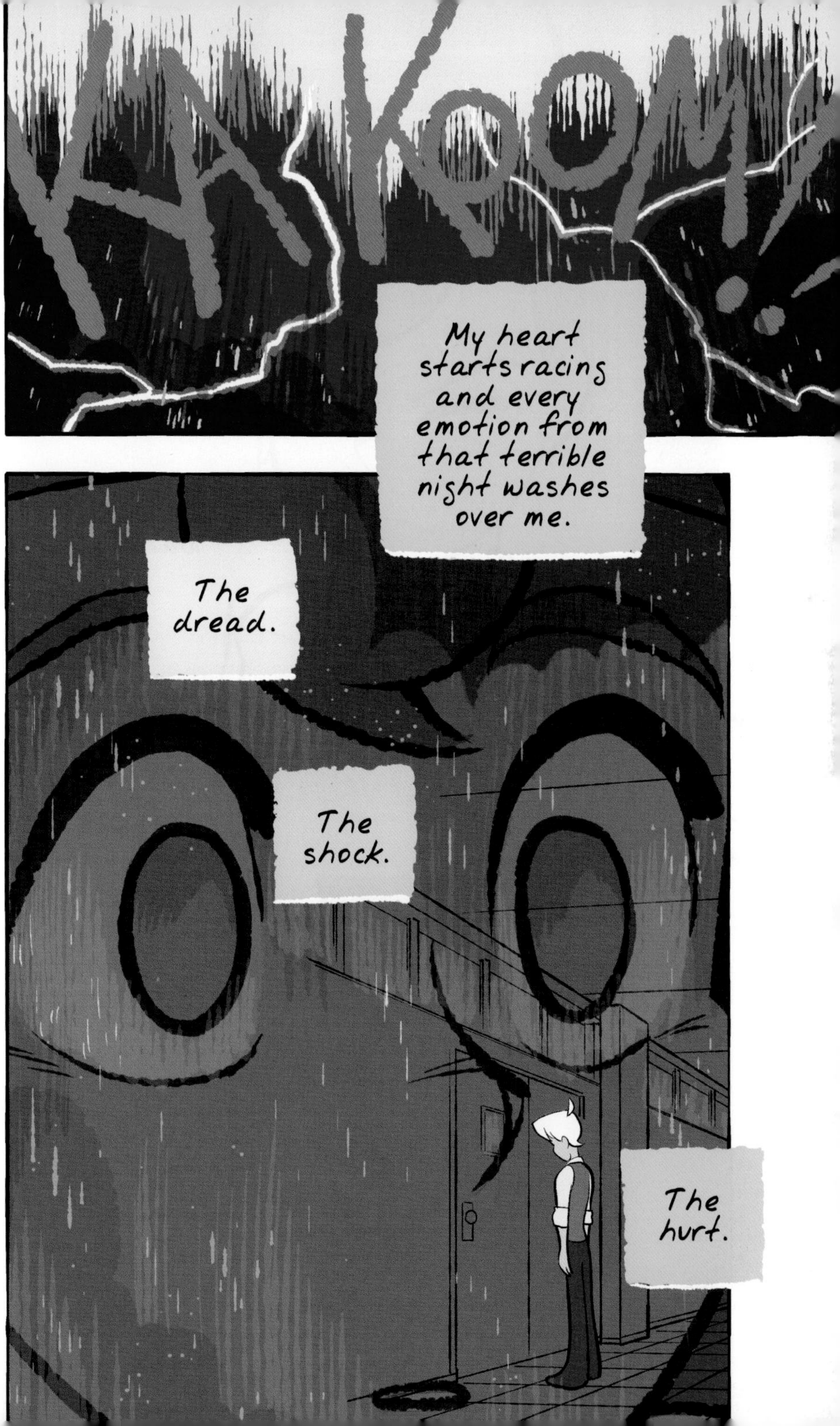
KA-KOOM!
My heart starts racing and every emotion from that terrible night washes over me.
The dread.
The shock.
The hurt.

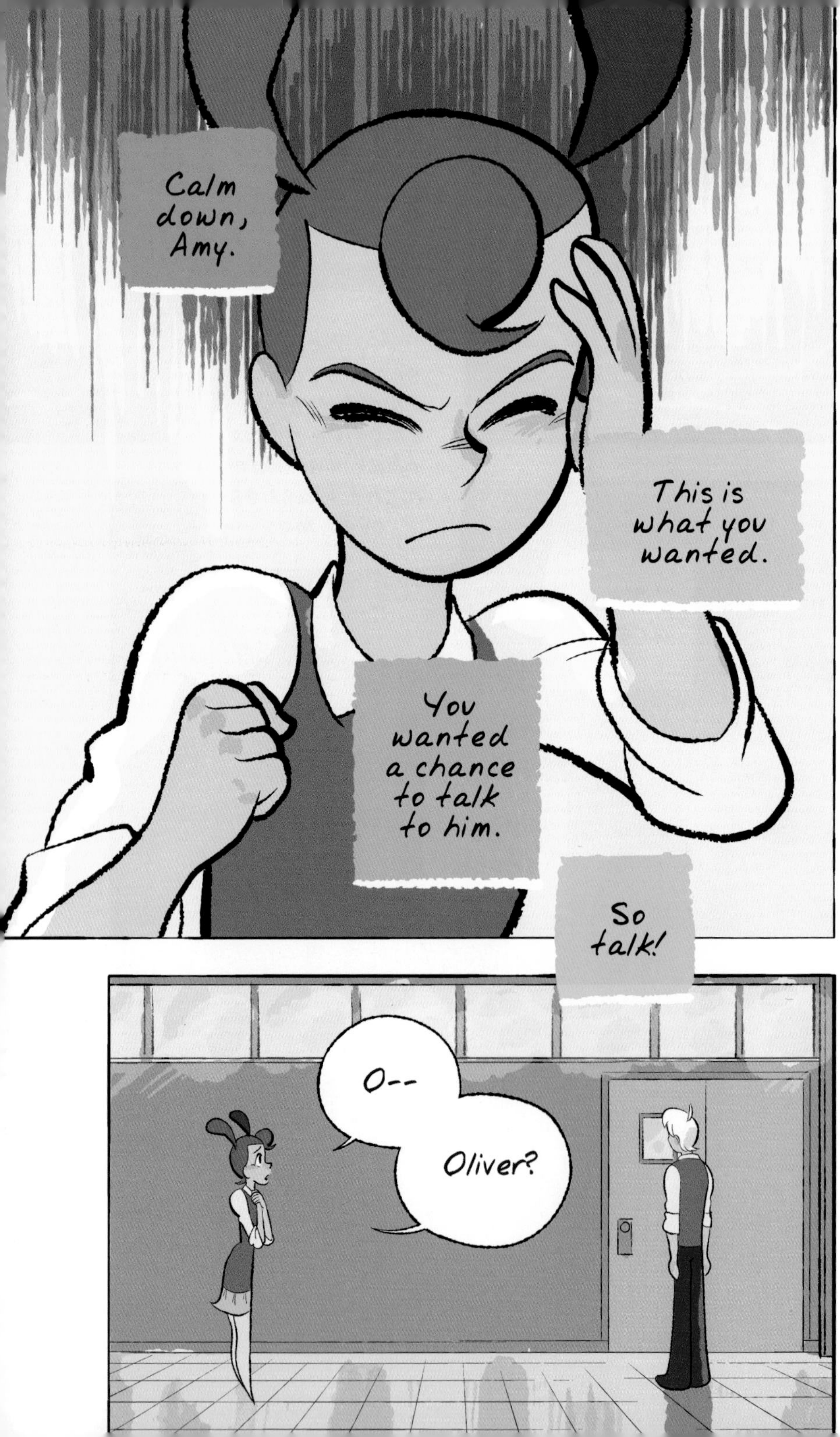
Calm down, Amy.
This is what you wanted.
You wanted a chance to talk to him.
So talk!
O--
Oliver?

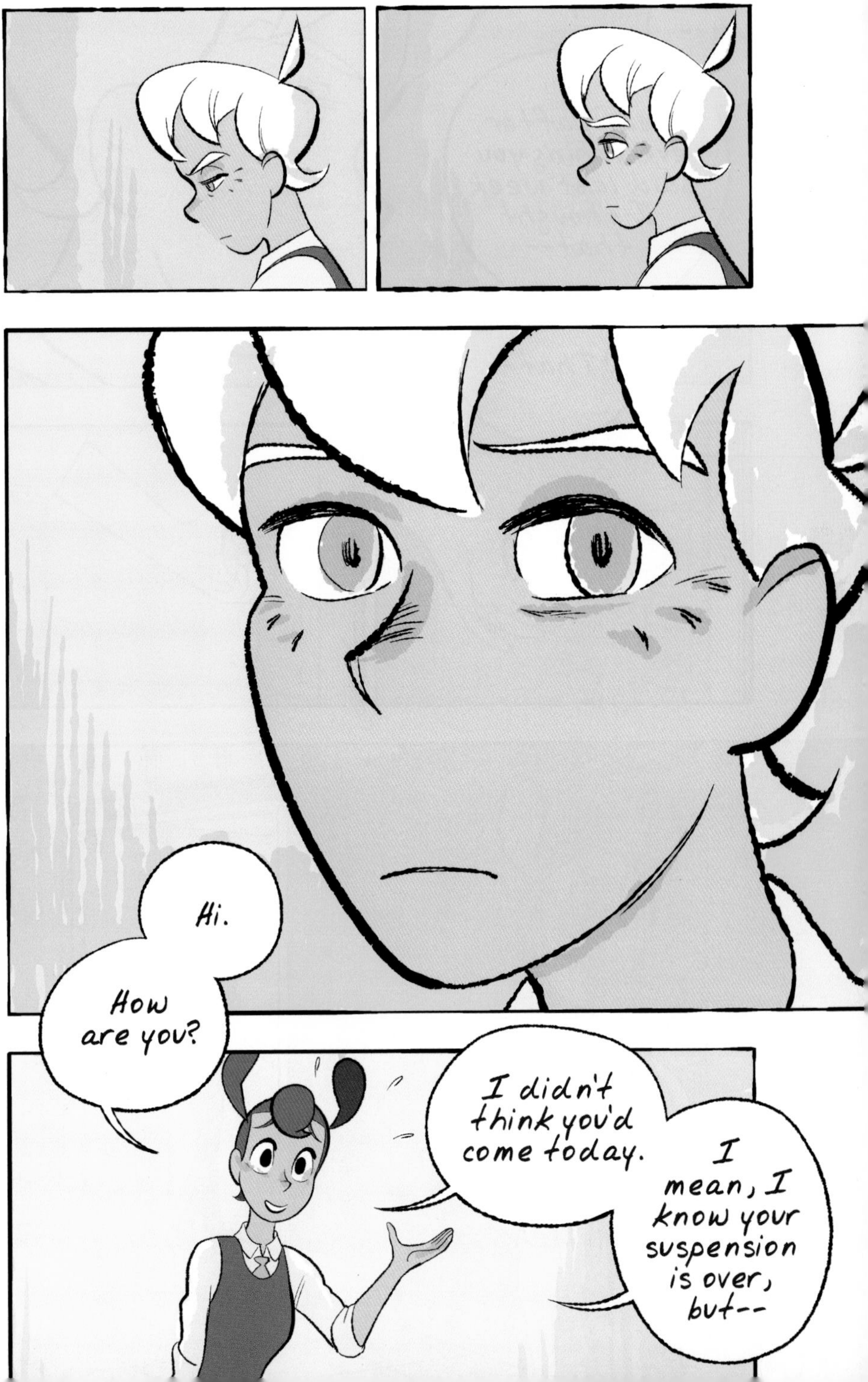
Hi.
How are you?
I didn't think you'd come today.
I mean, I know your suspension is over, but--

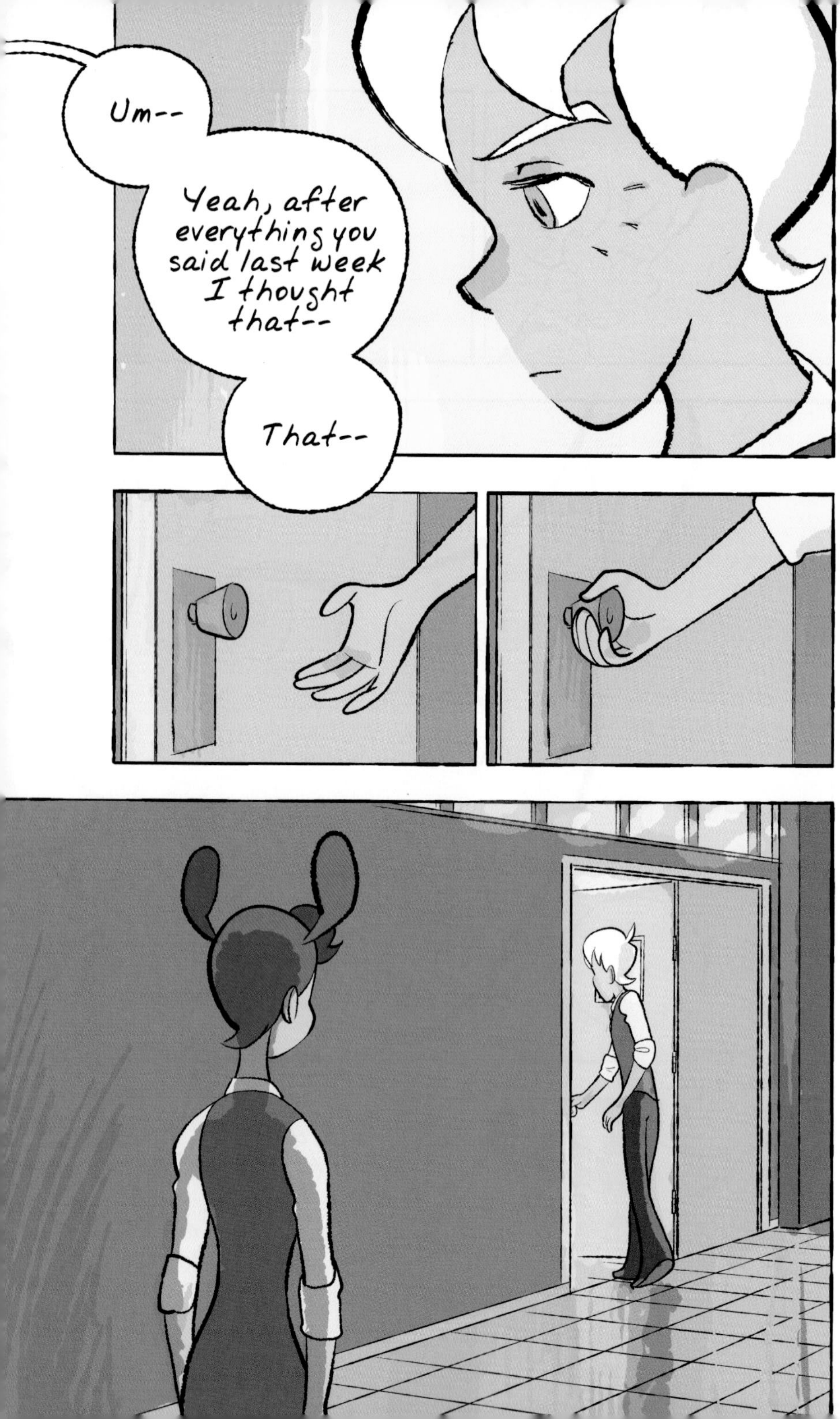
Um--
Yeah, after everything you said last week I thought that--
That--

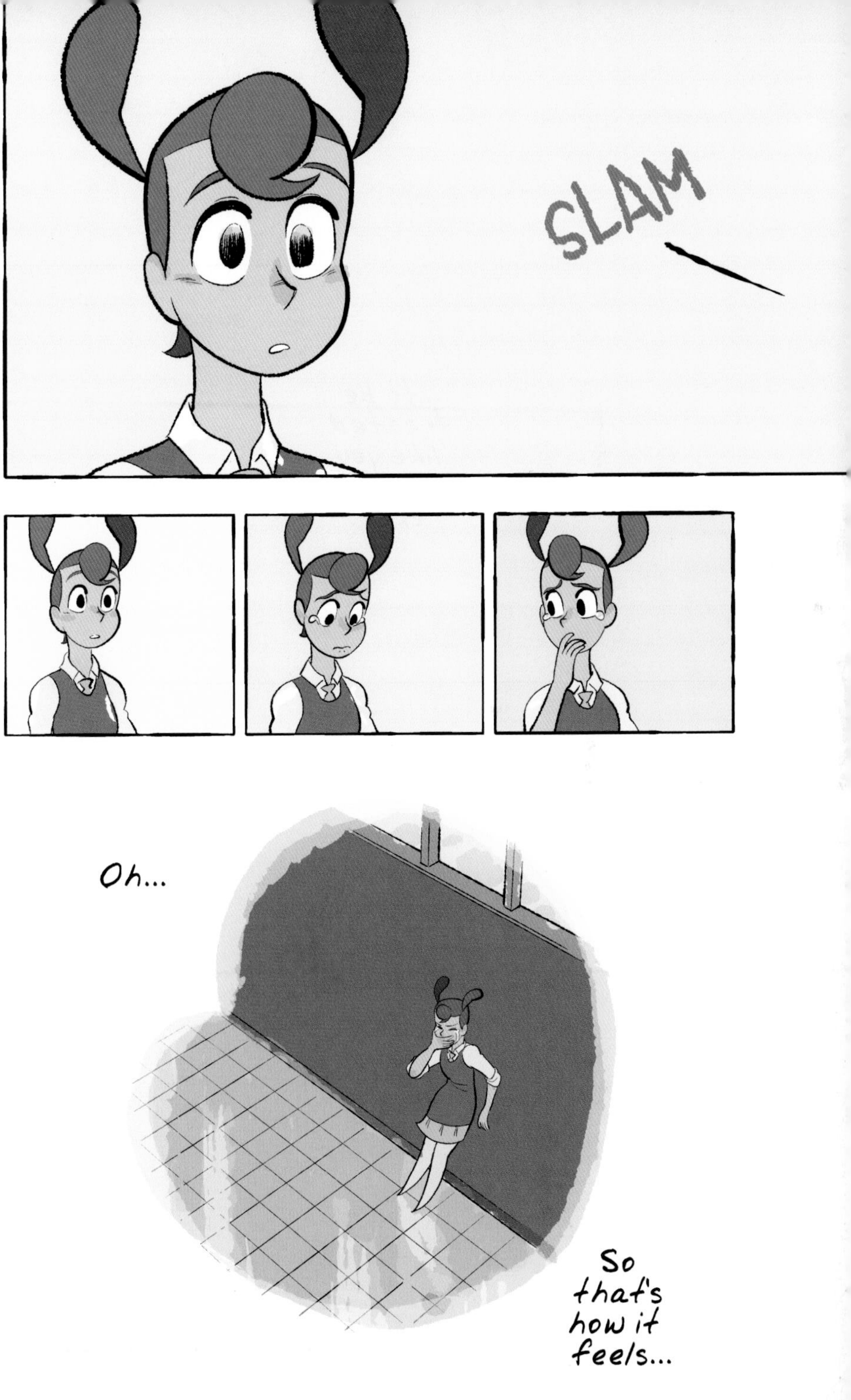
SLAM
Oh...
So that's how it feels...

...to be
treated
like you
don't
exist.

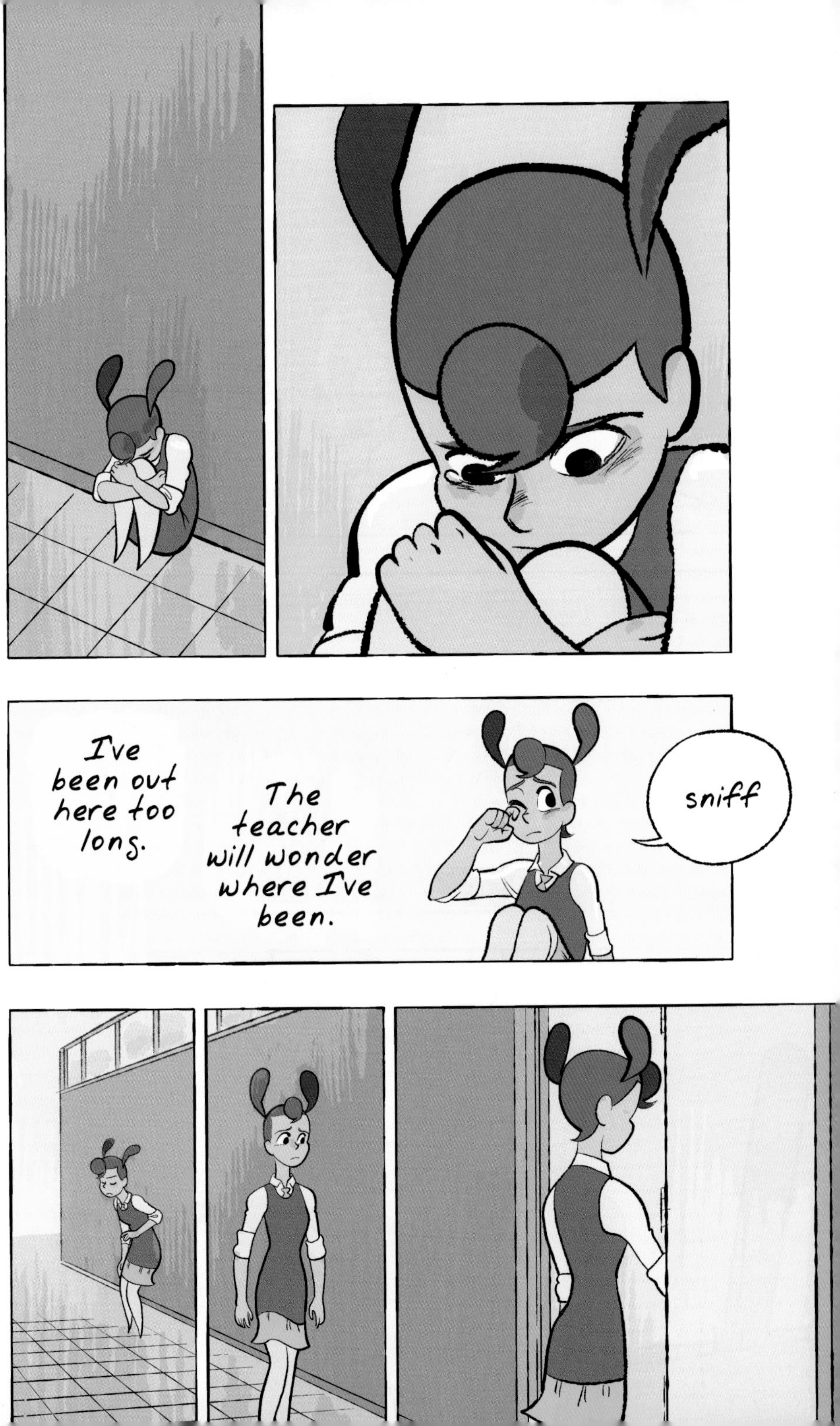
I've been out here too long.
The teacher will wonder where I've been.
sniff

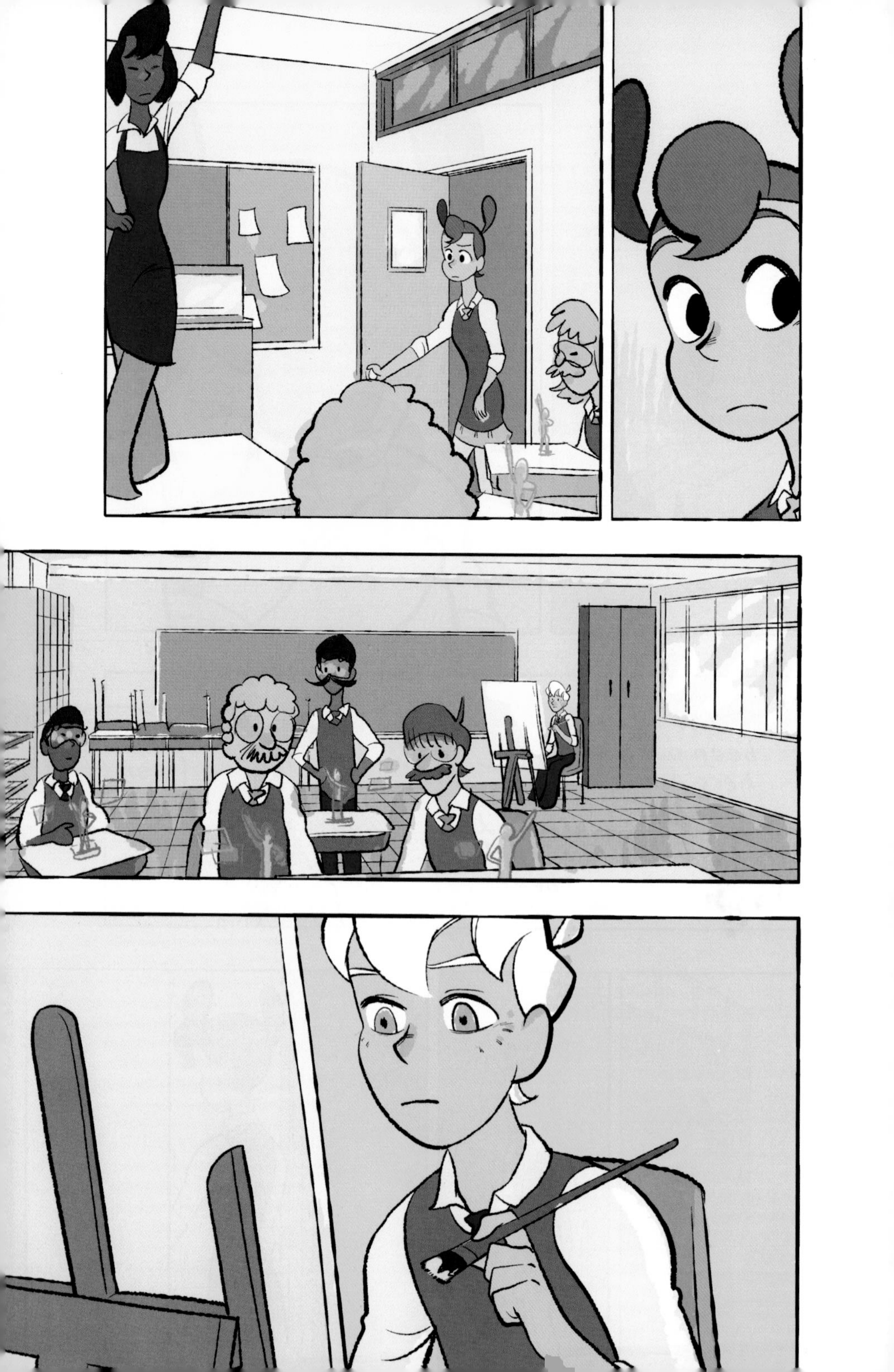

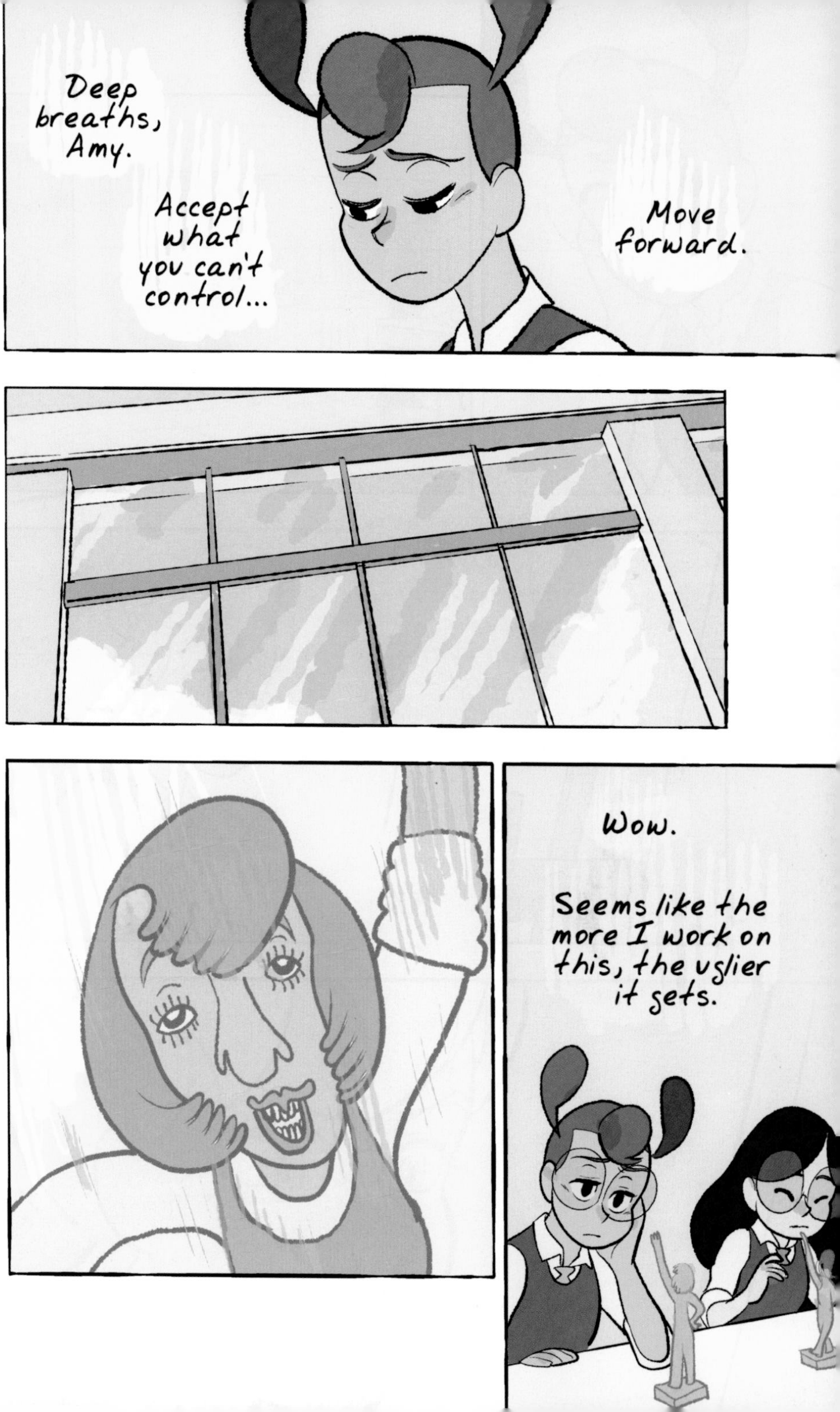
Deep breaths, Amy.
Accept what you can't control...
Move forward.
Wow.
Seems like the more I work on this, the uglier it gets.

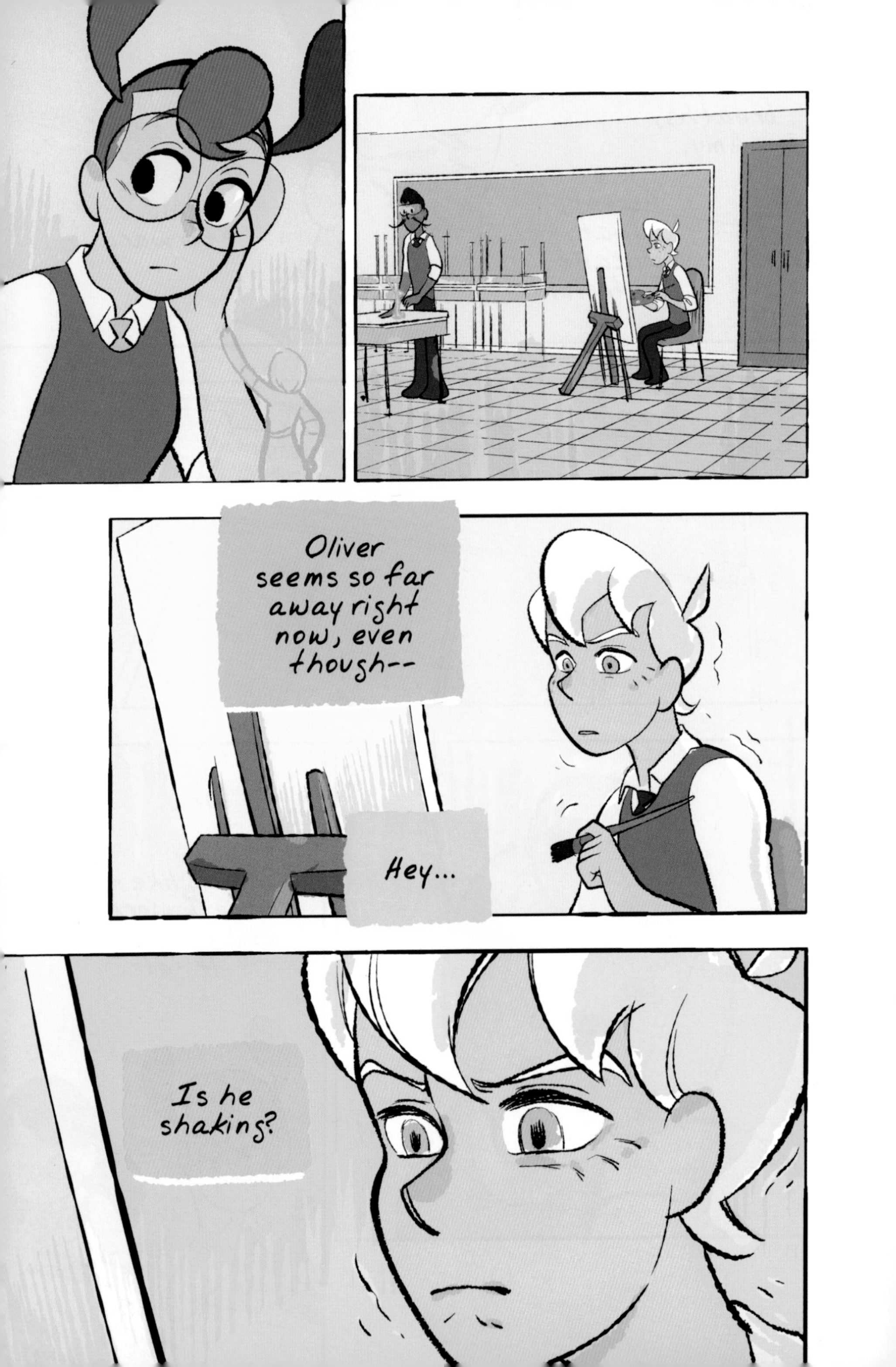
Oliver seems so far away right now, even though--
Hey...
Is he shaking?

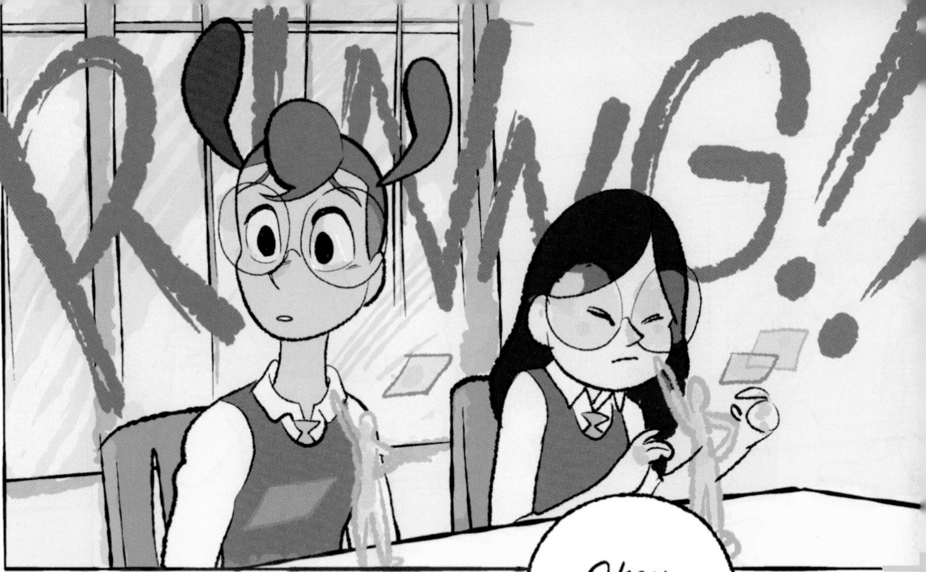
RRING!!

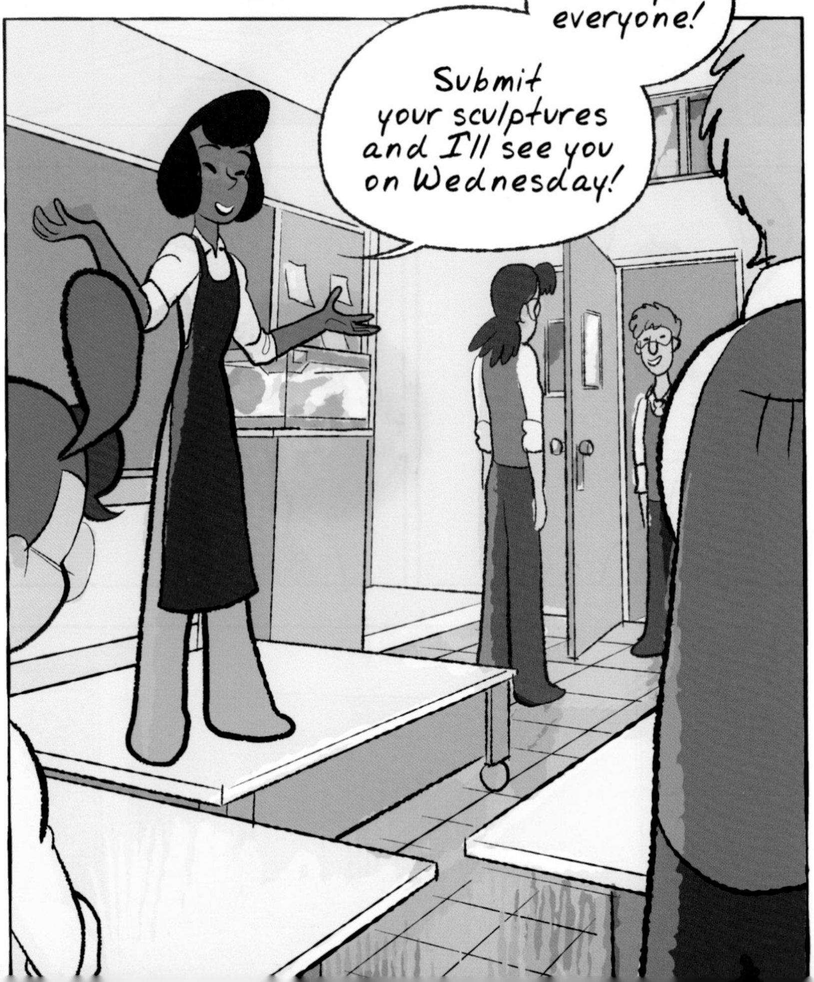
Okay, everyone!
Submit your sculptures and I'll see you on Wednesday!

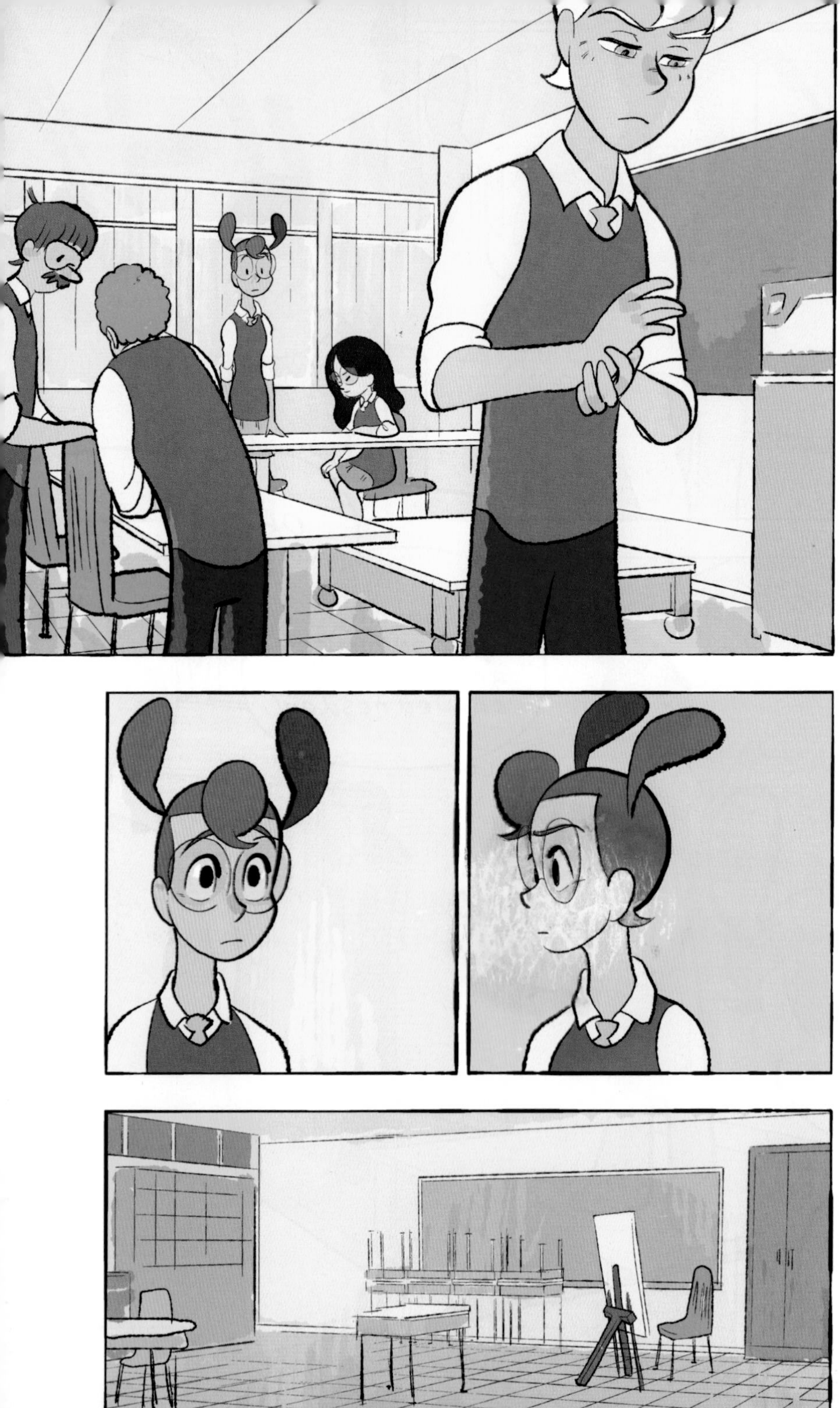

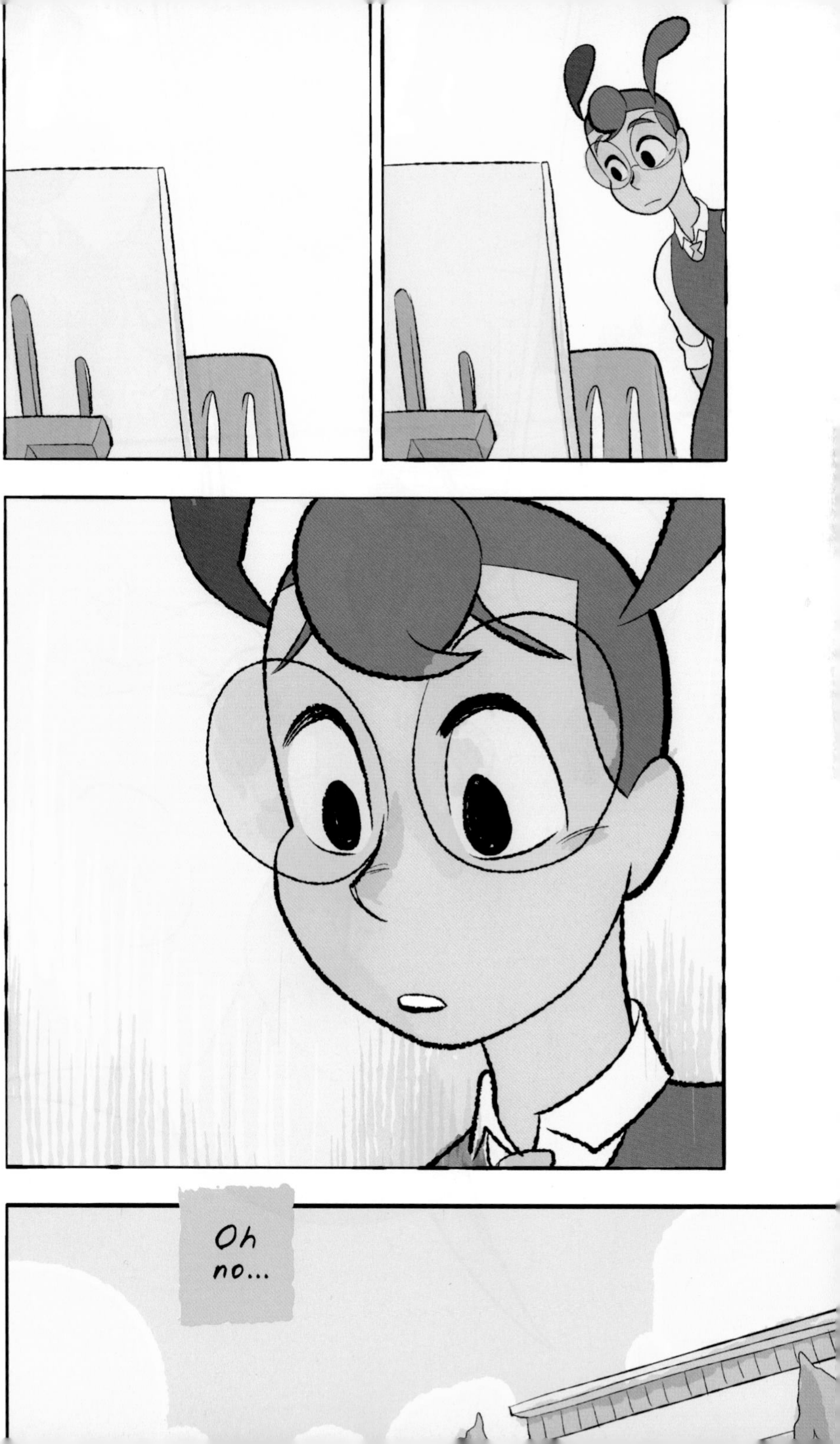
Oh
no...

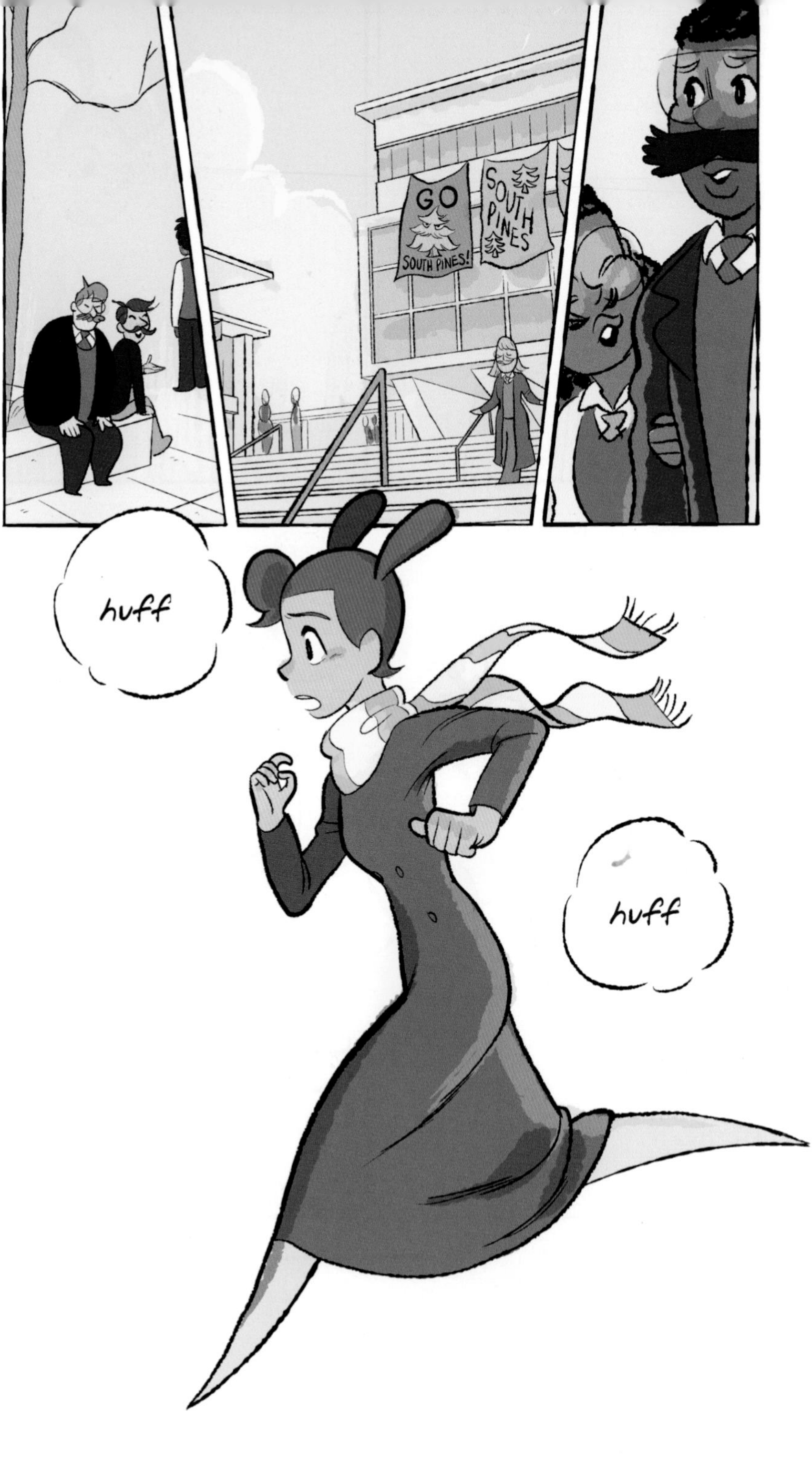
GO
SOUTH PINES!
SOUTH PINES
huff
huff

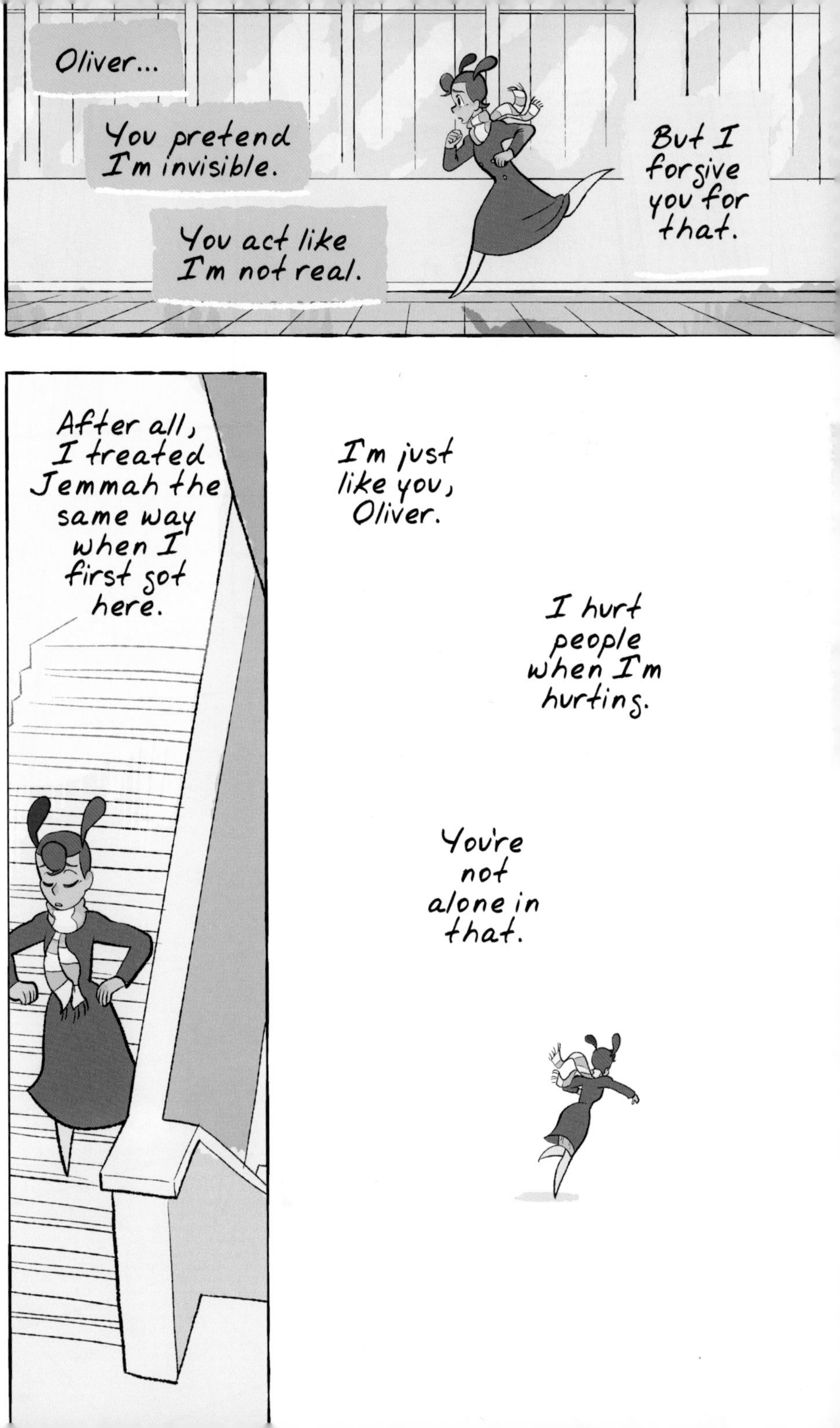
Oliver...
You pretend I'm invisible.
You act like I'm not real.
But I forgive you for that.
After all, I treated Jemmah the same way when I first got here.
I'm just like you, Oliver.
I hurt people when I'm hurting.
You're not alone in that.

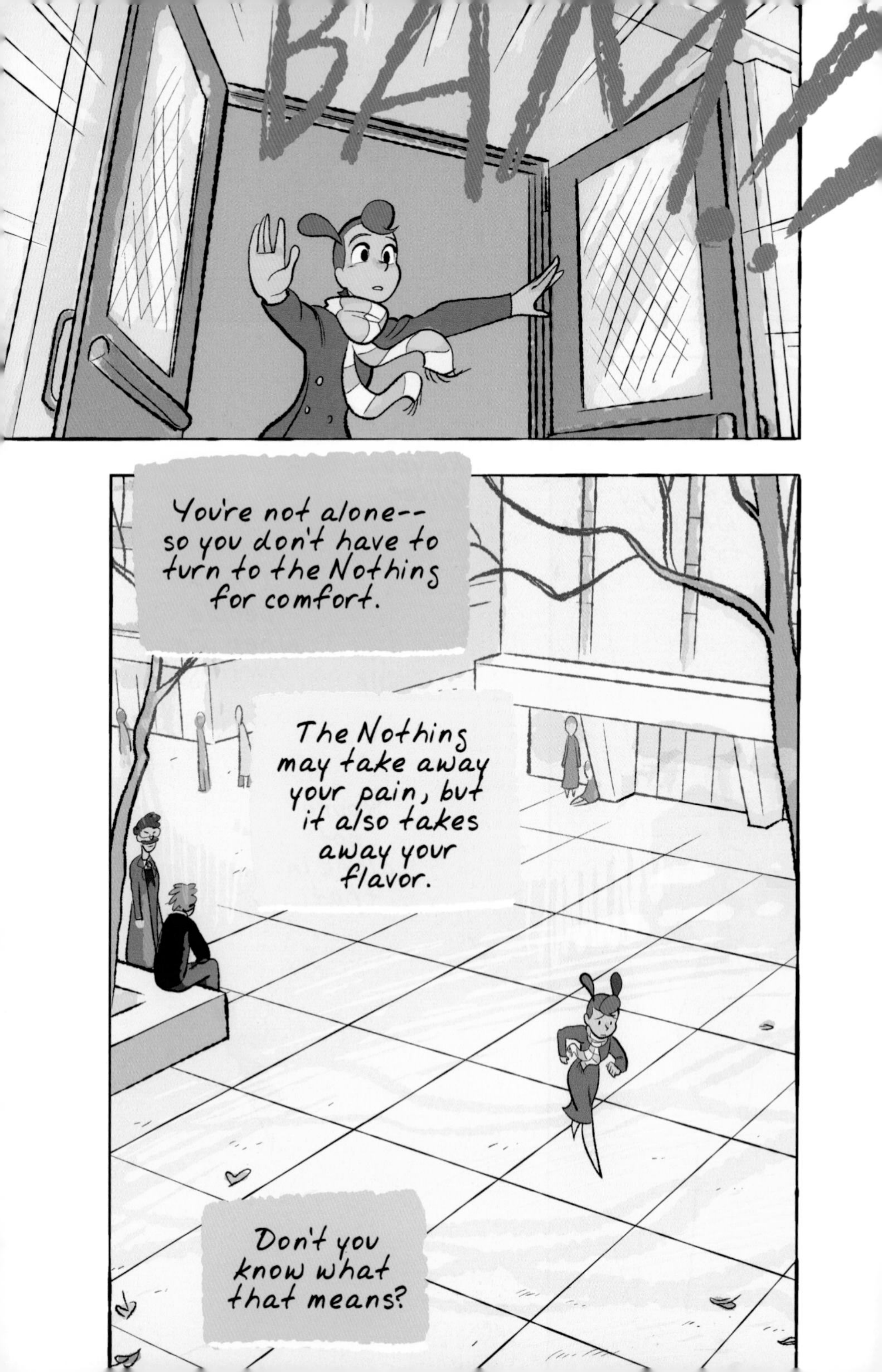
BAM!!
You're not alone--so you don't have to turn to the Nothing for comfort.
The Nothing may take away your pain, but it also takes away your flavor.
Don't you know what that means?

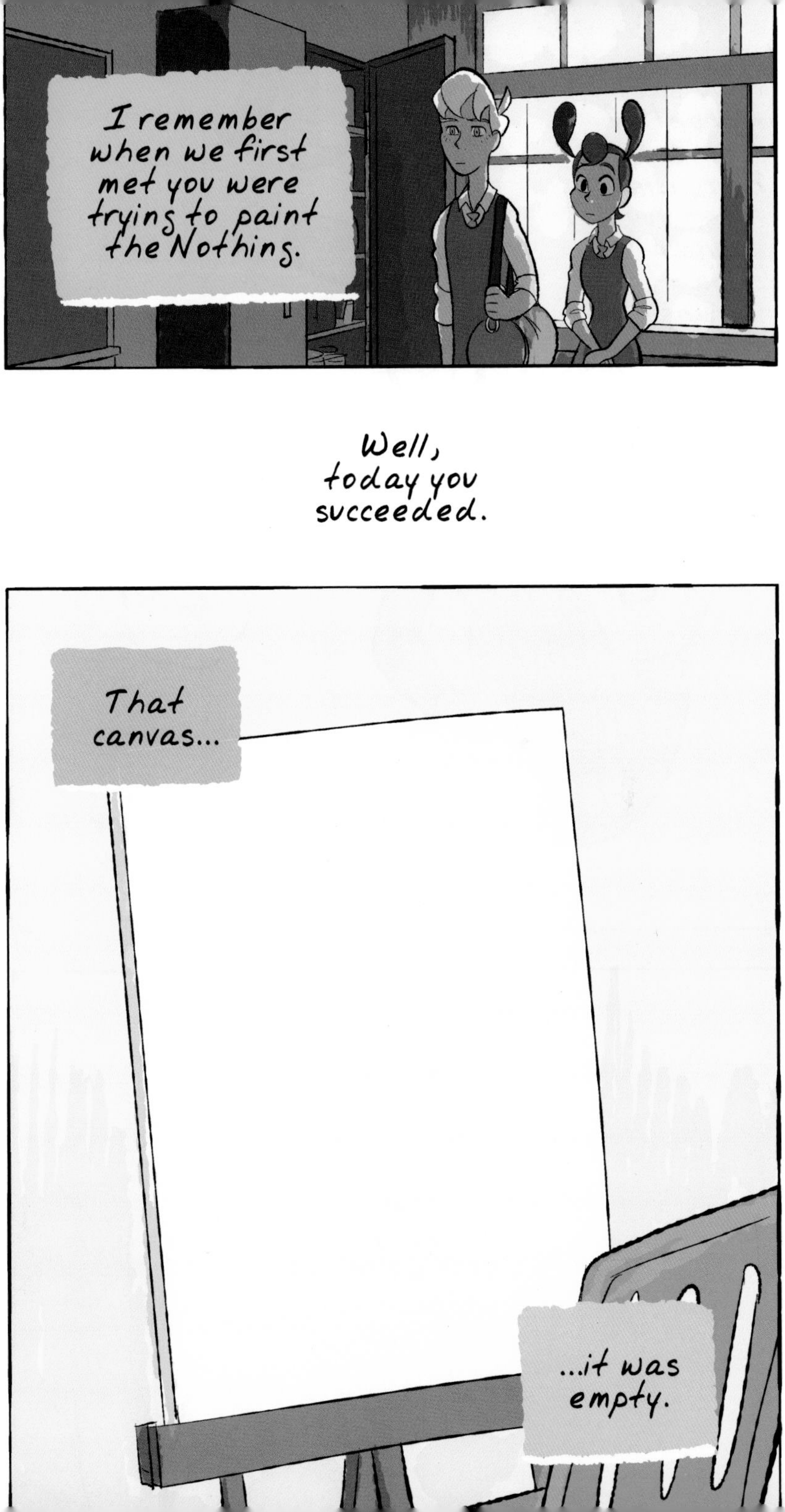
I remember when we first met you were trying to paint the Nothing.
Well, today you succeeded.
That canvas...
...it was empty.

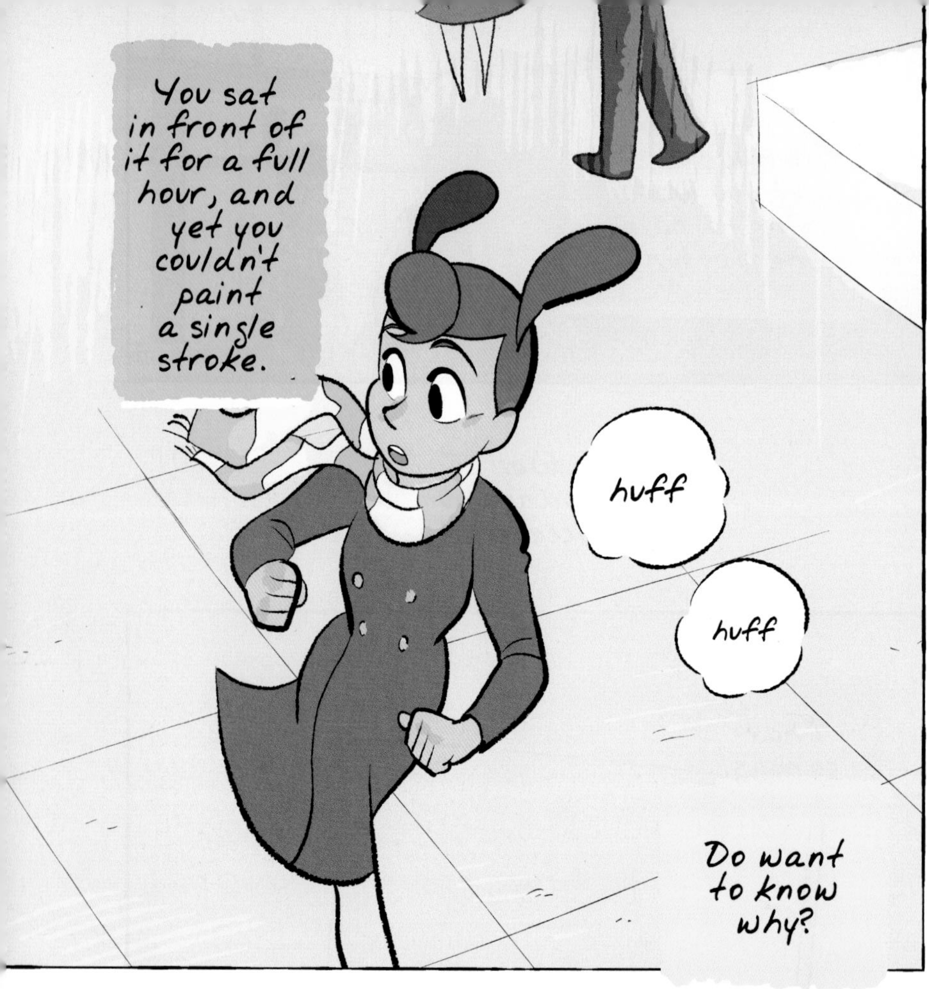
You sat in front of it for a full hour, and yet you couldn't paint a single stroke.
huff
huff
Do want to know why?
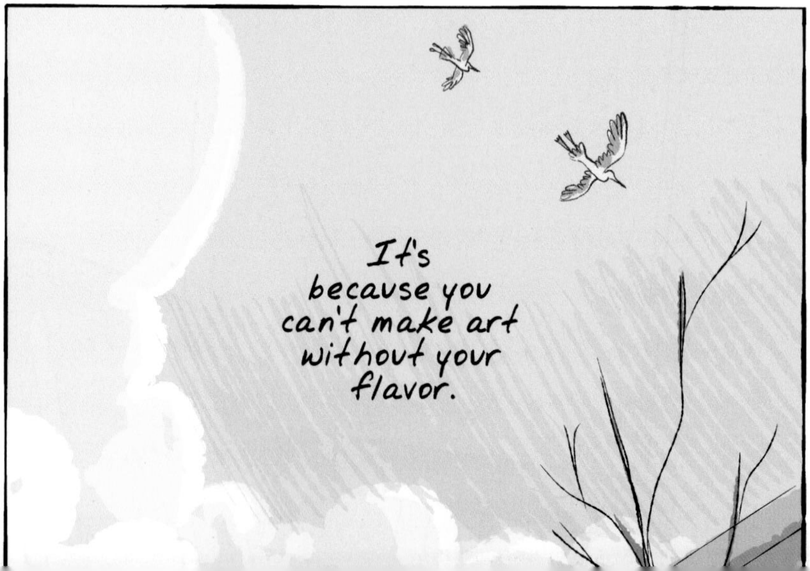
It's because you can't make art without your flavor.

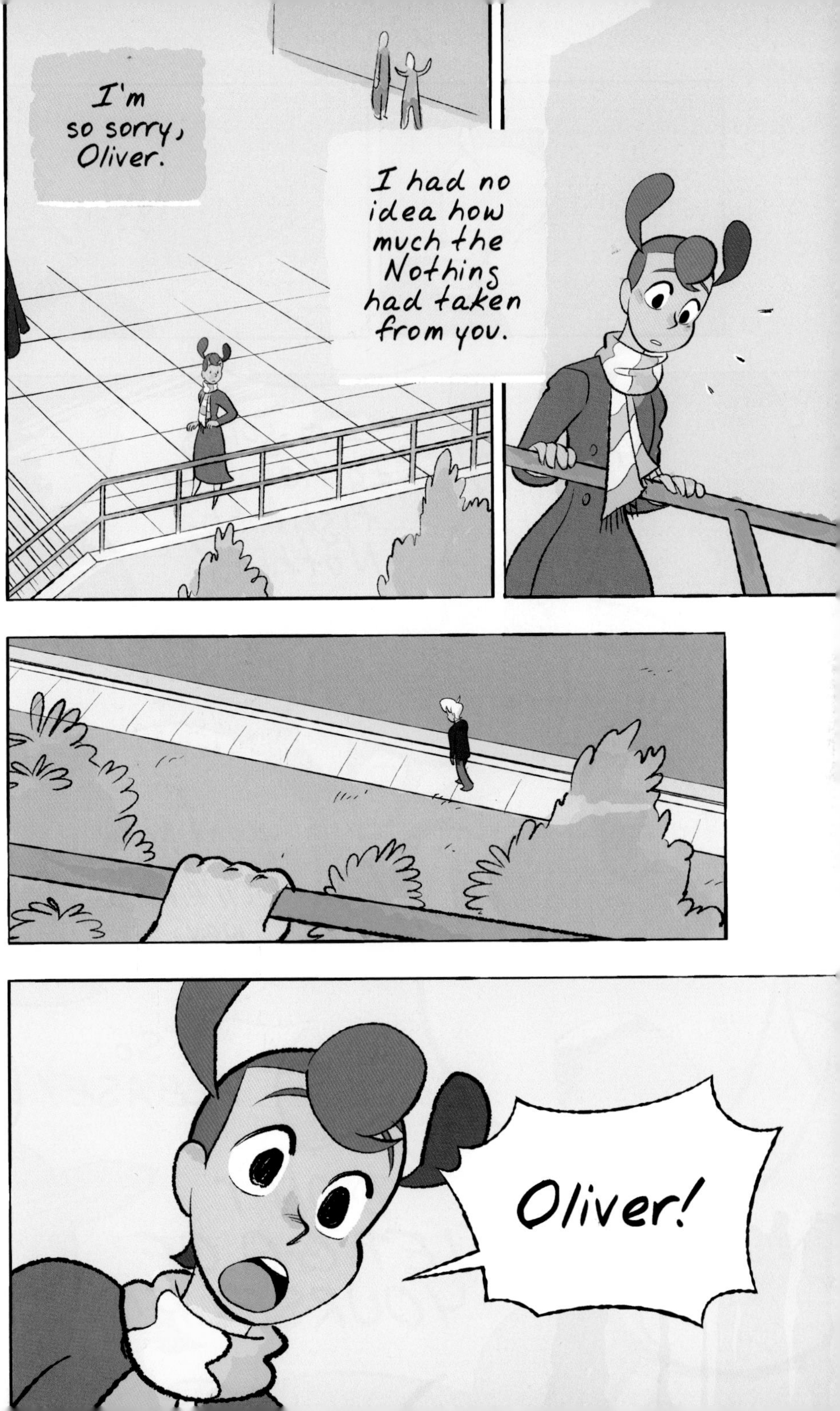
I'm so sorry, Oliver.
I had no idea how much the Nothing had taken from you.
Oliver!

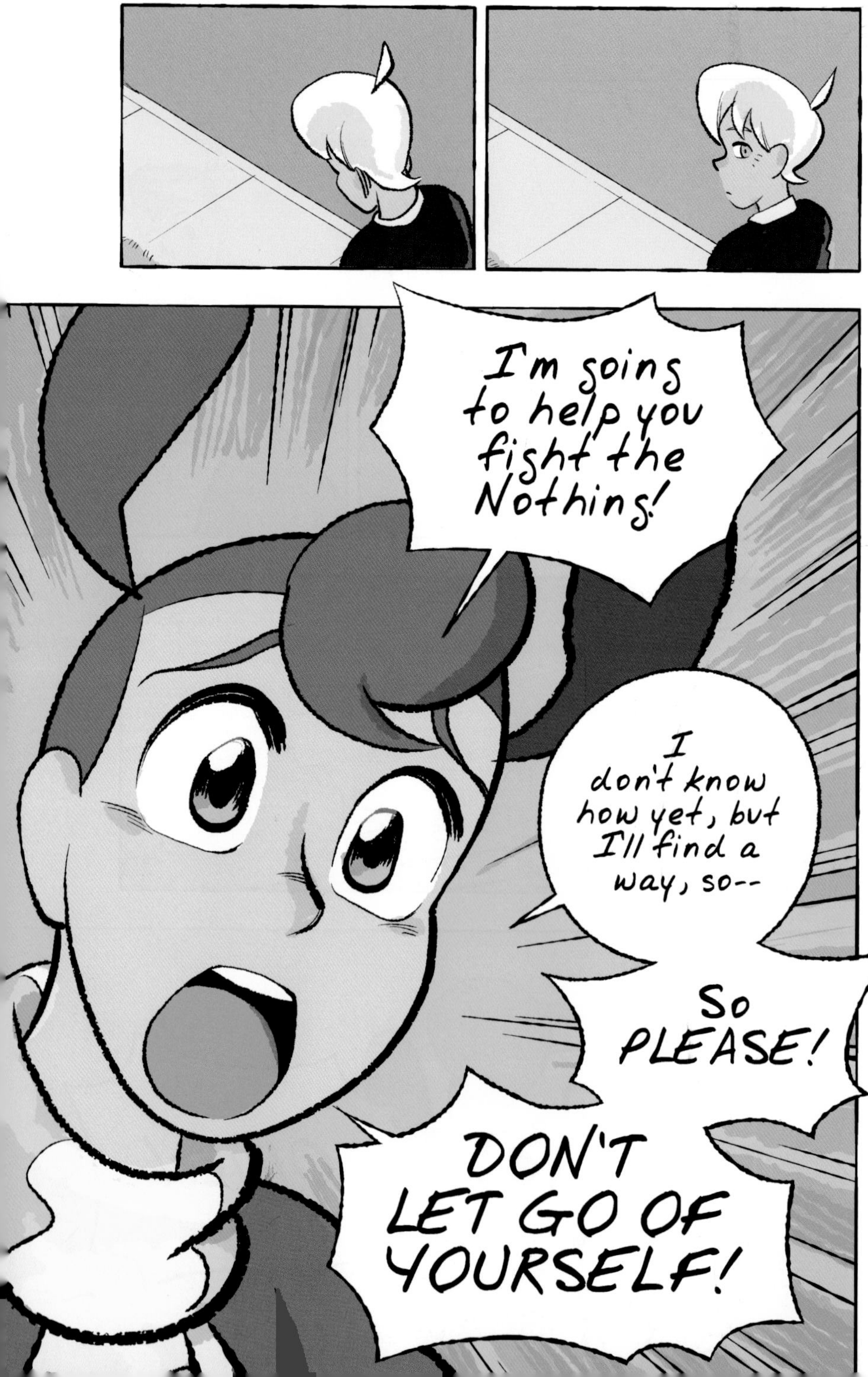
I'm going to help you fight the Nothing!
I don't know how yet, but I'll find a way, so--
So PLEASE!
DON'T LET GO OF YOURSELF!

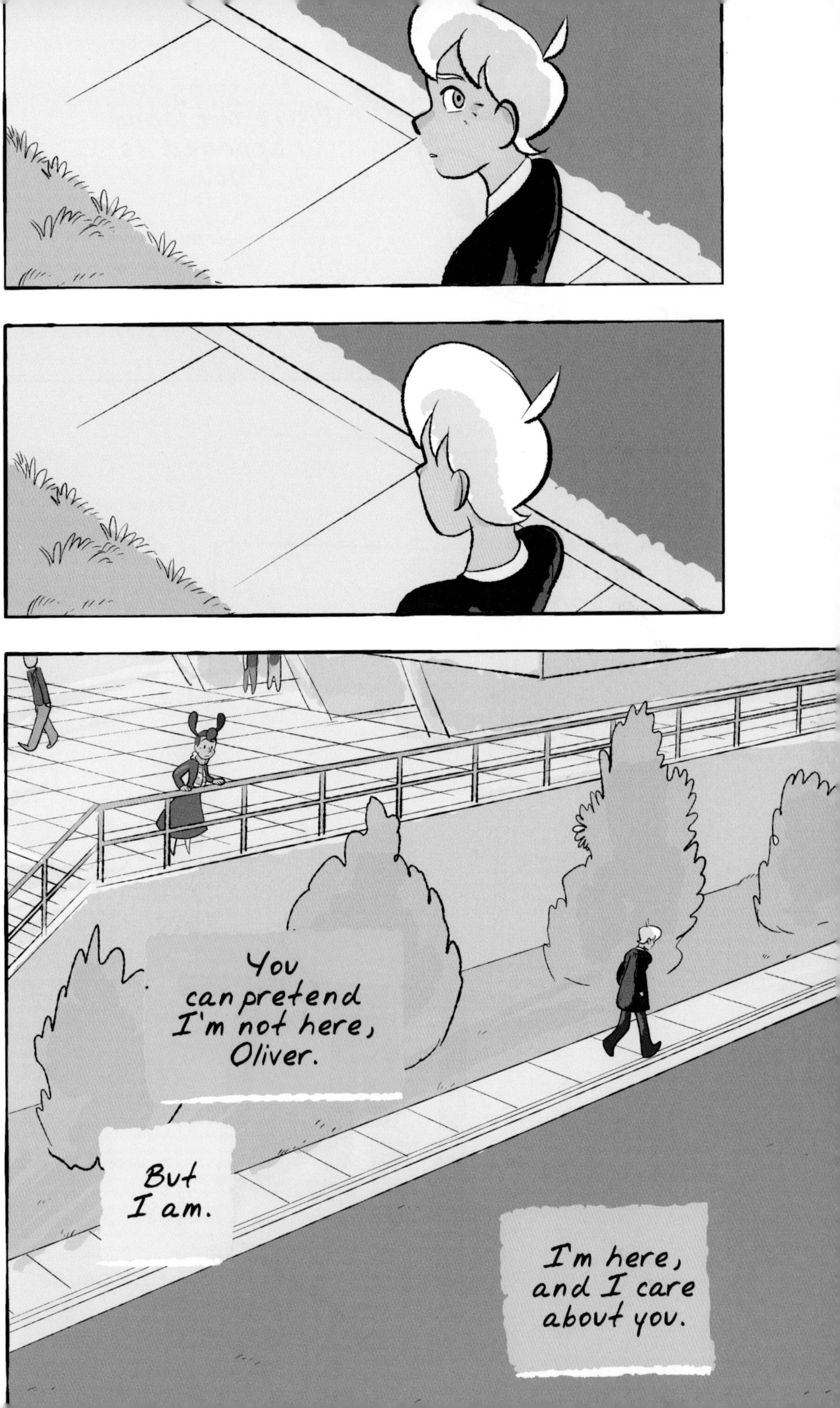
You can pretend I'm not here, Oliver.
But I am.
I'm here, and I care about you.

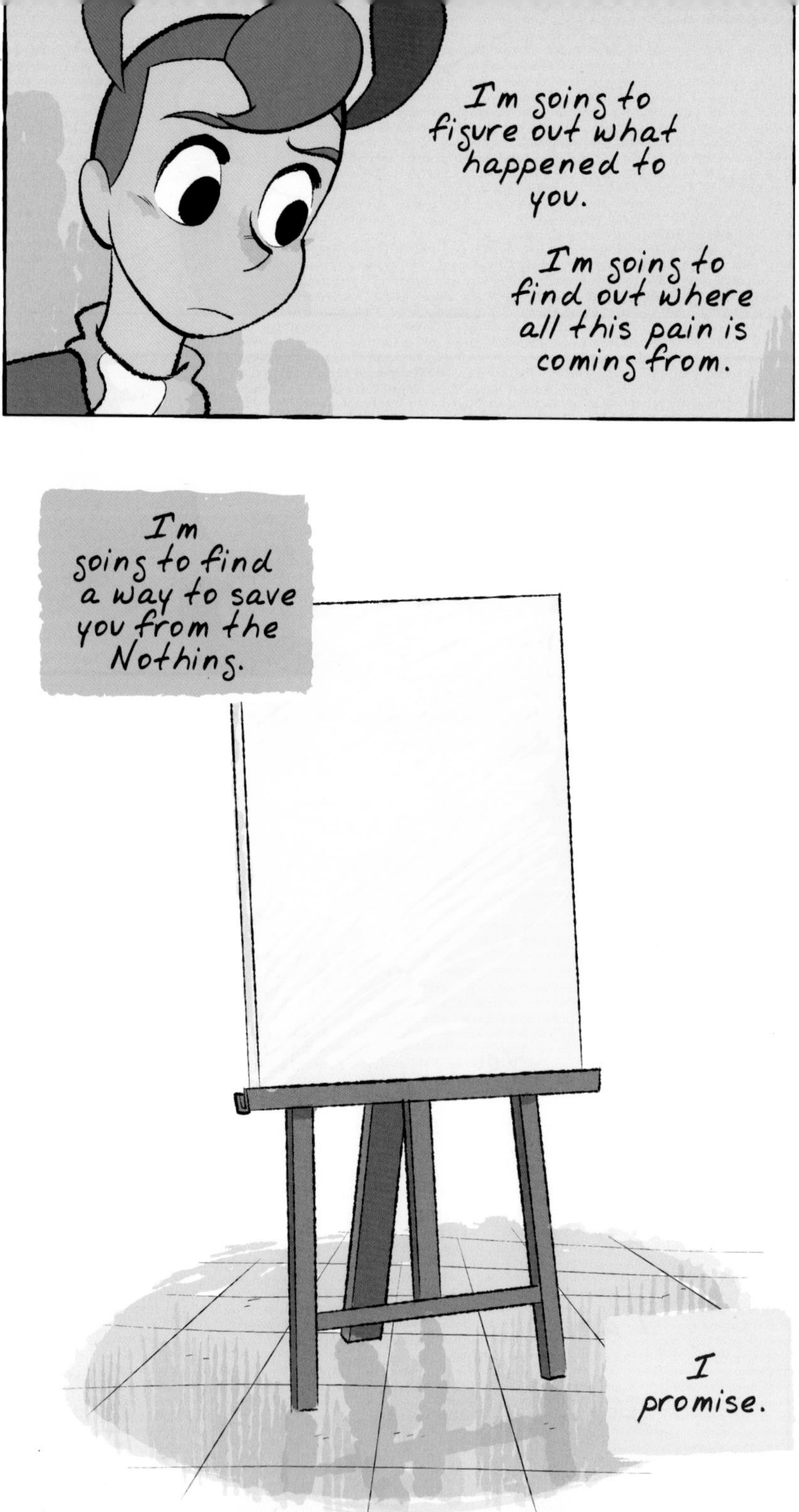
I'm going to figure out what happened to you.
I'm going to find out where all this pain is coming from.
I'm going to find a way to save you from the Nothing.
I promise.

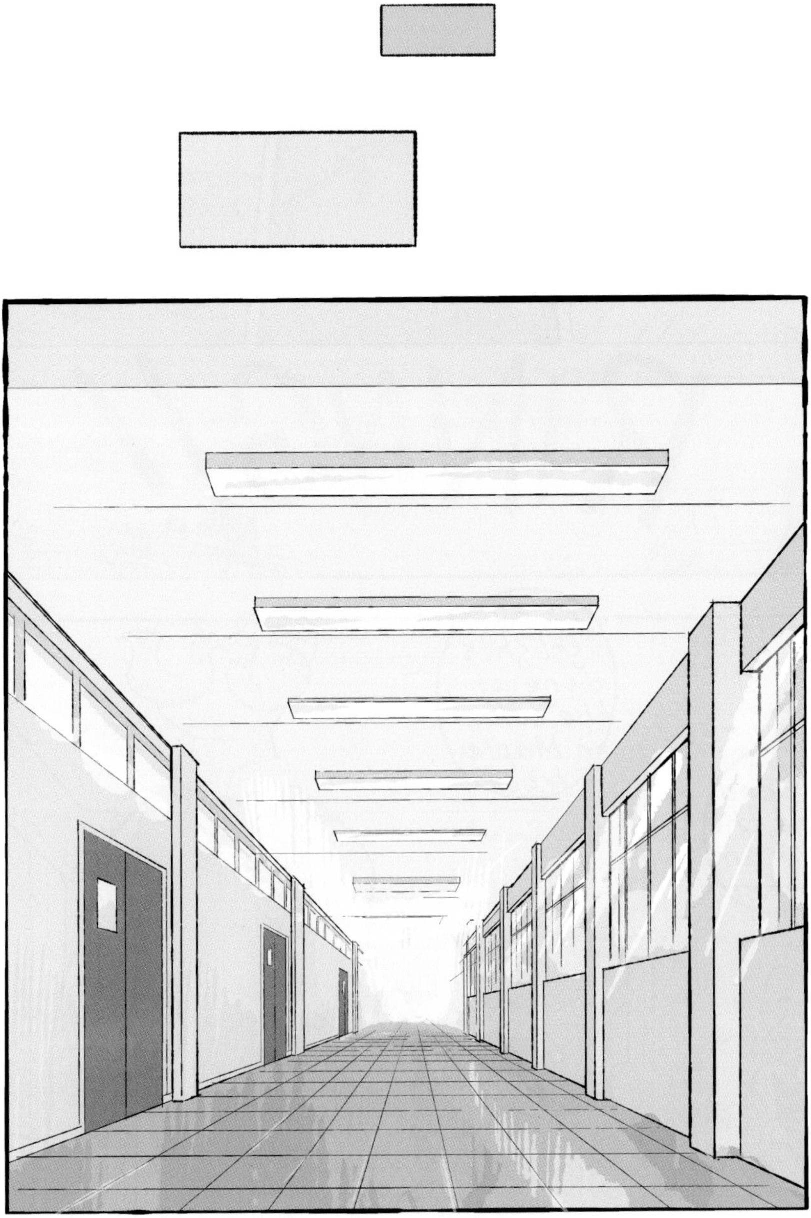

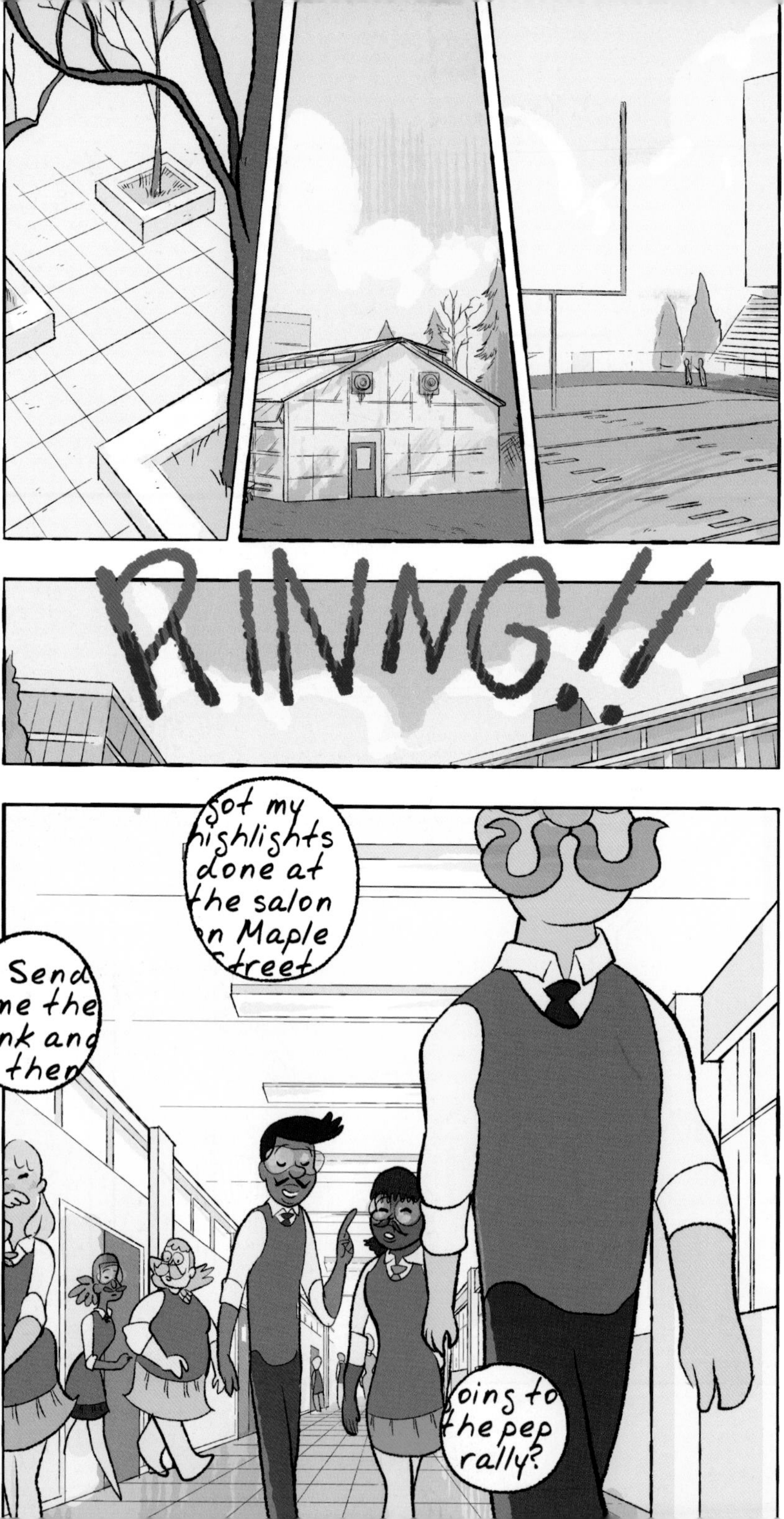
RINNG!!
got my highlights done at the salon on Maple Street
Send me the link and then
oing to the pep rally?

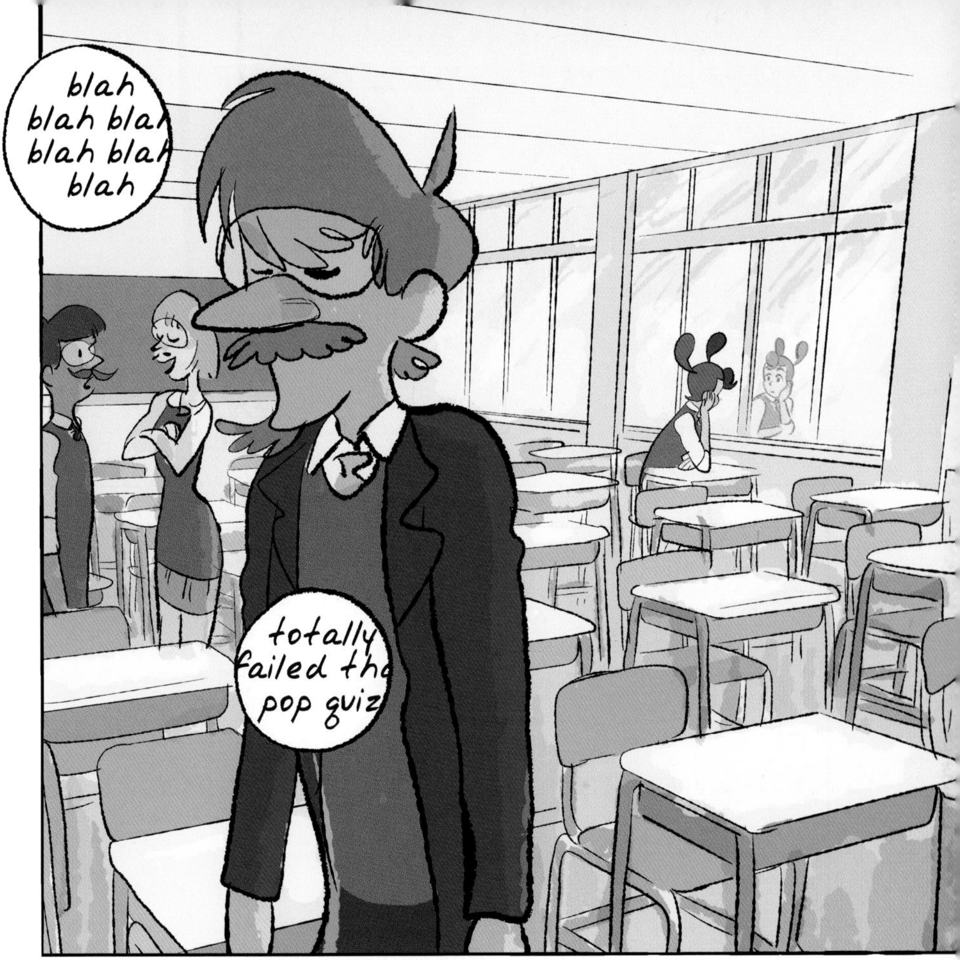
blah blah blah blah blah blah
totally failed the pop quiz

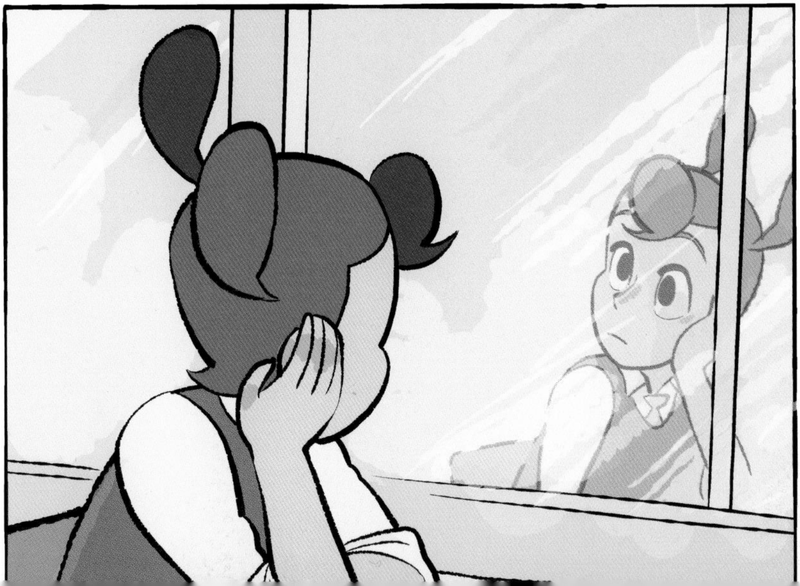

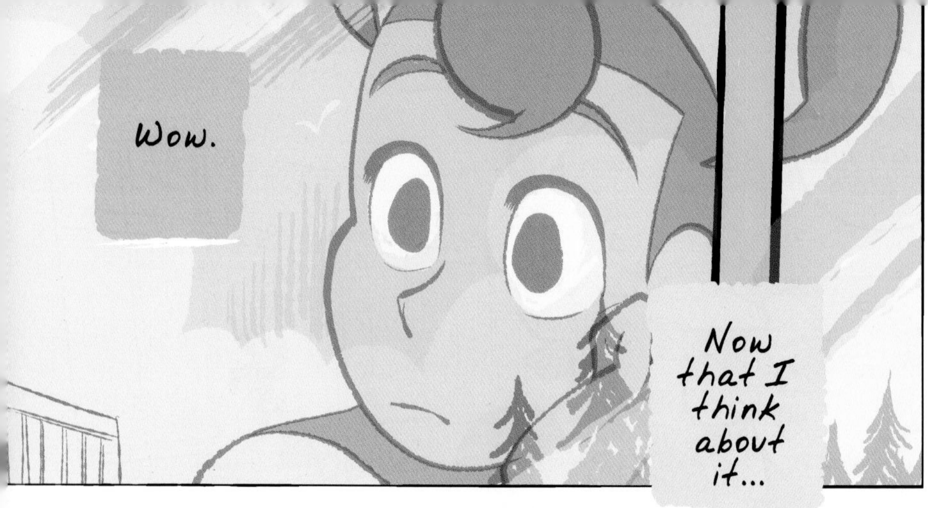
Wow.
Now that I think about it...

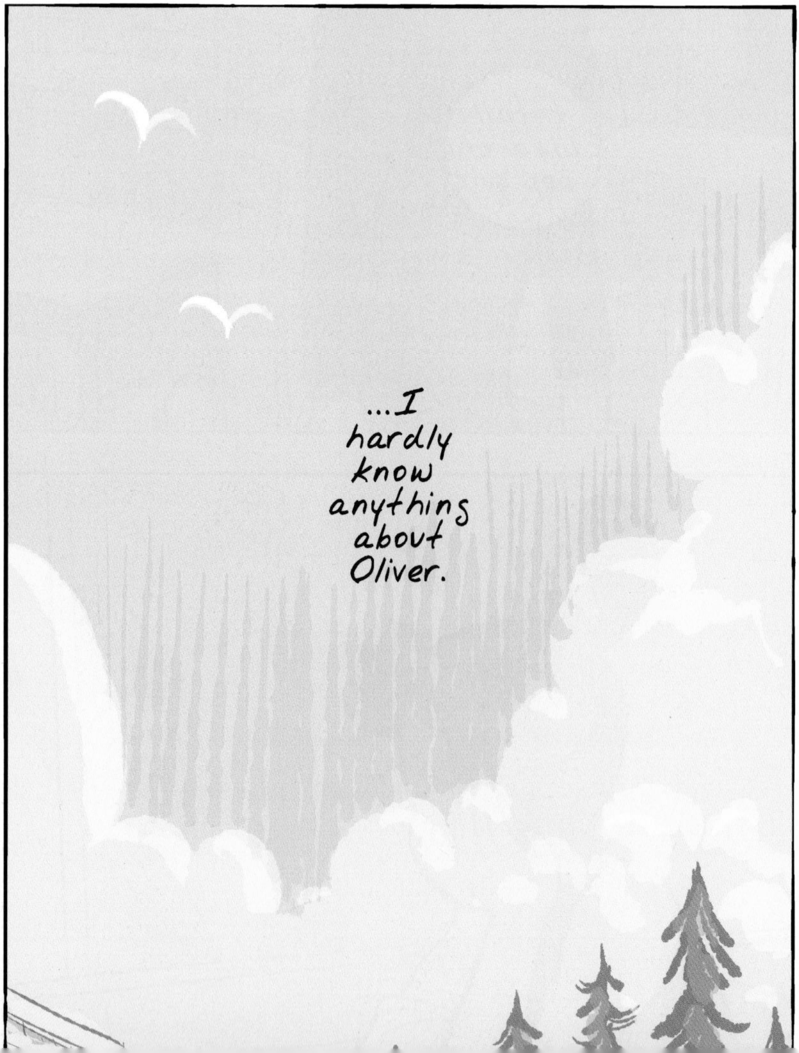
...I hardly know anything about Oliver.

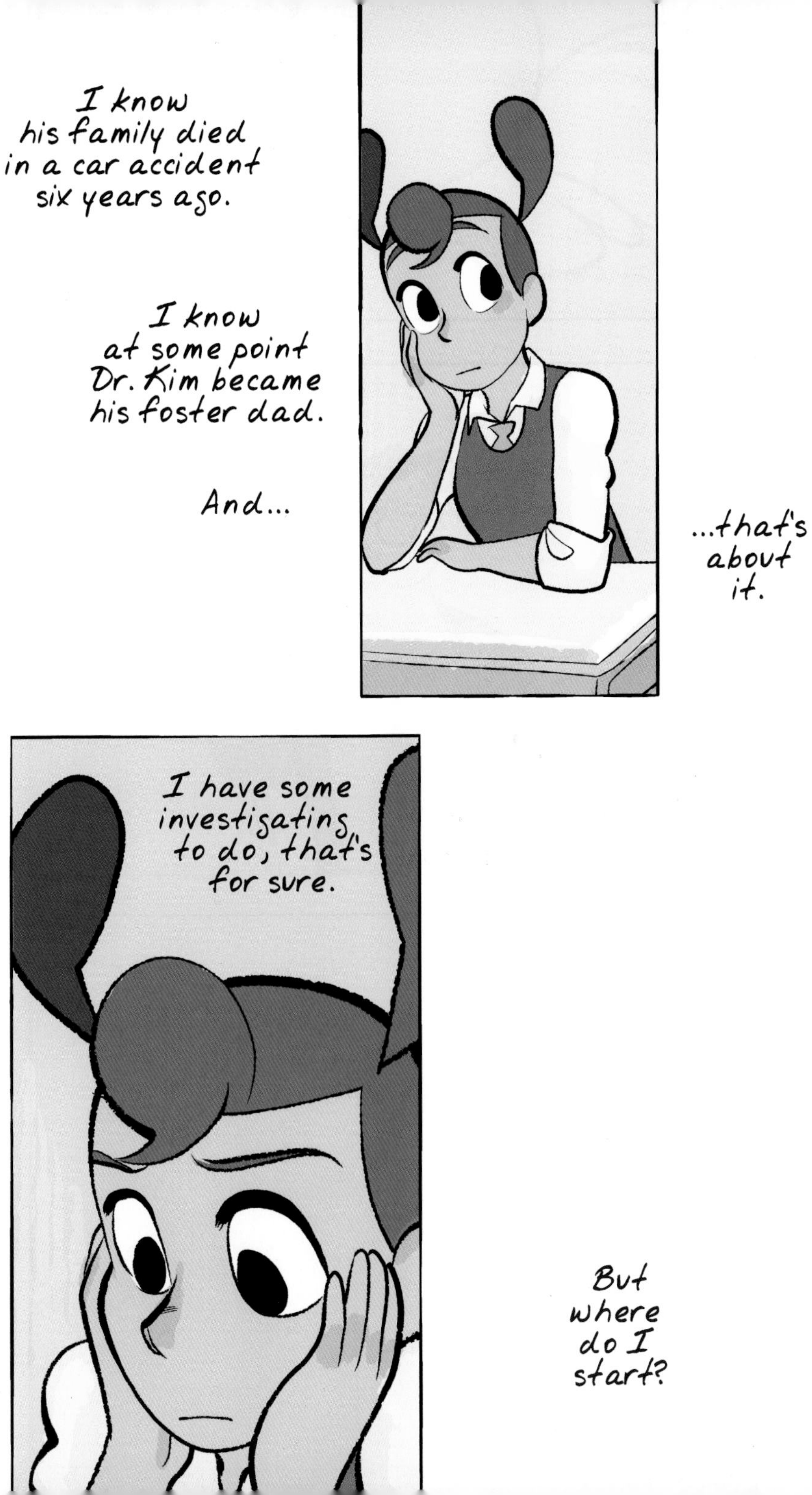
I know his family died in a car accident six years ago.
I know at some point Dr. Kim became his foster dad.
And...
...that's about it.
I have some investigating to do, that's for sure.
But where do I start?

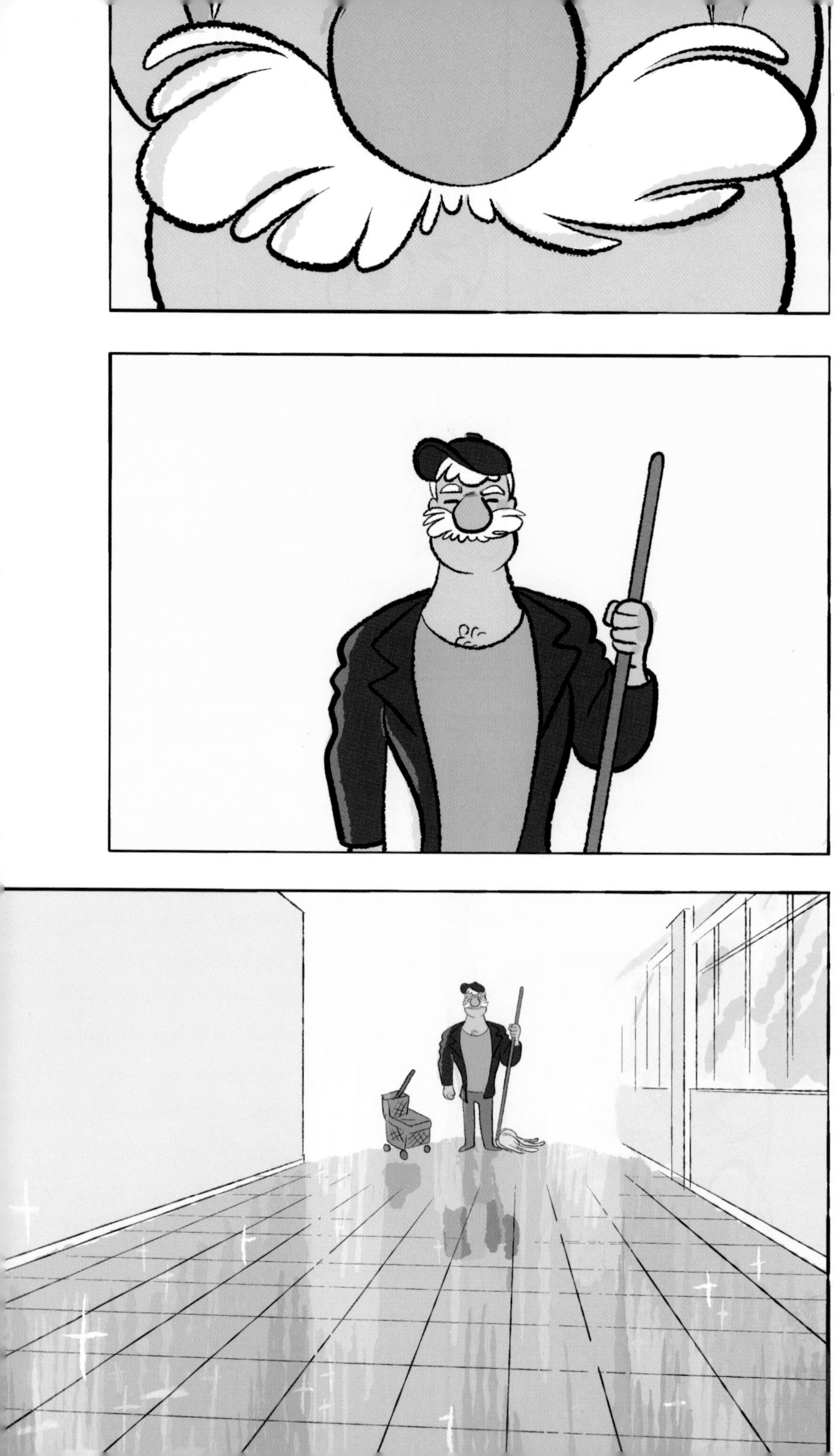

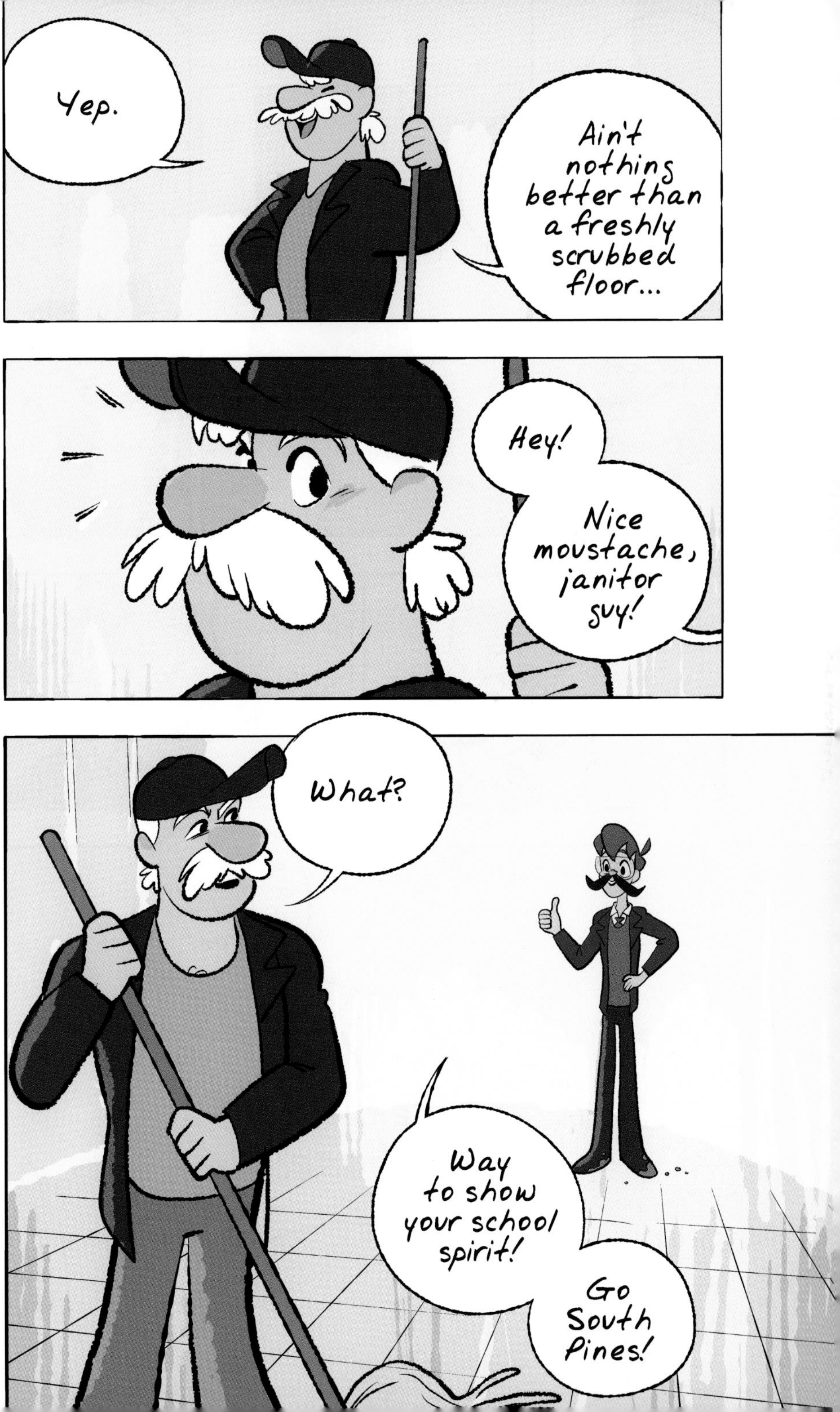
Yep.
Ain't nothing better than a freshly scrubbed floor...
Hey!
Nice moustache, janitor guy!
What?
Way to show your school spirit!
Go South Pines!

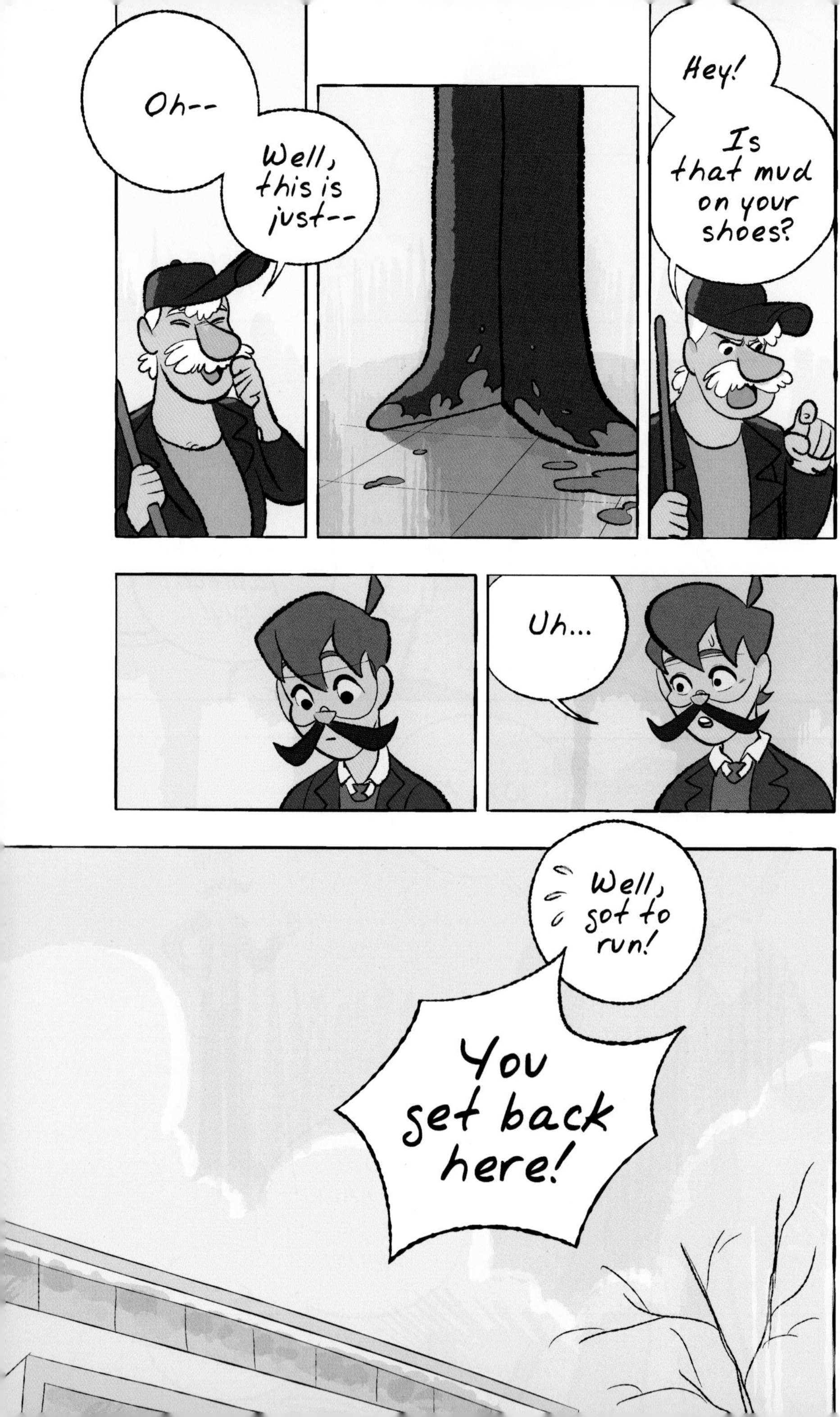
Oh--
Well, this is just--
Hey!
Is that mud on your shoes?
Uh...
Well, got to run!
You get back here!

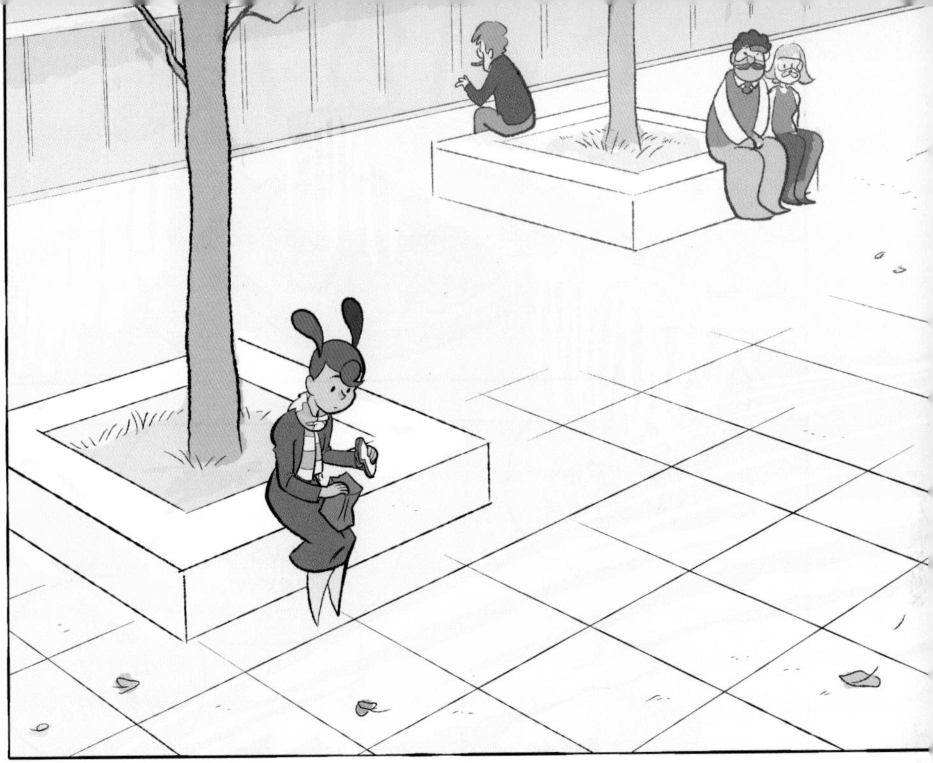

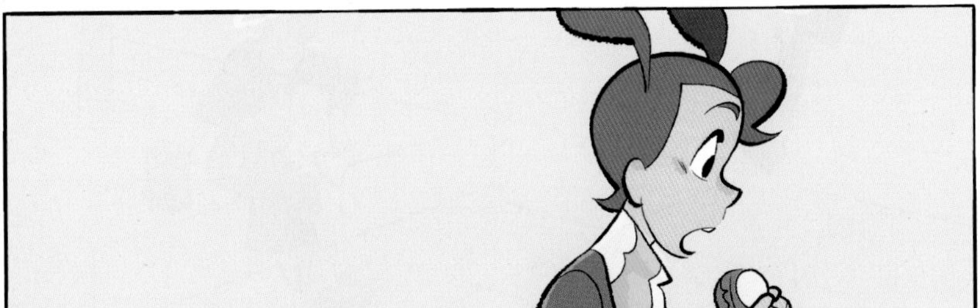

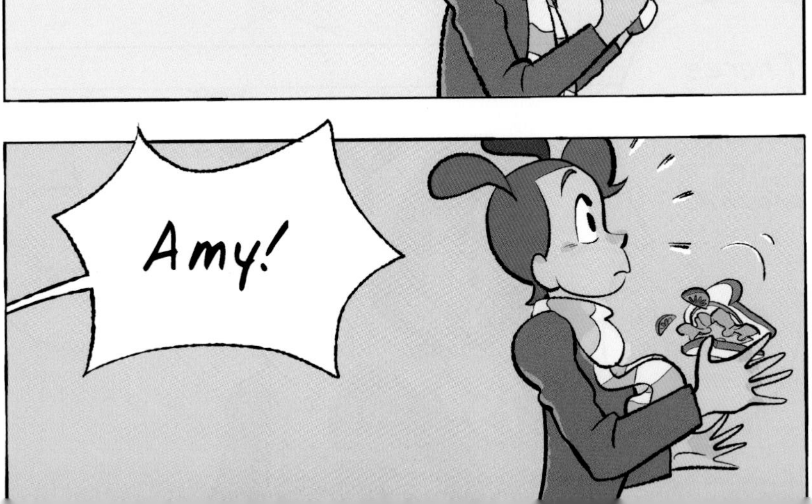
Amy!

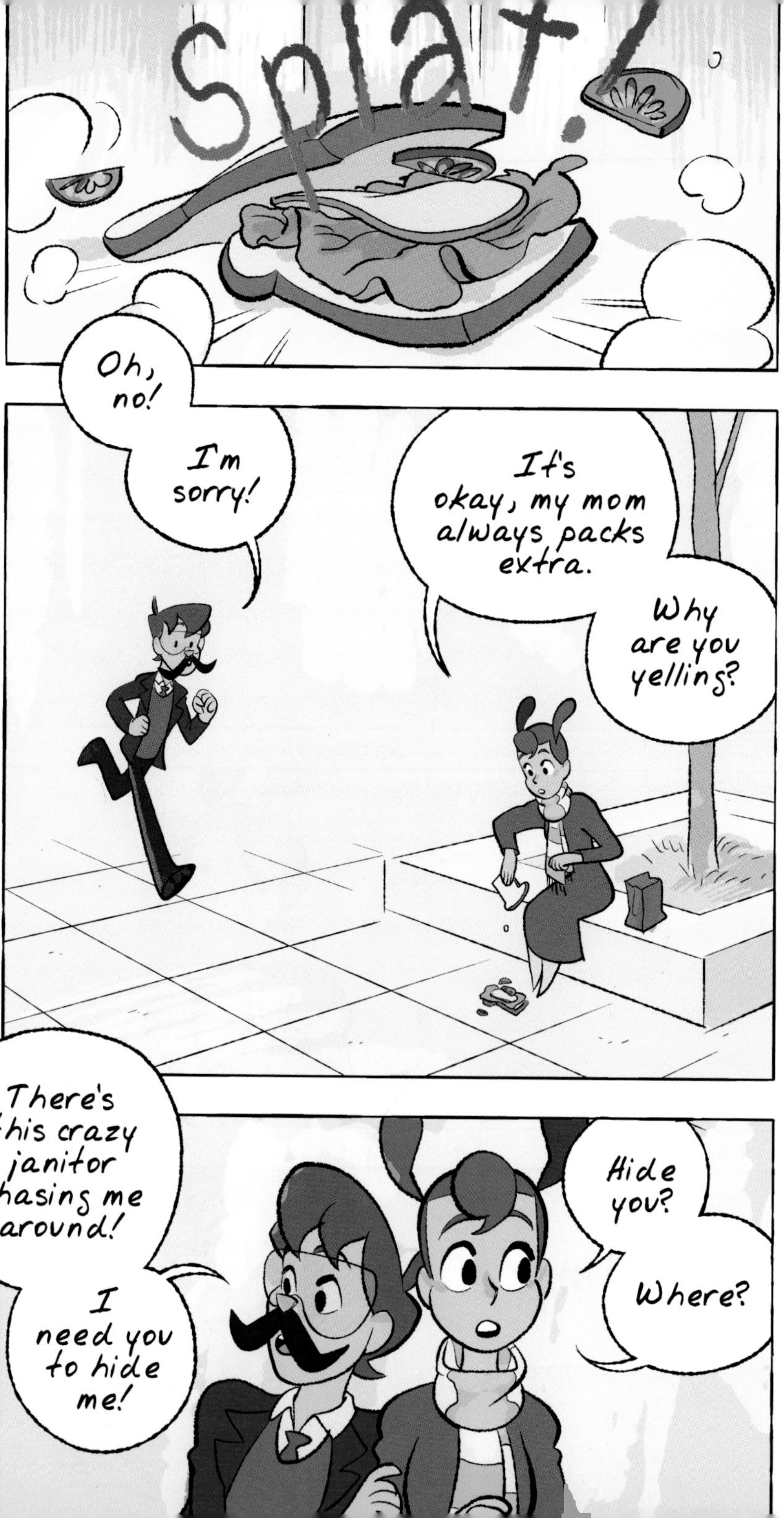
Splat!
Oh, no!
I'm sorry!
It's okay, my mom always packs extra.
Why are you yelling?
There's this crazy janitor chasing me around!
I need you to hide me!
Hide you?
Where?

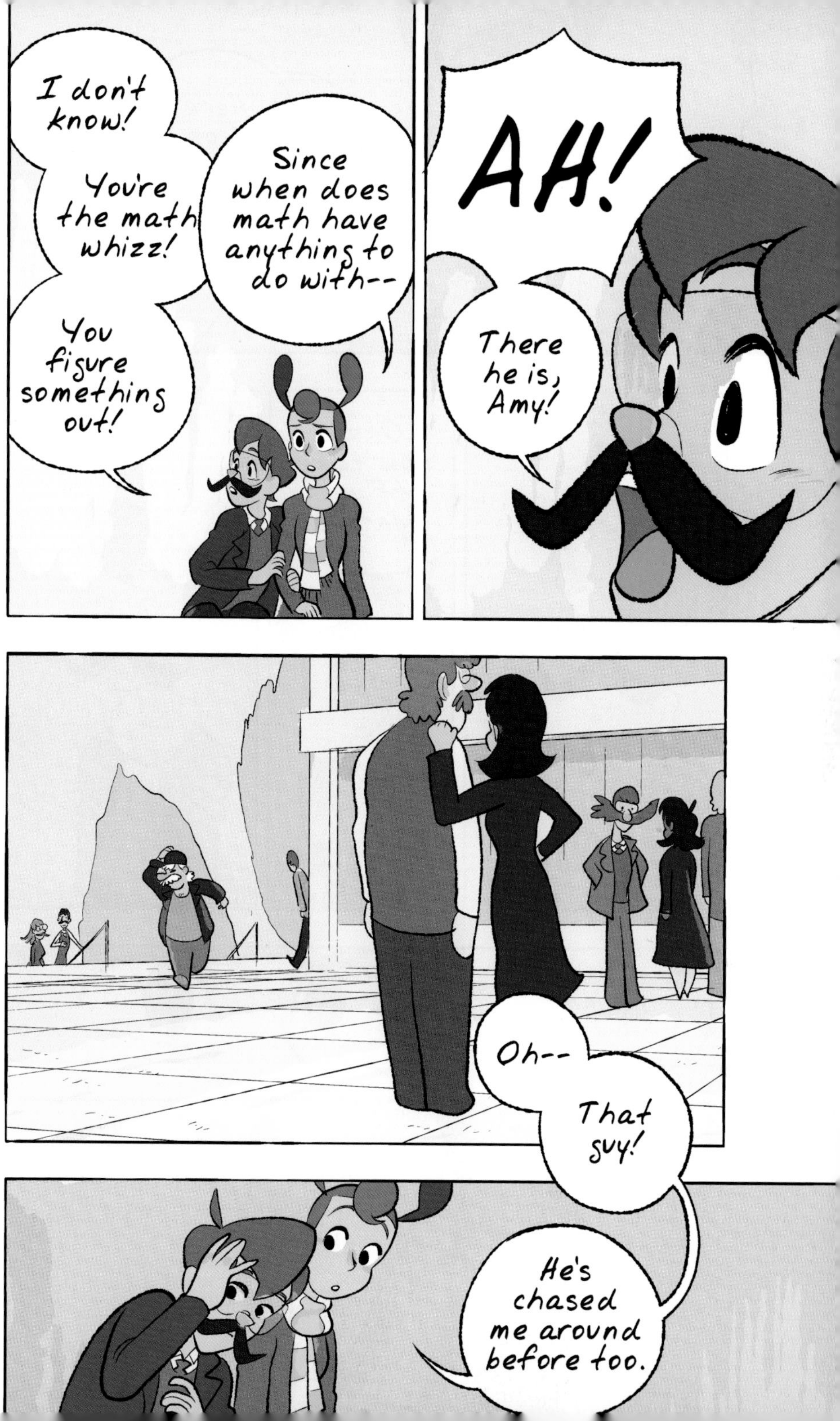

I don't know!
You're the math whizz!
You figure something out!
Since when does math have anything to do with--
AH!
There he is, Amy!
Oh--
That guy!
He's chased me around before too.

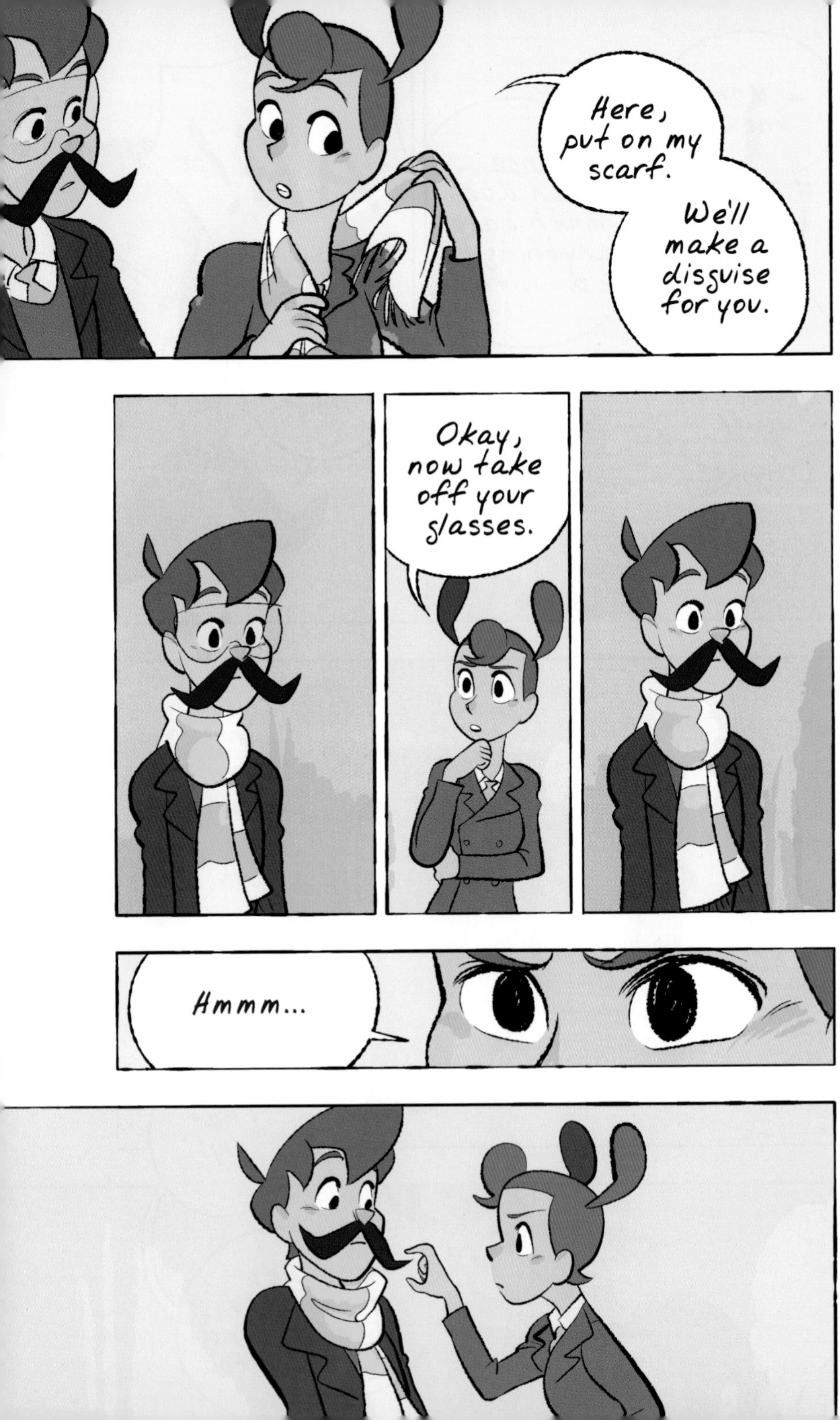
Here, put on my scarf.
We'll make a disguise for you.
Okay, now take off your glasses.
Hmmm...

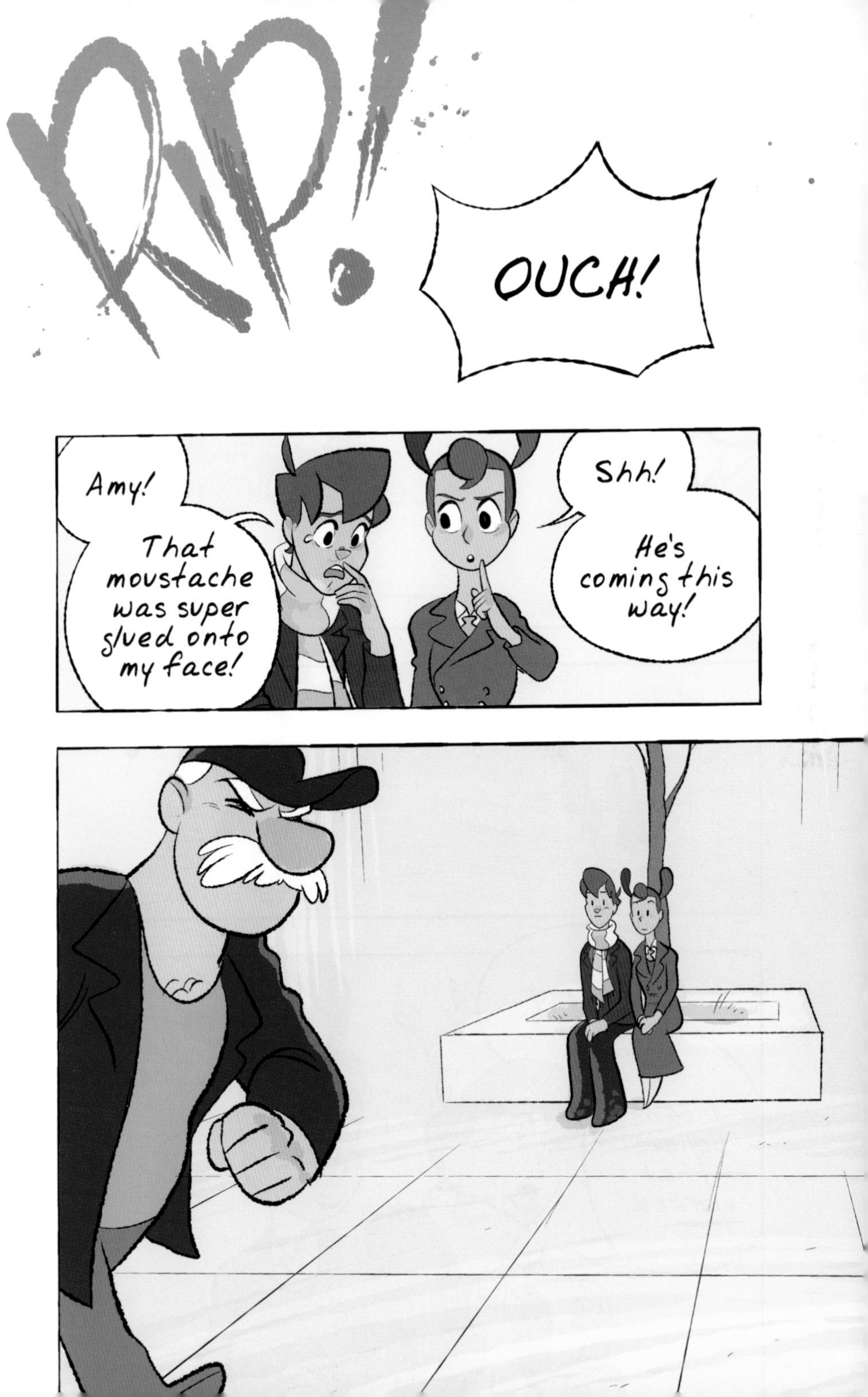
RIP!
OUCH!
Amy!
That moustache was super glued onto my face!
Shh!
He's coming this way!

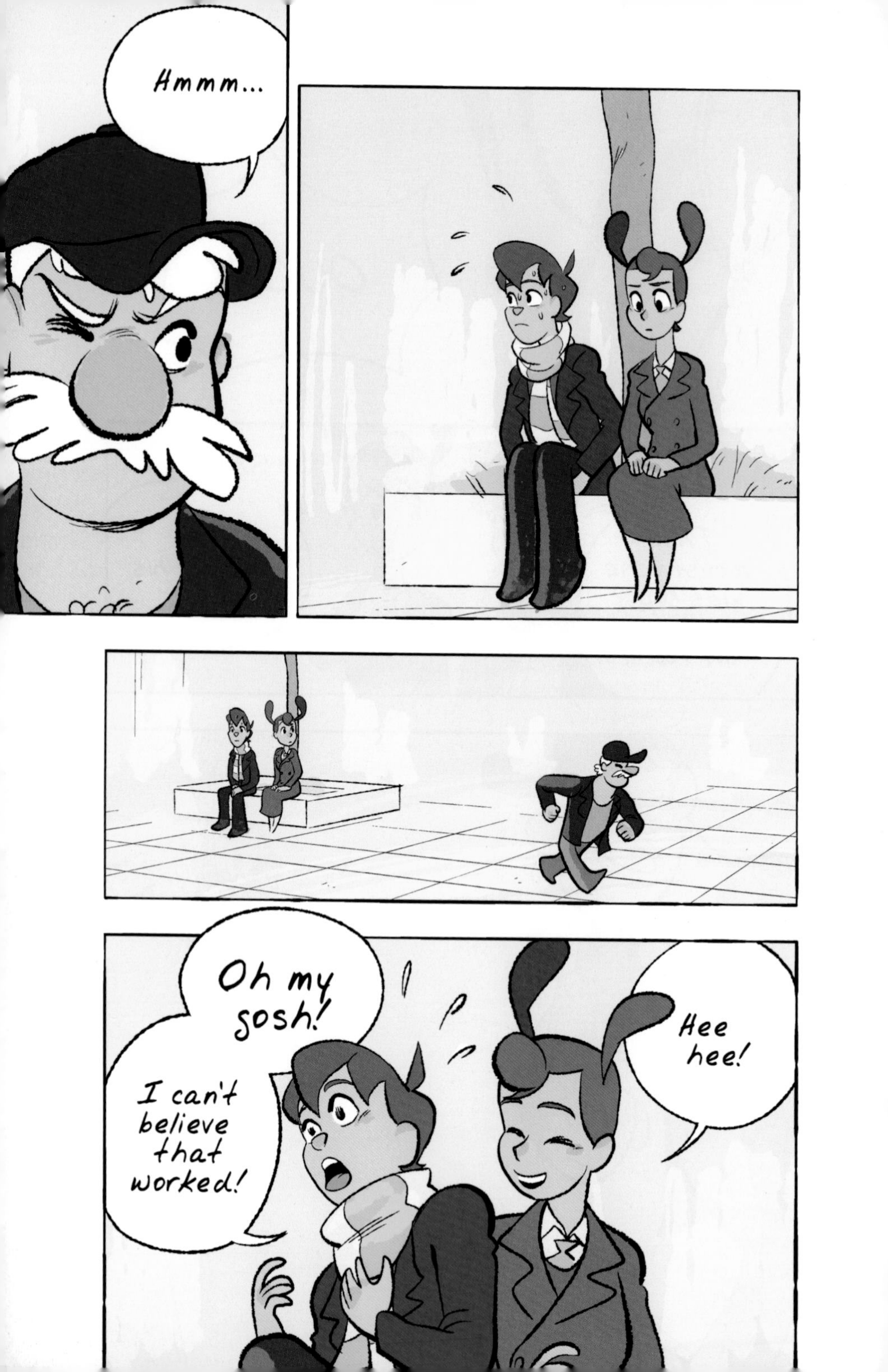
Hmmm...
Oh my gosh!
I can't believe that worked!
Hee hee!

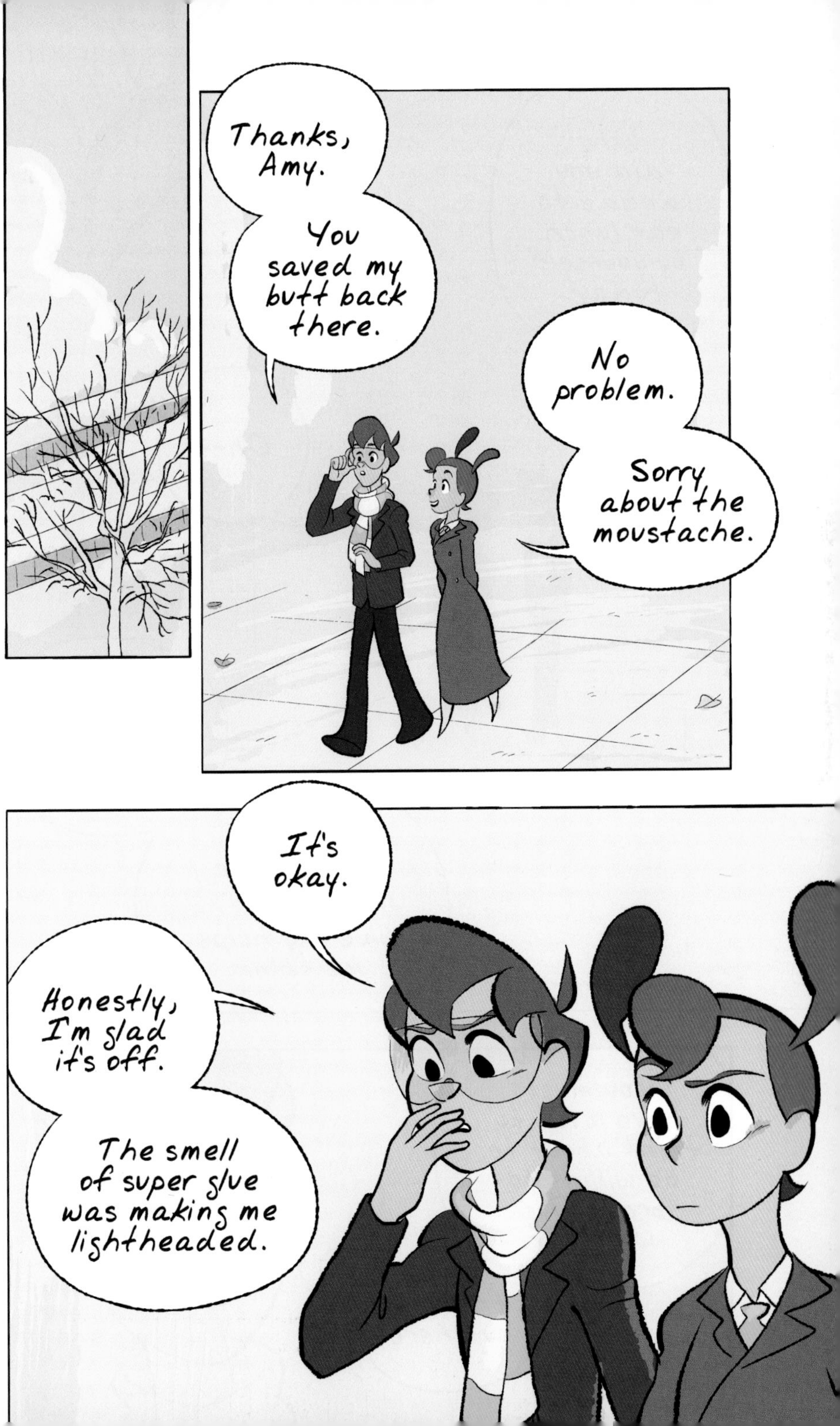

Thanks, Amy.
You saved my butt back there.
No problem.
Sorry about the moustache.
It's okay.
Honestly, I'm glad it's off.
The smell of super glue was making me lightheaded.

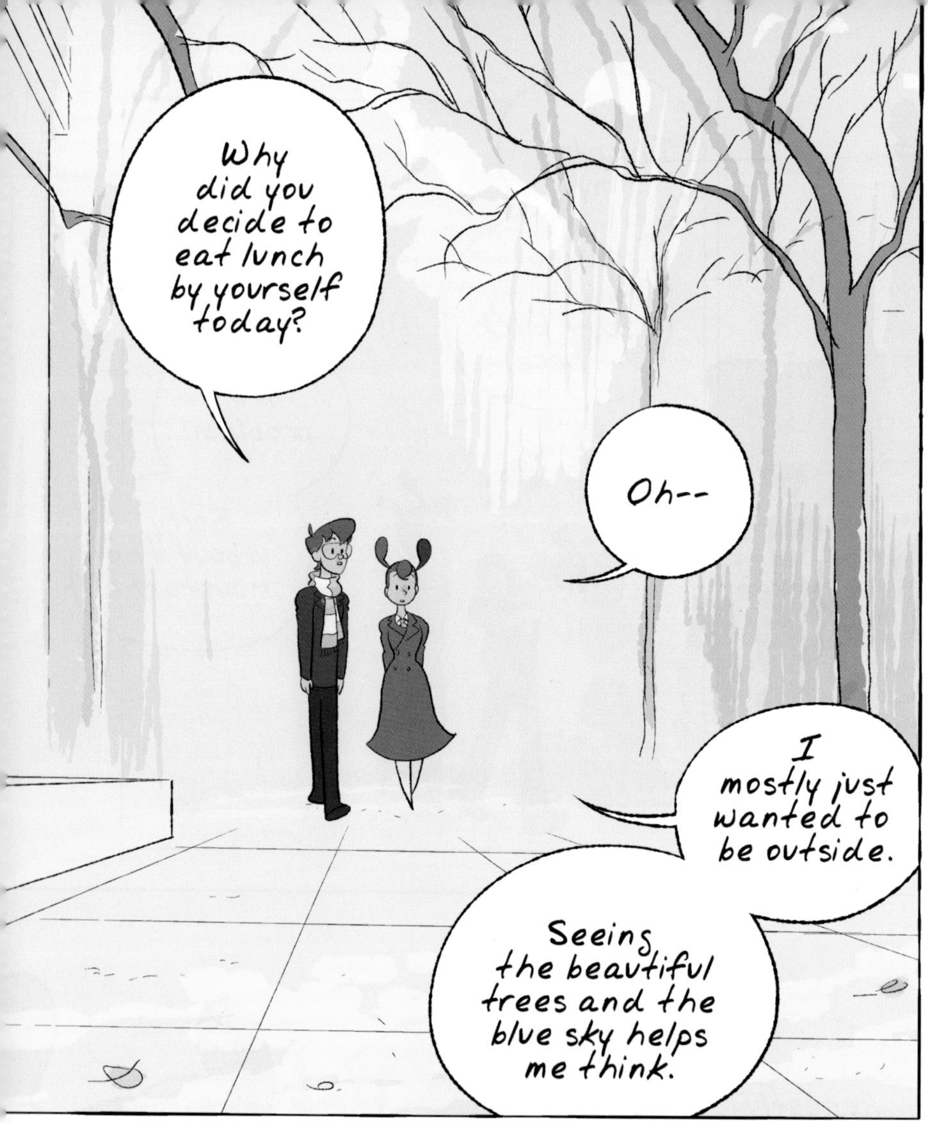
Why did you decide to eat lunch by yourself today?
Oh--
I mostly just wanted to be outside.
Seeing the beautiful trees and the blue sky helps me think.

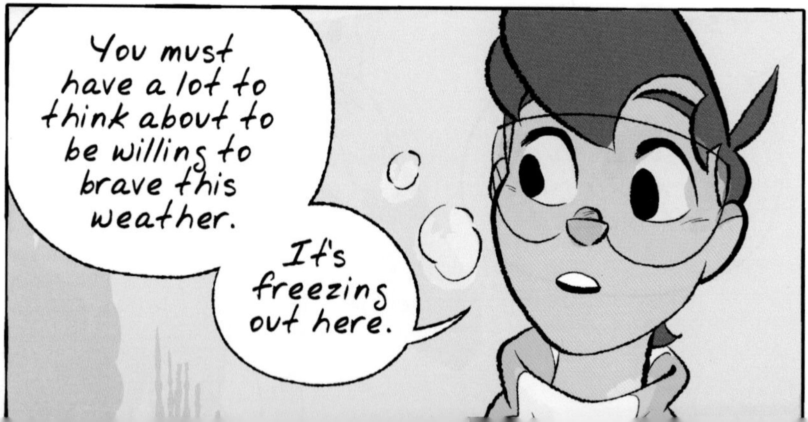
You must have a lot to think about to be willing to brave this weather.
It's freezing out here.

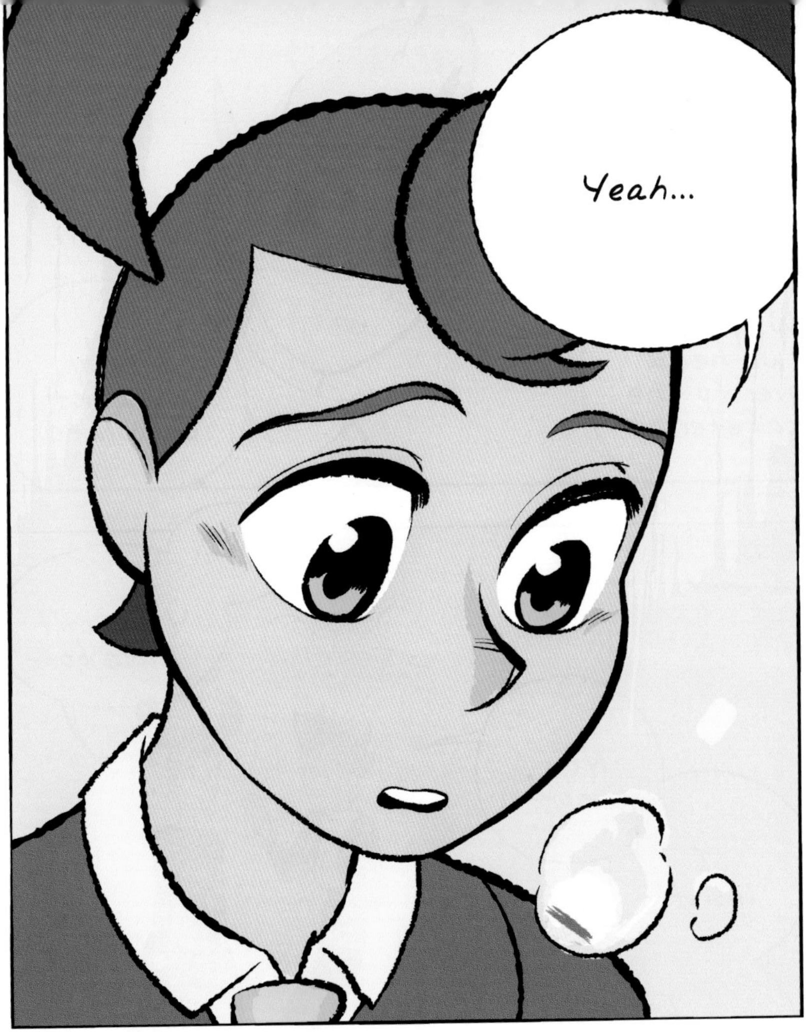
Yeah...

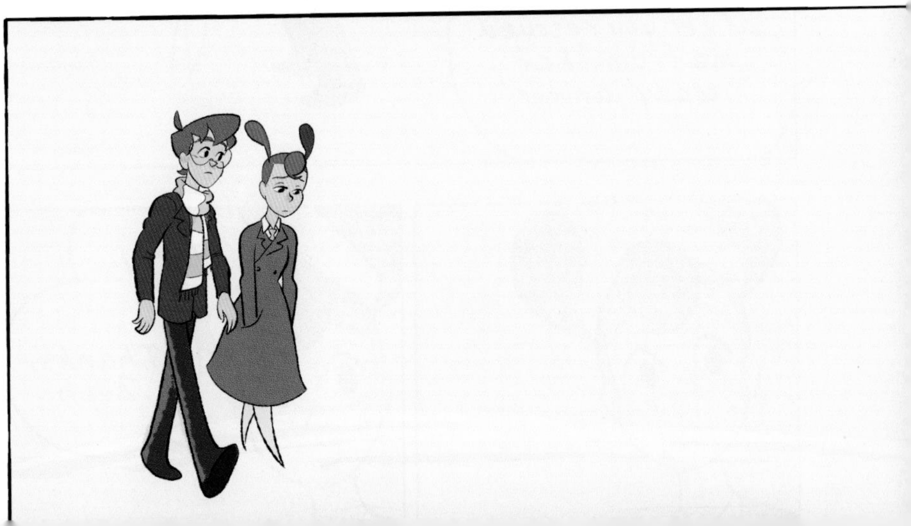

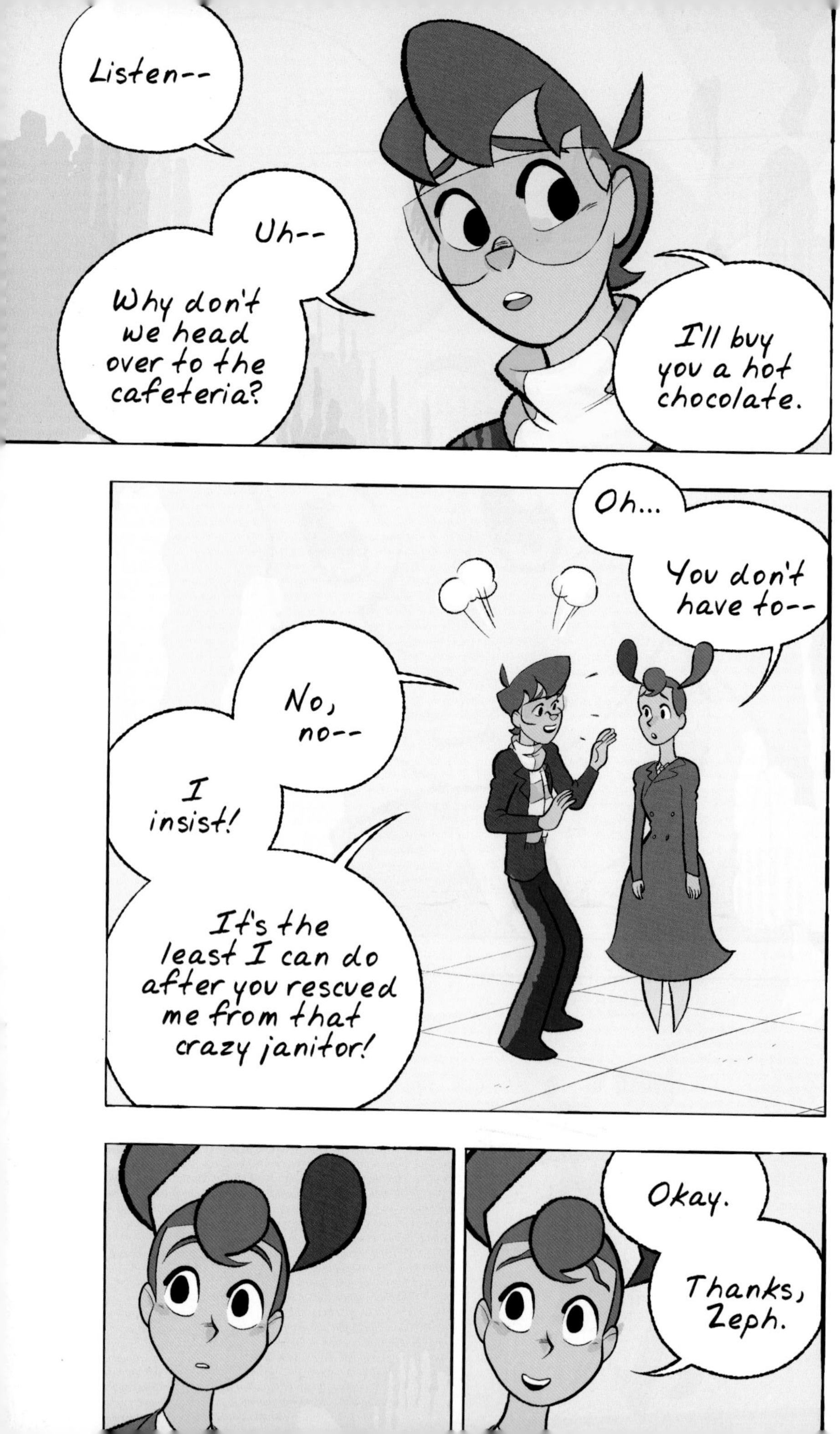
Listen--
Uh--
Why don't we head over to the cafeteria?
I'll buy you a hot chocolate.
Oh...
You don't have to--
No, no--
I insist!
It's the least I can do after you rescued me from that crazy janitor!
Okay.
Thanks, Zeph.

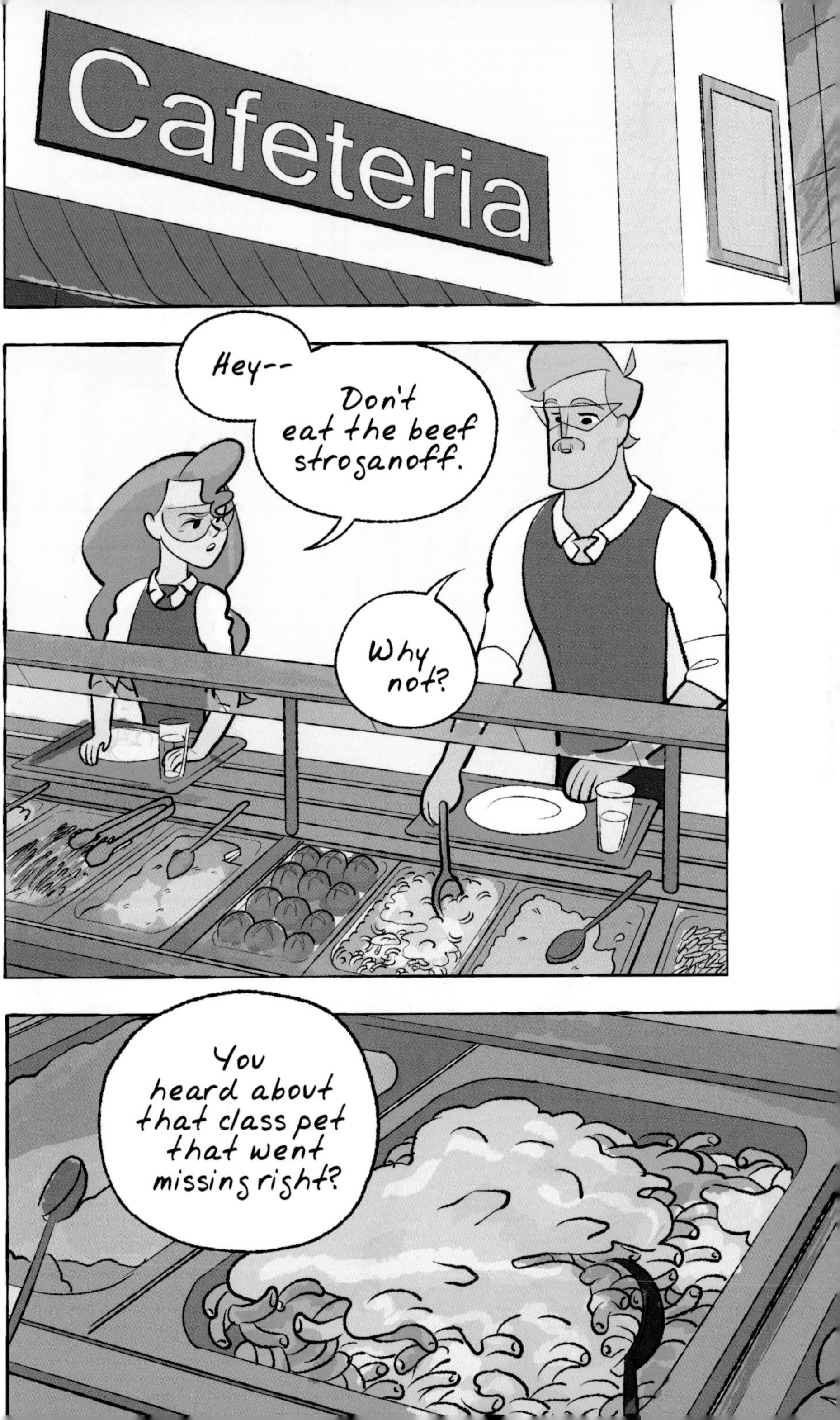
Cafeteria
Hey-- Don't eat the beef stroganoff.
Why not?
You heard about that class pet that went missing right?

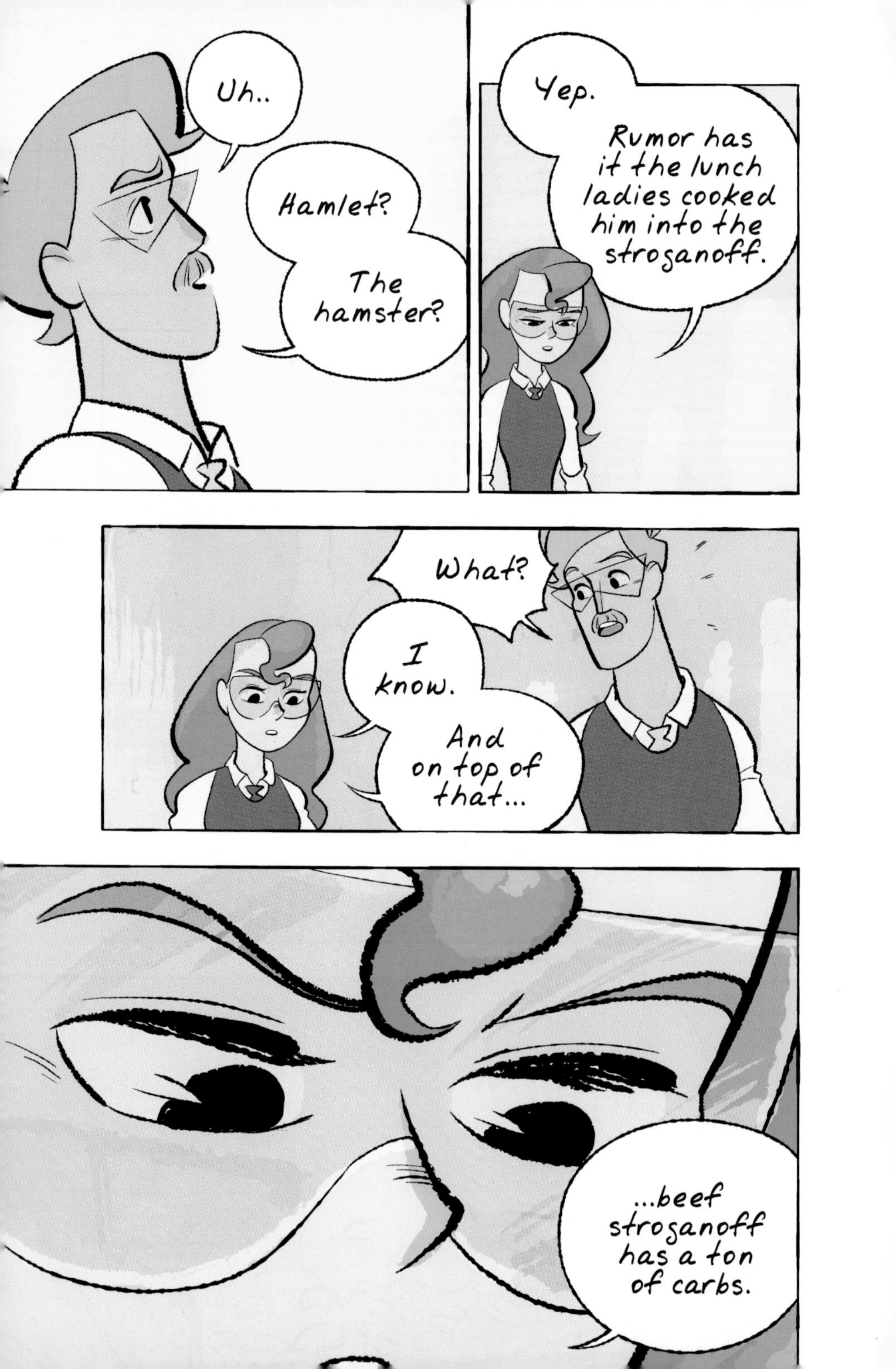
Uh..
Hamlet?
The hamster?
Yep.
Rumor has it the lunch ladies cooked him into the stroganoff.
What?
I know.
And on top of that...
...beef stroganoff has a ton of carbs.

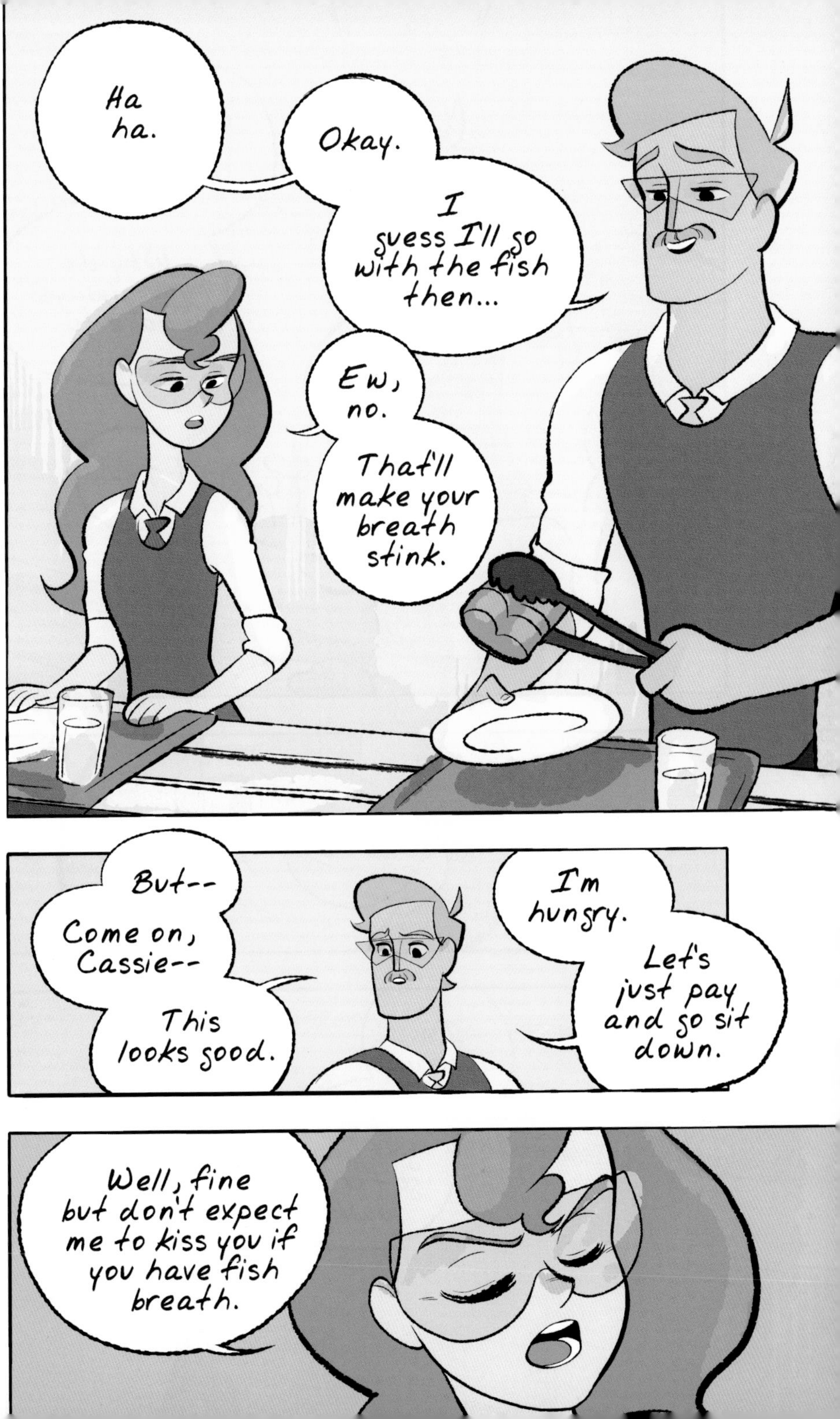
Ha ha.
Okay.
I guess I'll go with the fish then...
Ew, no.
That'll make your breath stink.
But--
Come on, Cassie--
This looks good.
I'm hungry.
Let's just pay and go sit down.
Well, fine but don't expect me to kiss you if you have fish breath.

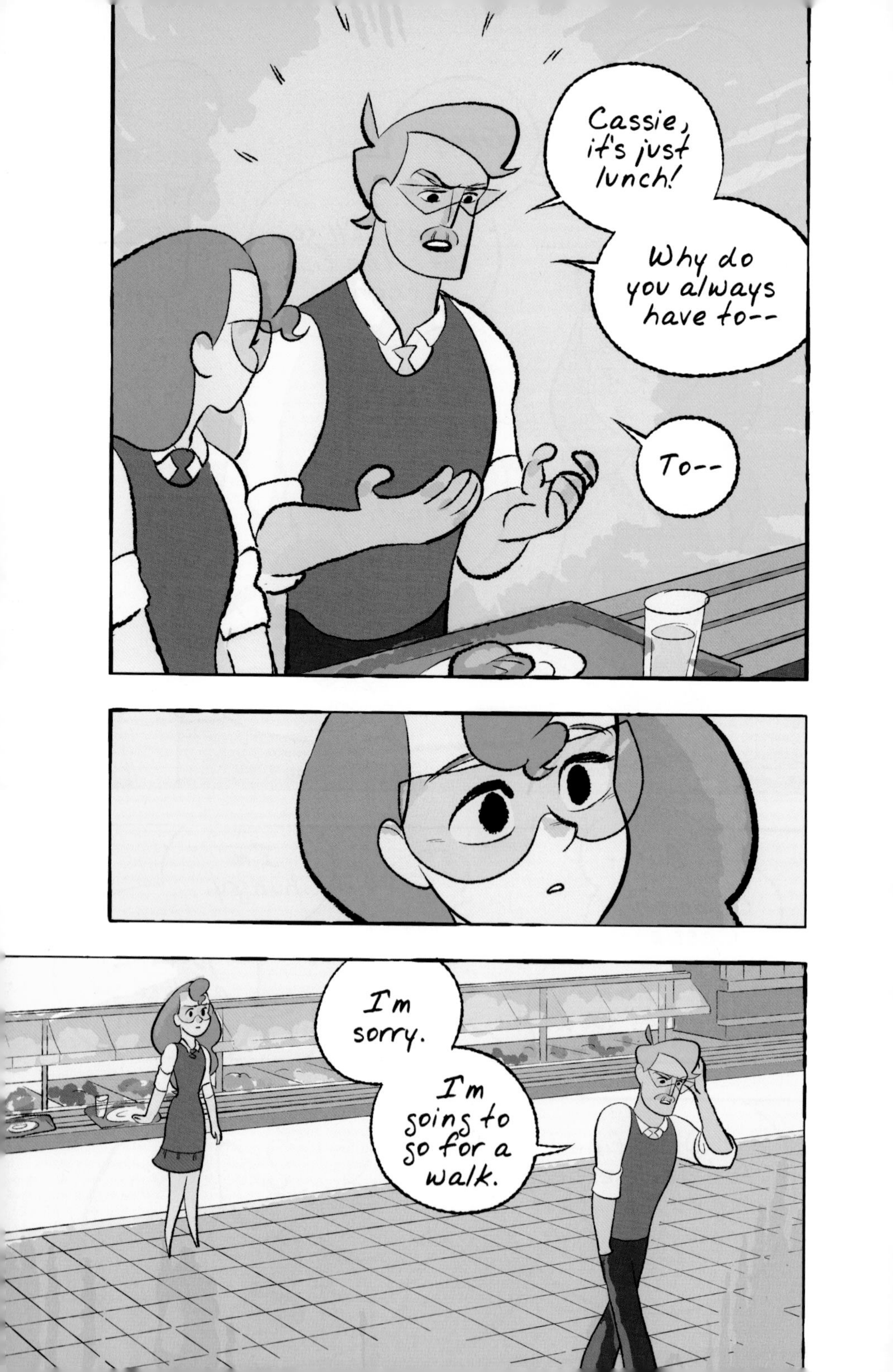

Cassie, it's just lunch!
Why do you always have to--
To--
I'm sorry.
I'm soing to so for a walk.

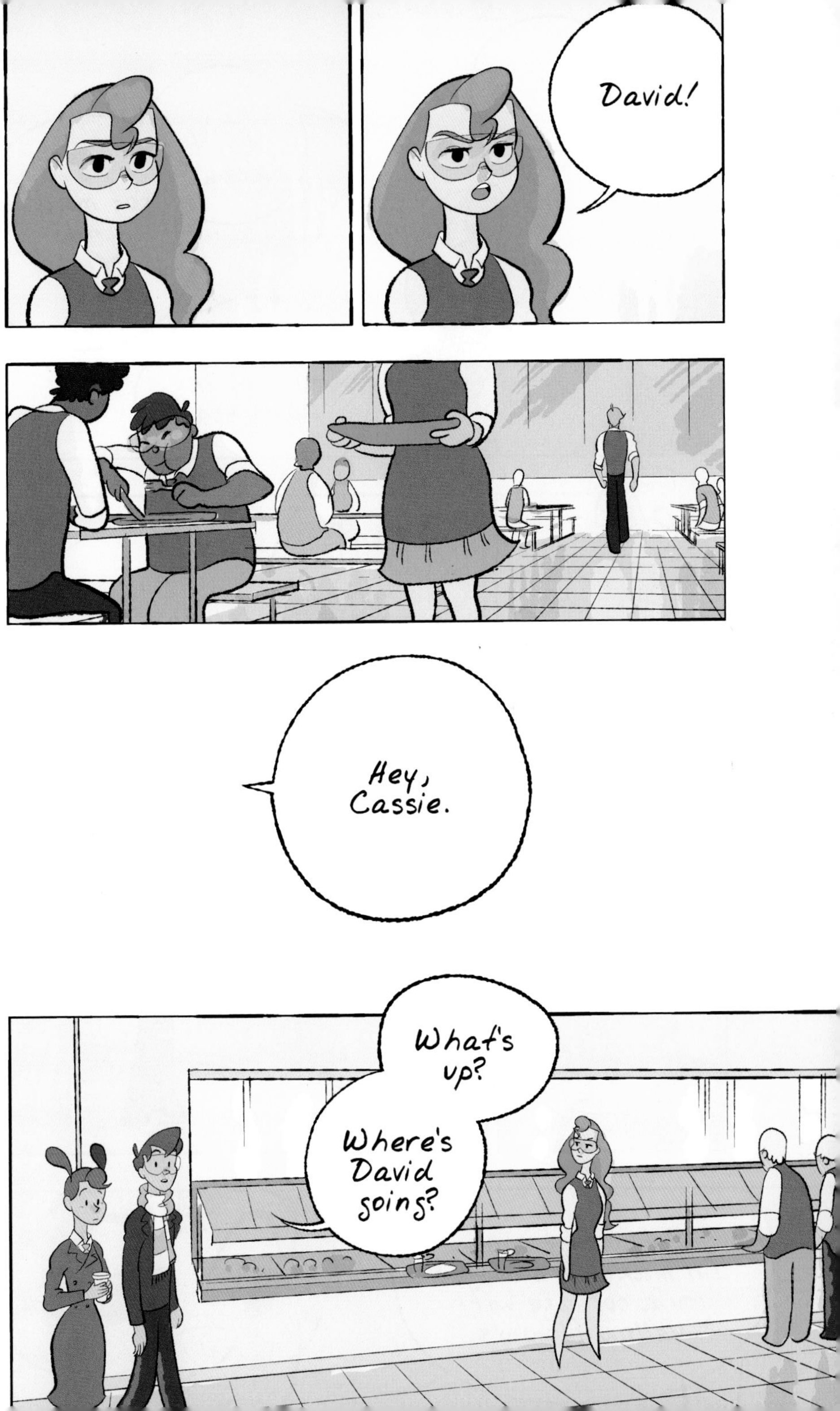
David!
Hey, Cassie.
What's up?
Where's David going?

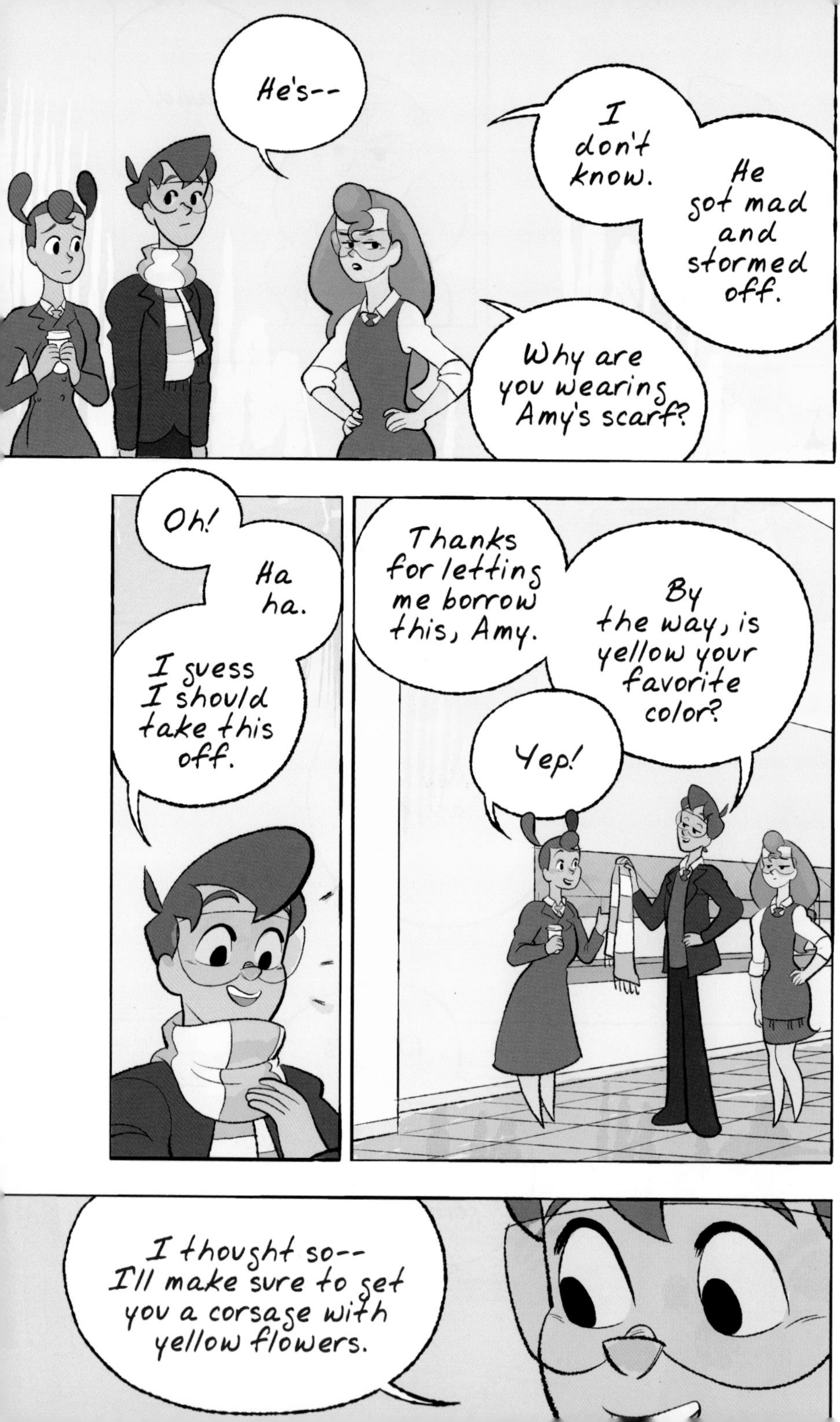
He's--
I don't know.
He got mad and stormed off.
Why are you wearing Amy's scarf?
Oh!
Ha ha.
I guess I should take this off.
Thanks for letting me borrow this, Amy.
By the way, is yellow your favorite color?
Yep!
I thought so-- I'll make sure to get you a corsage with yellow flowers.

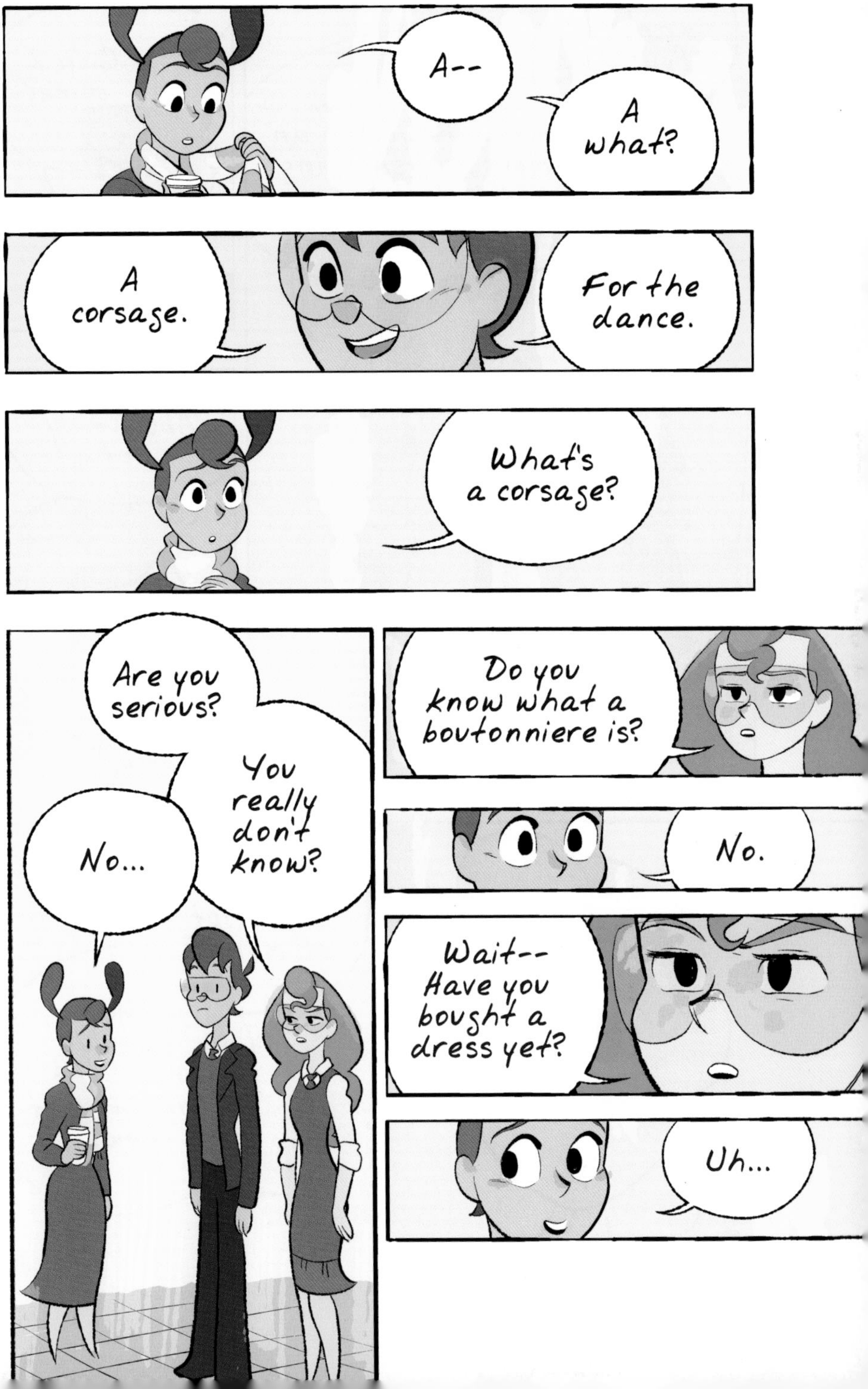
A--
A what?
A corsage.
For the dance.
What's a corsage?
Are you serious?
No...
You really don't know?
Do you know what a boutonniere is?
No.
Wait-- Have you bought a dress yet?
Uh...

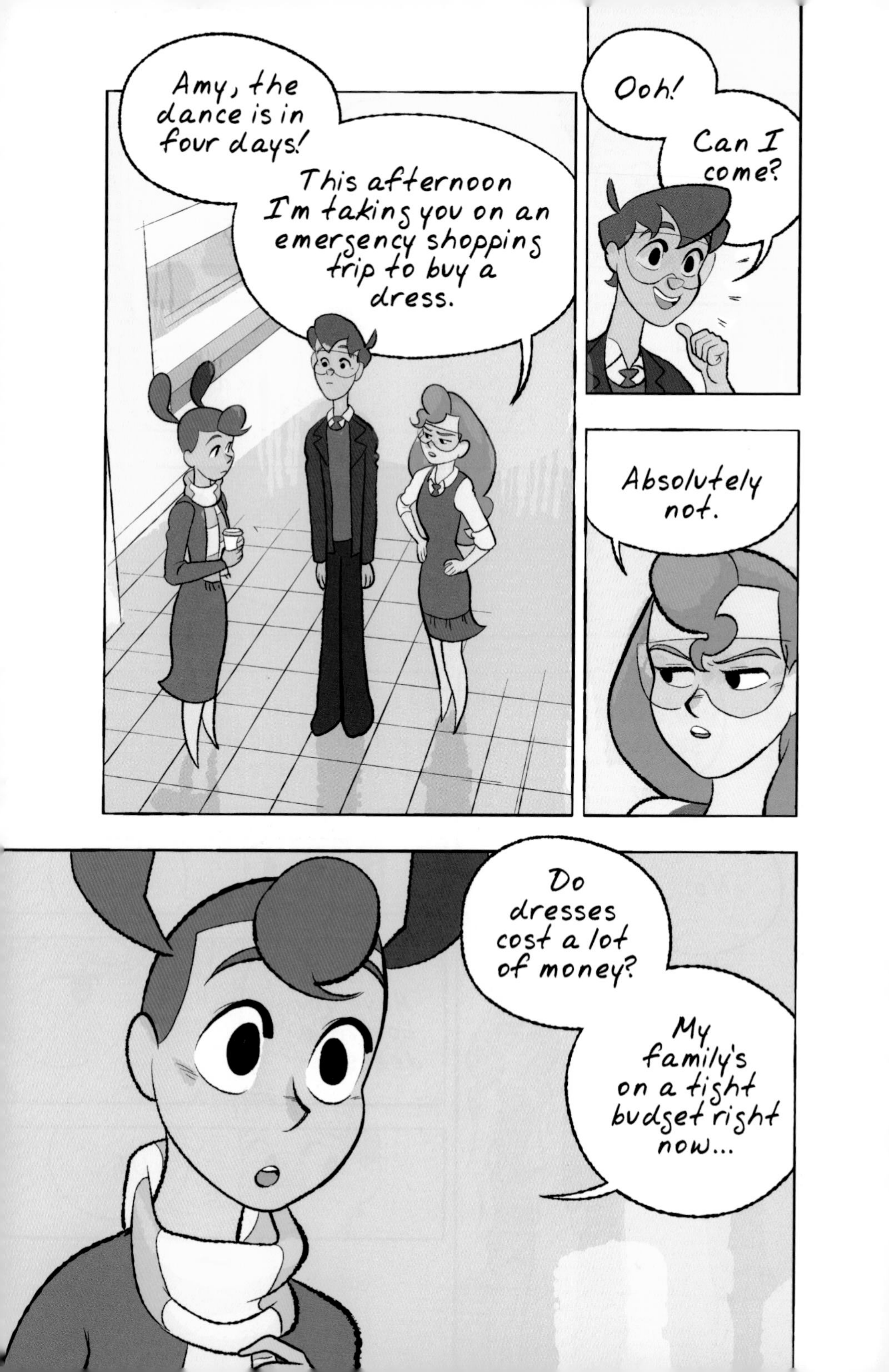
Amy, the dance is in four days!
This afternoon I'm taking you on an emergency shopping trip to buy a dress.
Ooh!
Can I come?
Absolutely not.
Do dresses cost a lot of money?
My family's on a tight budget right now...

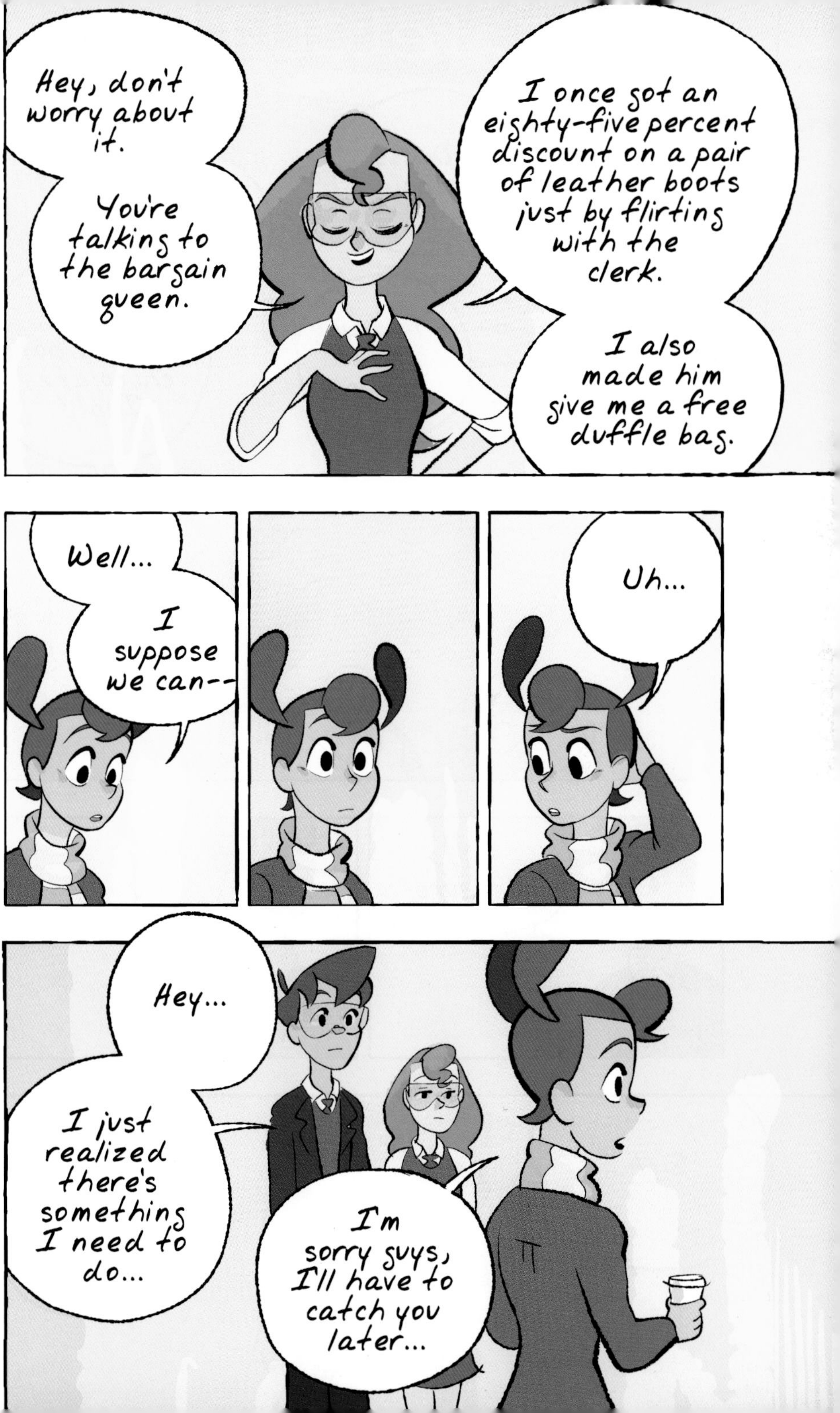
Hey, don't worry about it.
You're talking to the bargain queen.
I once got an eighty-five percent discount on a pair of leather boots just by flirting with the clerk.
I also made him give me a free duffle bag.
Well...
I suppose we can--
Uh...
Hey...
I just realized there's something I need to do...
I'm sorry guys, I'll have to catch you later...

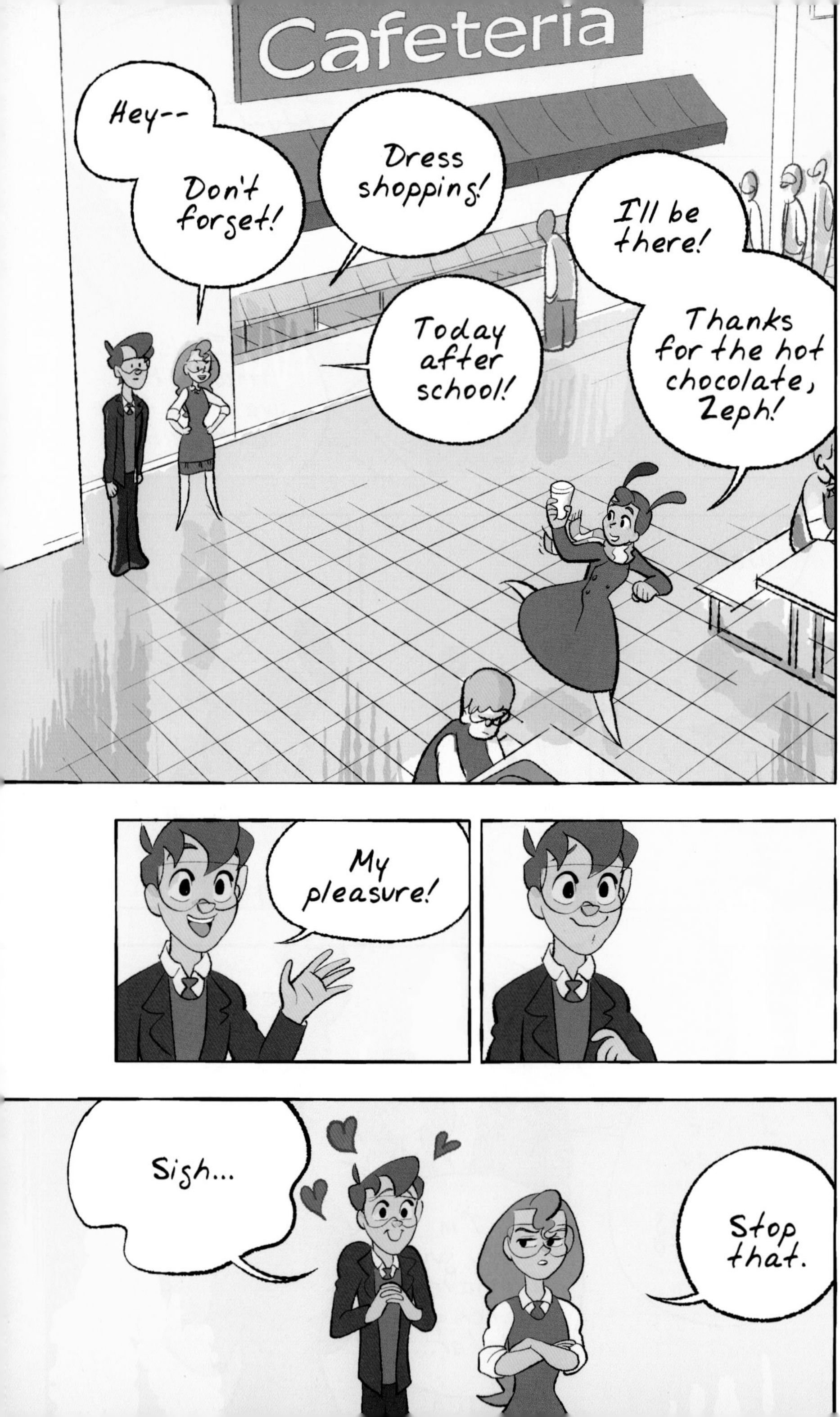
Cafeteria
Hey--
Don't forget!
Dress shopping!
Today after school!
I'll be there!
Thanks for the hot chocolate, Zeph!
My pleasure!
Sigh...
Stop that.

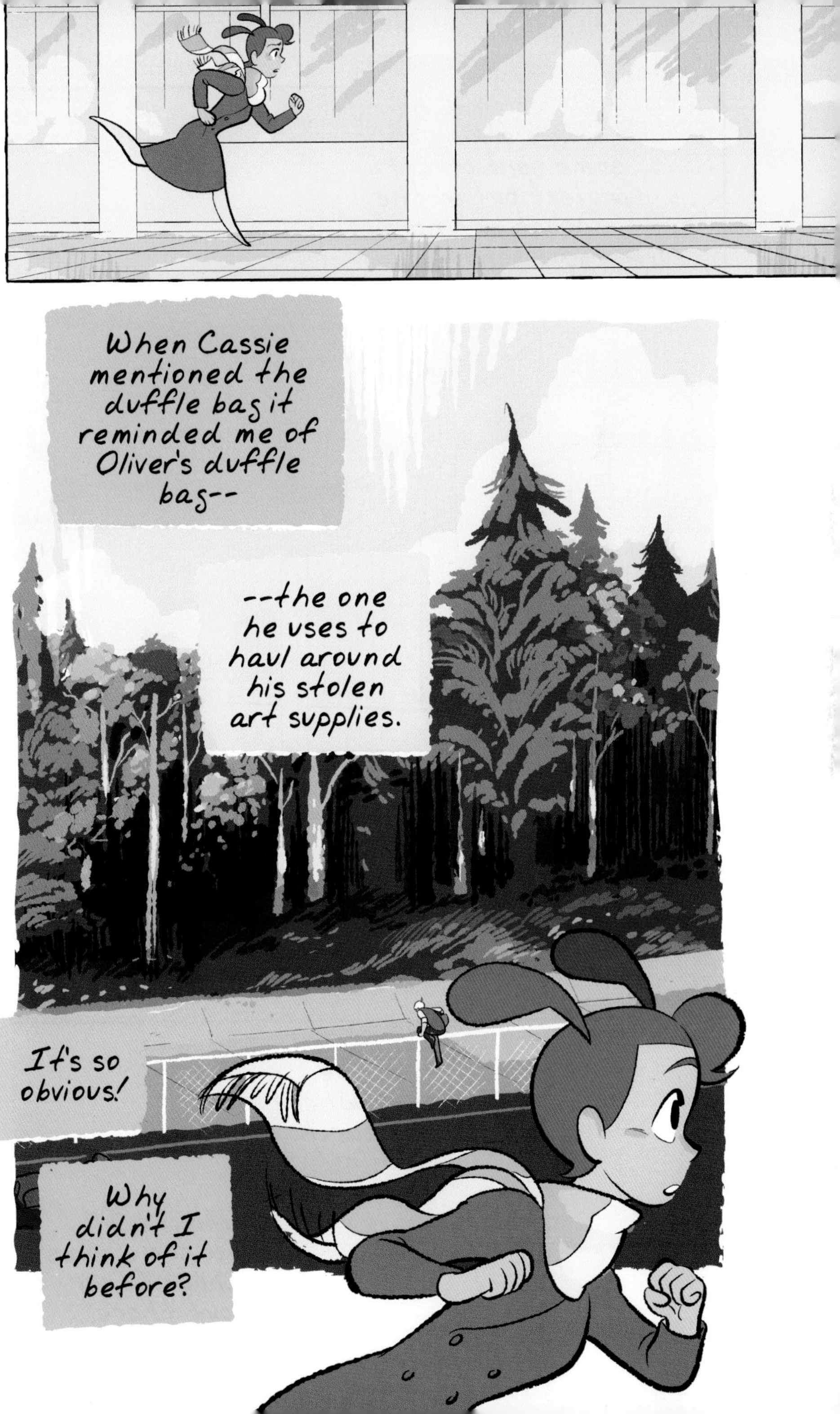
When Cassie mentioned the duffle bag it reminded me of Oliver's duffle bag--
--the one he uses to haul around his stolen art supplies.
It's so obvious!
Why didn't I think of it before?

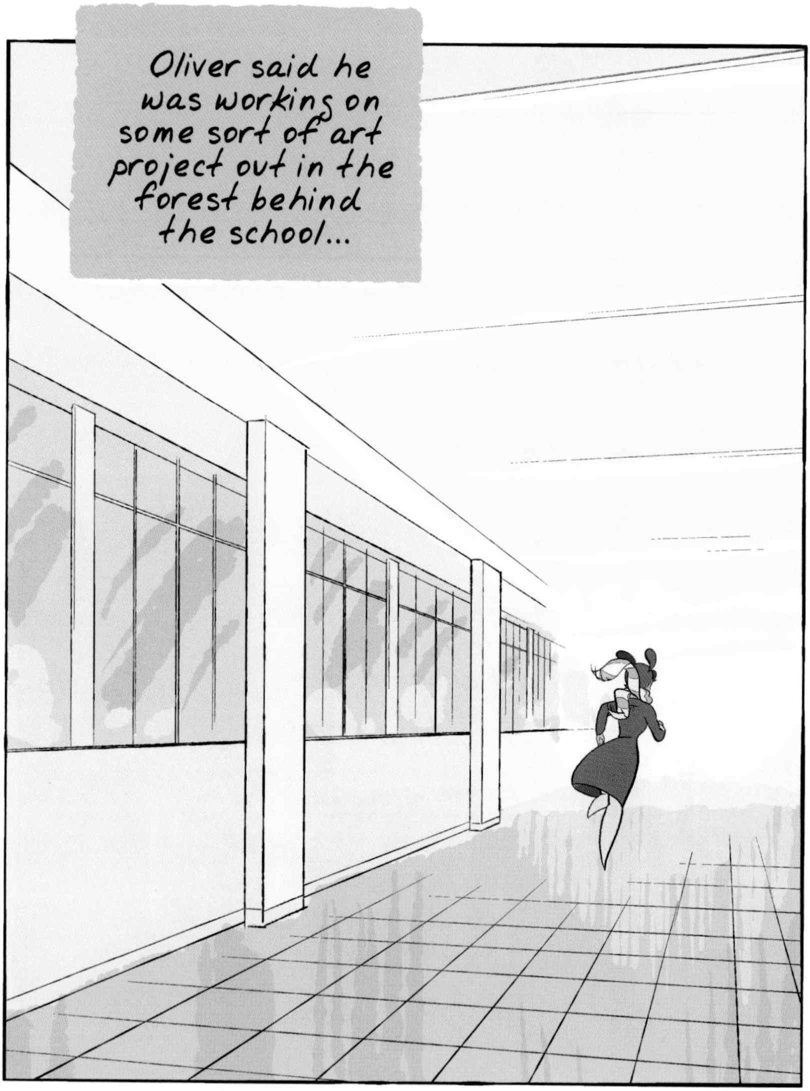
Oliver said he was working on some sort of art project out in the forest behind the school...

Maybe that's where my search begins!

Maybe I'll find some clues about Oliver out there!

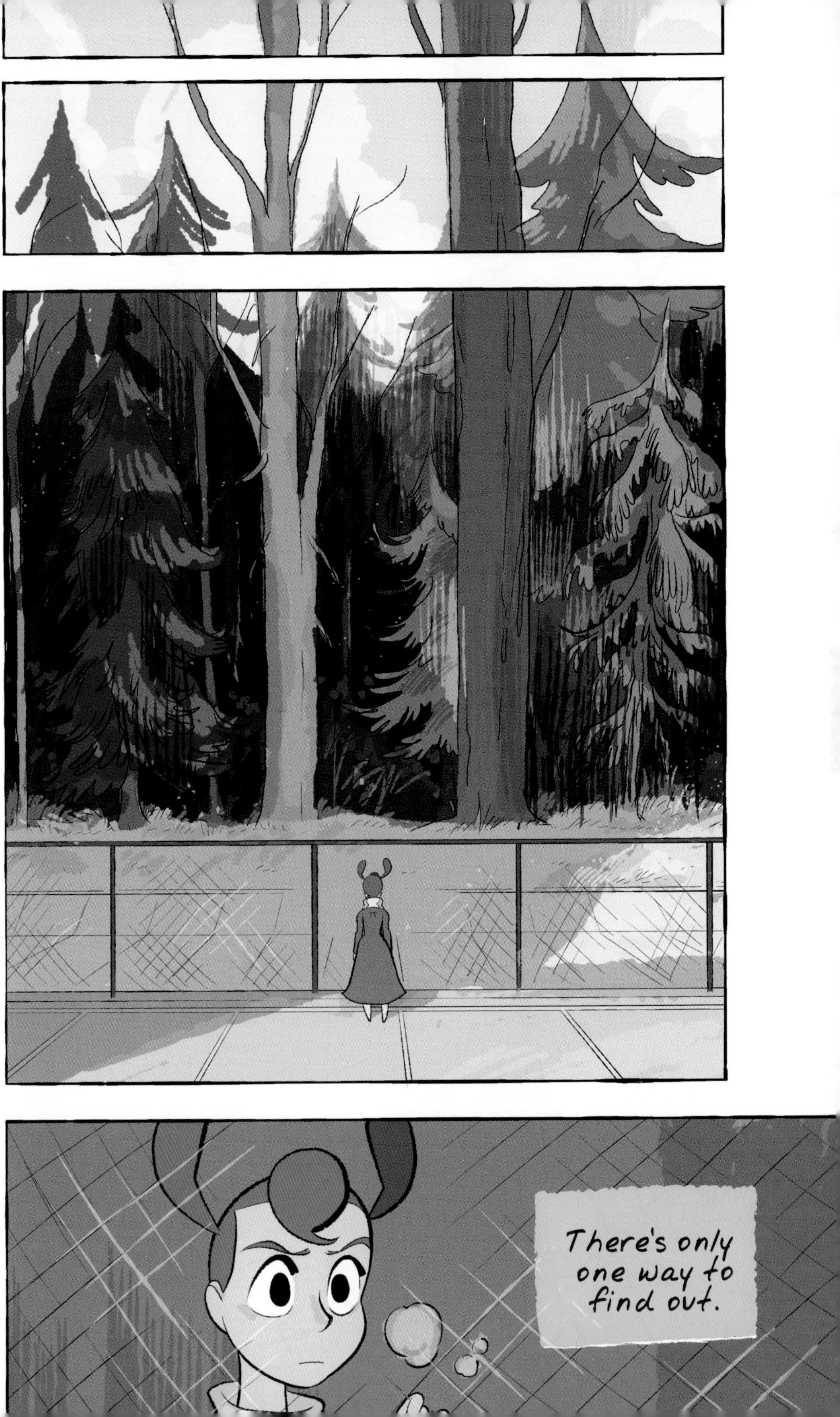
There's only one way to find out.

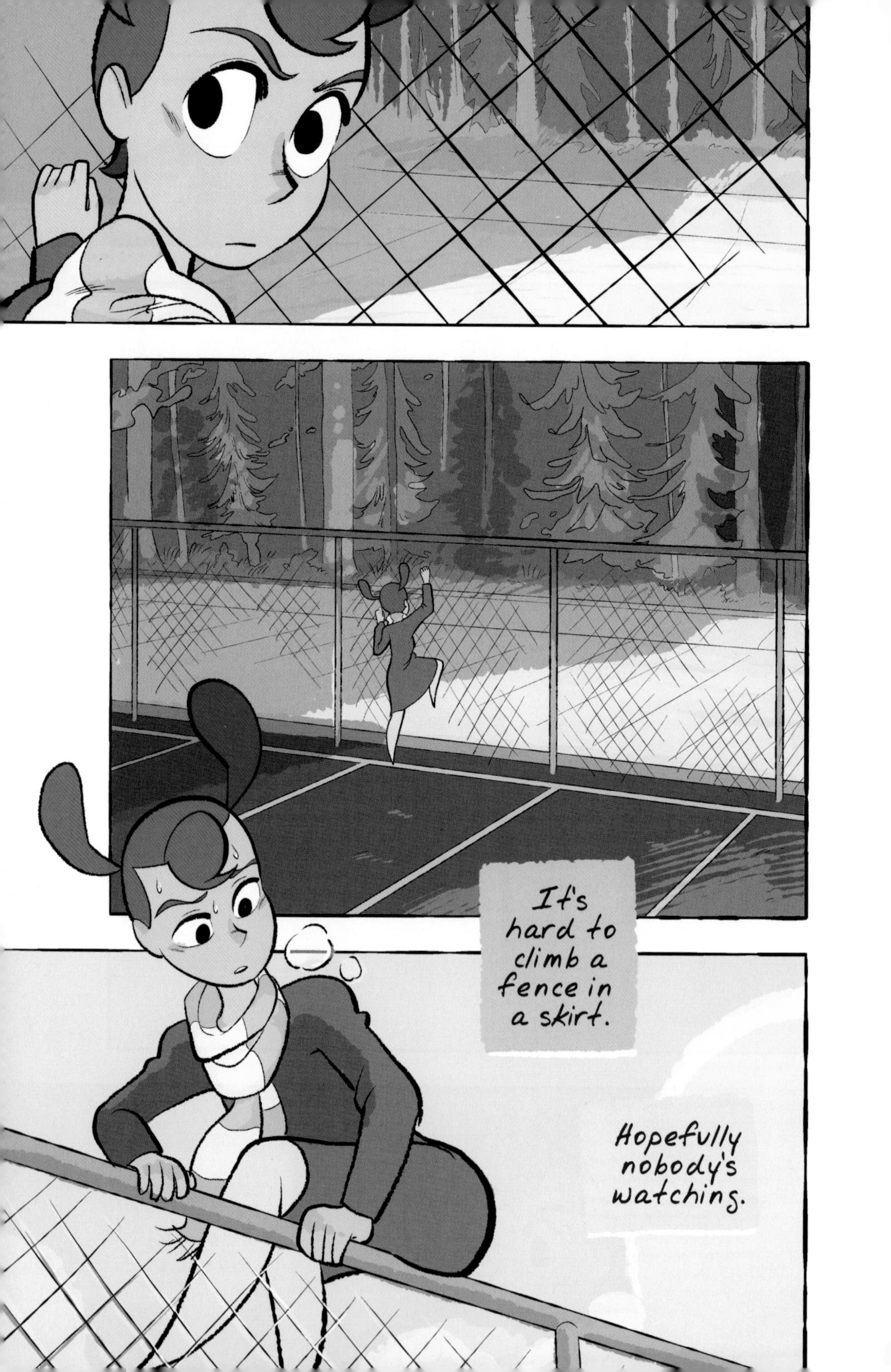
It's hard to climb a fence in a skirt.
Hopefully nobody's watching.

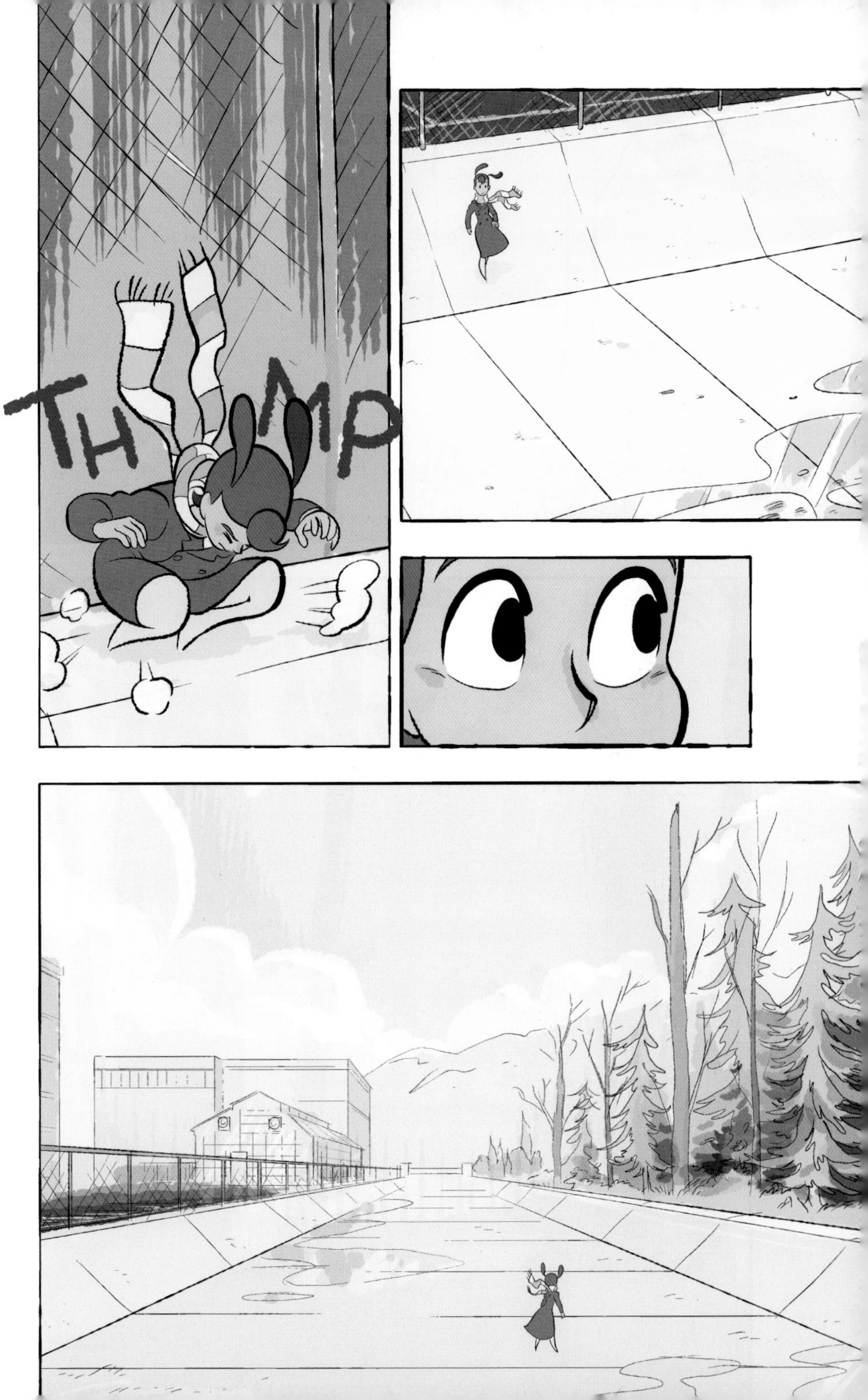
THUMP

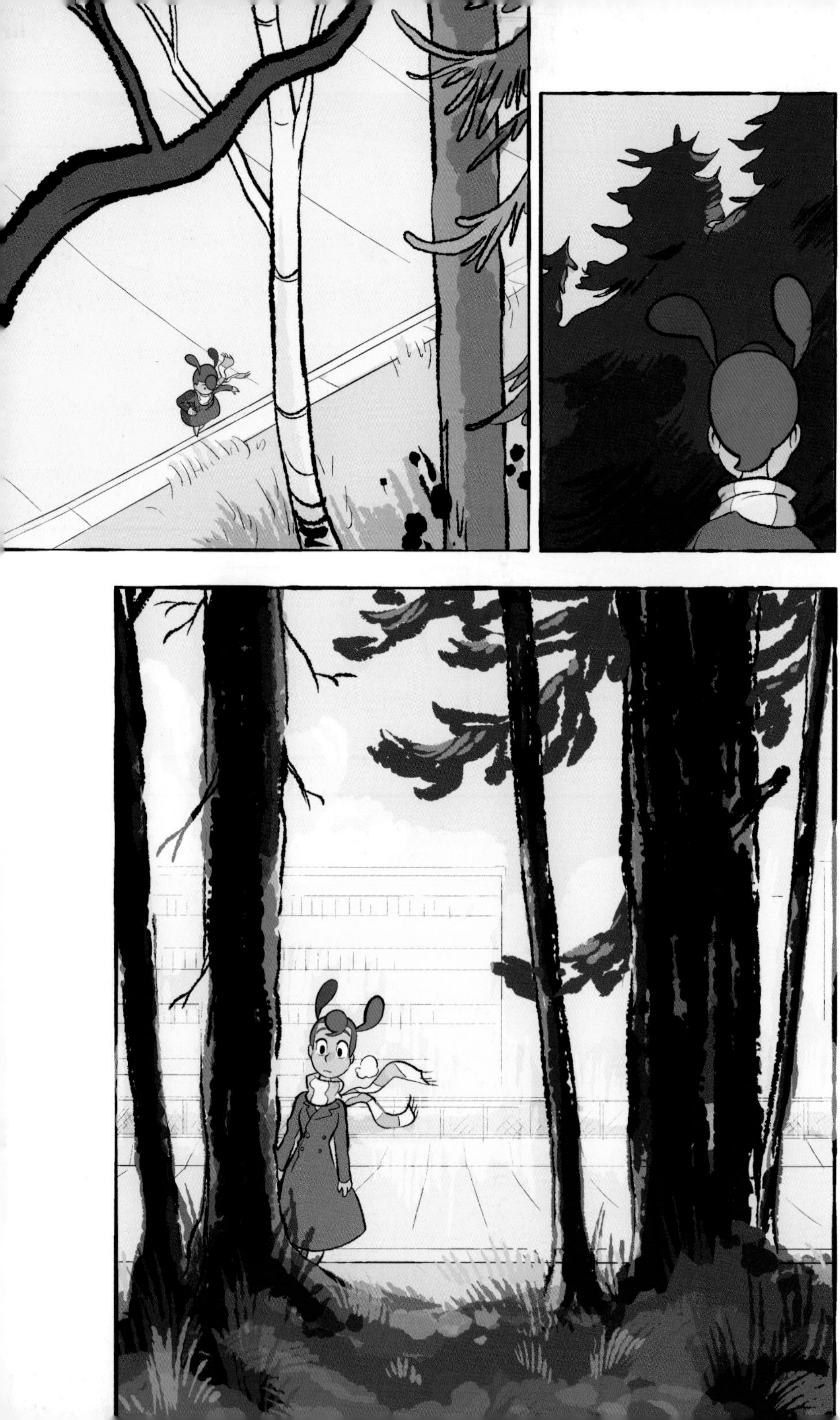

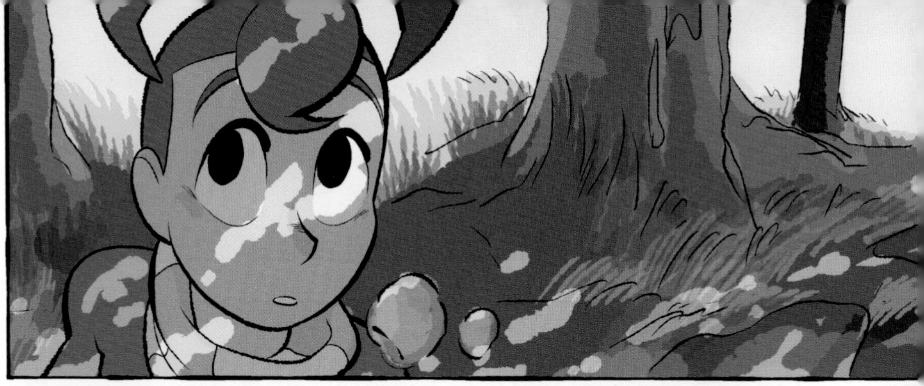
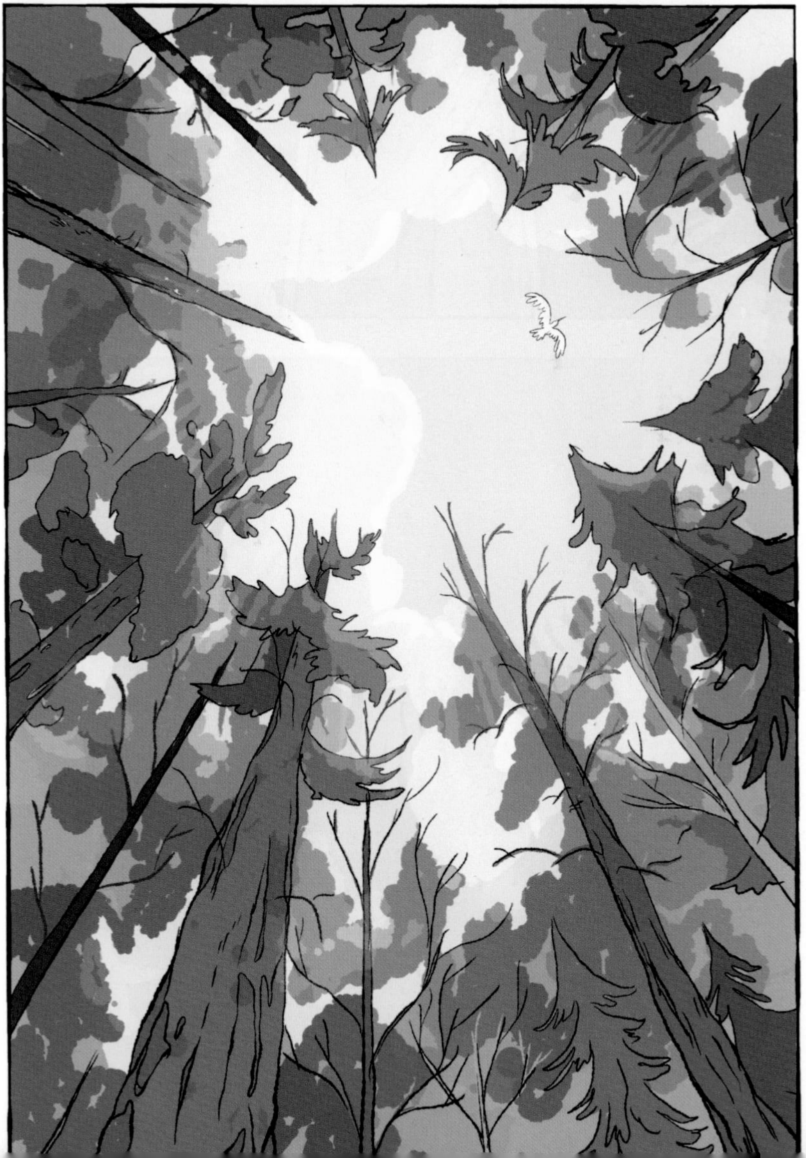

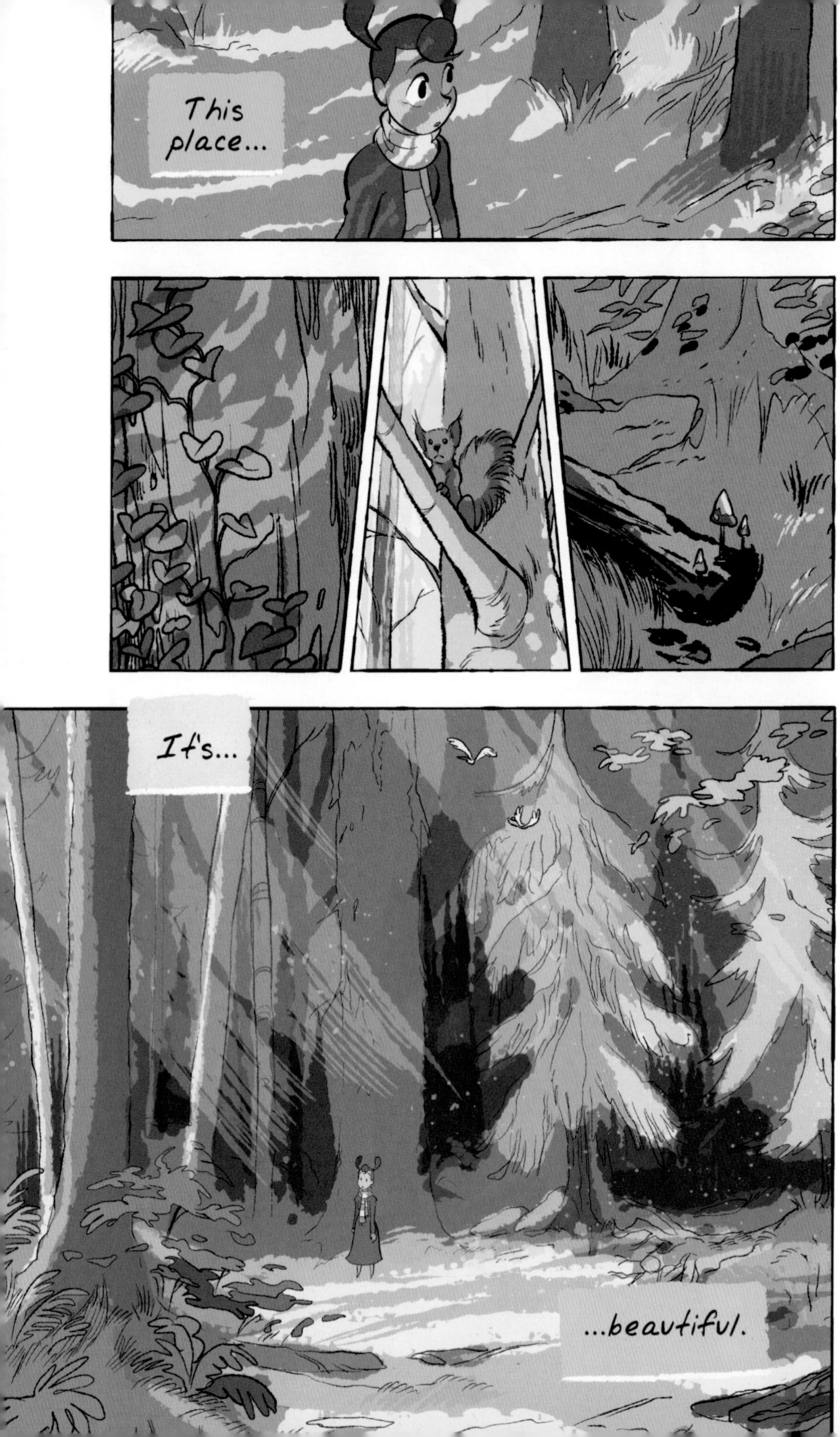
This place...
It's...
...beautiful.

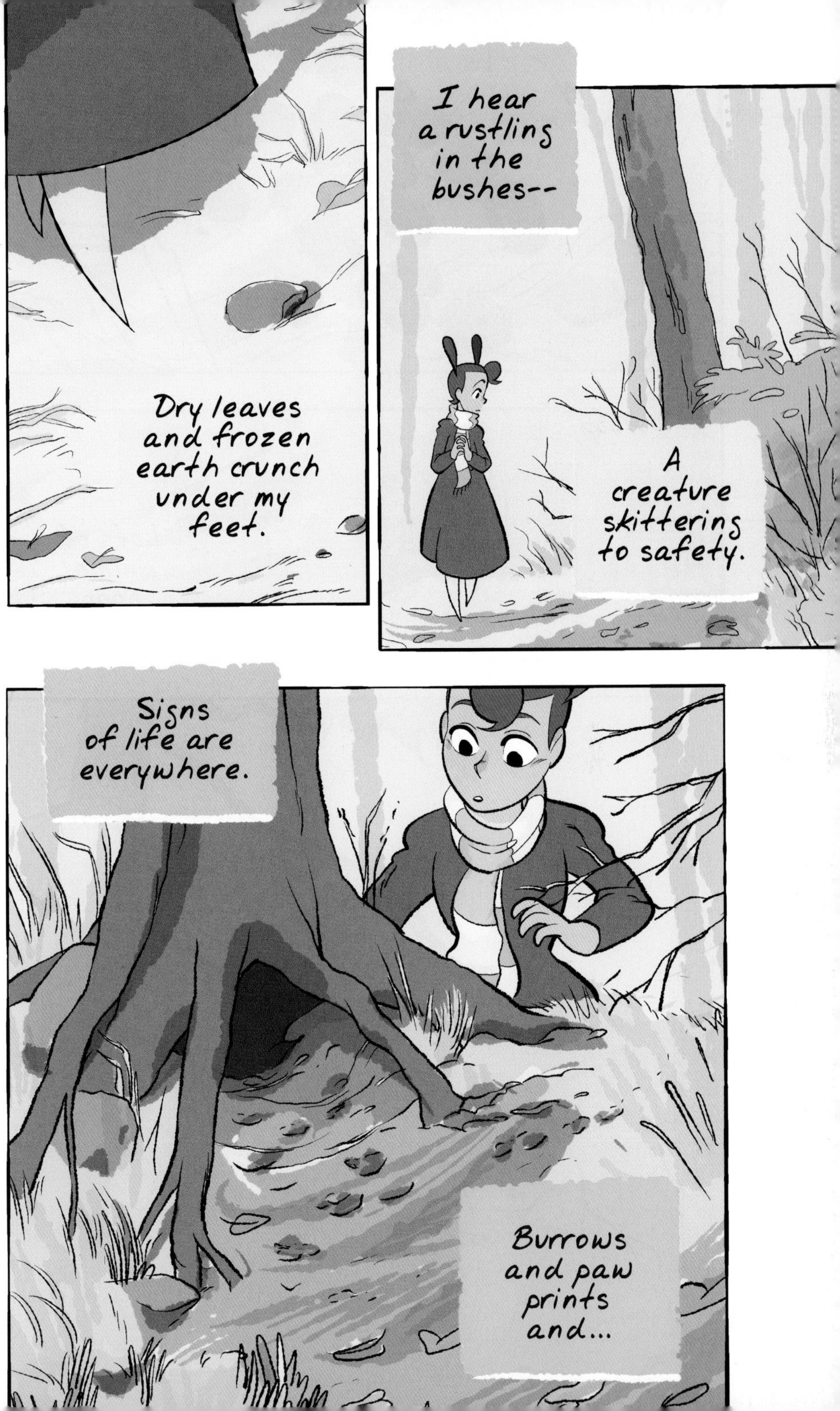
Dry leaves and frozen earth crunch under my feet.
I hear a rustling in the bushes--
A creature skittering to safety.
Signs of life are everywhere.
Burrows and paw prints and...

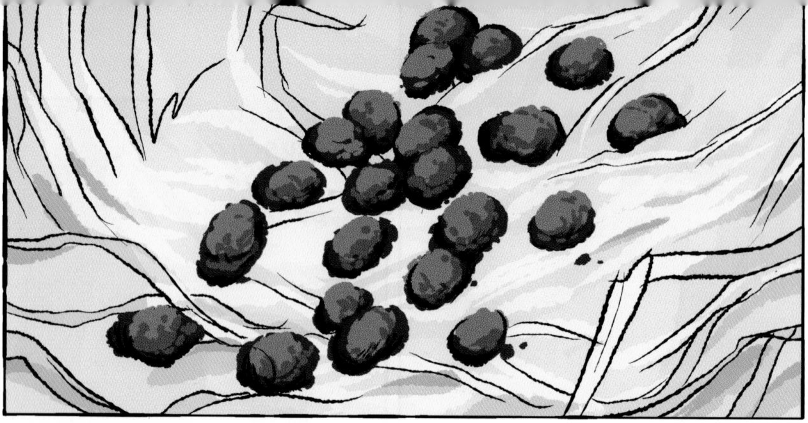

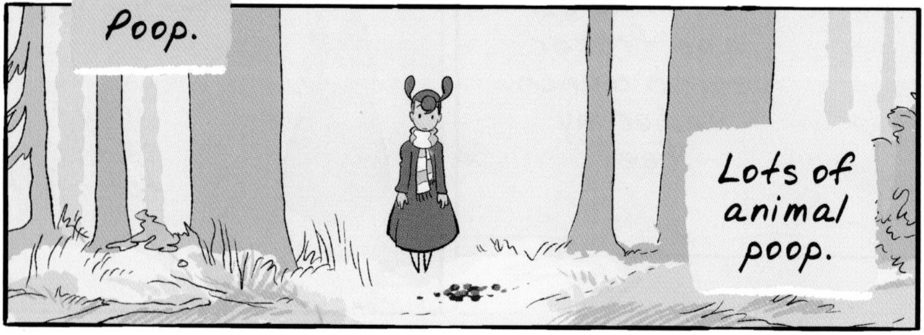
Poop.
Lots of animal poop.

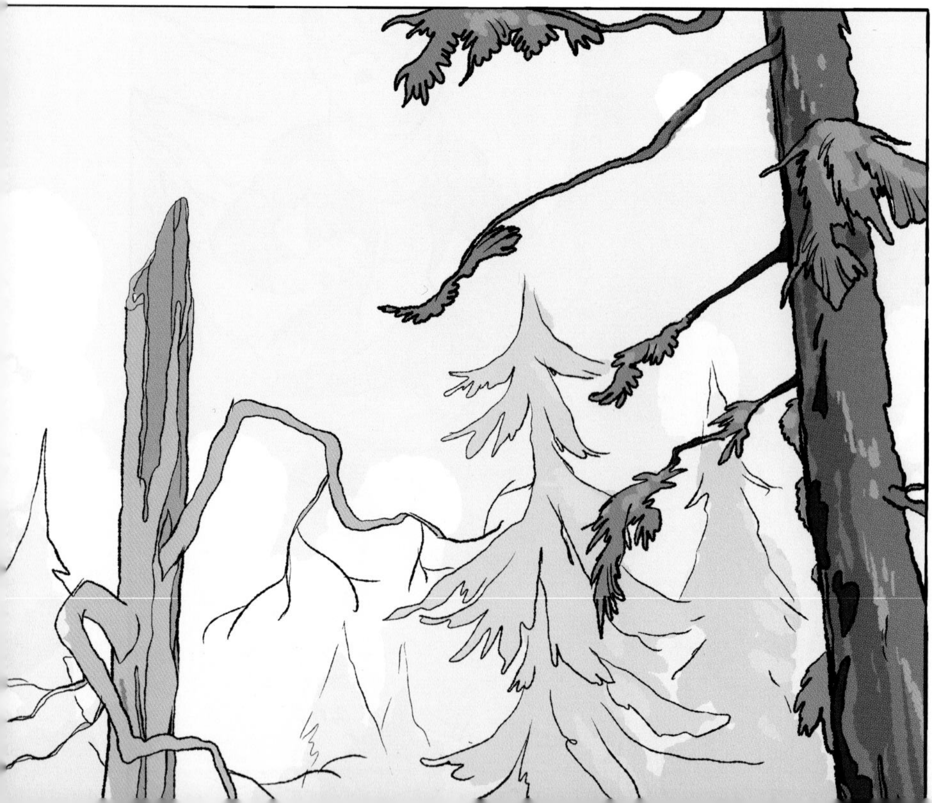

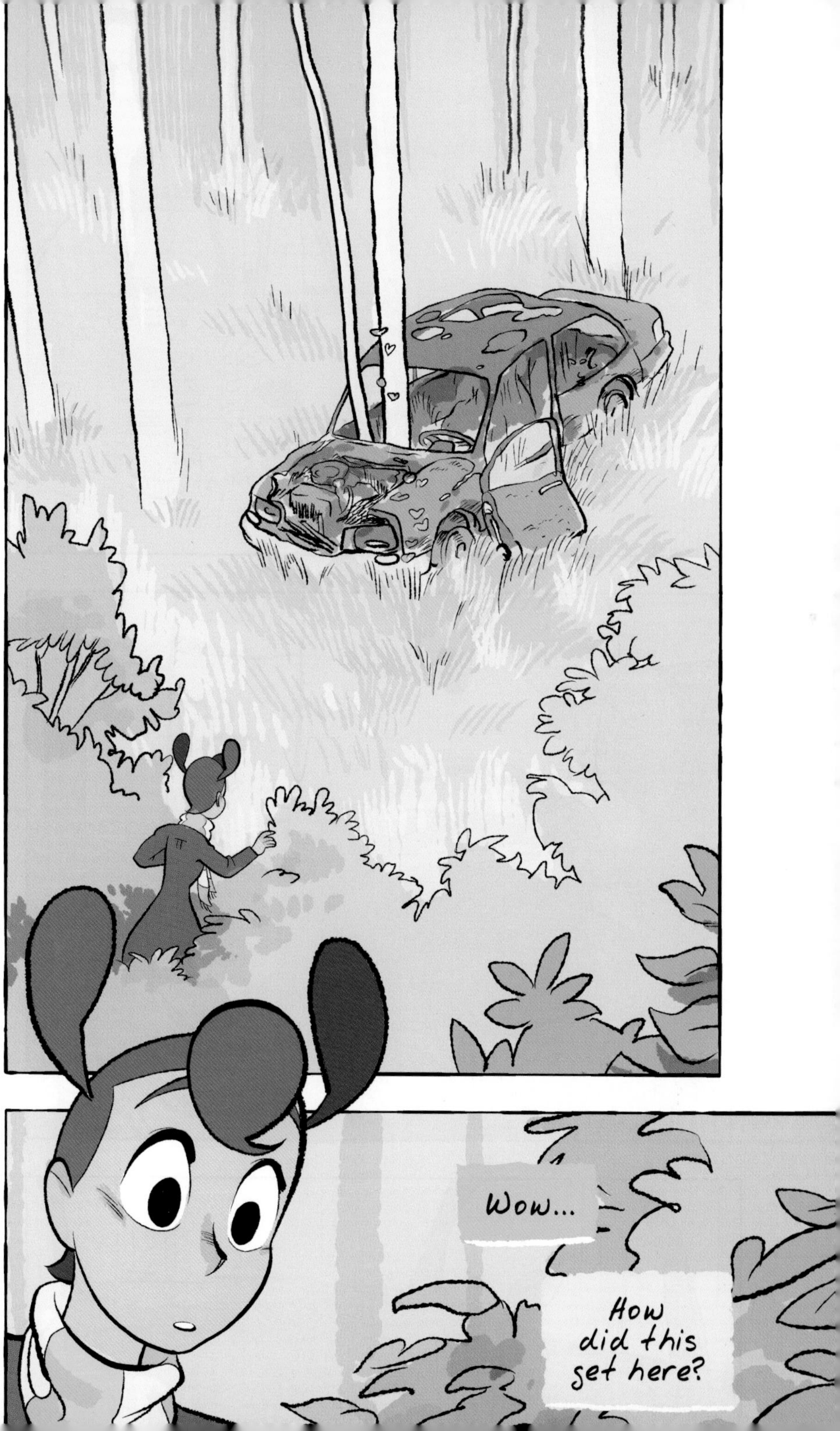
Wow...
How did this get here?

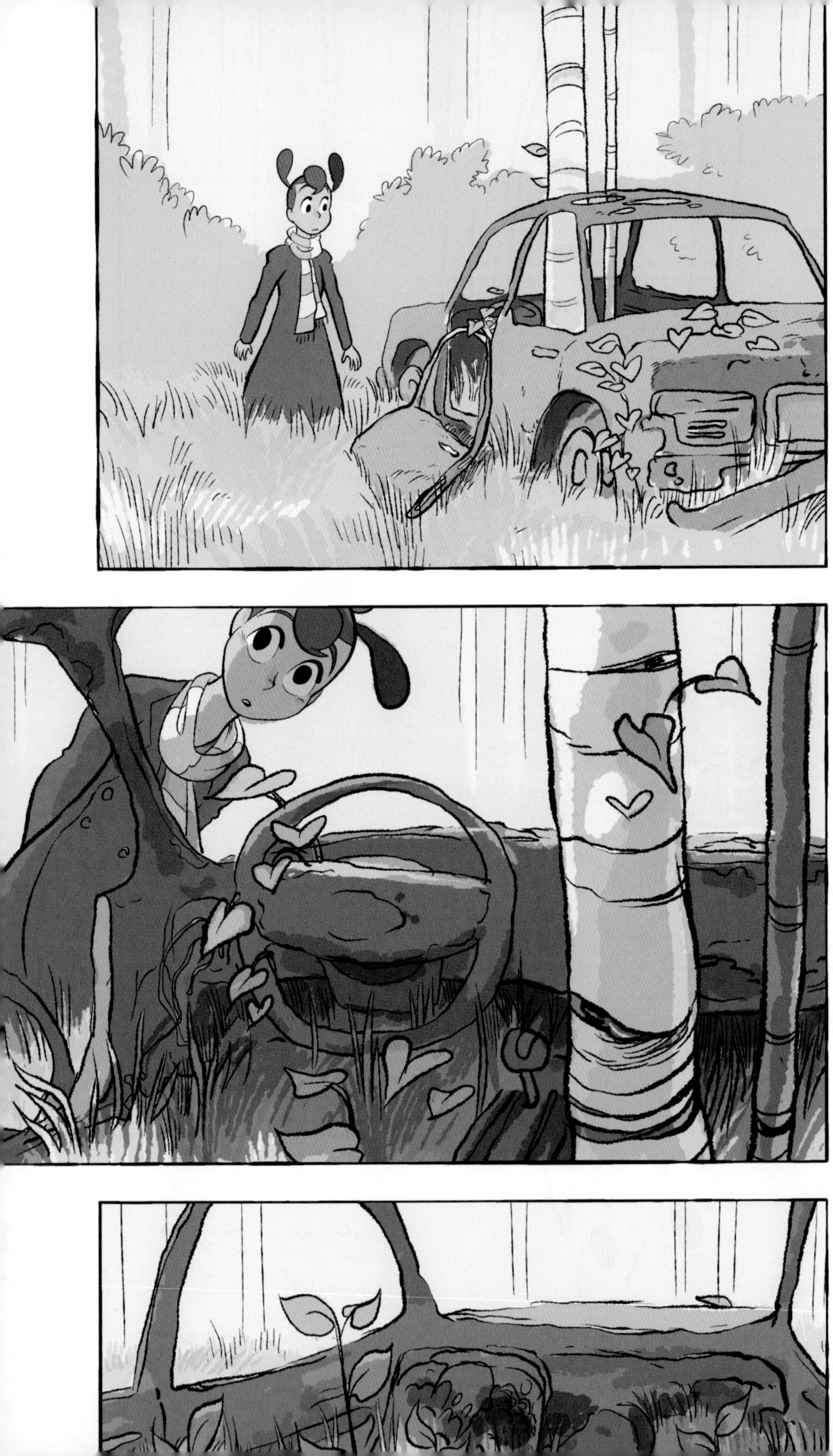

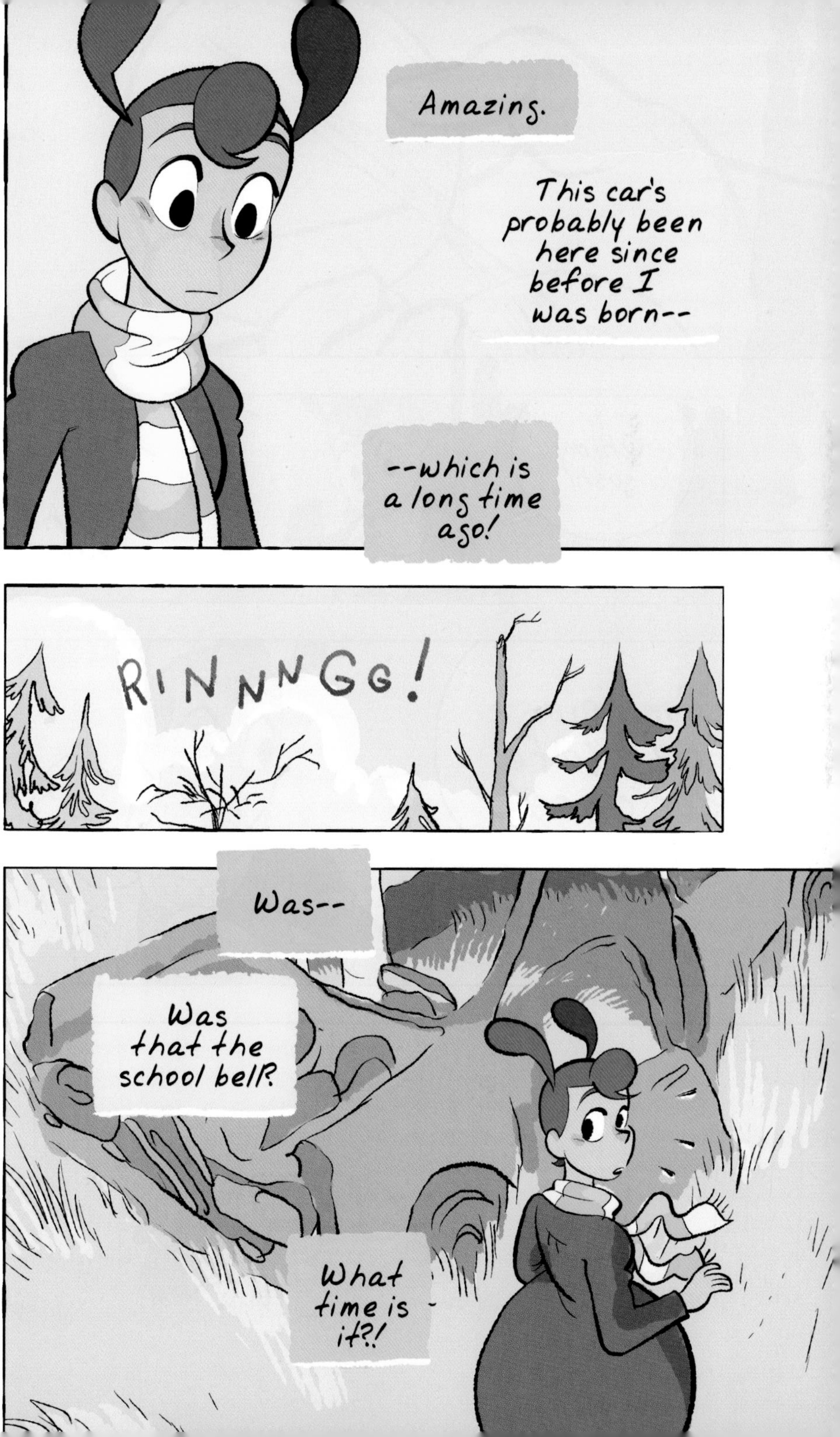
Amazing.
This car's probably been here since before I was born--
--which is a long time ago!
RINNNGG!
Was--
Was that the school bell?
What time is it?!

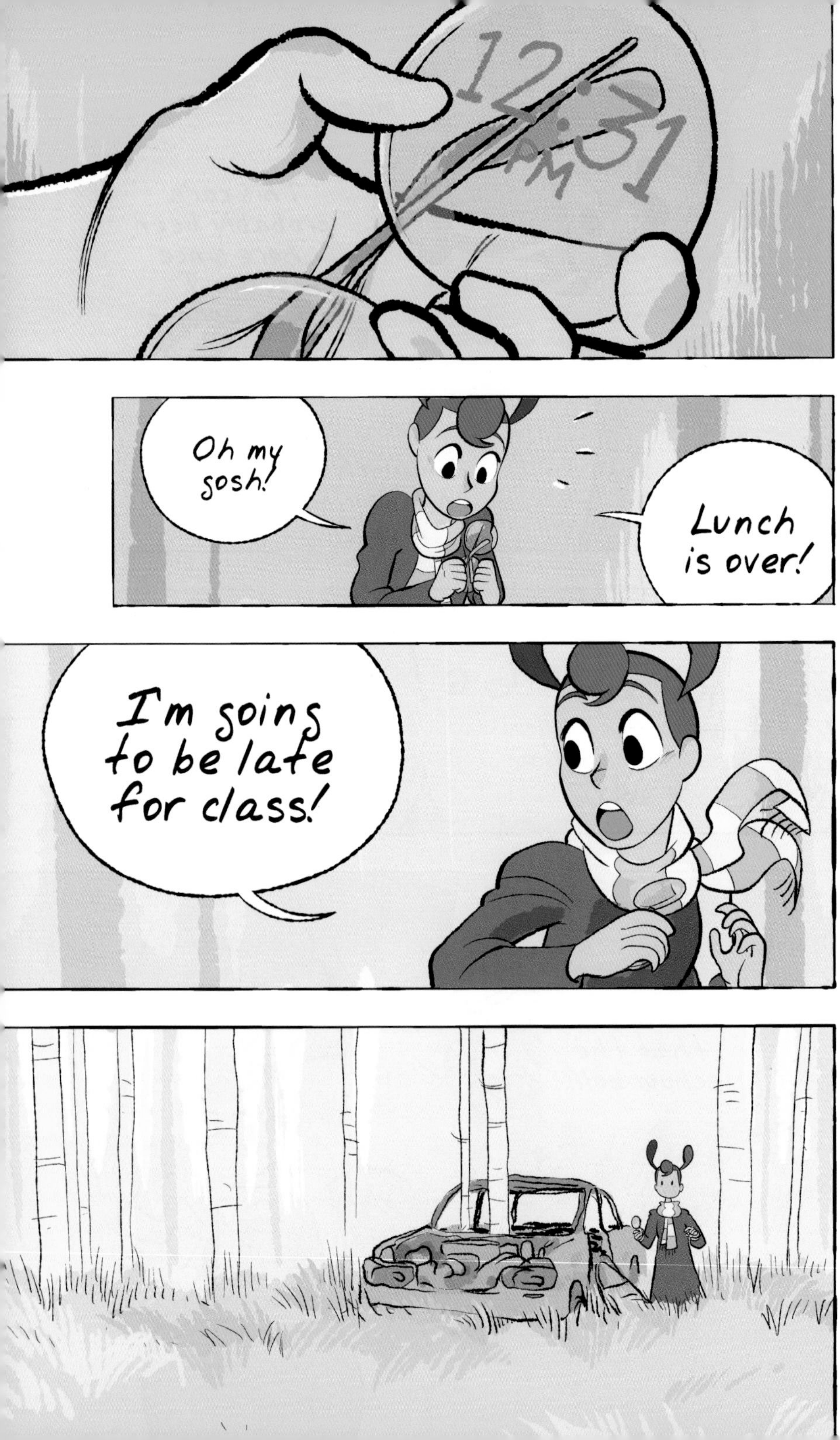
12:31 PM
Oh my gosh!
Lunch is over!
I'm going to be late for class!

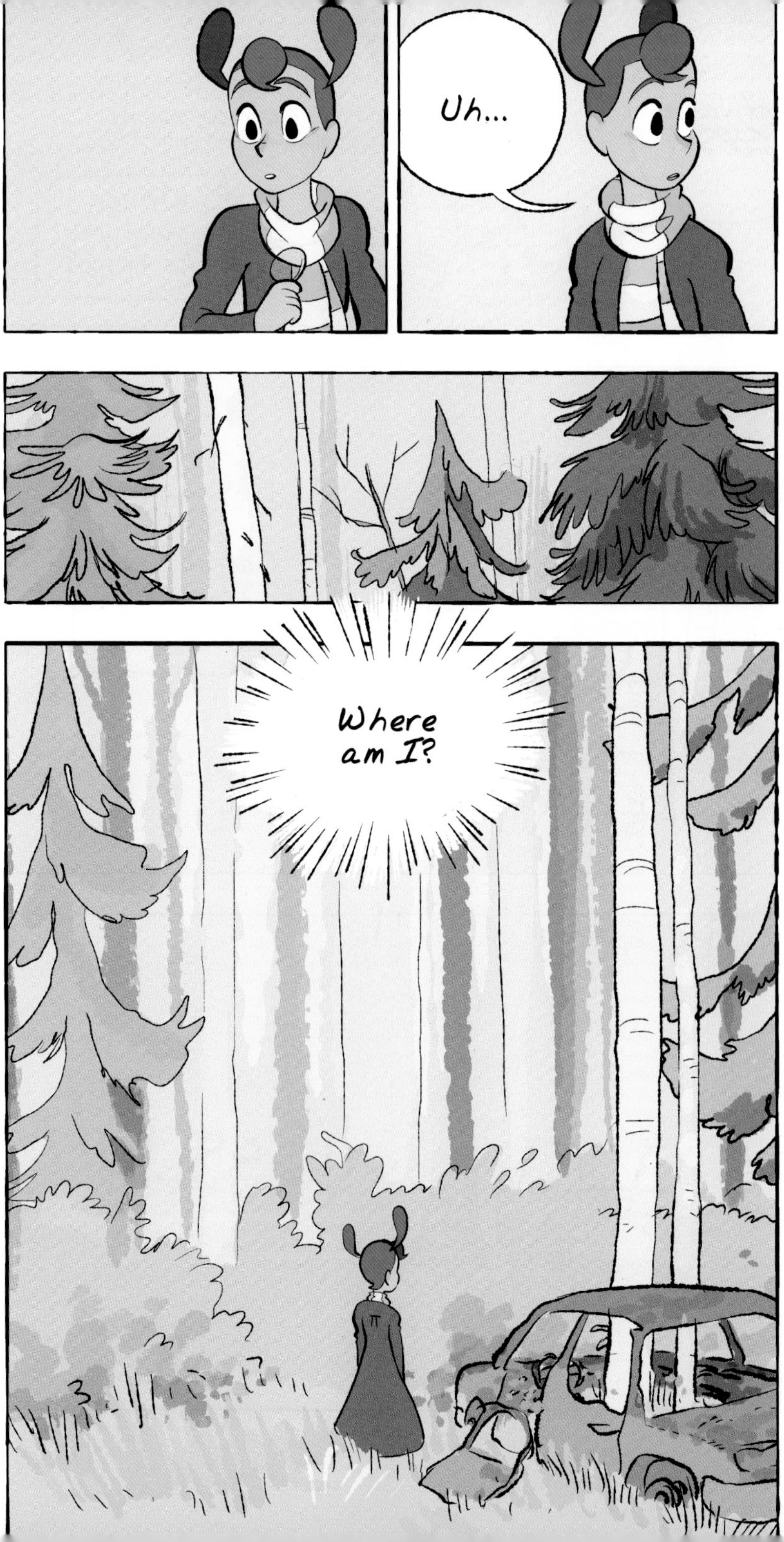
Uh...
Where am I?

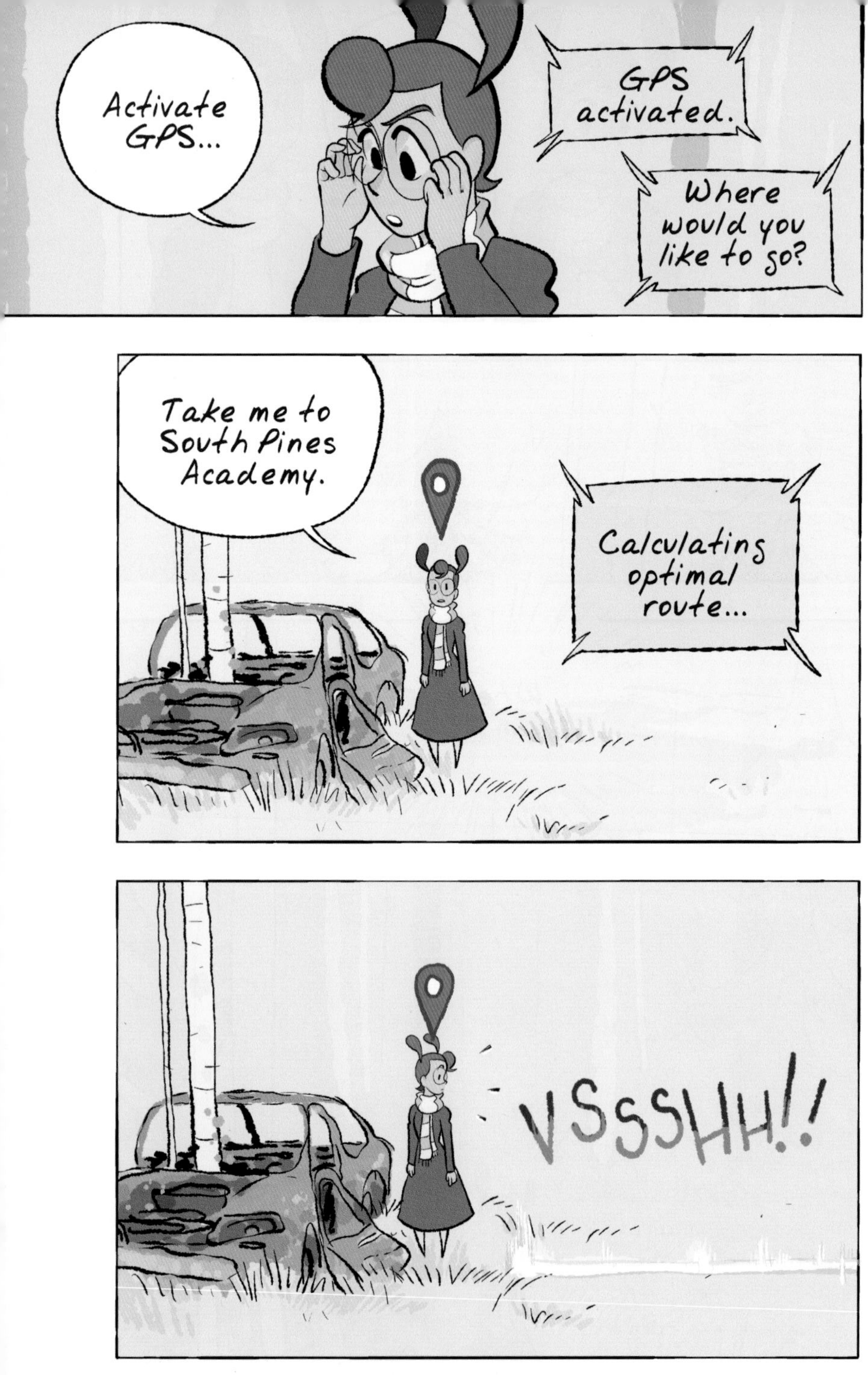
Activate GPS...
GPS activated.
Where would you like to go?
Take me to South Pines Academy.
Calculating optimal route...
VSSSHH!!

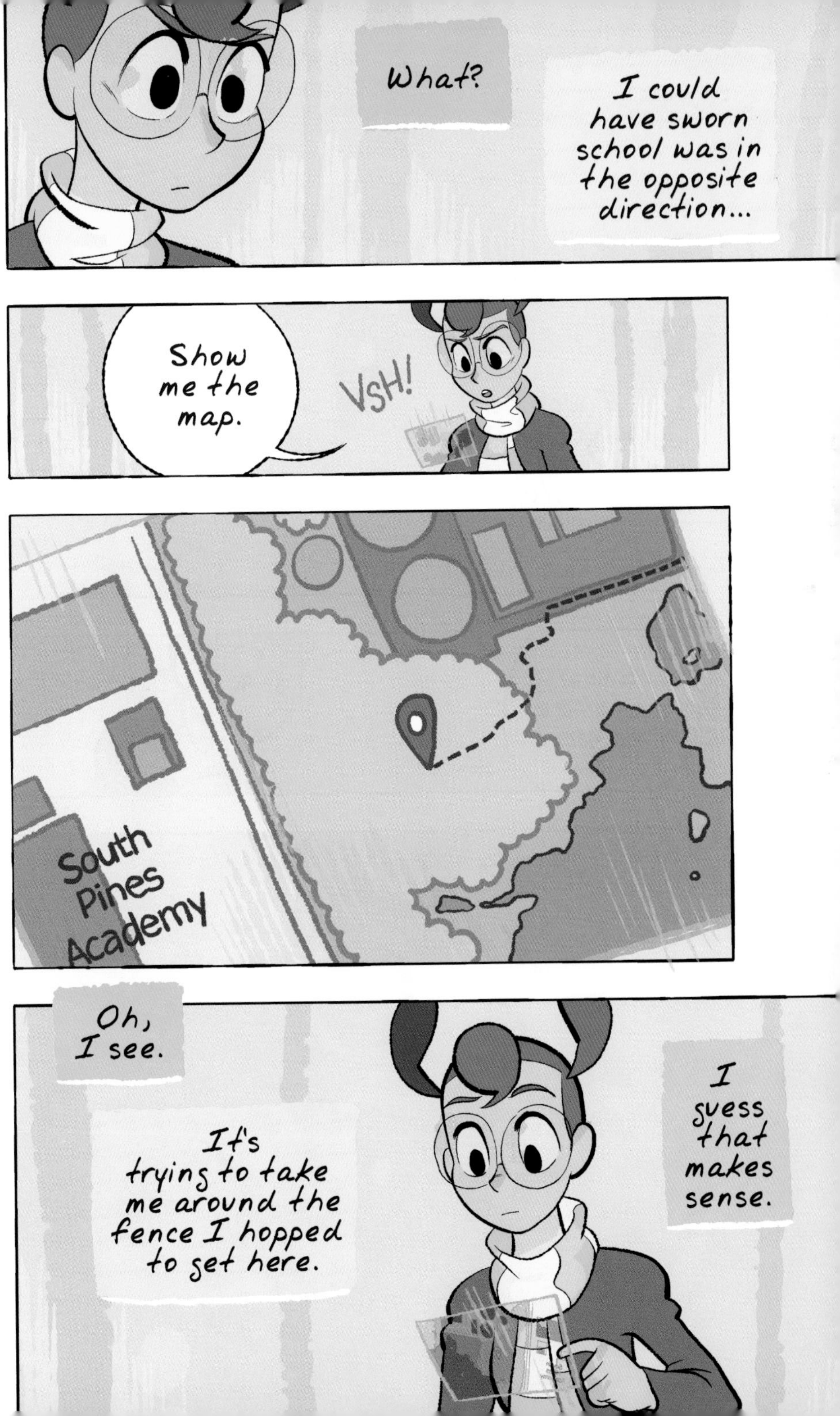
What?
I could have sworn school was in the opposite direction...
Show me the map.
VSH!
South Pines Academy
Oh, I see.
It's trying to take me around the fence I hopped to get here.
I guess that makes sense.

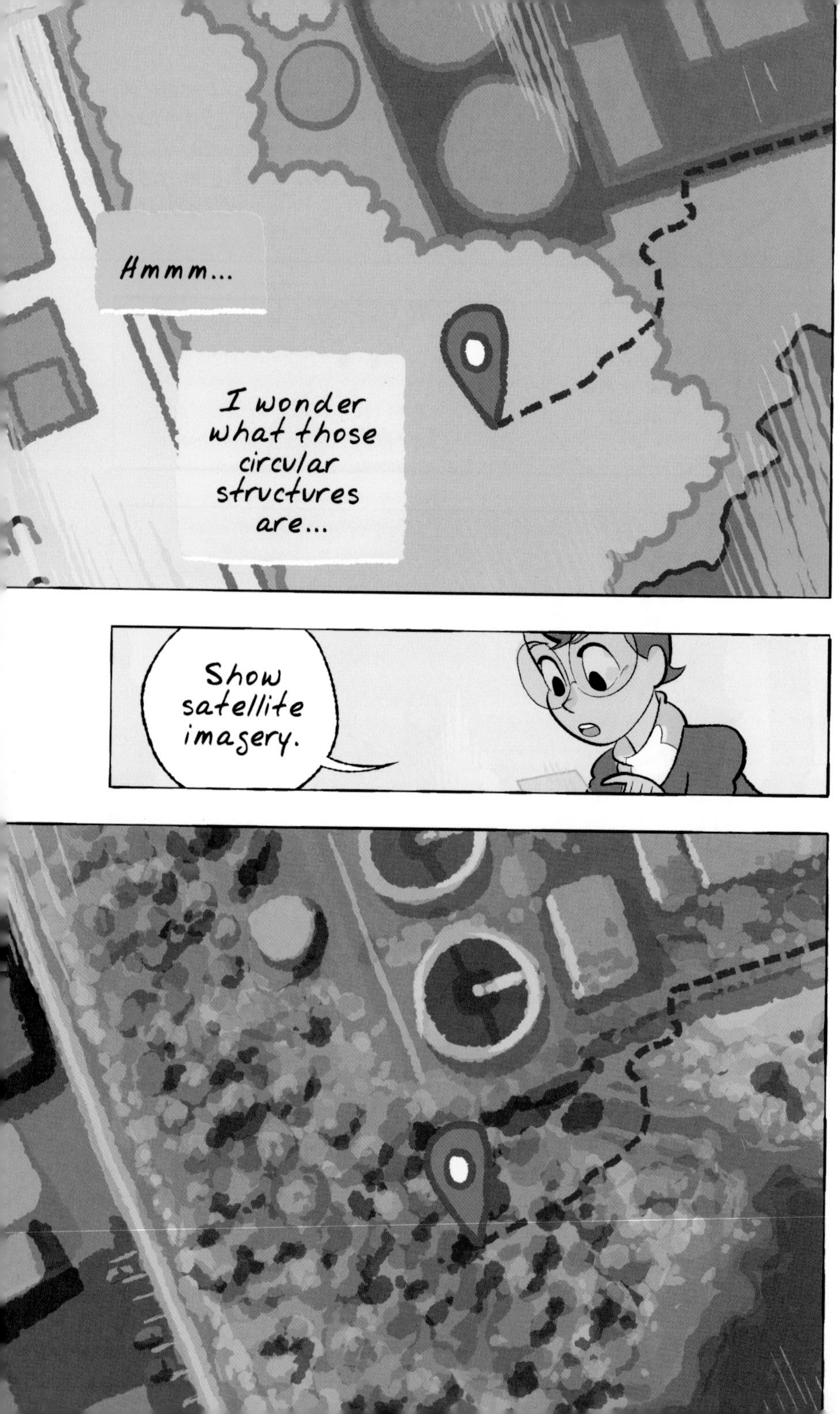
Hmmm...
I wonder what those circular structures are...
Show satellite imagery.

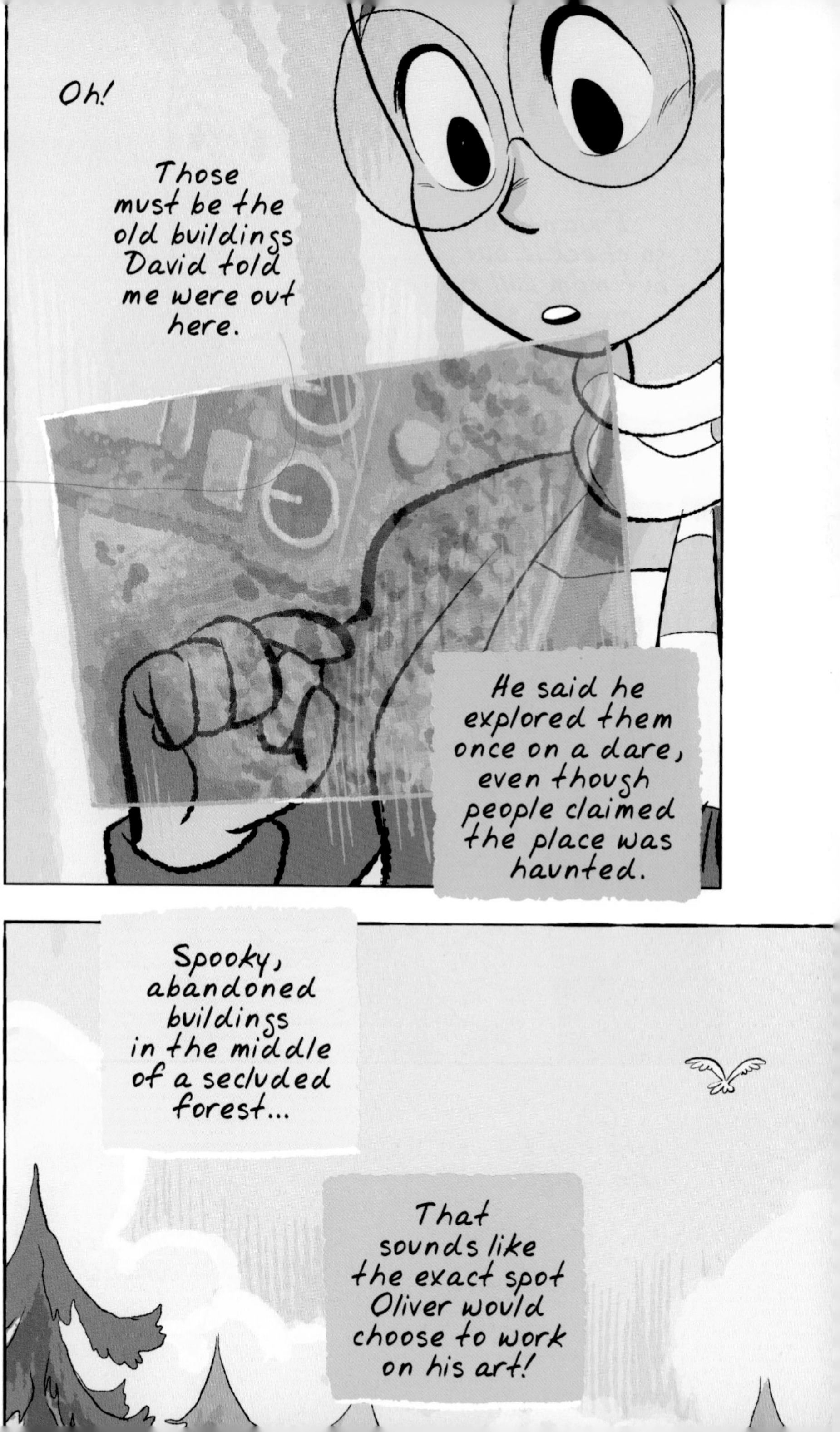
Oh!
Those must be the old buildings David told me were out here.
He said he explored them once on a dare, even though people claimed the place was haunted.
Spooky, abandoned buildings in the middle of a secluded forest...
That sounds like the exact spot Oliver would choose to work on his art!

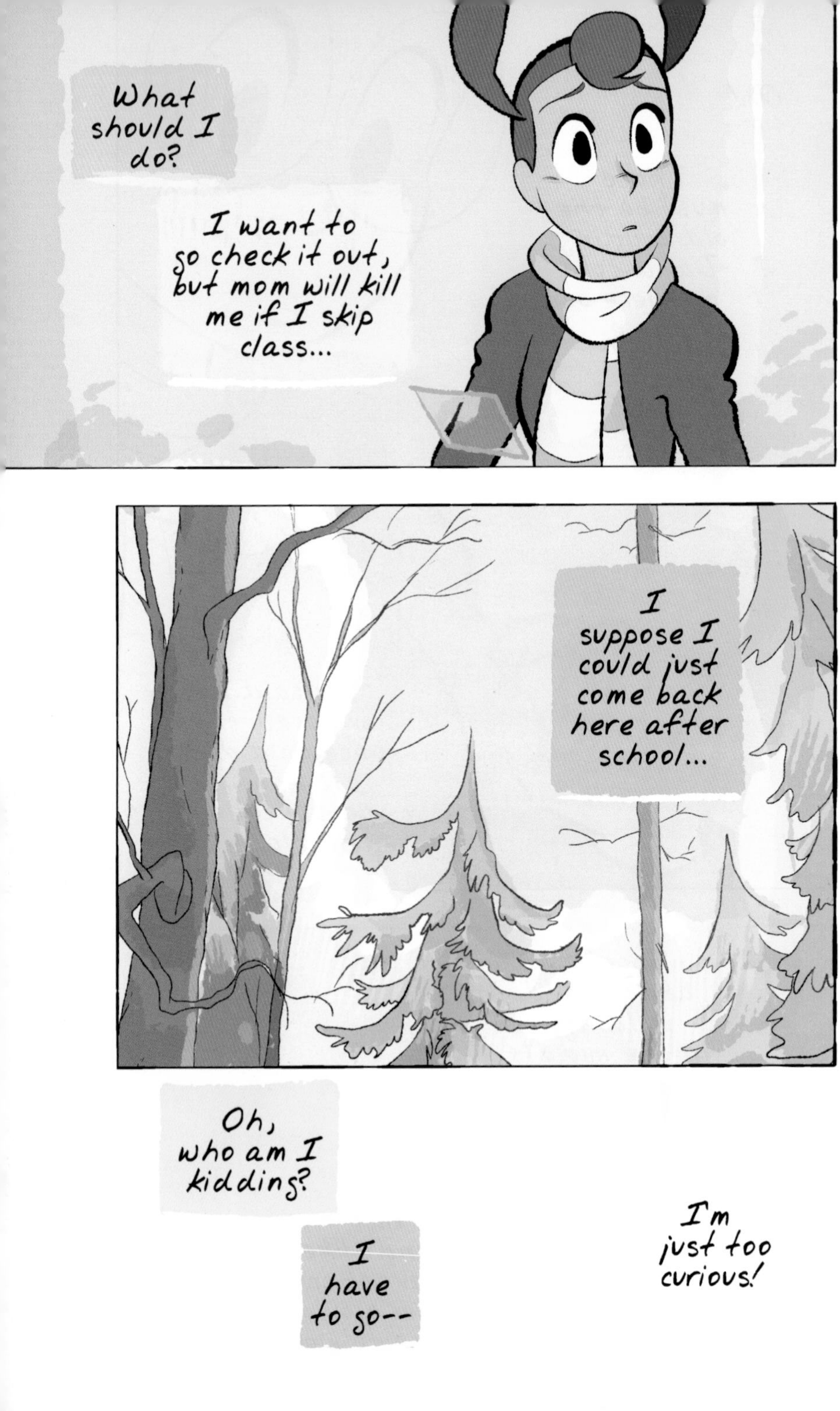
What should I do?
I want to go check it out, but mom will kill me if I skip class...
I suppose I could just come back here after school...
Oh, who am I kidding?
I have to go--
I'm just too curious!

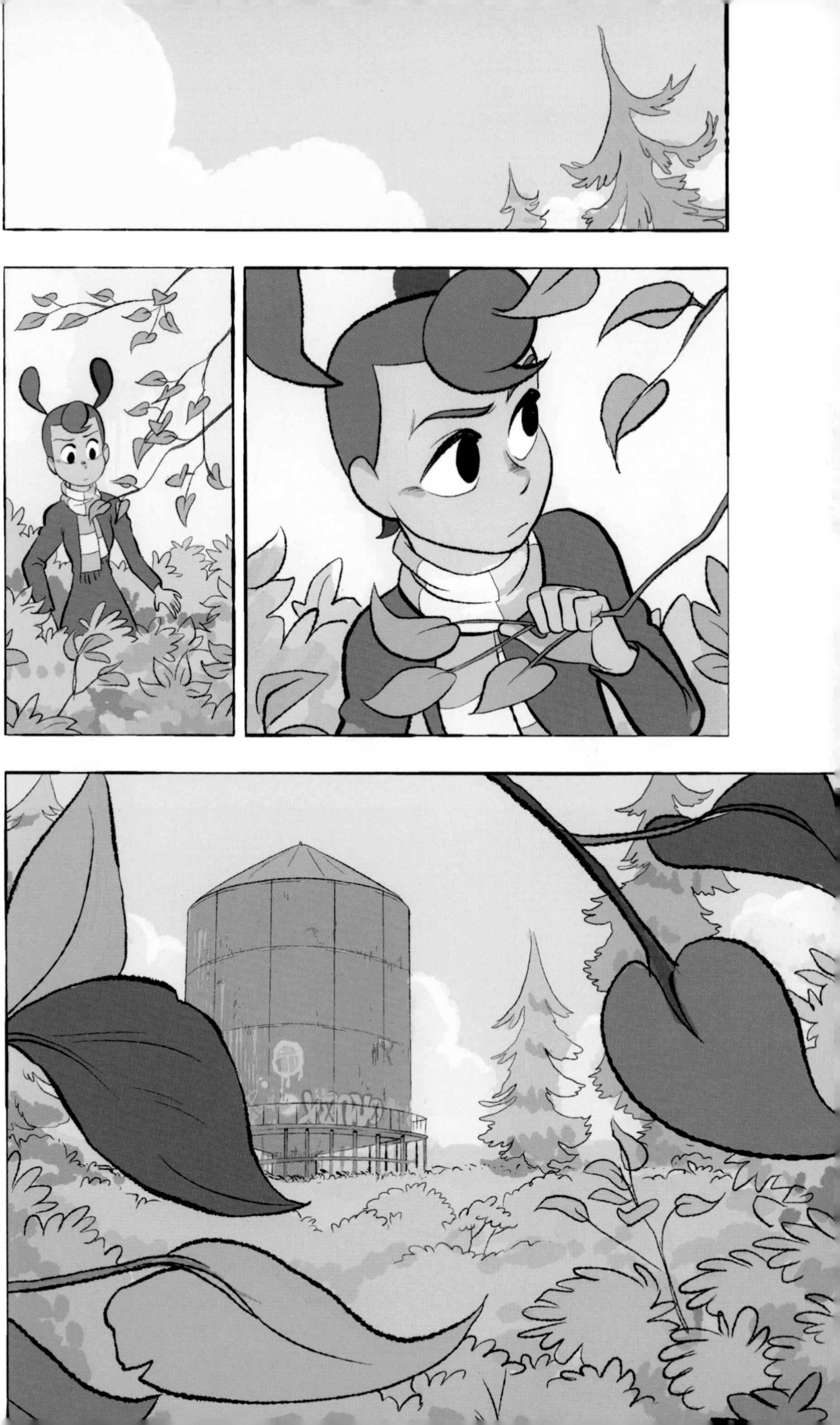

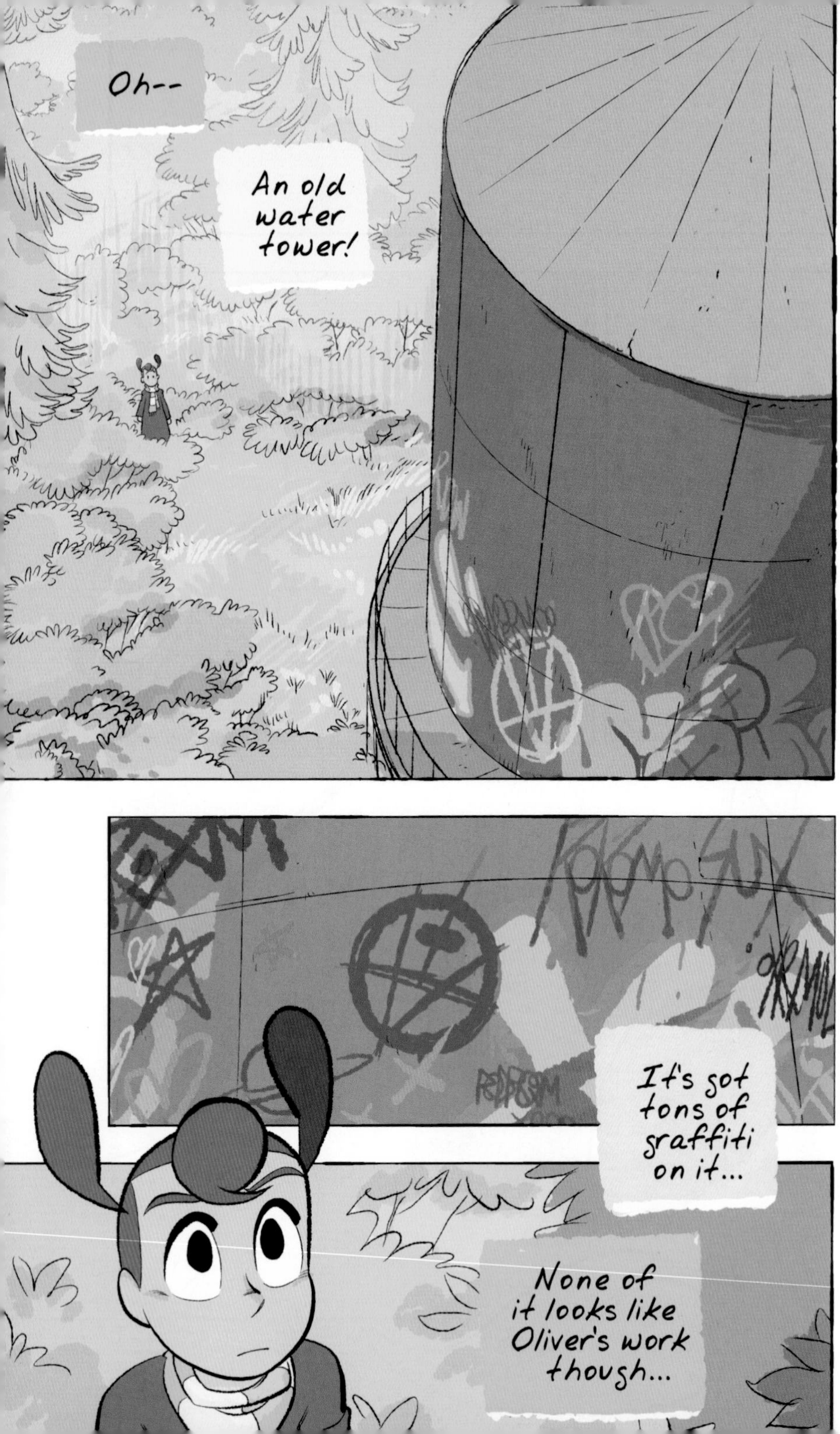
Oh--
An old water tower!
It's got tons of graffiti on it...
None of it looks like Oliver's work though...

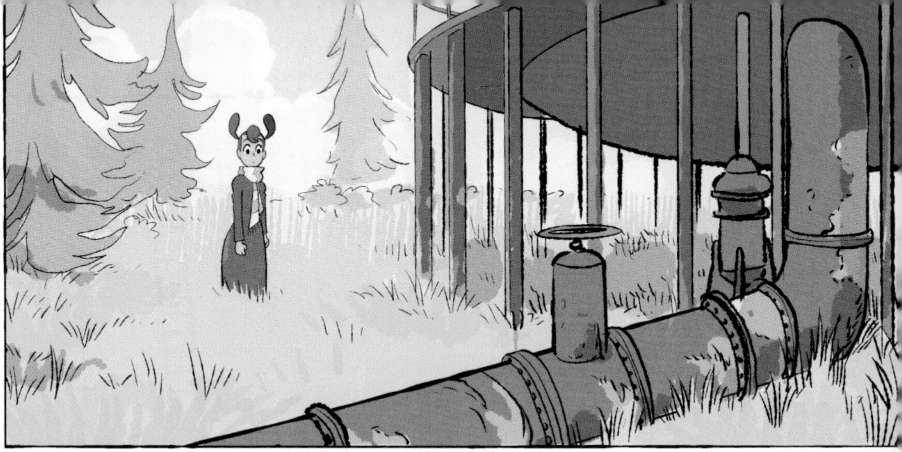
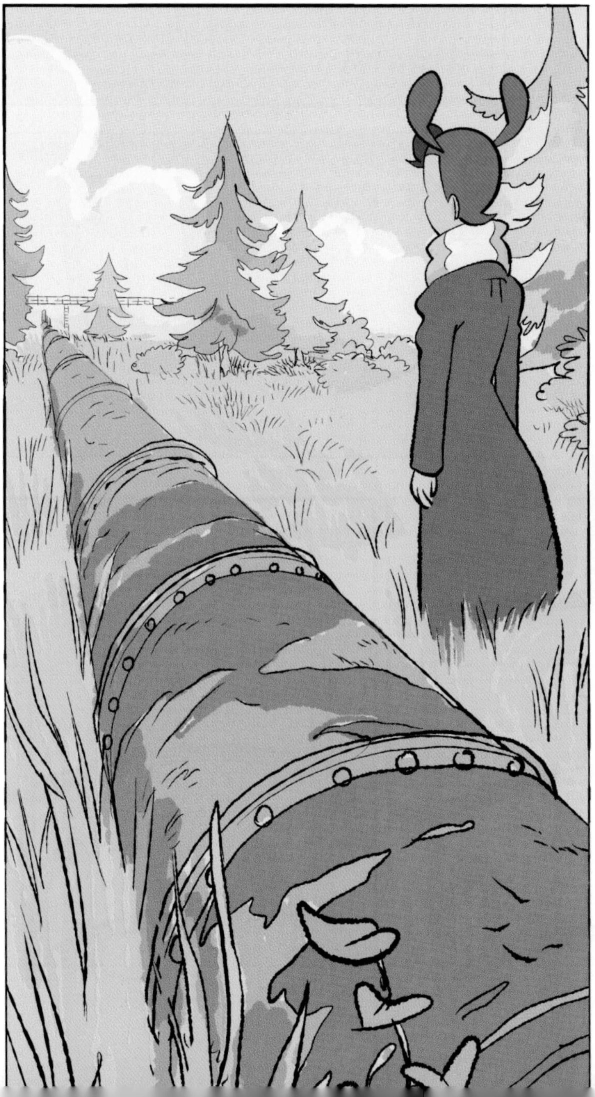
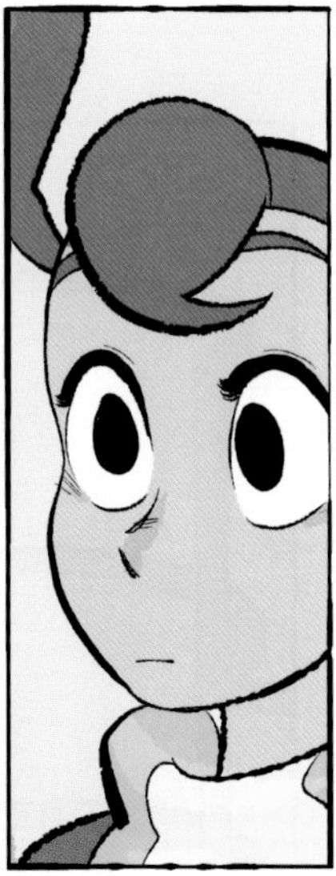

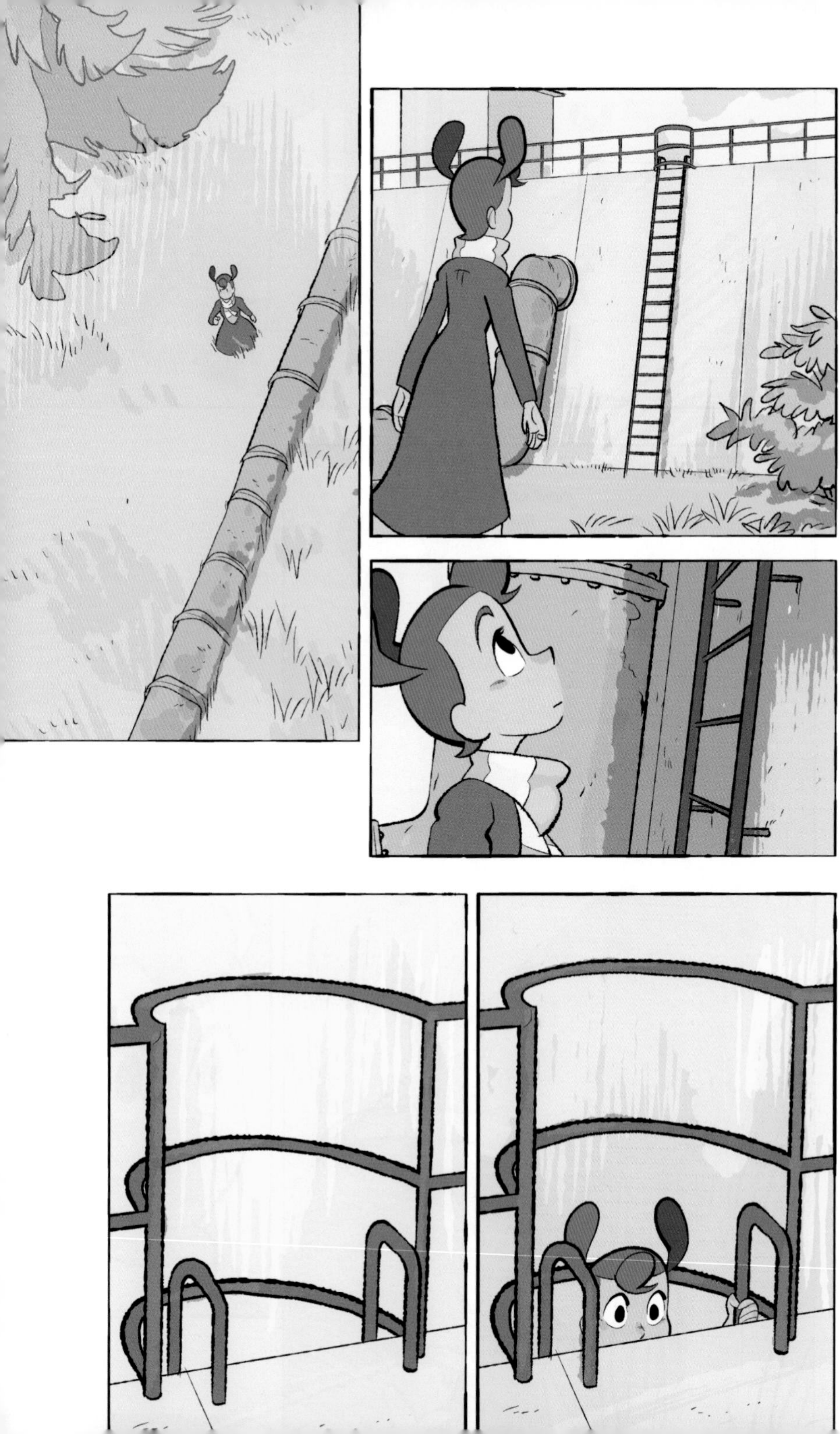

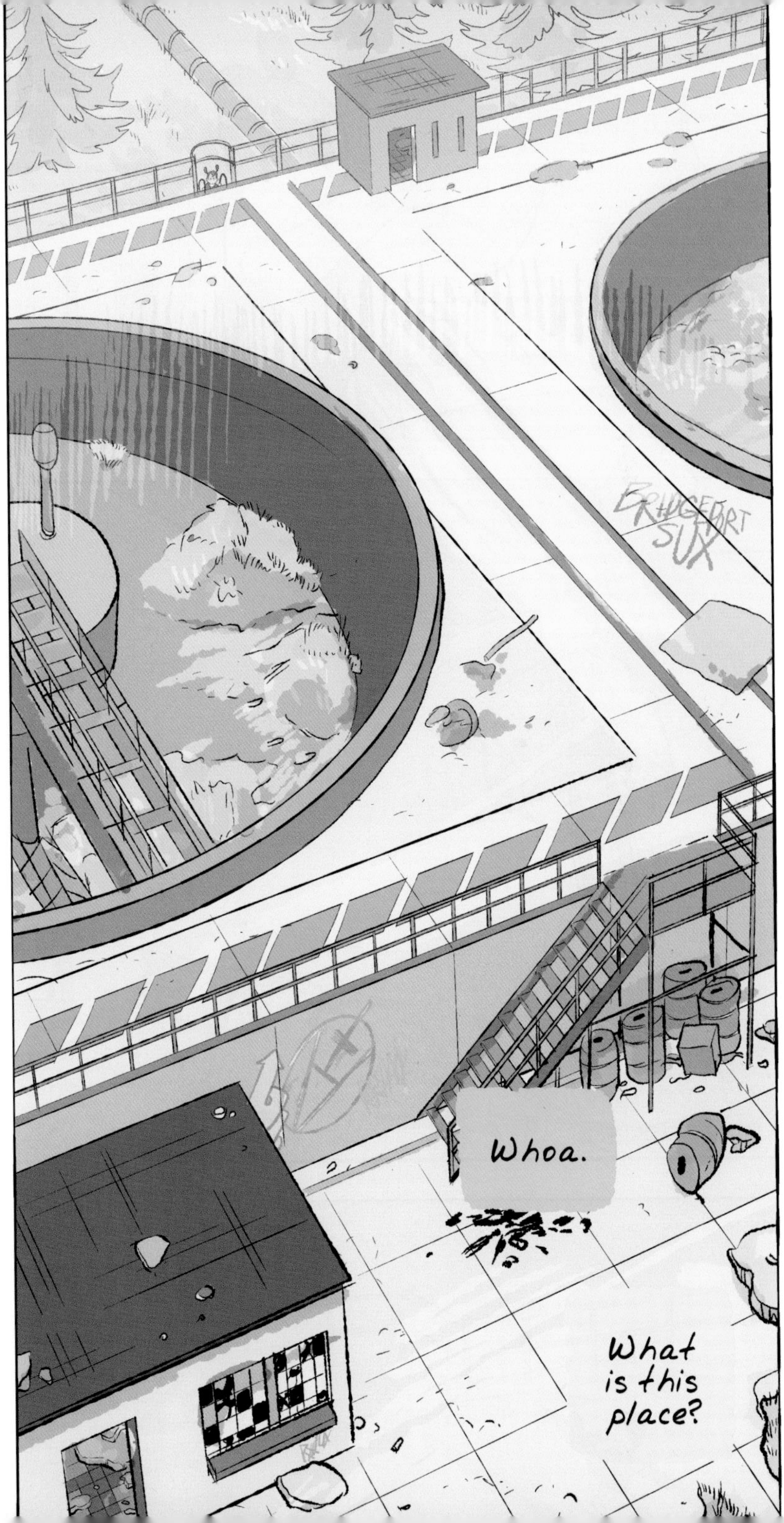
Whoa.
What is this place?

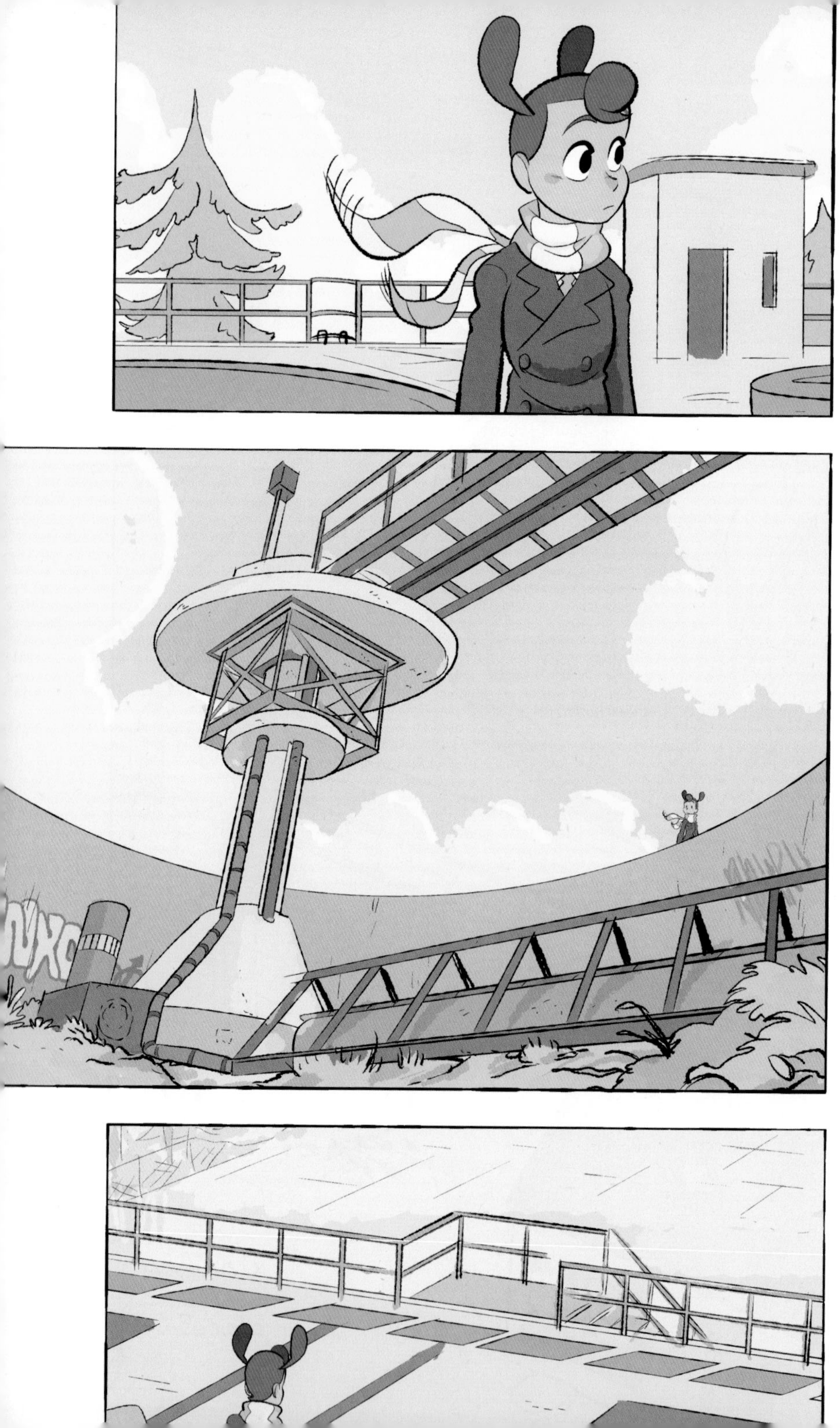

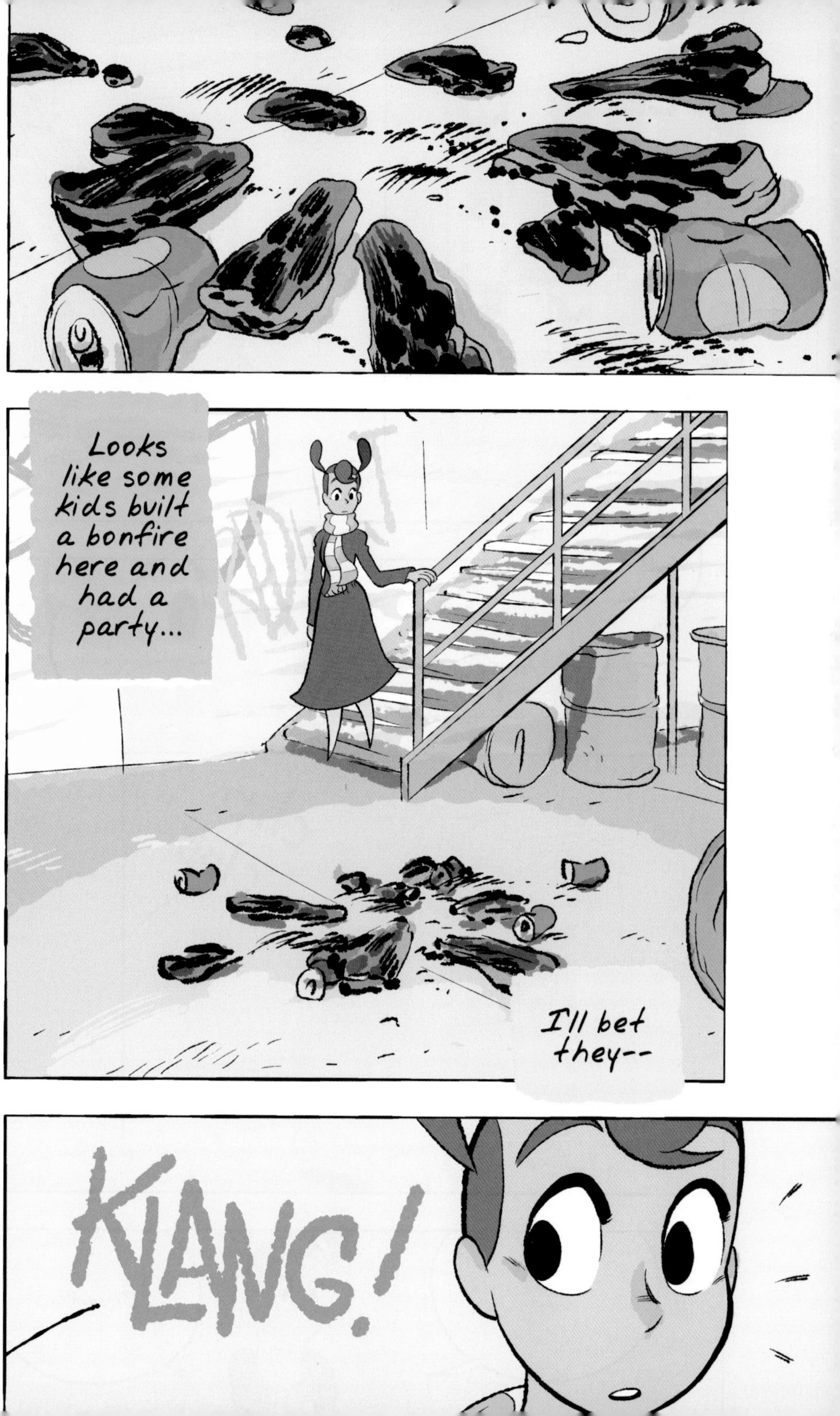

Looks like some kids built a bonfire here and had a party...
I'll bet they--
KLANG!

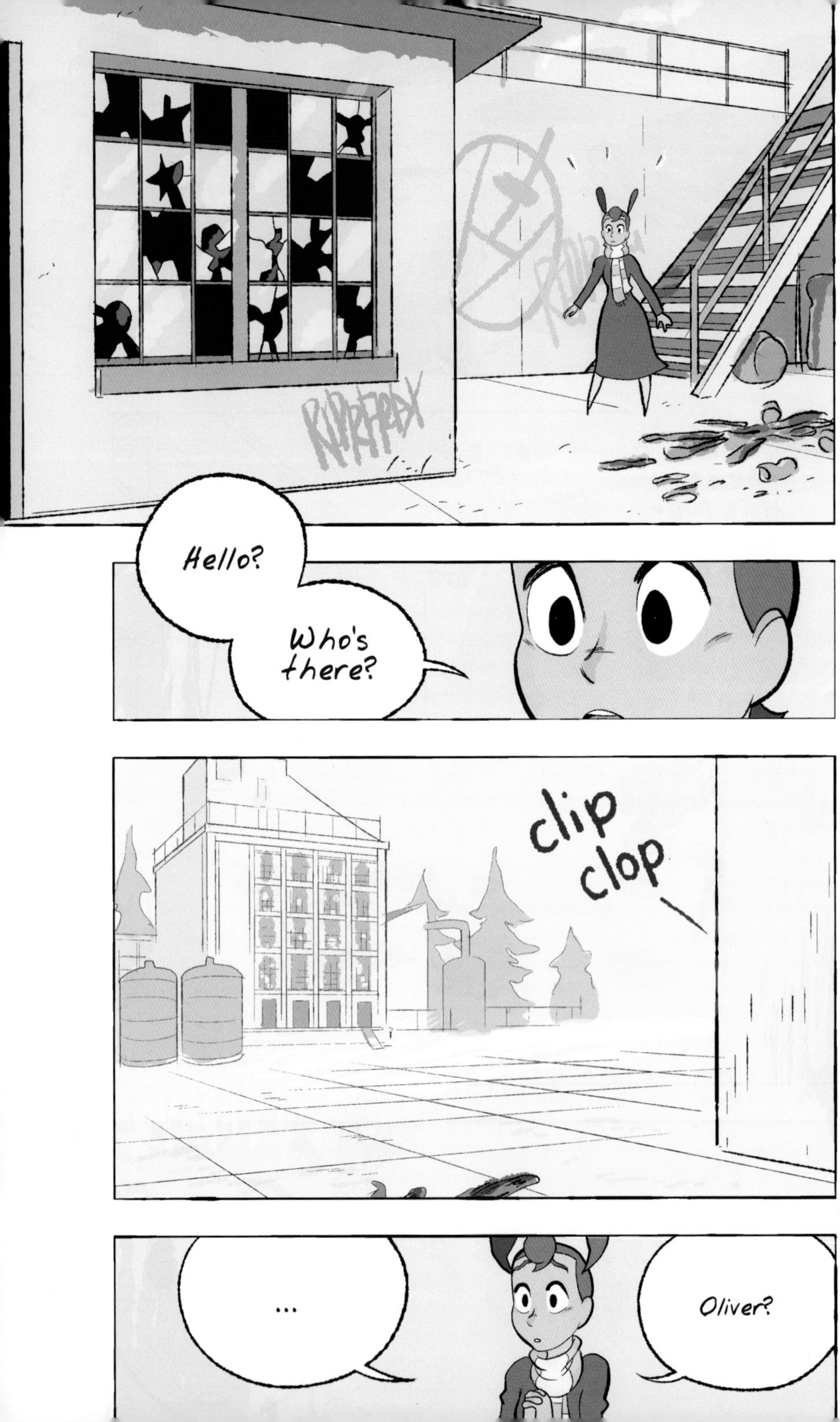
Hello?
Who's there?
clip
clop
...
Oliver?

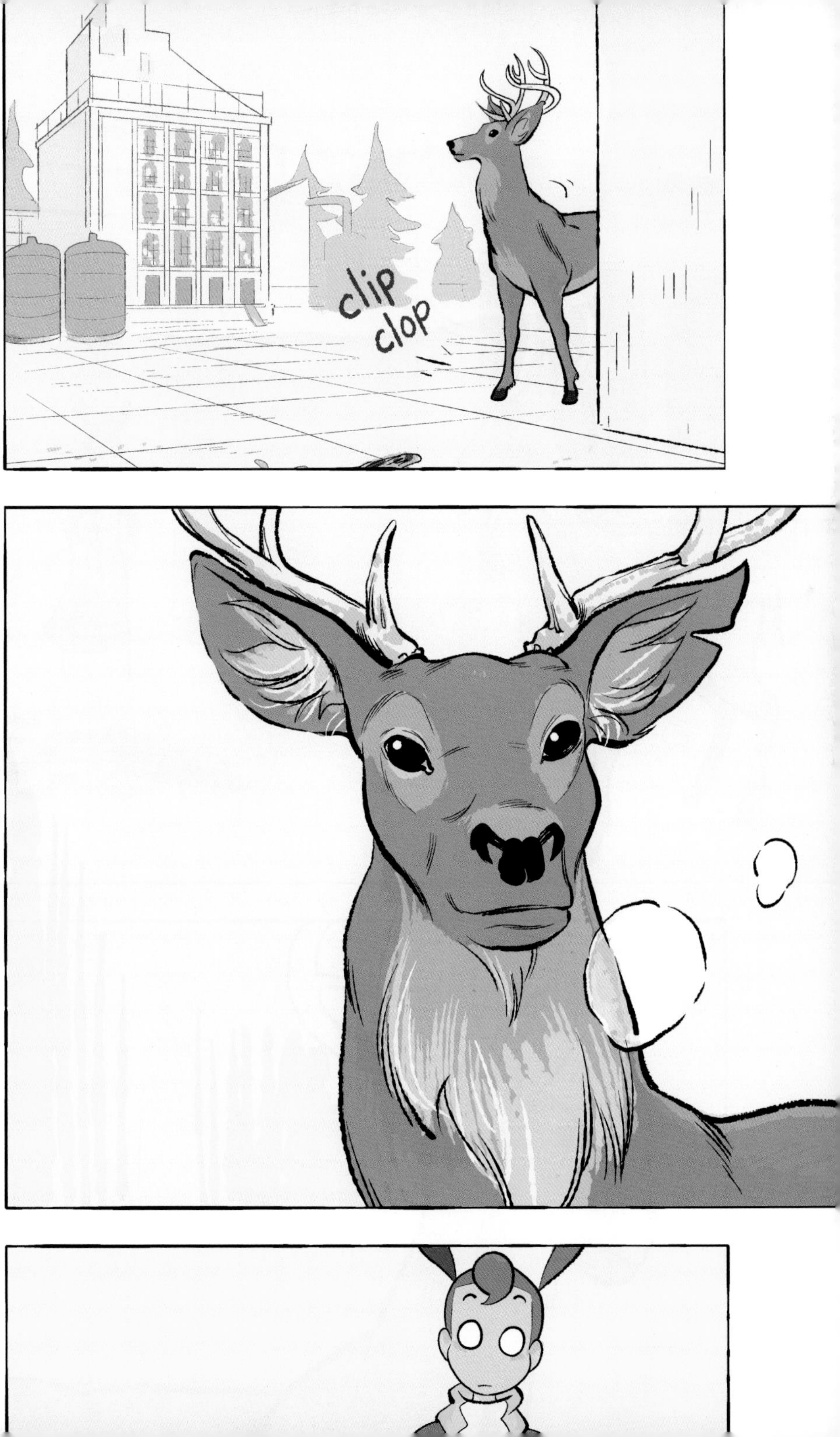
clip
clop

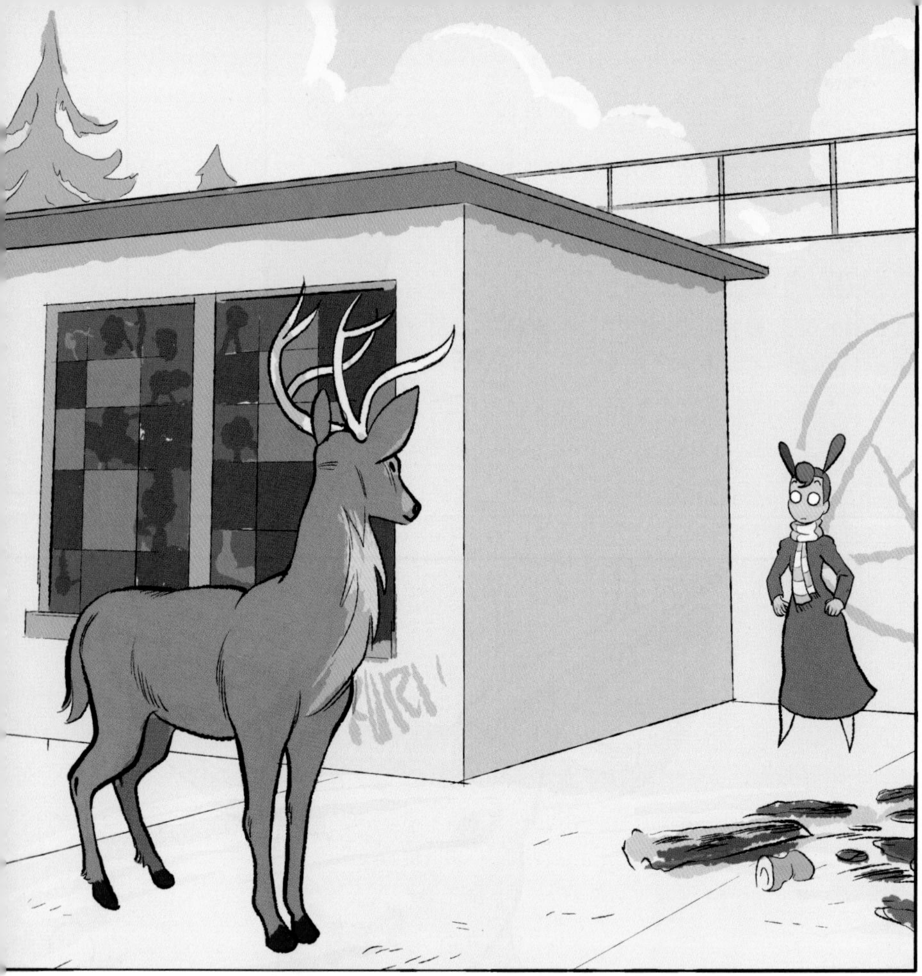

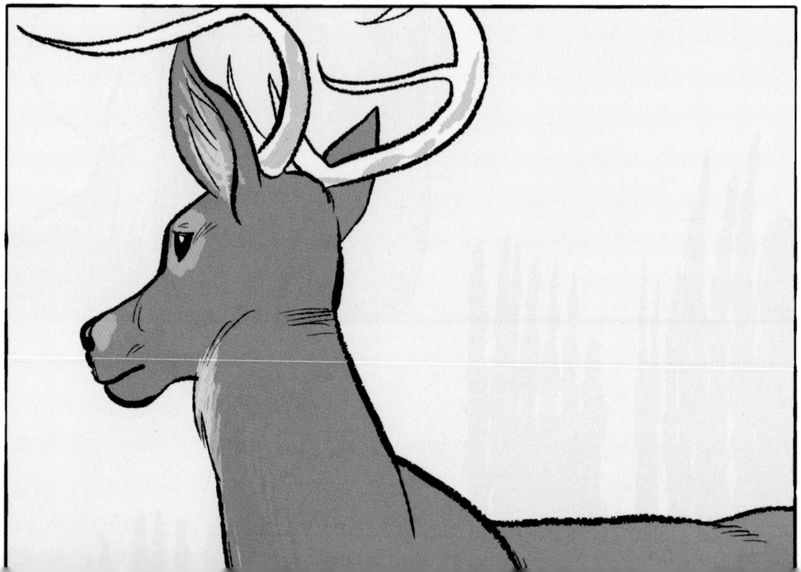

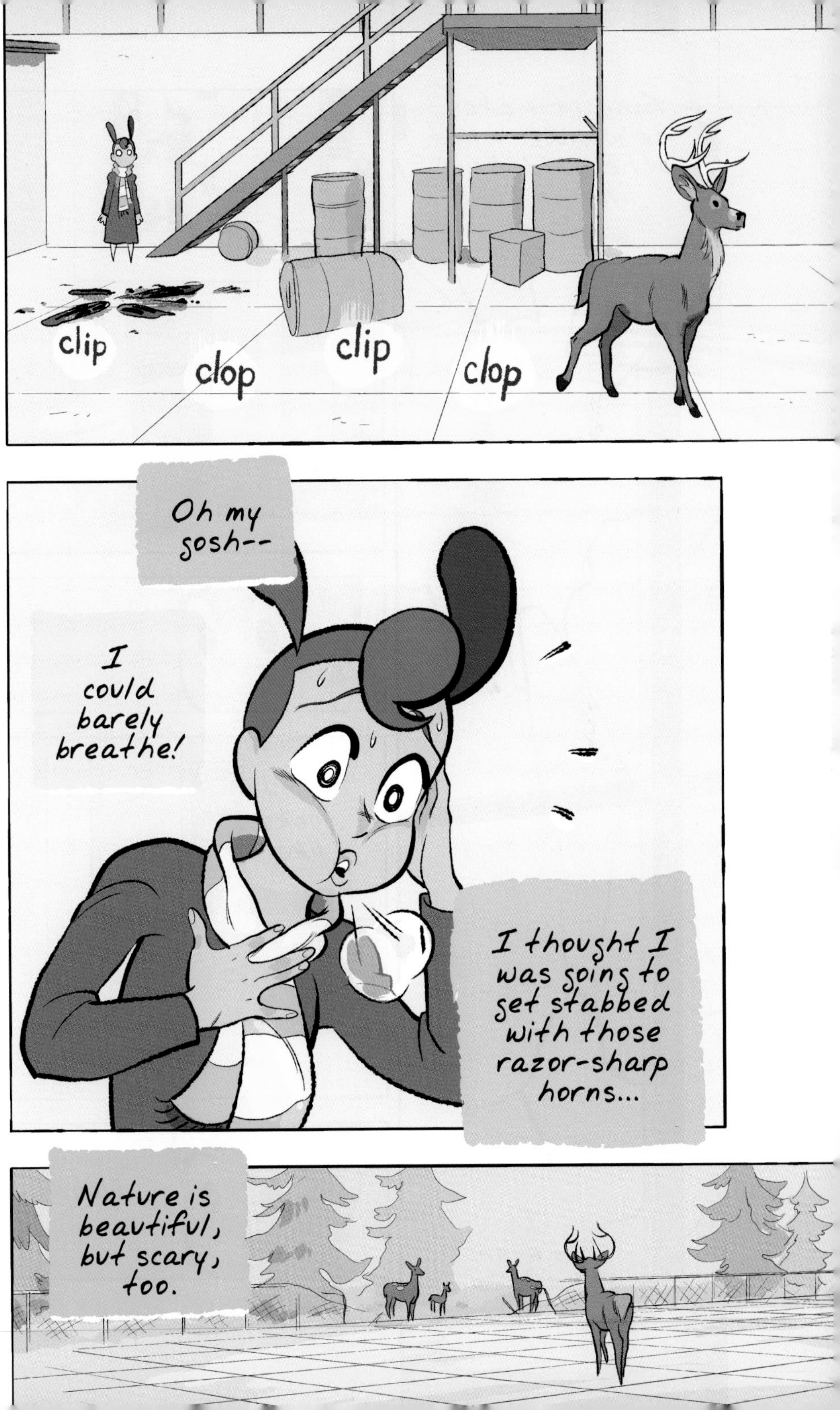
clip
clop
clip
clop
Oh my gosh--
I could barely breathe!
I thought I was going to get stabbed with those razor-sharp horns...
Nature is beautiful, but scary, too.

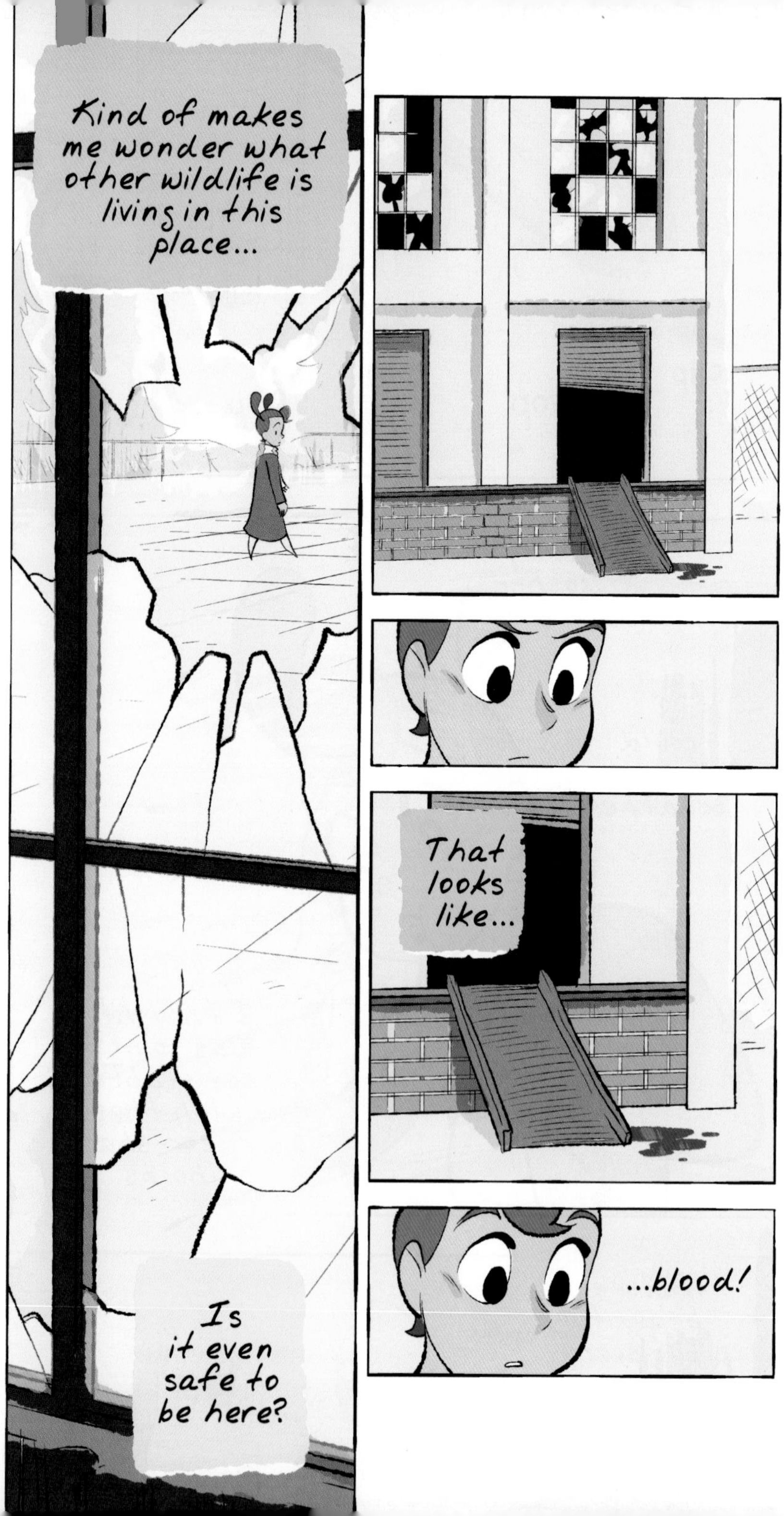
Kind of makes me wonder what other wildlife is living in this place...
Is it even safe to be here?
That looks like...
...blood!

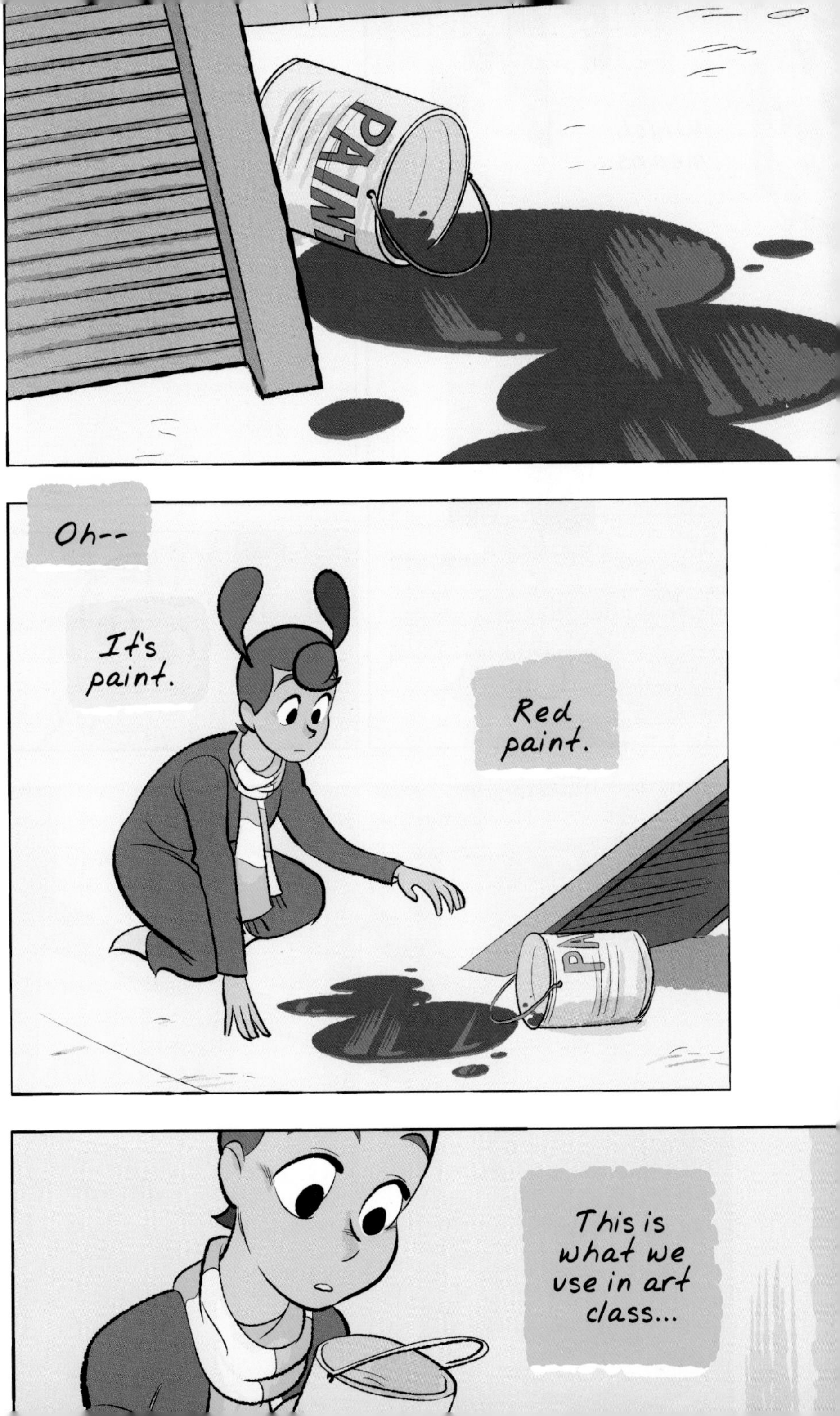
Oh--
It's paint.
Red paint.
This is what we use in art class...

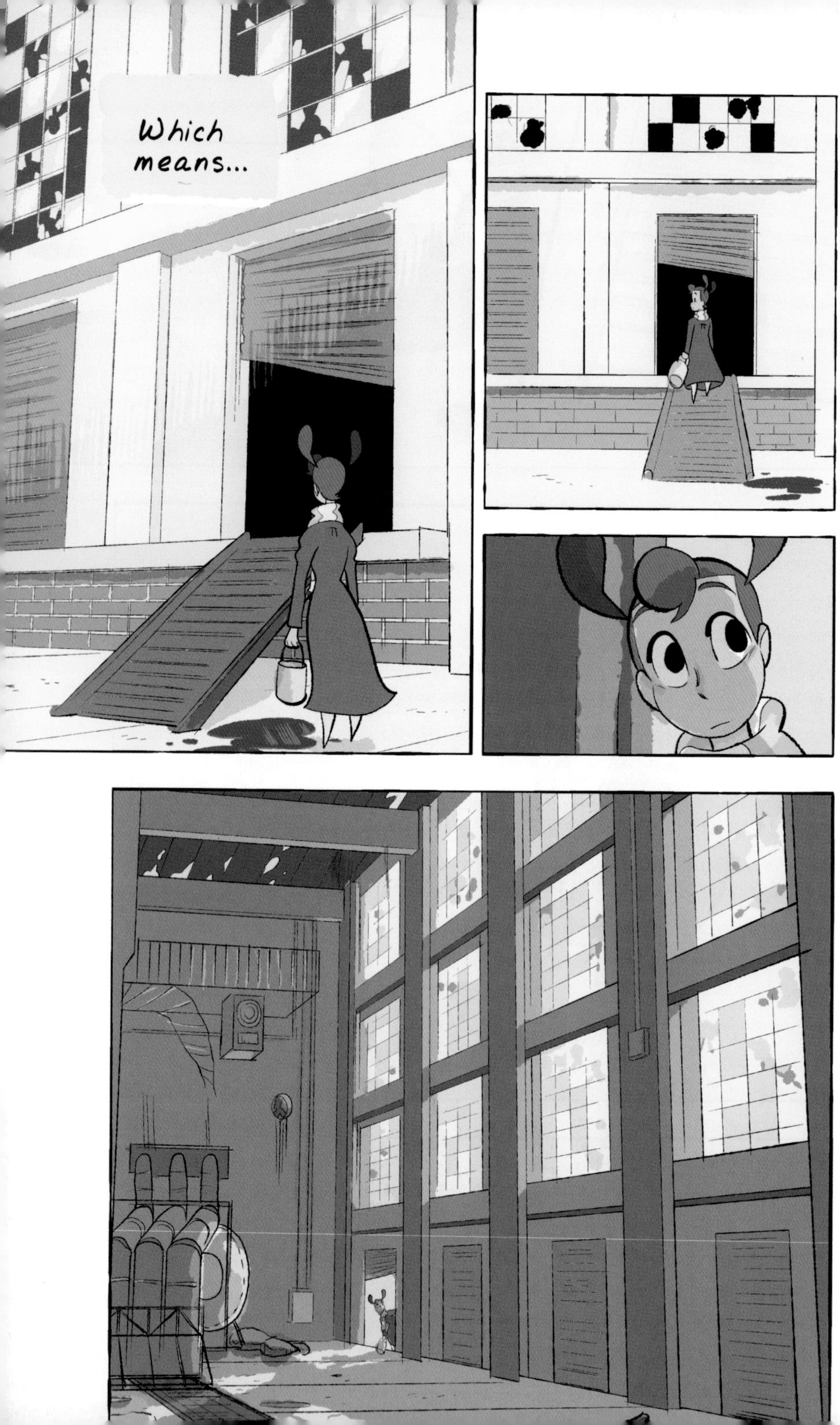
Which means...

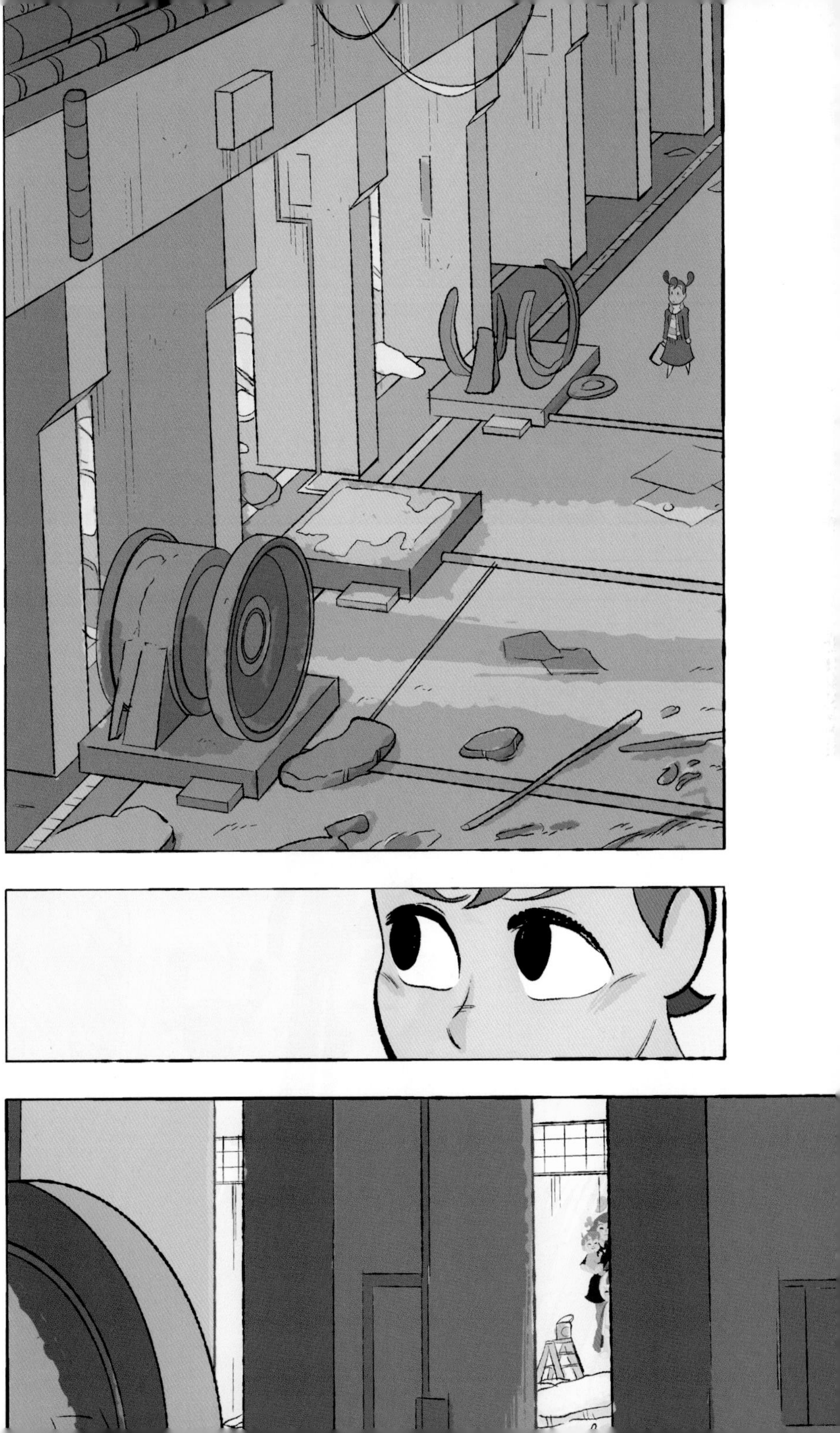

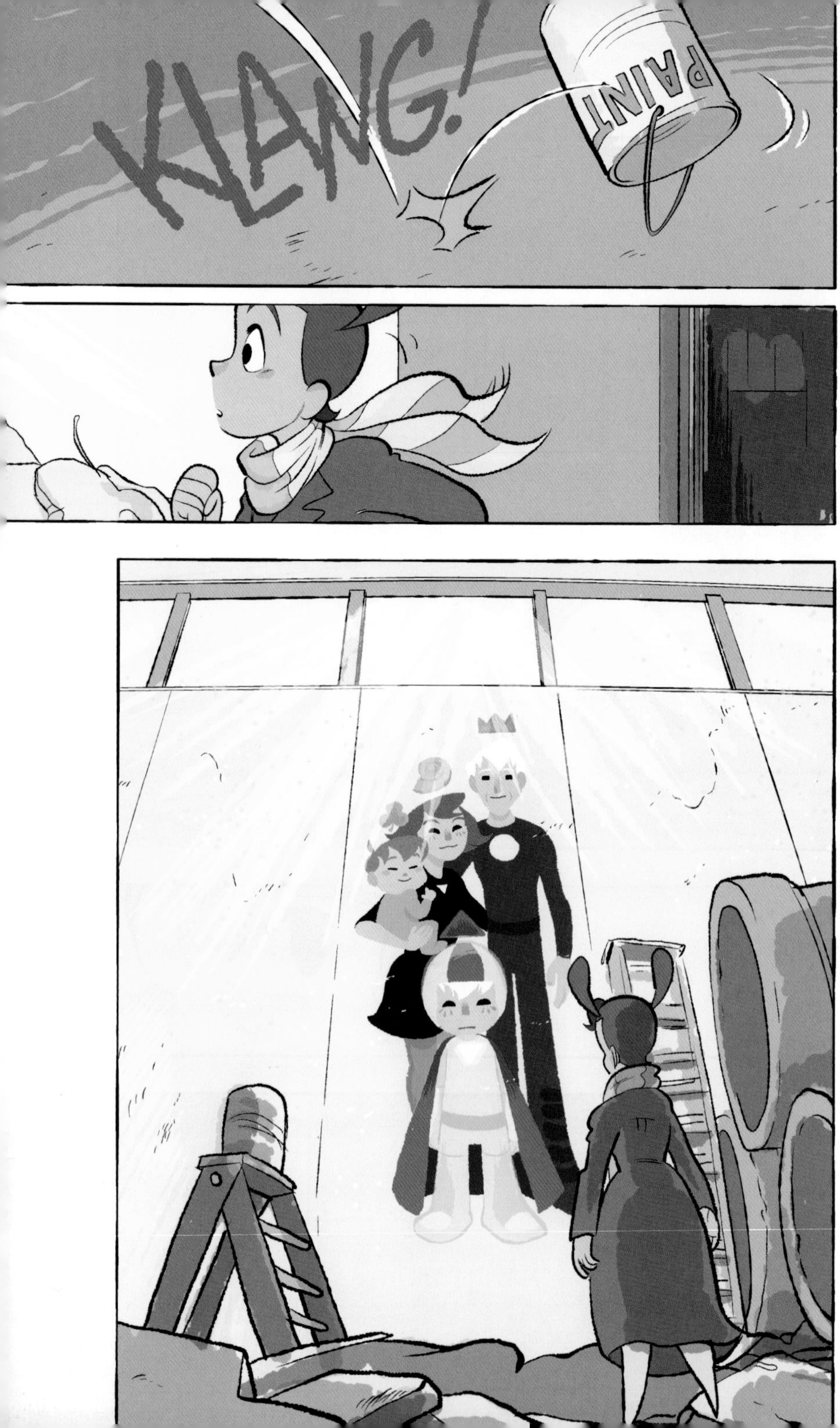
KLANG!
PAINT

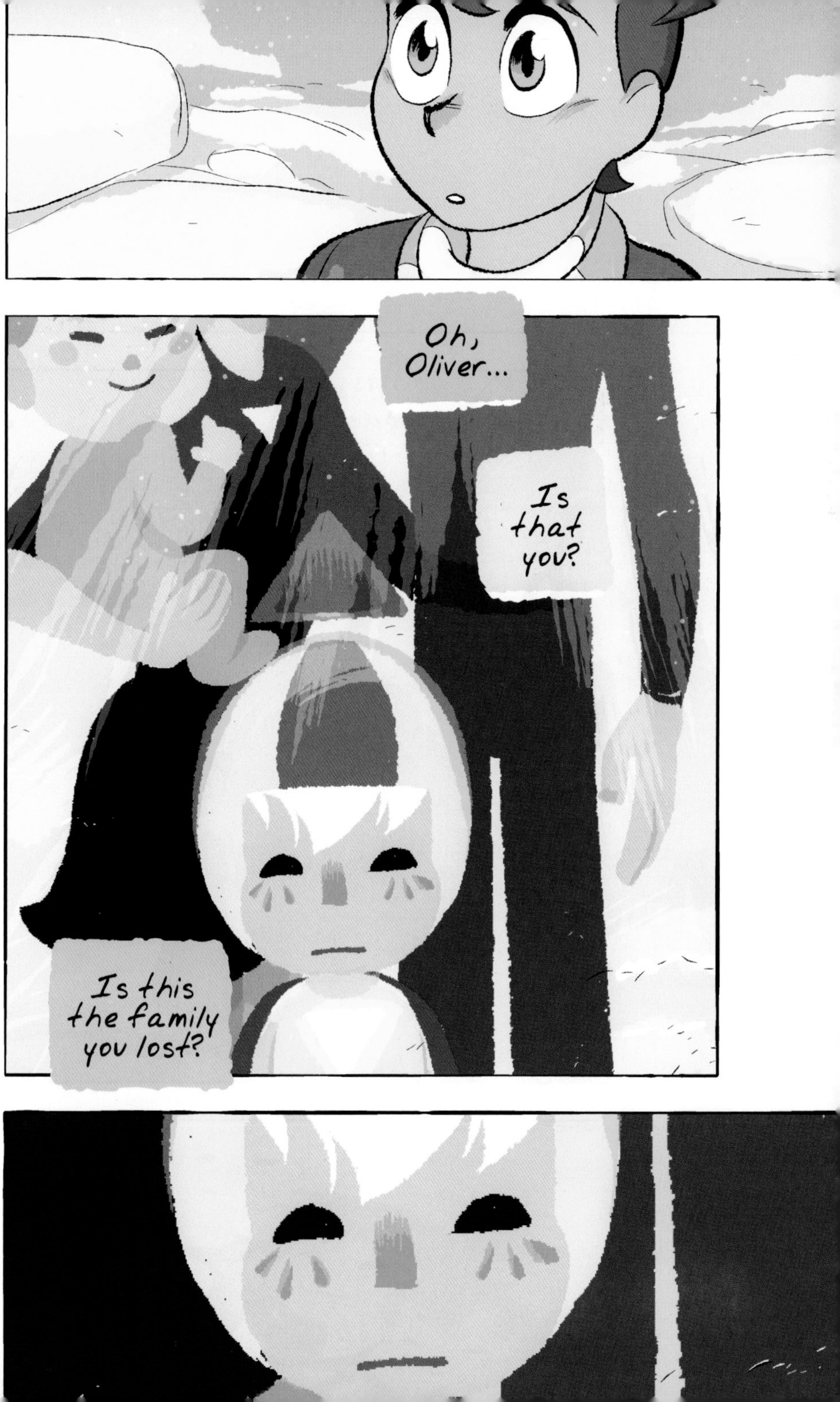
Oh, Oliver...
Is that you?
Is this the family you lost?

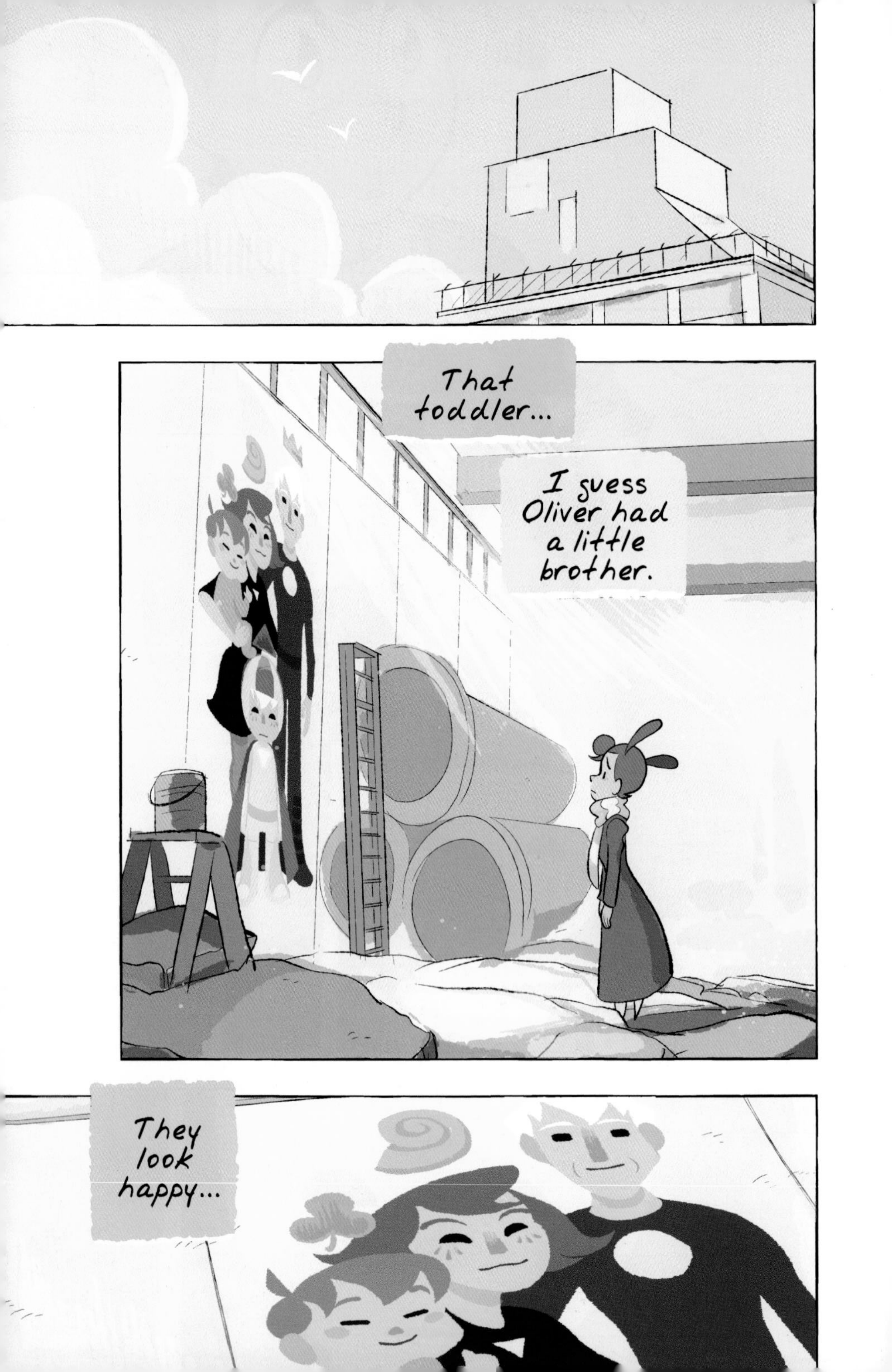
That toddler...
I guess Oliver had a little brother.
They look happy...

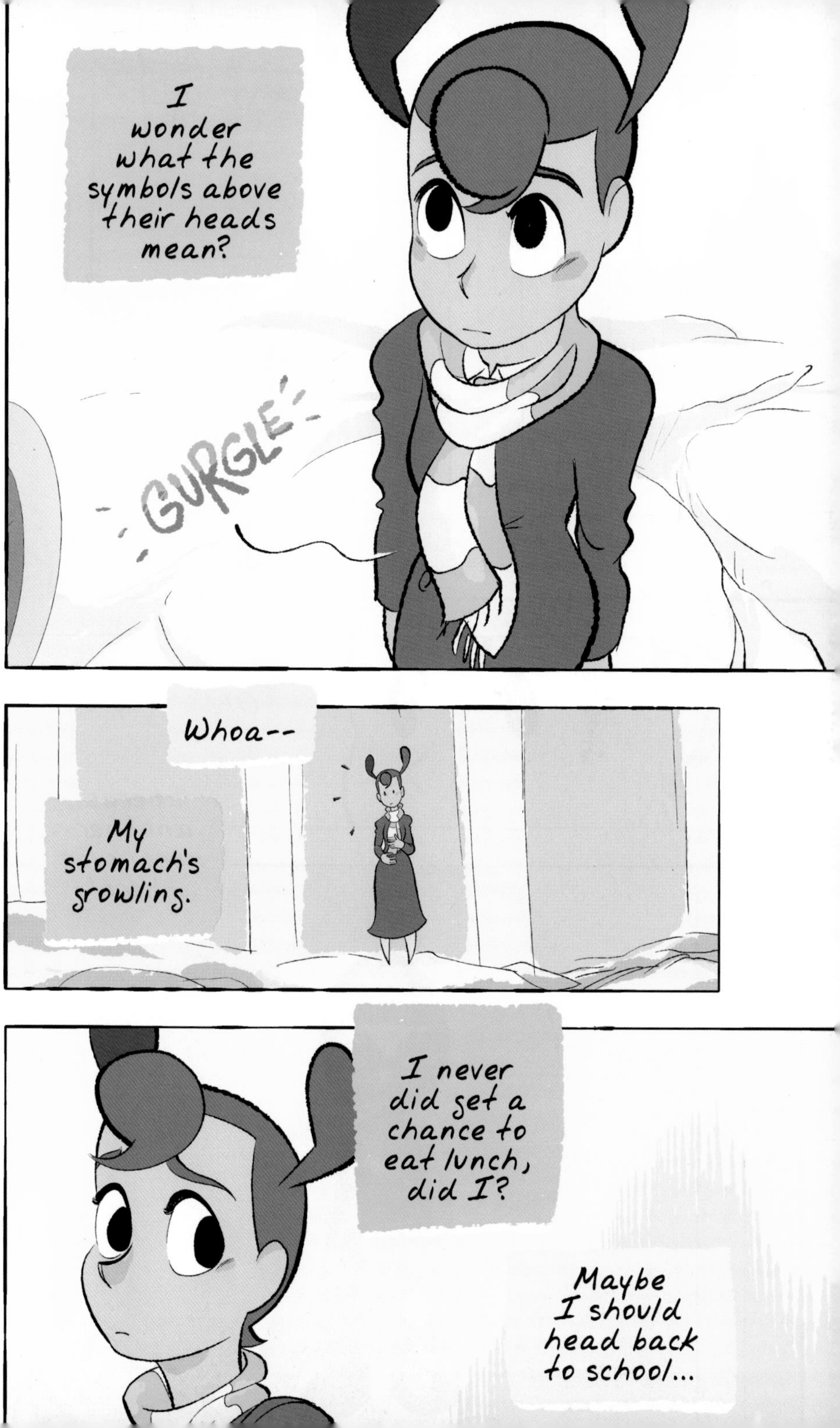
I wonder what the symbols above their heads mean?
GURGLE
Whoa--
My stomach's growling.
I never did get a chance to eat lunch, did I?
Maybe I should head back to school...

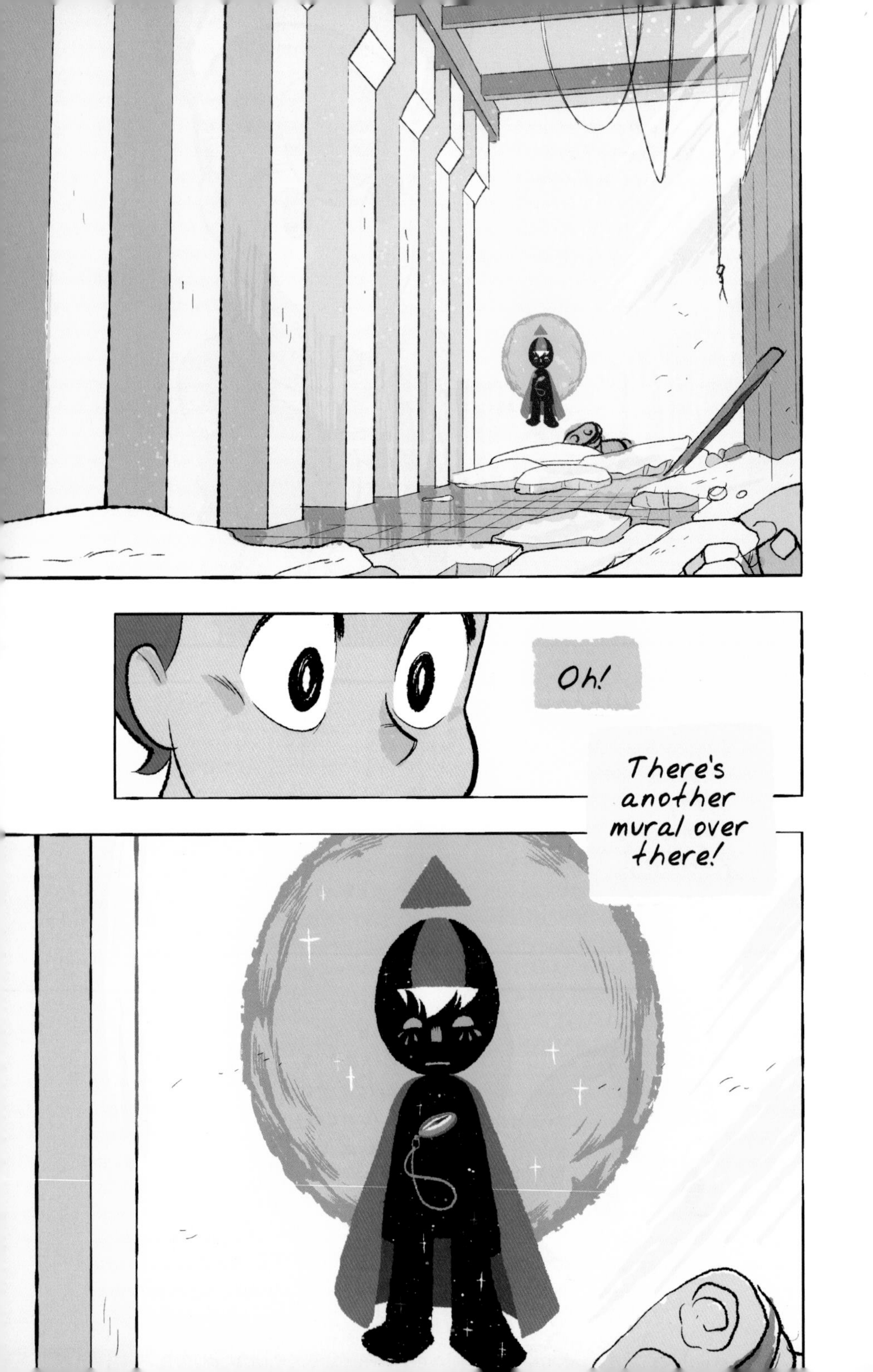
Oh!
There's another mural over there!

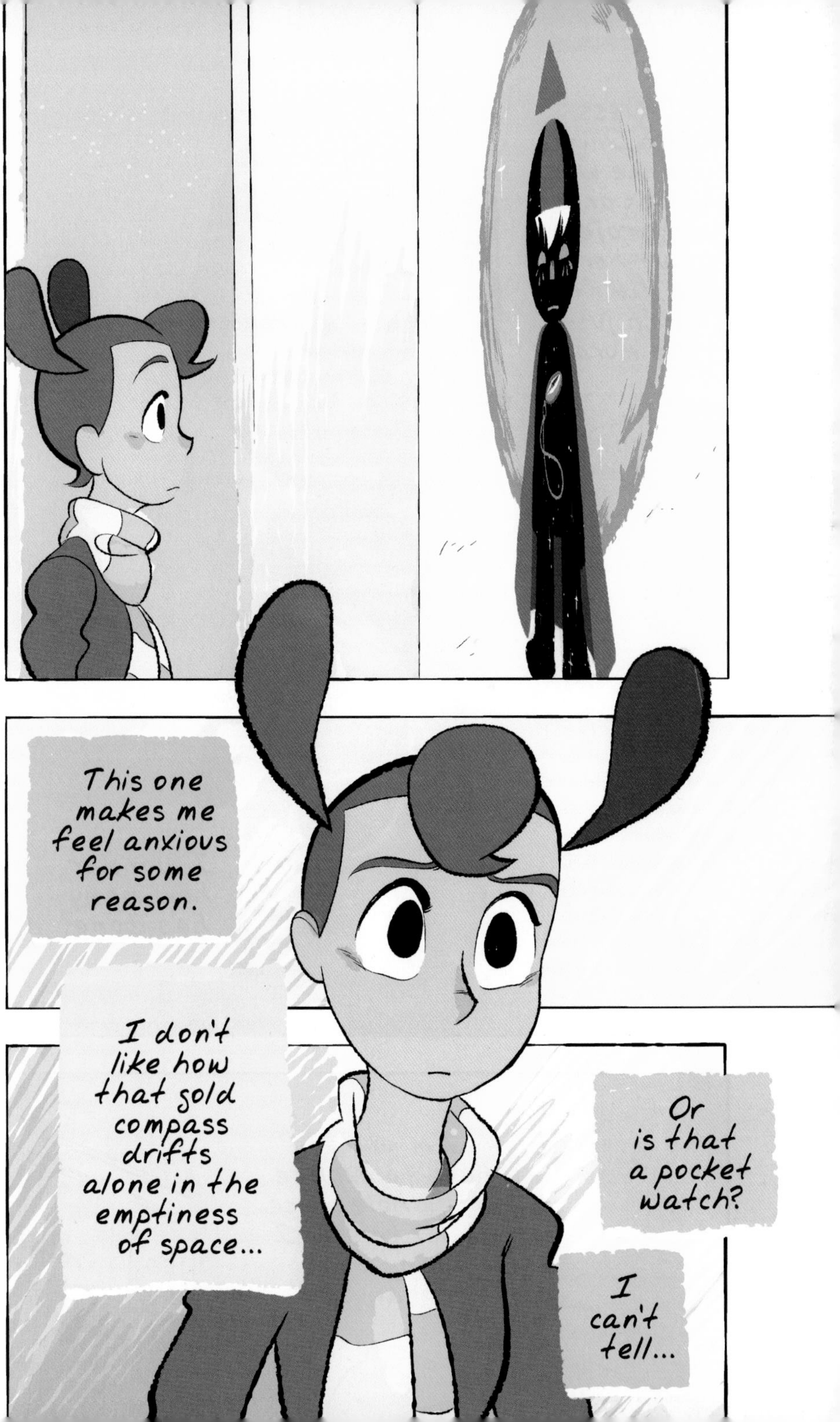
This one makes me feel anxious for some reason.
I don't like how that gold compass drifts alone in the emptiness of space...
Or is that a pocket watch?
I can't tell...

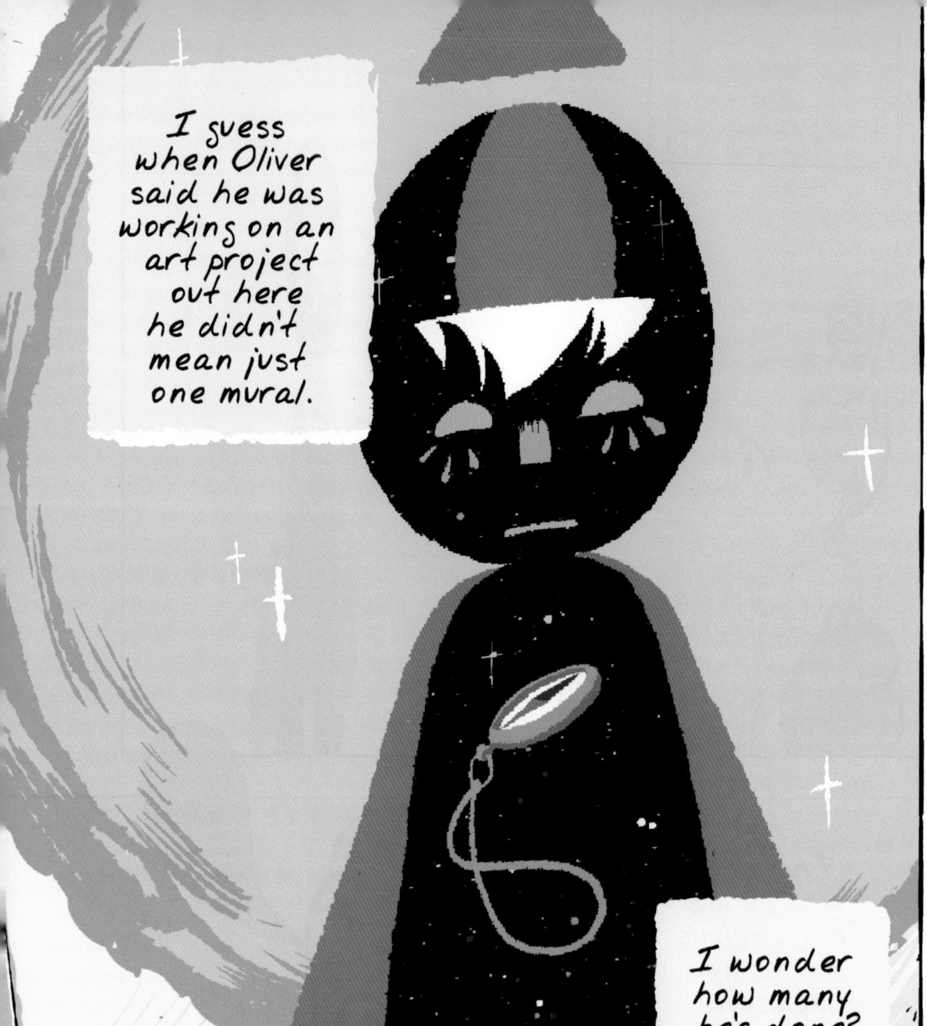
I guess when Oliver said he was working on an art project out here he didn't mean just one mural.
I wonder how many he's done?
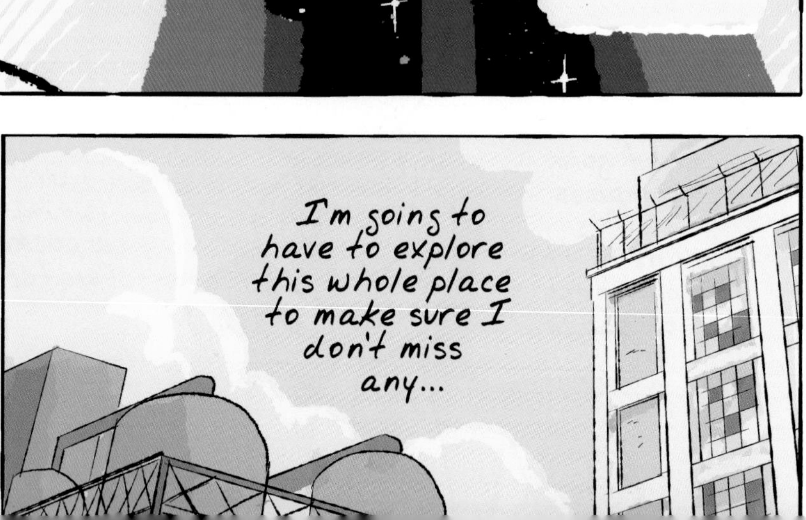
I'm going to have to explore this whole place to make sure I don't miss any...

ON
OFF
NO
TRESSPASSIN

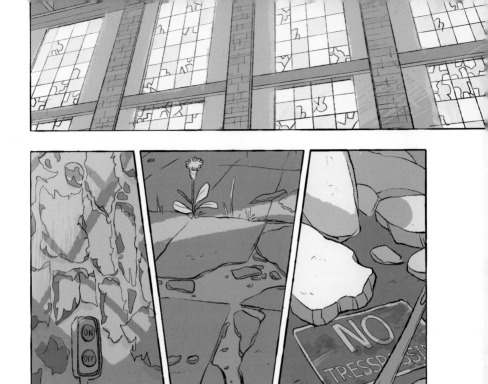

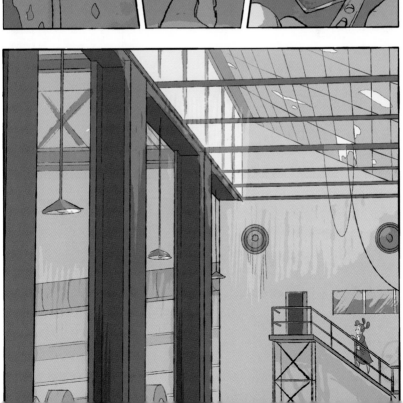

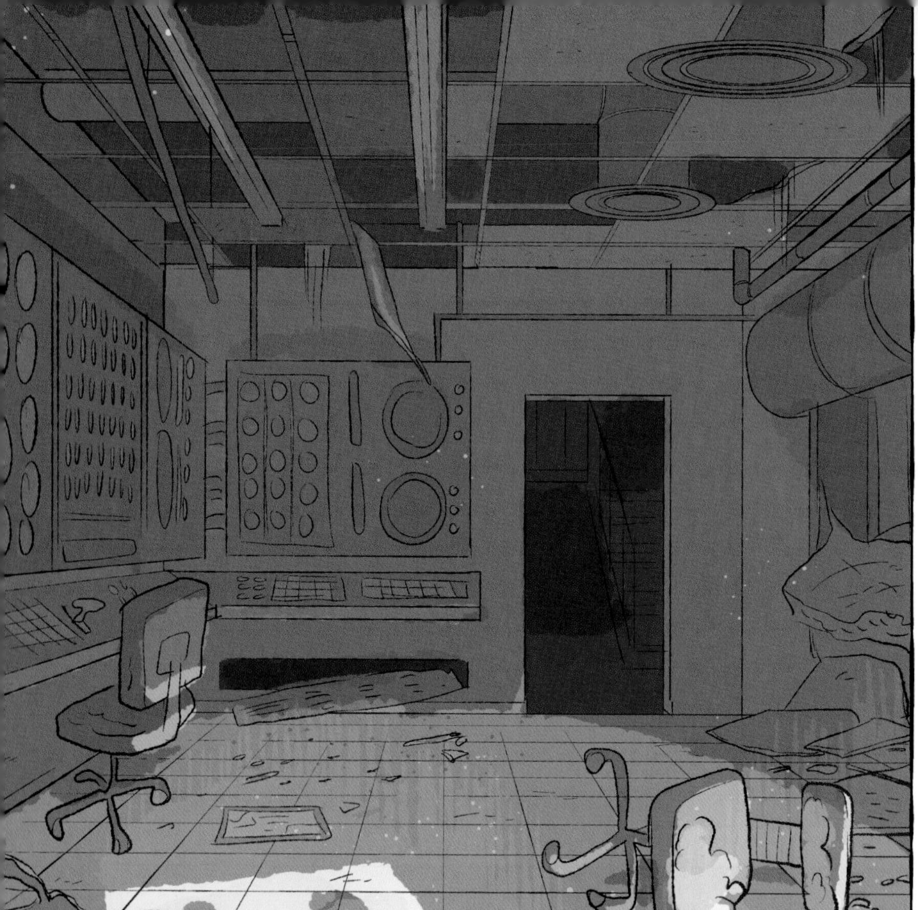

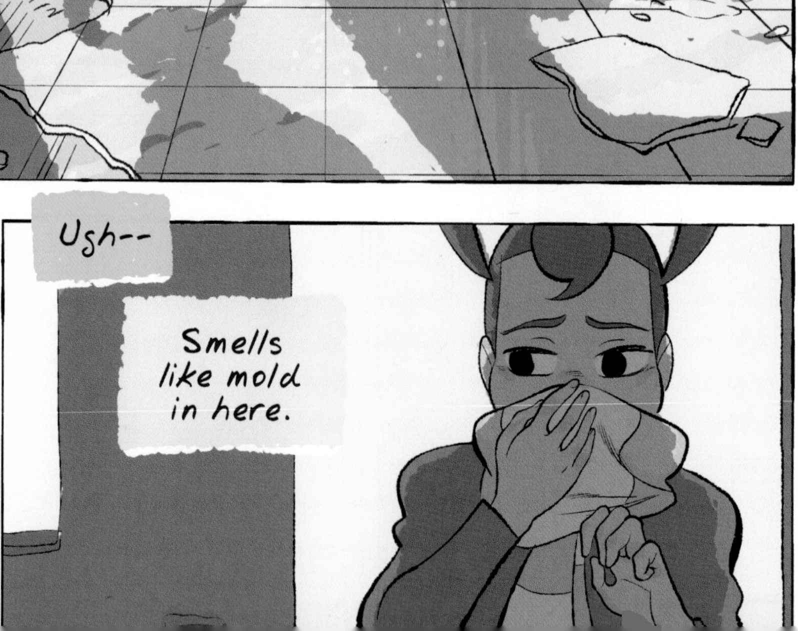
Ugh--
Smells like mold in here.

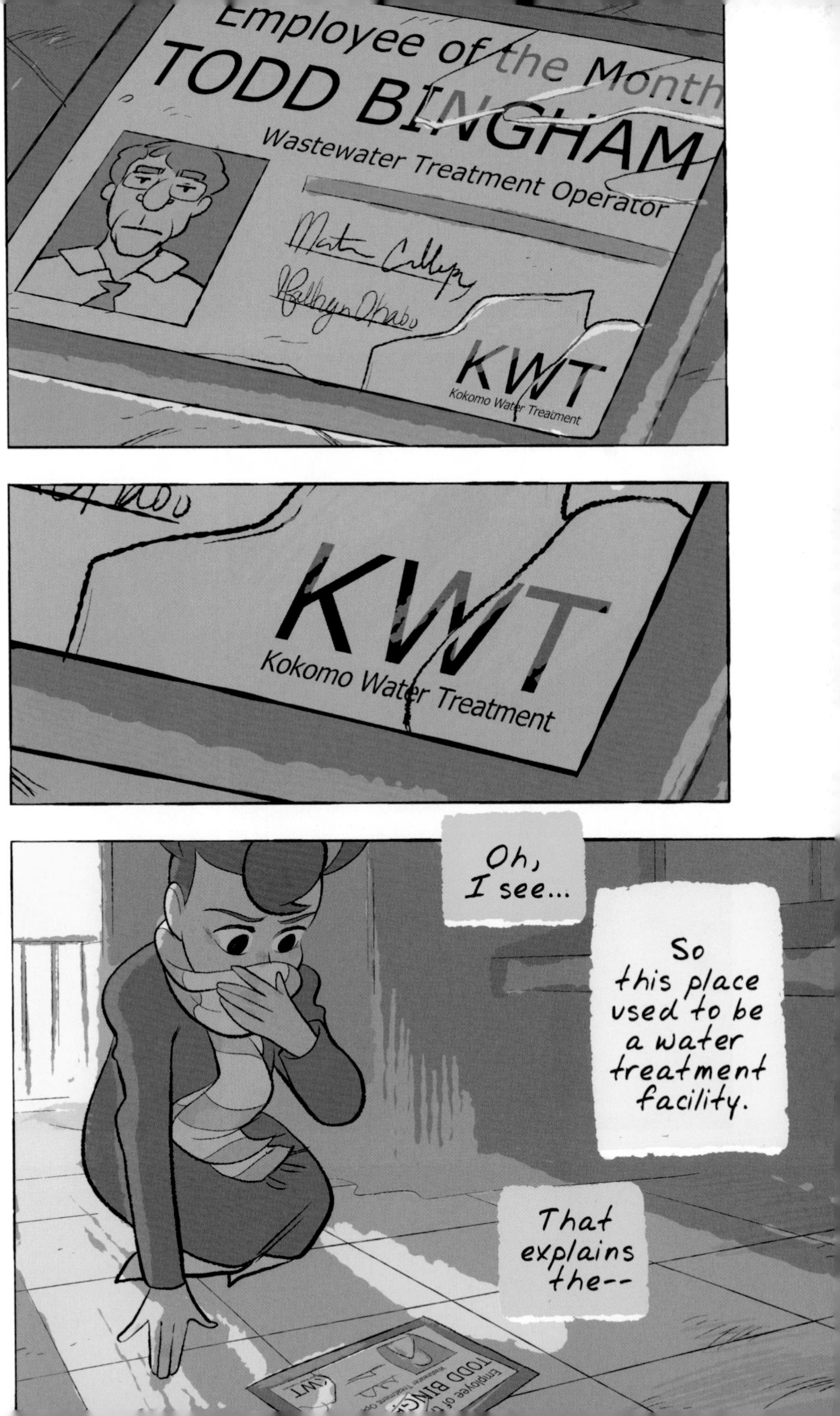
Employee of the Month
TODD BINGHAM
Wastewater Treatment Operator
KWT
Kokomo Water Treatment
KWT
Kokomo Water Treatment
Oh, I see...
So this place used to be a water treatment facility.
That explains the--

The mold is burning my lungs...

Got to keep moving.

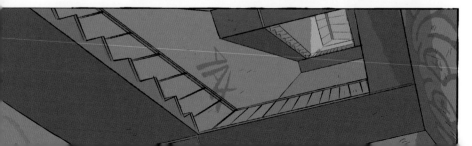

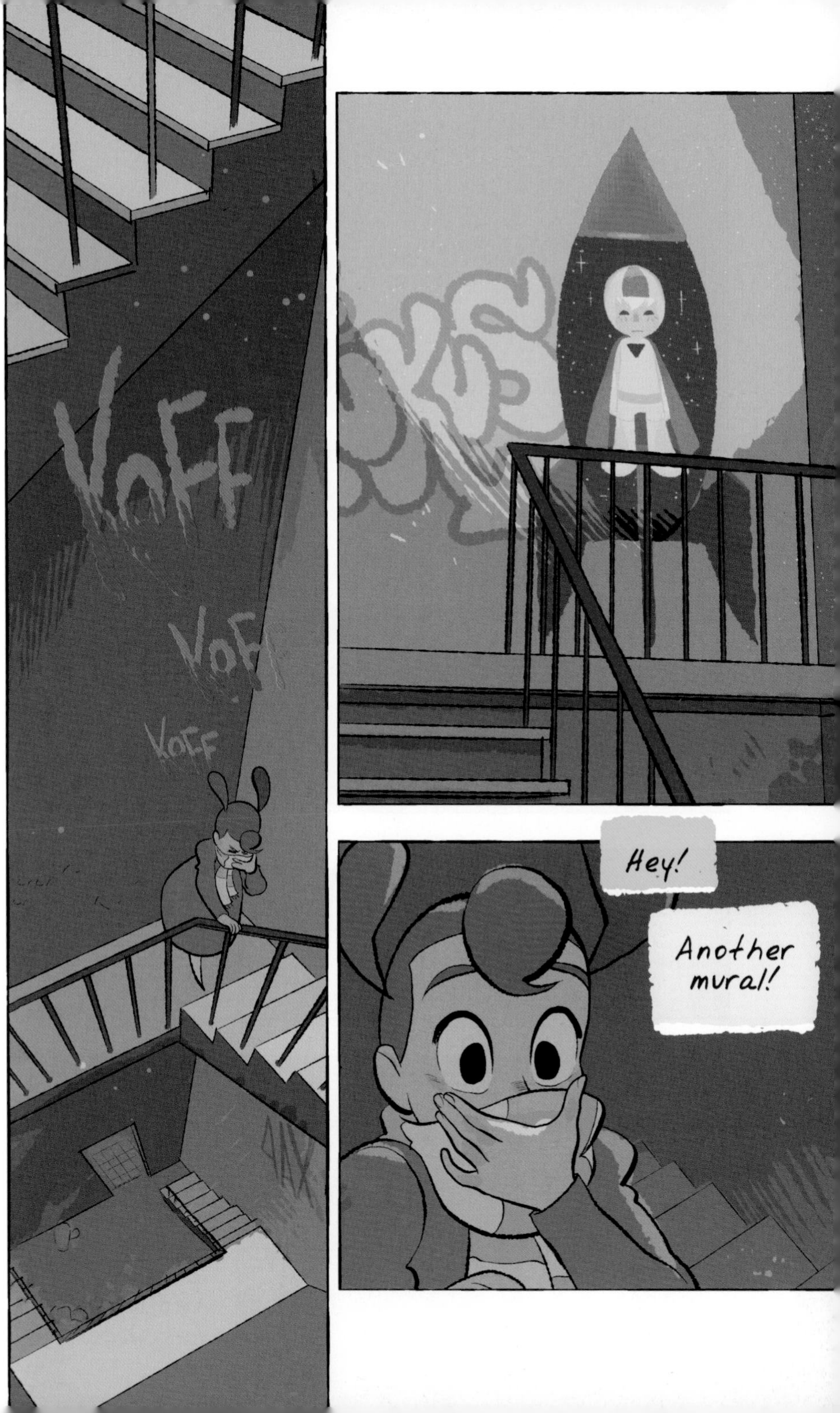
KOFF
KOFF
KOFF
Hey!
Another mural!

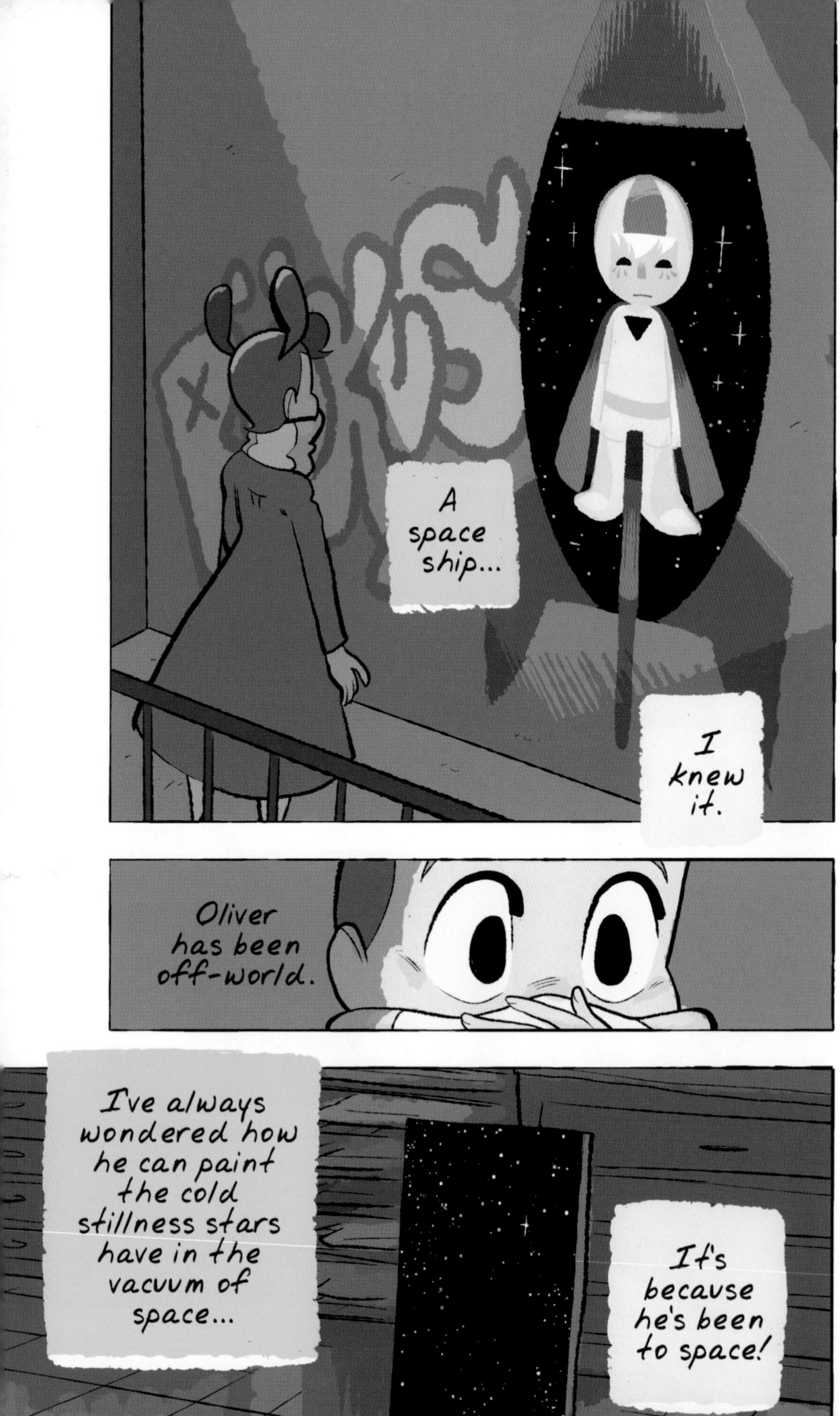
A space ship...
I knew it.
Oliver has been off-world.
I've always wondered how he can paint the cold stillness stars have in the vacuum of space...
It's because he's been to space!

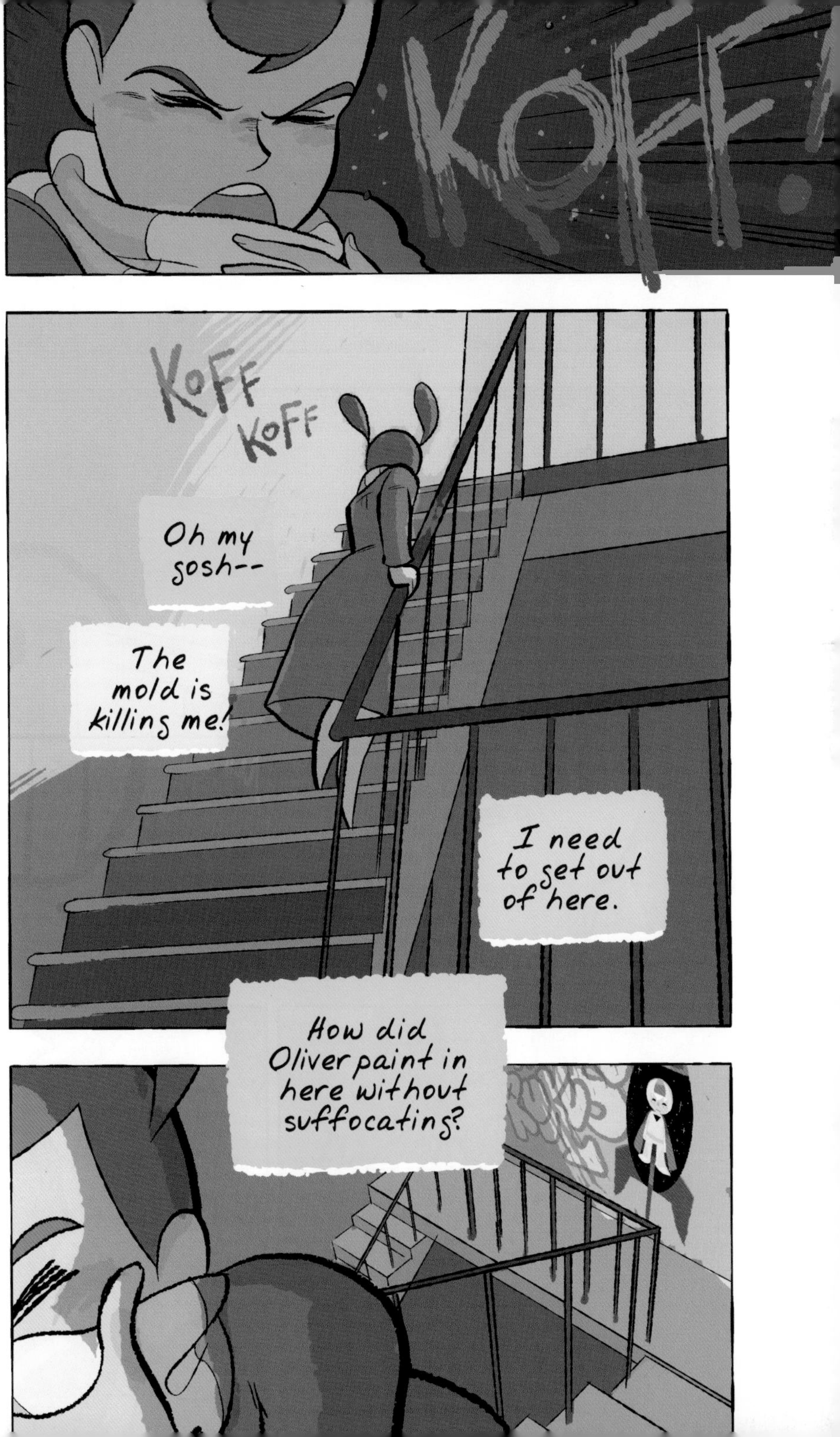
KOFF!
KOFF
KOFF
Oh my gosh--
The mold is killing me!
I need to get out of here.
How did Oliver paint in here without suffocating?

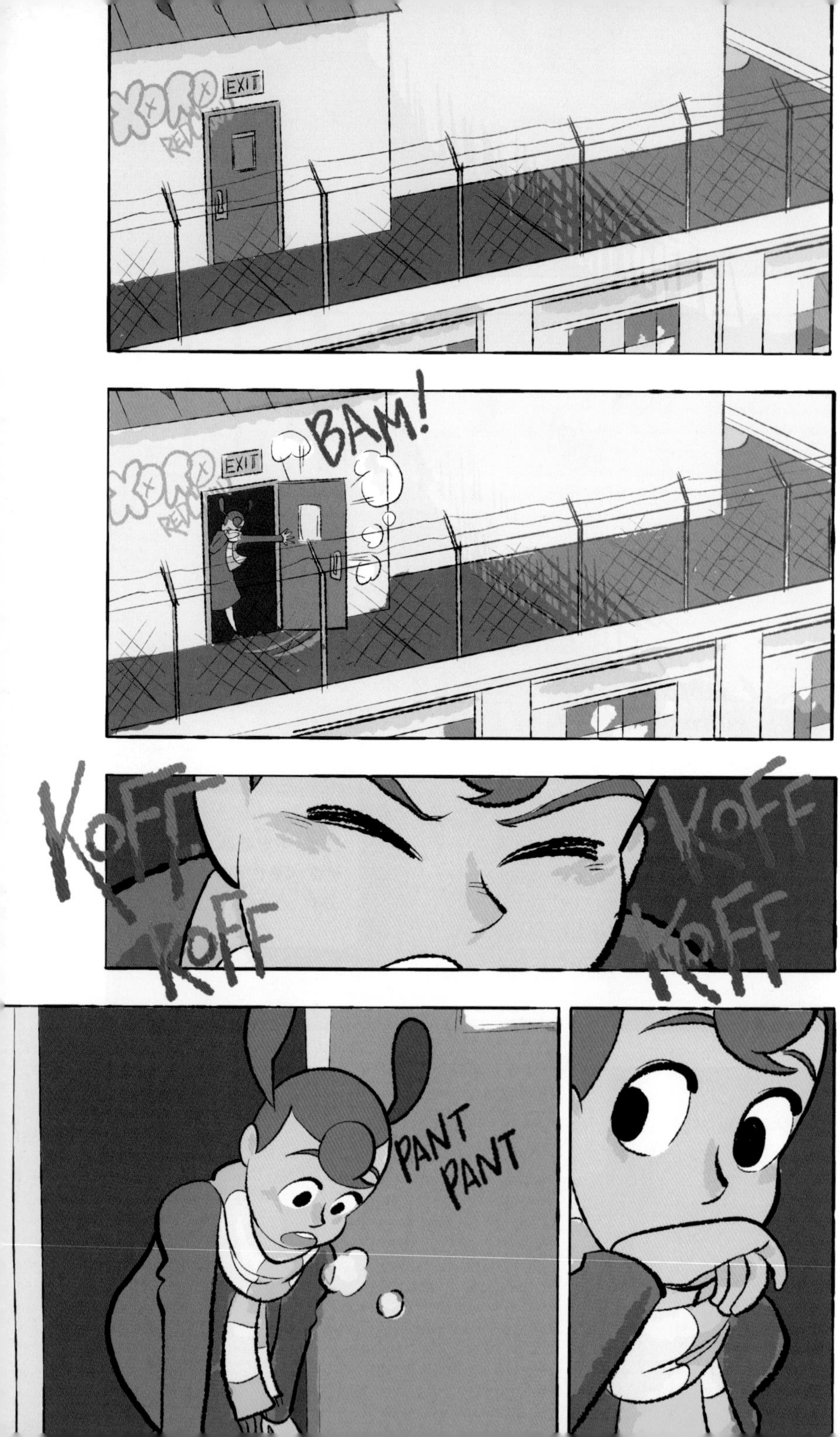
EXIT
EXIT
BAM!
KOFF
KOFF
KOFF
KOFF
PANT
PANT

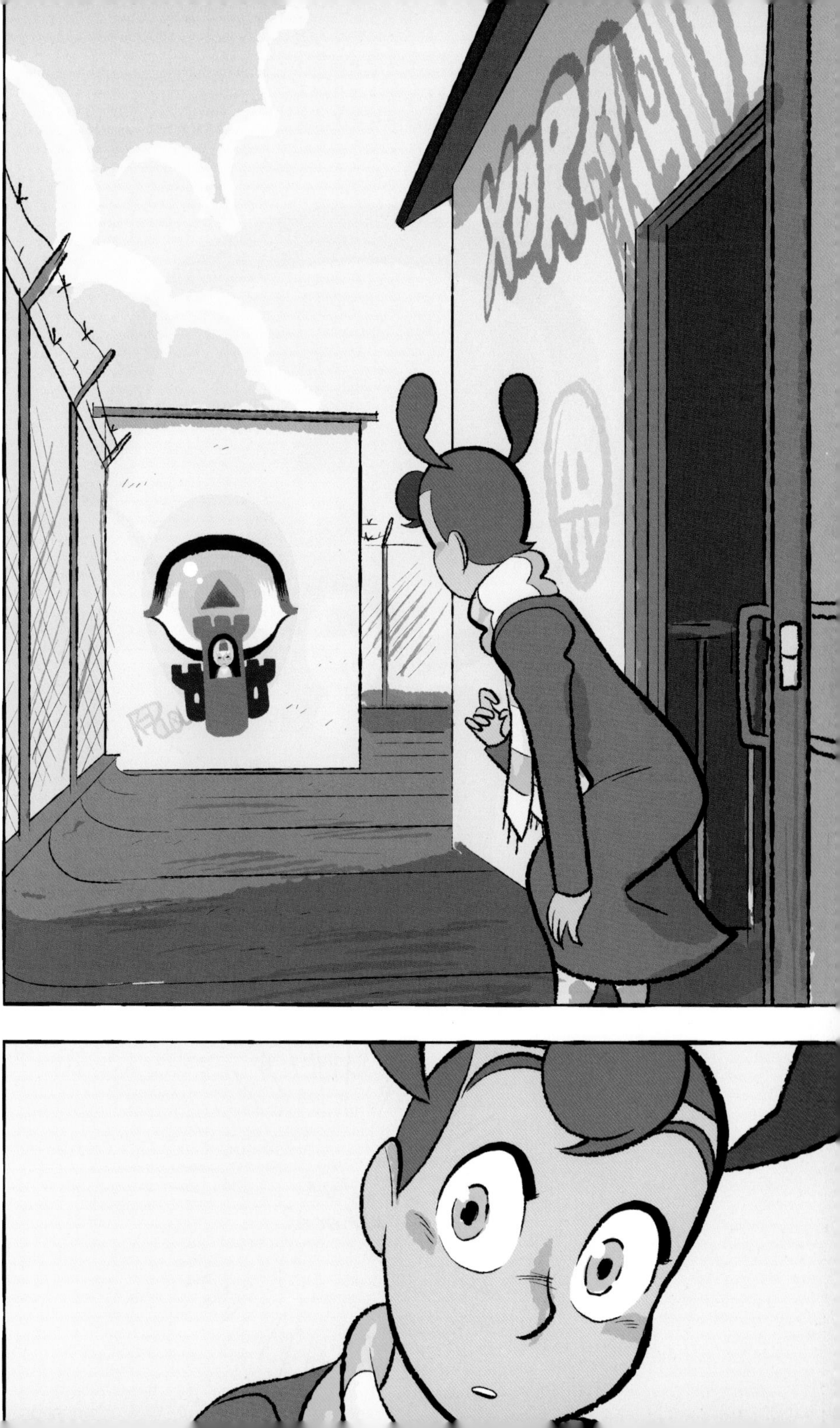

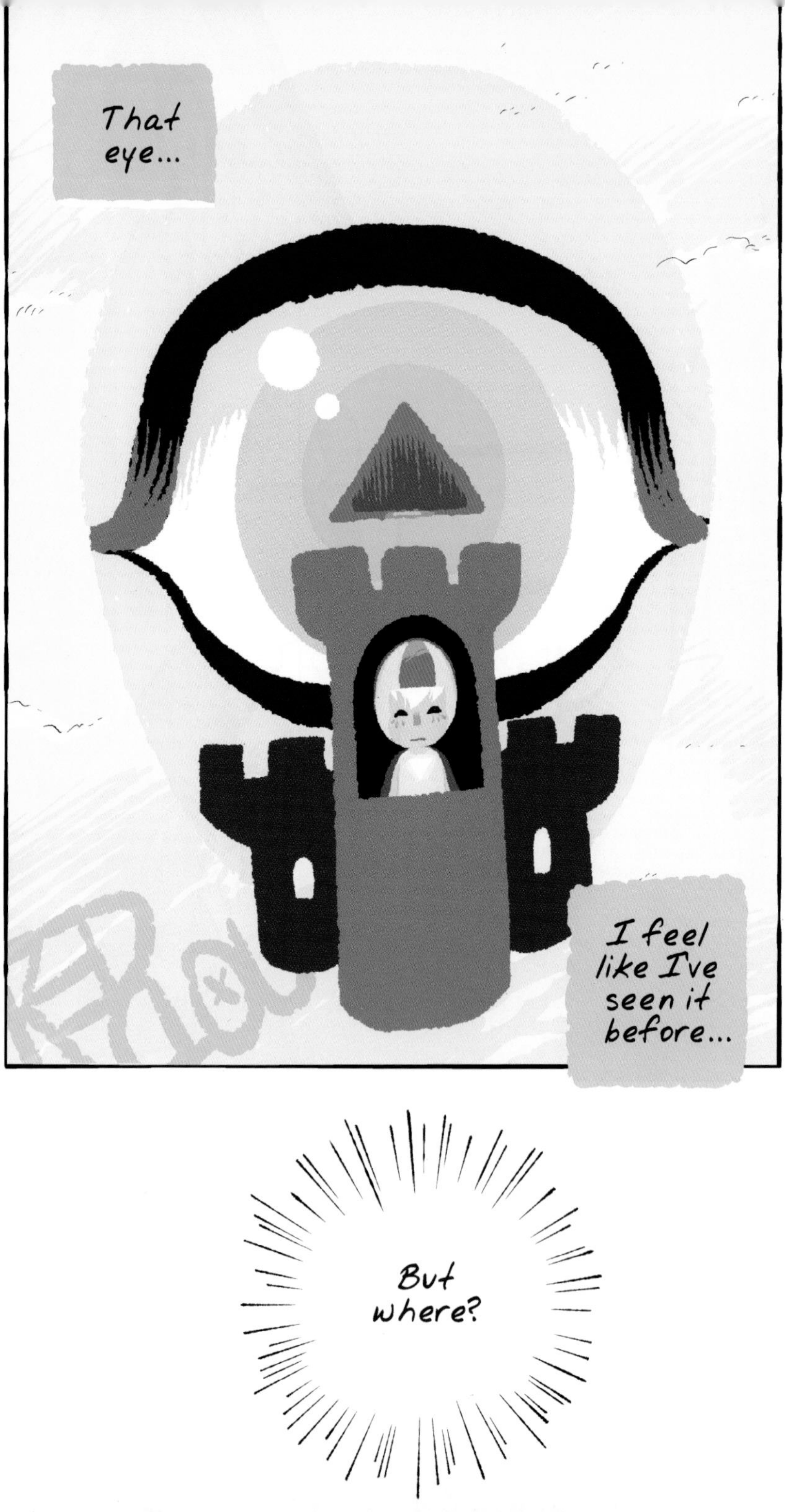
That eye...
I feel like Ive seen it before...
But where?

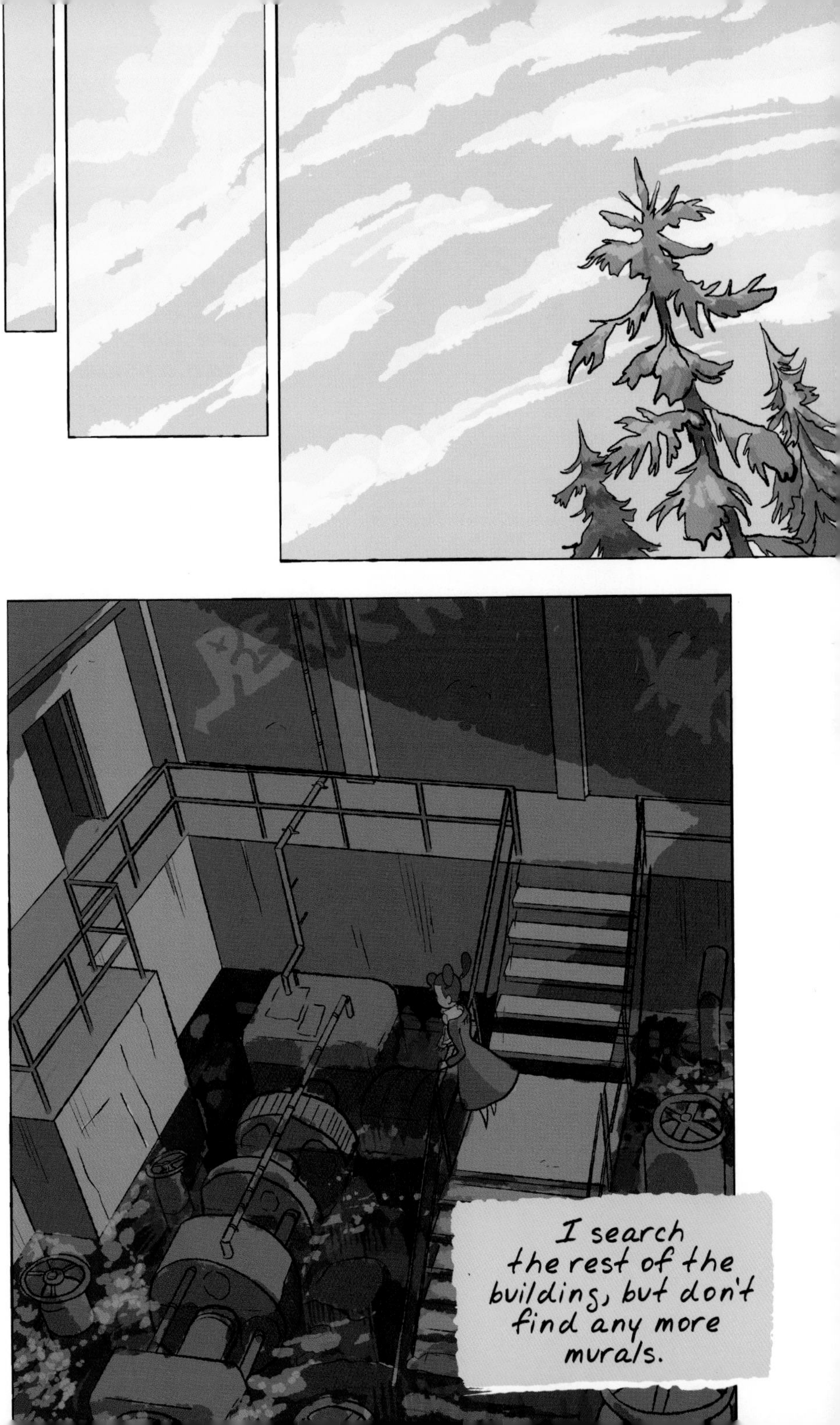
I search the rest of the buildings, but don't find any more murals.

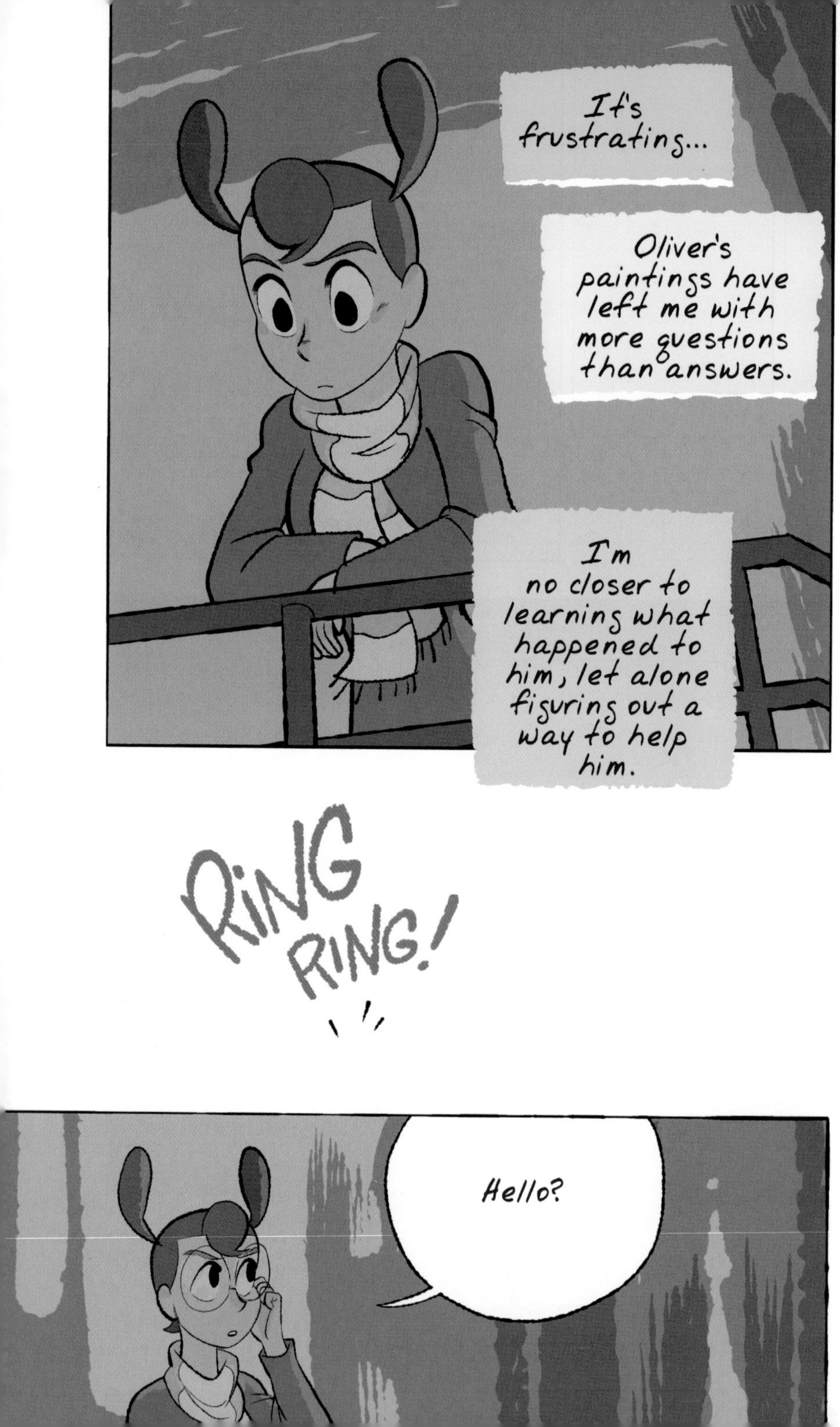
It's frustrating...
Oliver's paintings have left me with more questions than answers.
I'm no closer to learning what happened to him, let alone figuring out a way to help him.
RING RING!
Hello?

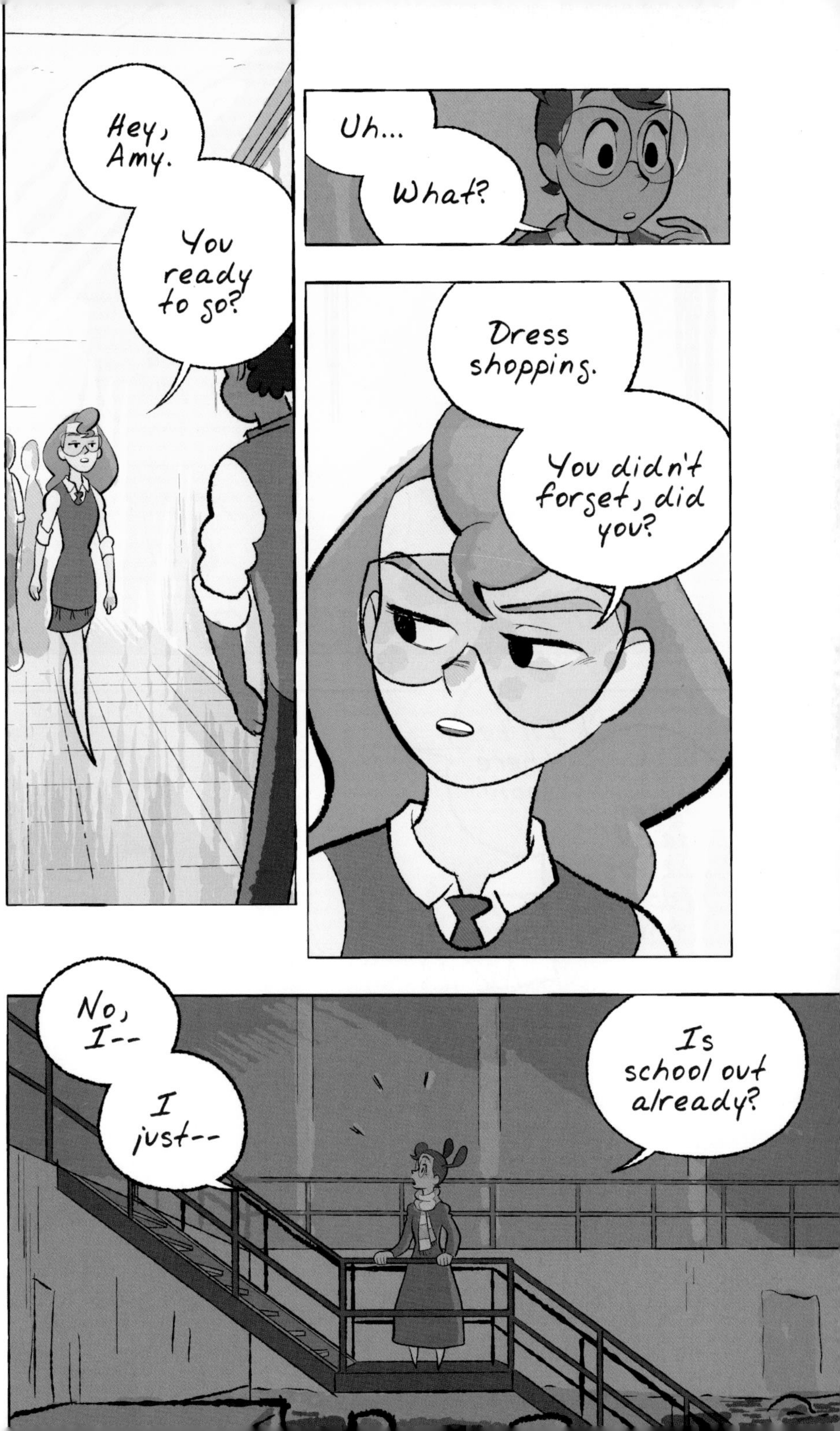
Hey, Amy.
You ready to go?
Uh...
What?
Dress shopping.
You didn't forget, did you?
No, I--
I just--
Is school out already?

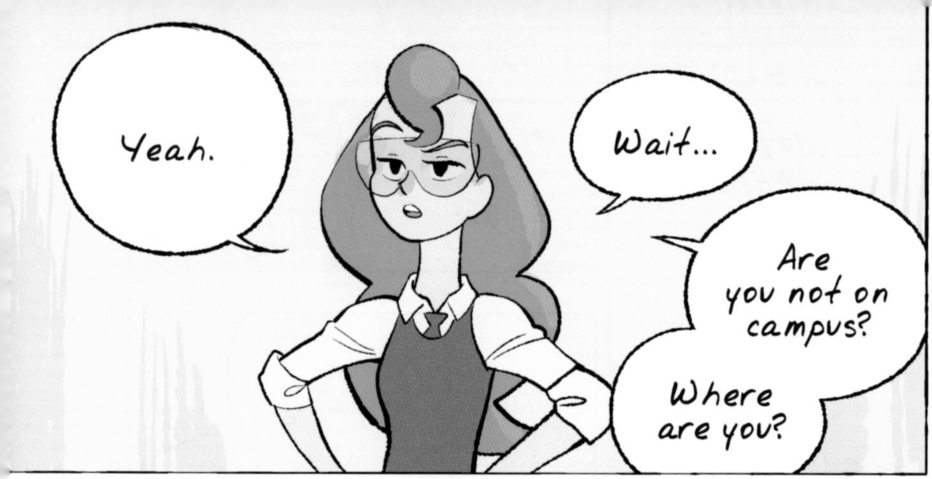
Yeah.
Wait...
Are you not on campus?
Where are you?

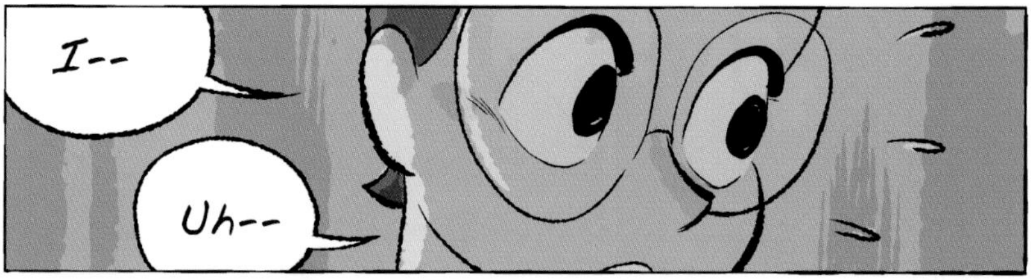
I--
Uh--

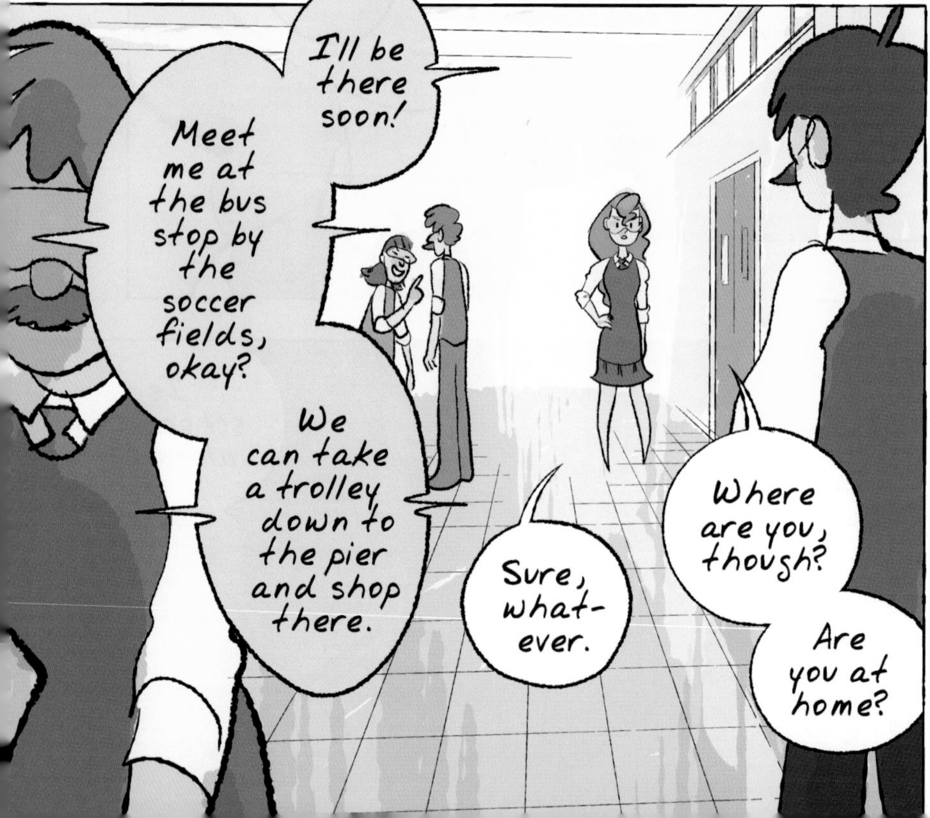
I'll be there soon!
Meet me at the bus stop by the soccer fields, okay?
We can take a trolley down to the pier and shop there.
Sure, what-ever.
Where are you, though?
Are you at home?

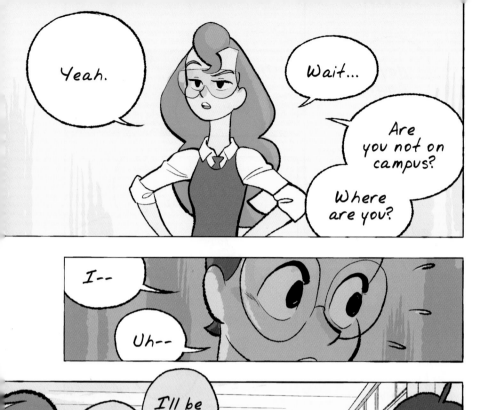

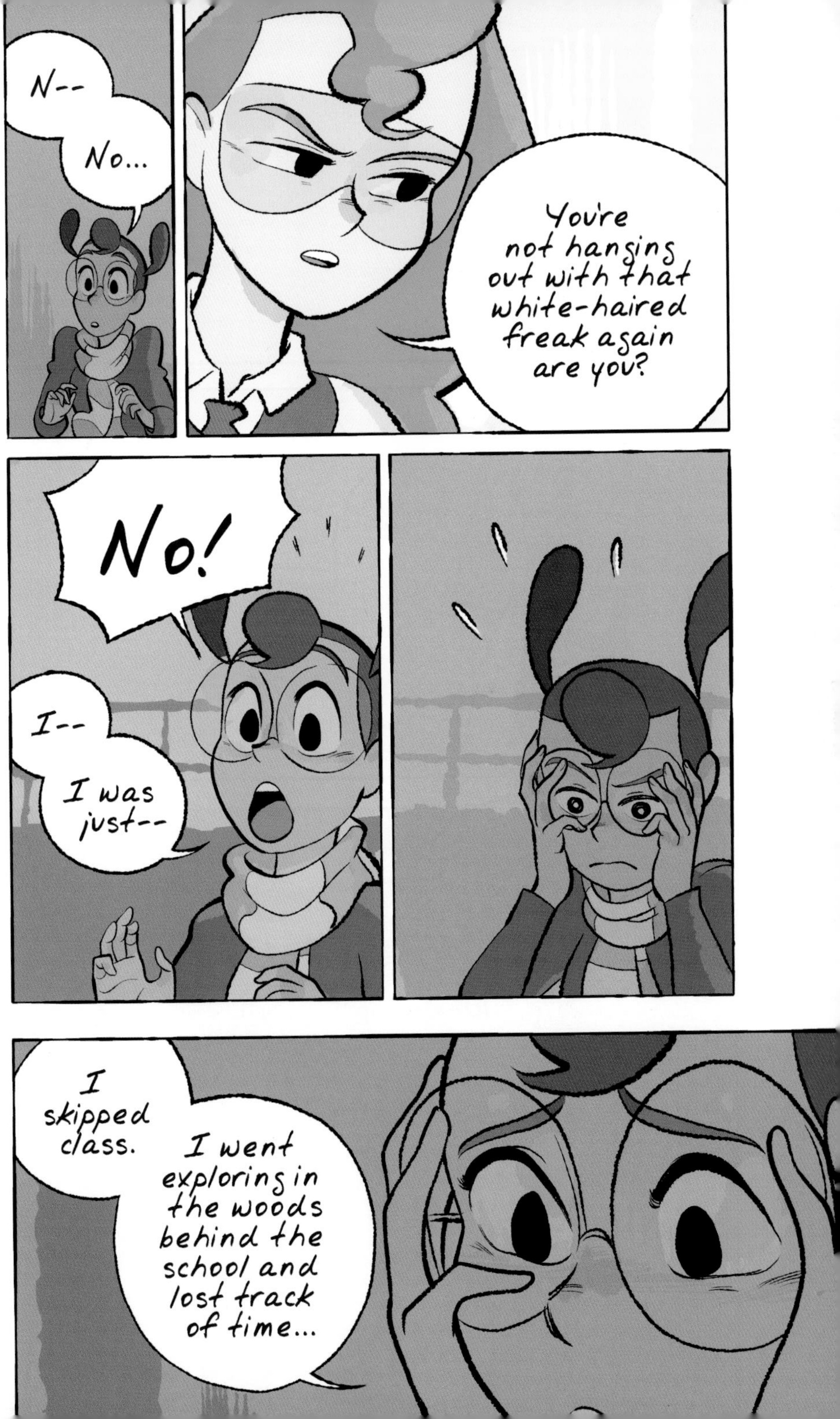
N--
No...
You're not hanging out with that white-haired freak again are you?
No!
I--
I was just--
I skipped class.
I went exploring in the woods behind the school and lost track of time...

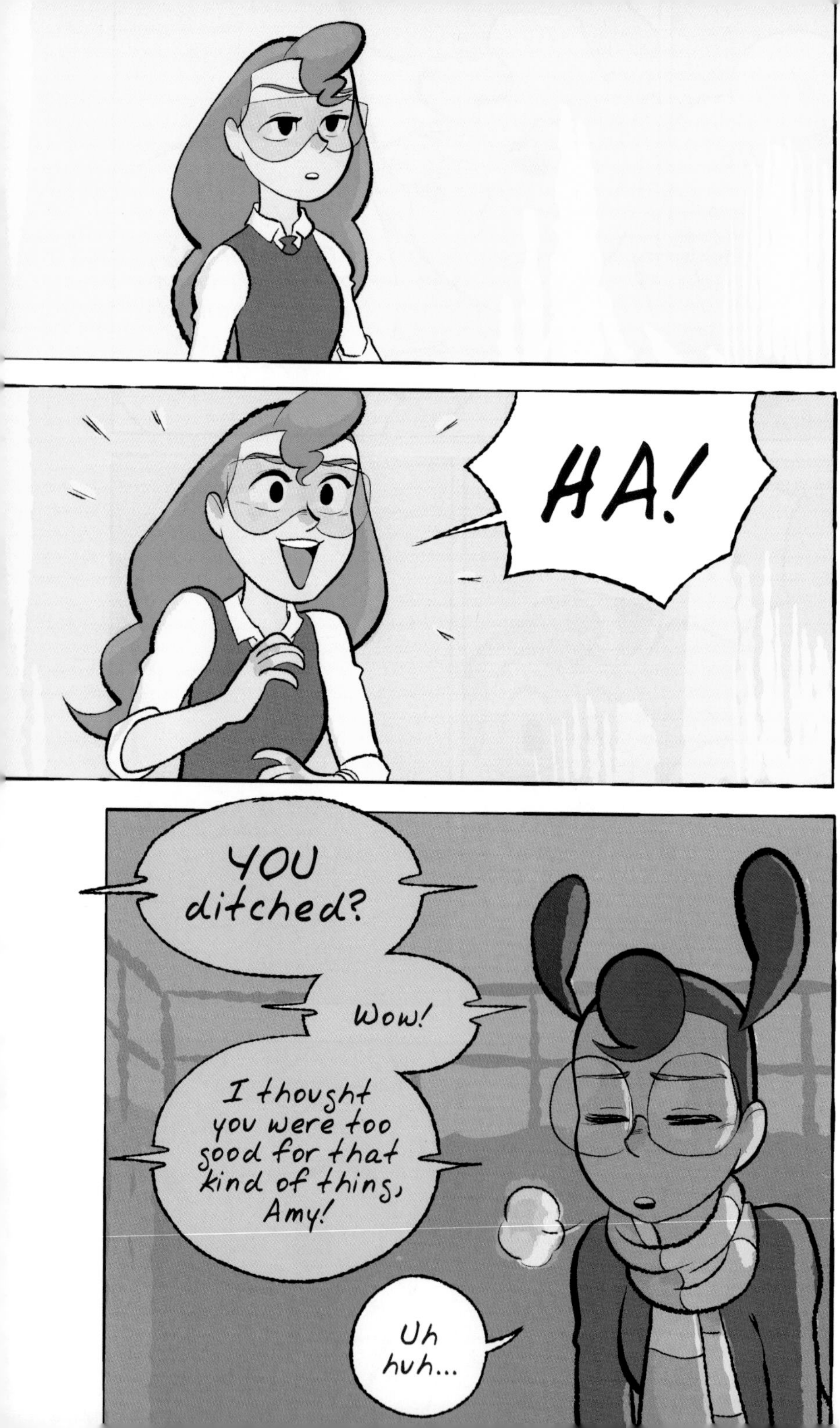
HA!
YOU ditched?
Wow!
I thought you were too good for that kind of things, Amy!
Uh huh...

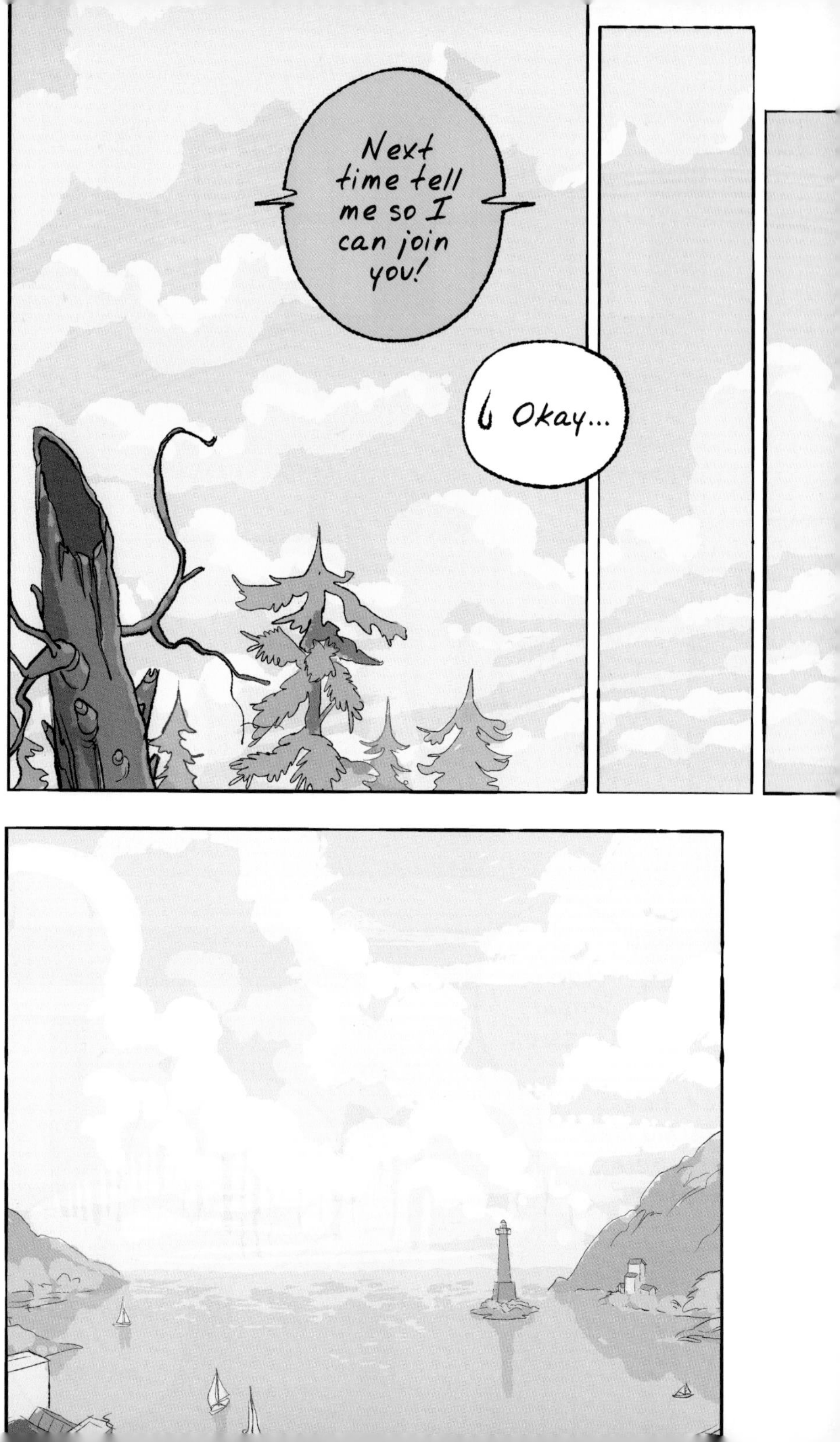
Next time tell me so I can join you!
Okay...

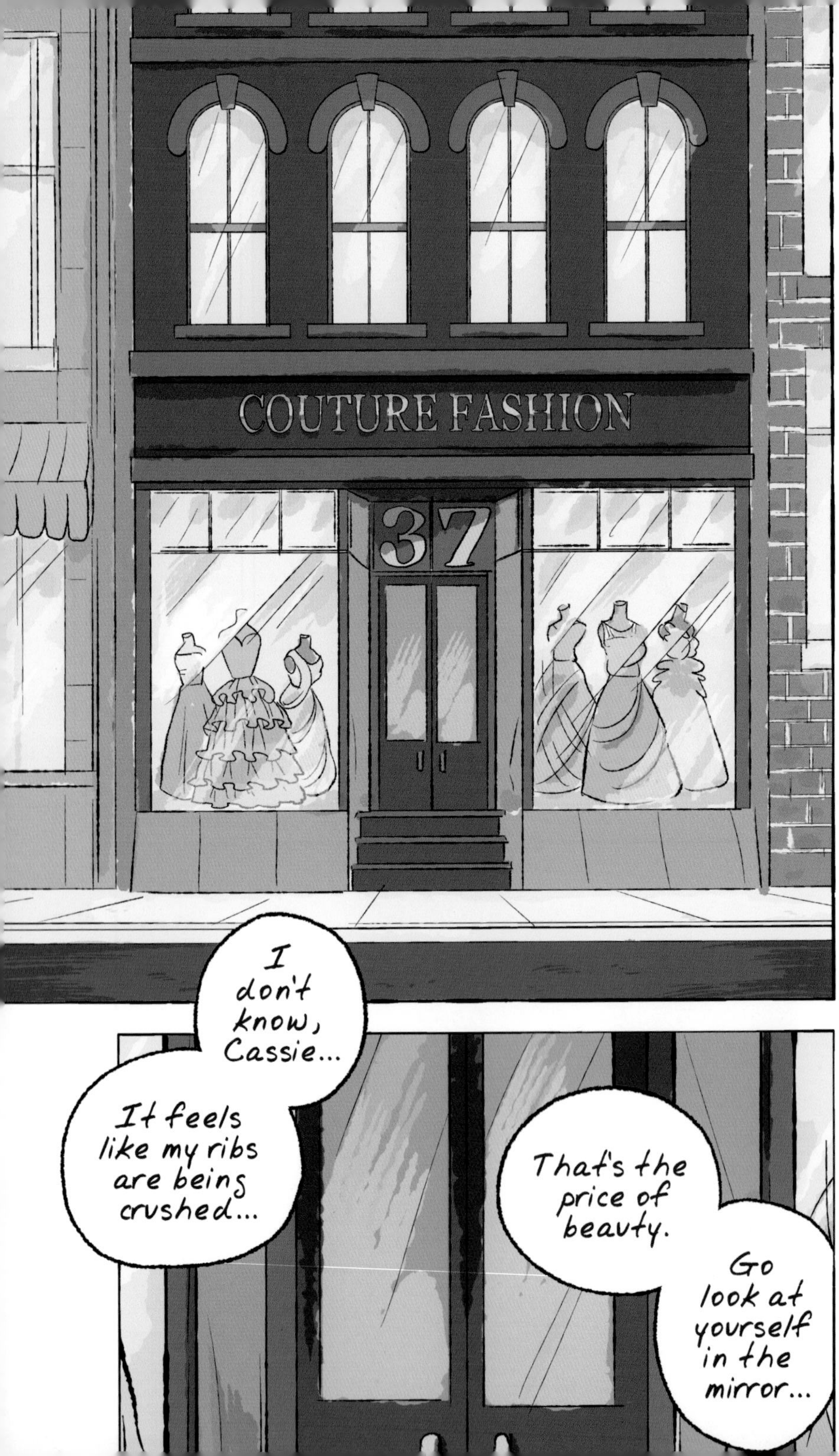
COUTURE FASHION
37
I don't know, Cassie...
It feels like my ribs are being crushed...
That's the price of beauty.
Go look at yourself in the mirror...

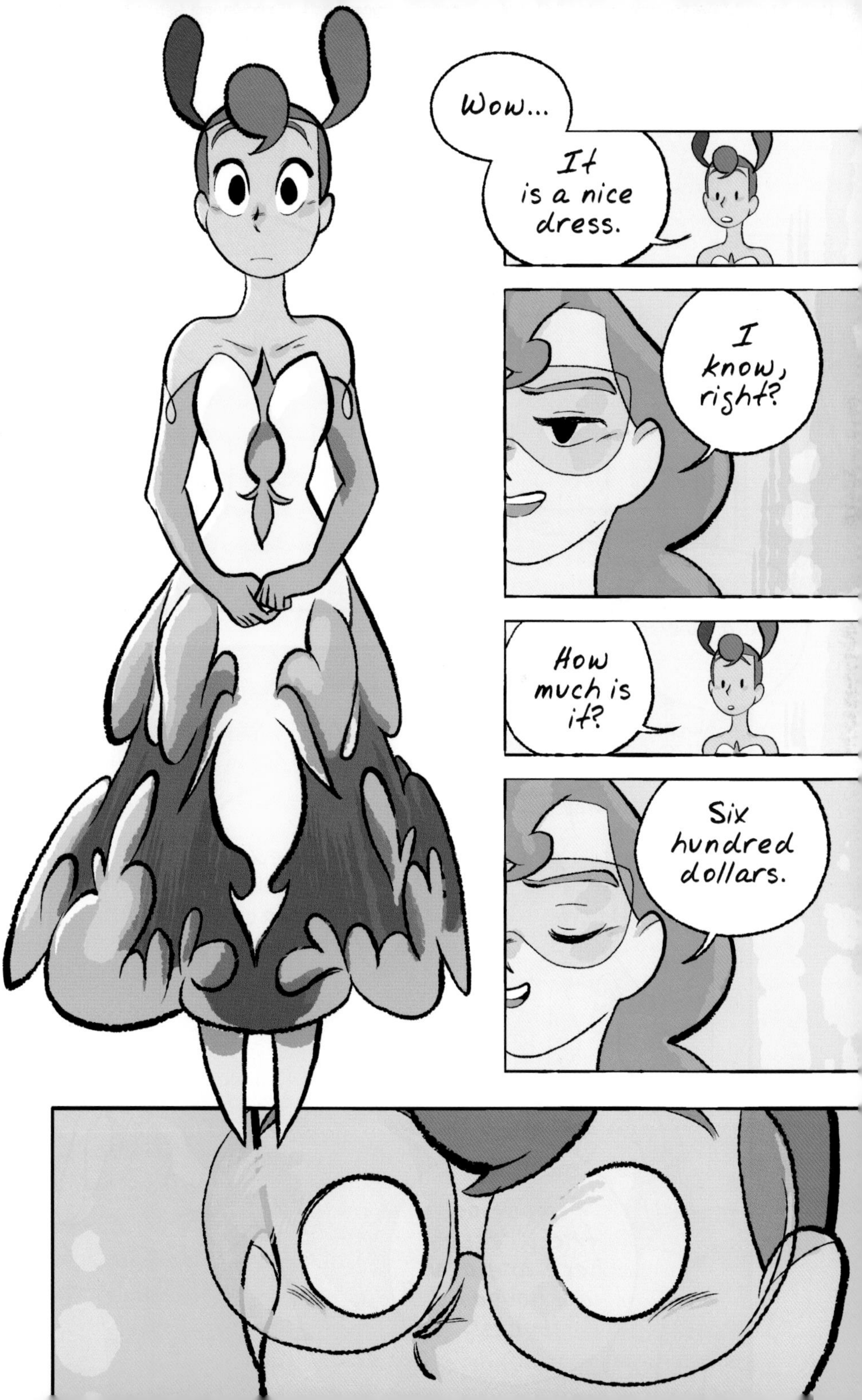
Wow...
It is a nice dress.
I know, right?
How much is it?
Six hundred dollars.

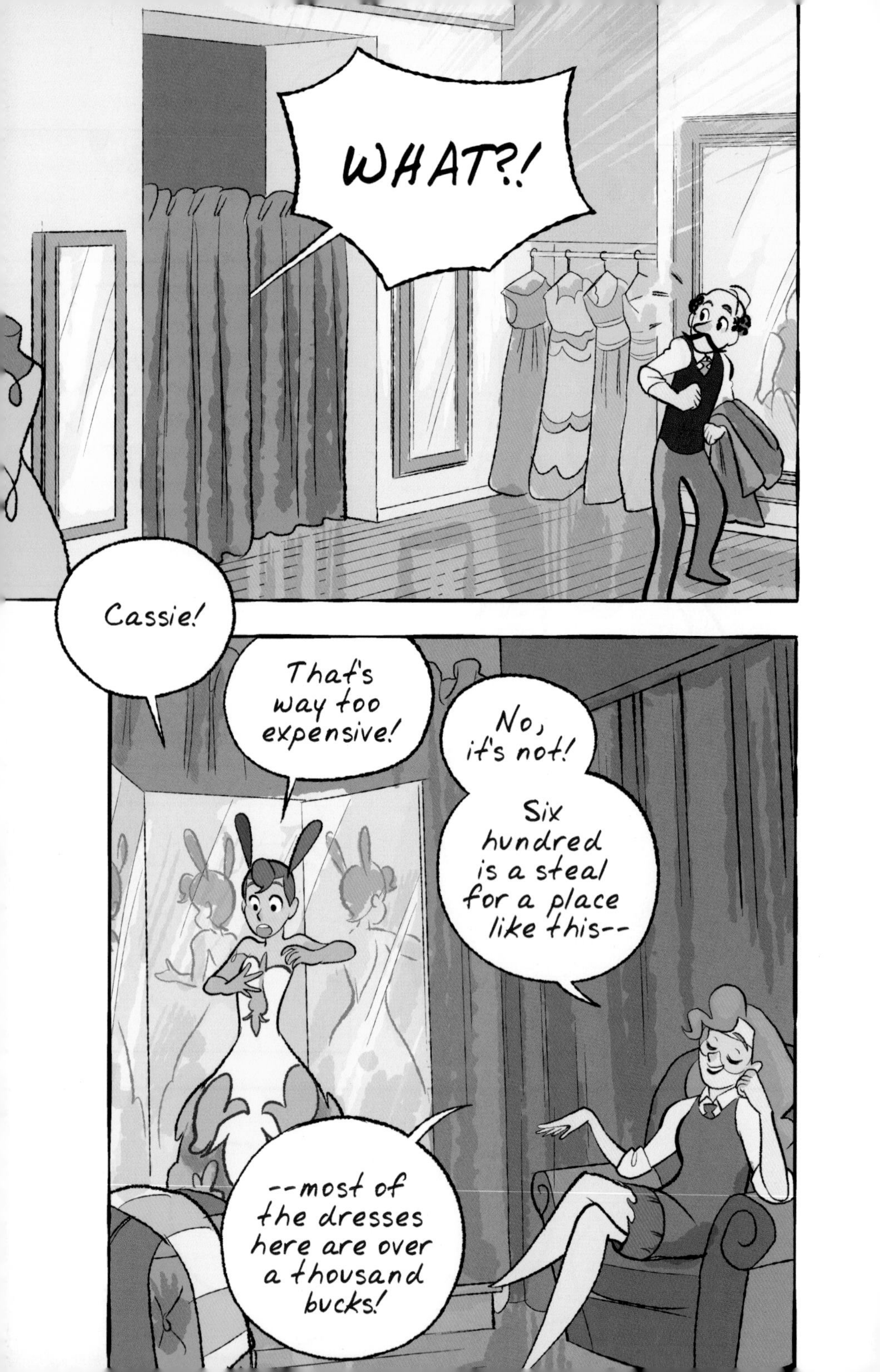
WHAT?!
Cassie!
That's way too expensive!
No, it's not!
Six hundred is a steal for a place like this--
--most of the dresses here are over a thousand bucks!

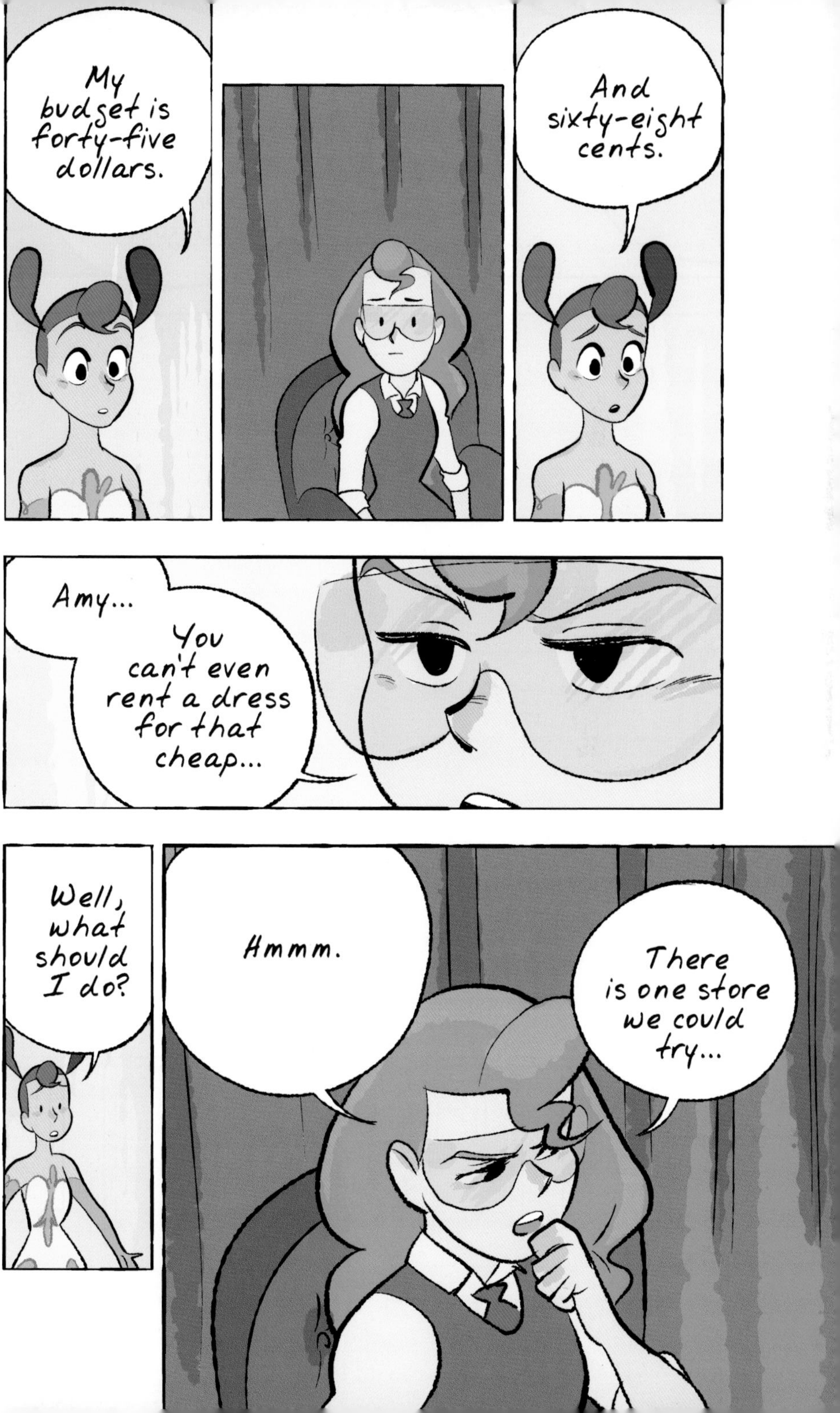
My budget is forty-five dollars.
And sixty-eight cents.
Amy...
You can't even rent a dress for that cheap...
Well, what should I do?
Hmmm.
There is one store we could try...

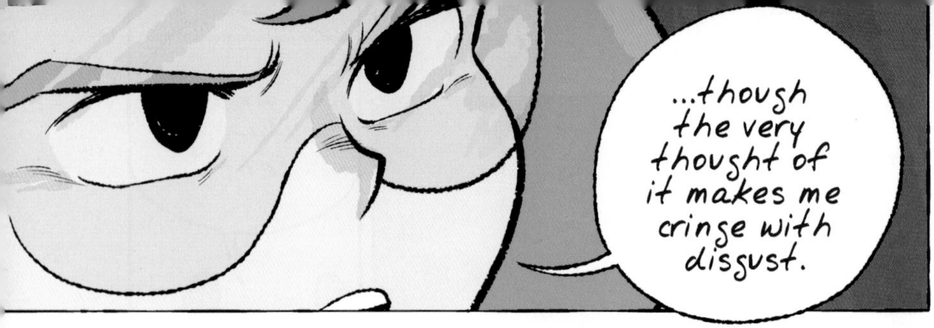
...though the very thought of it makes me cringe with disgust.

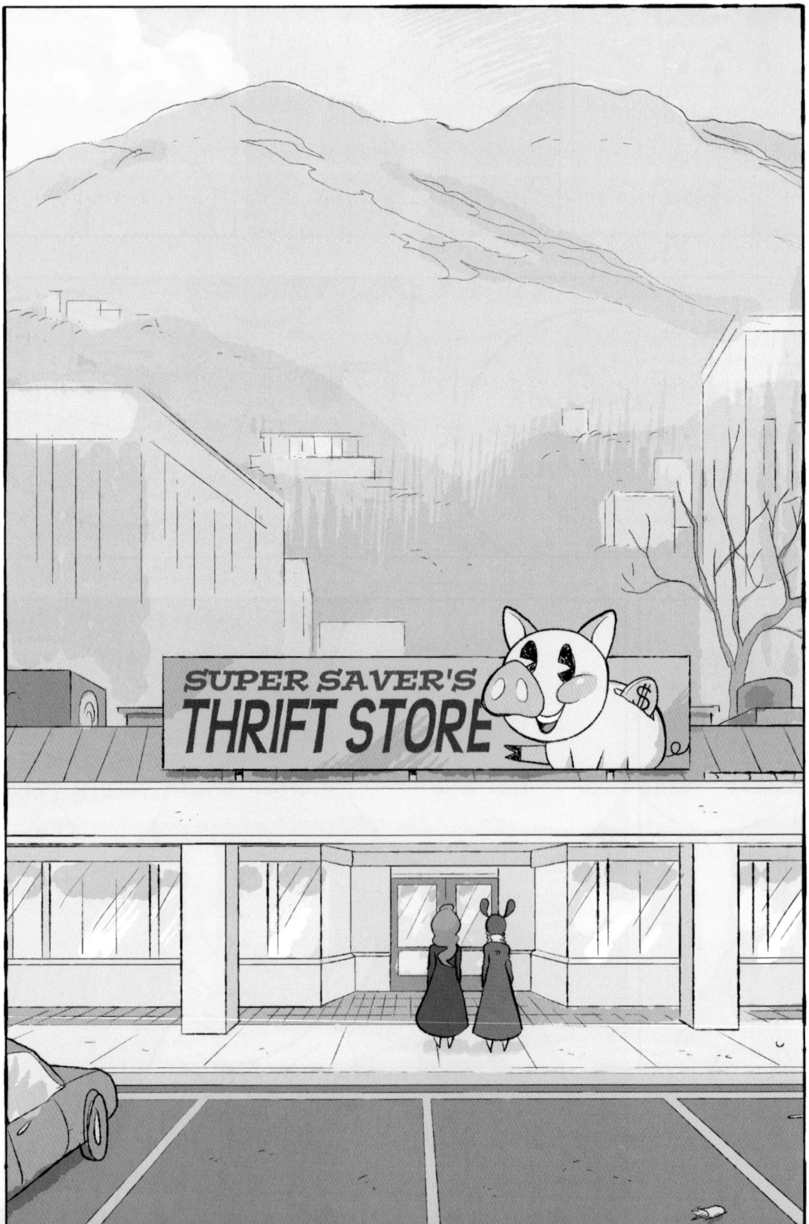
SUPER SAVER'S
THRIFT STORE

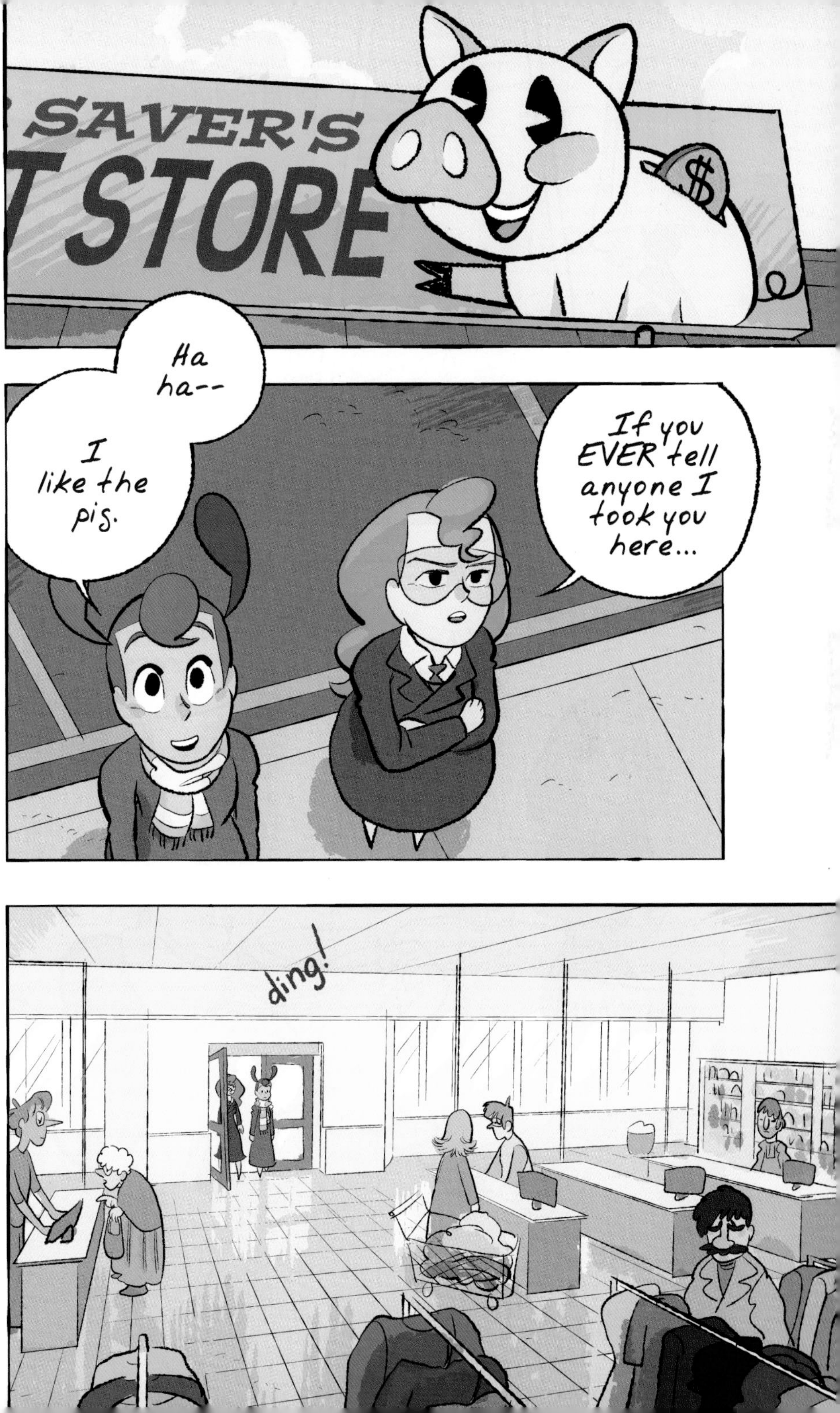
SAVER'S
T STORE
$
Ha ha--
I like the pig.
If you EVER tell anyone I took you here...
ding!

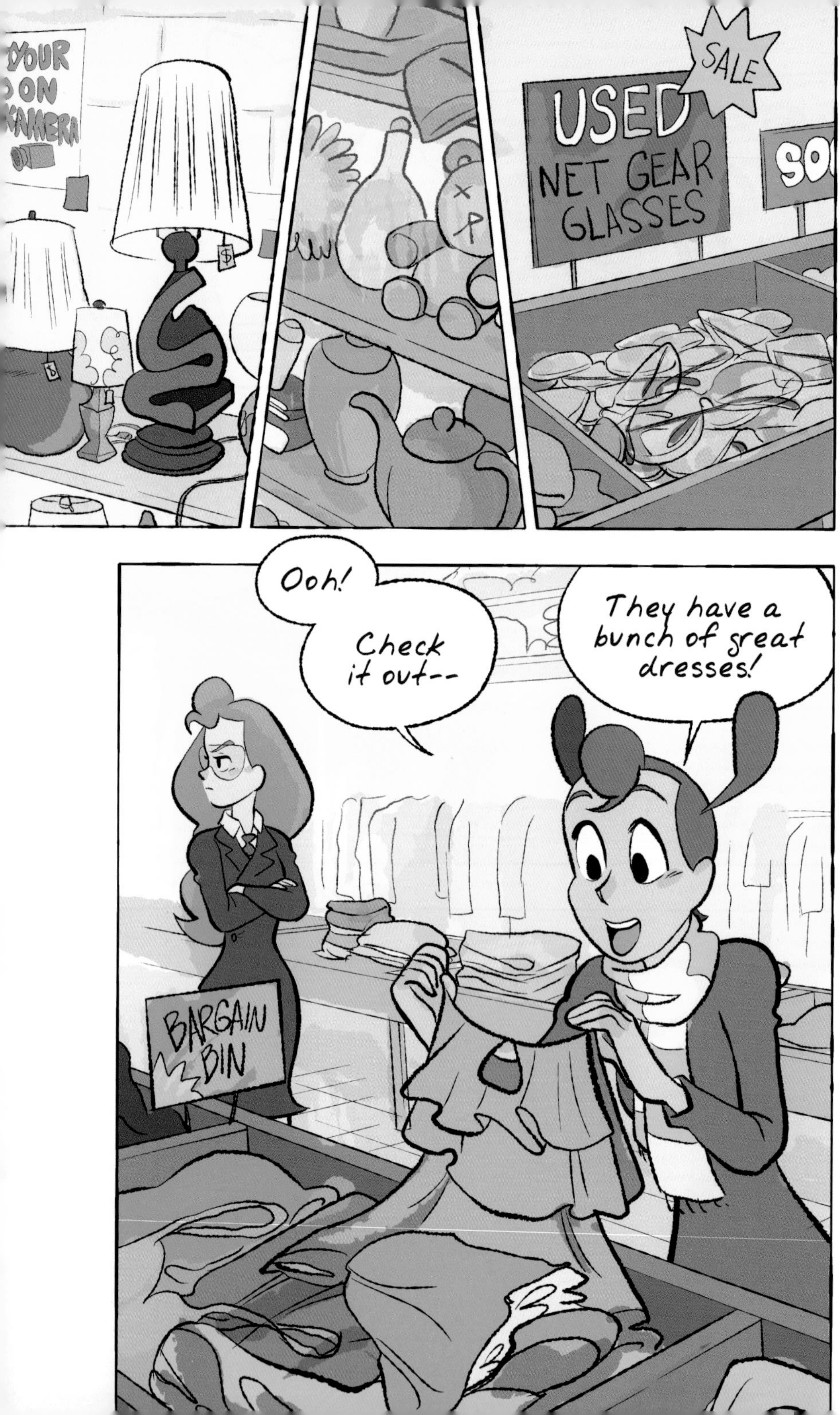

YOUR
ON
KAMERA
USED NET GEAR GLASSES
SALE
Ooh!
Check it out--
They have a bunch of great dresses!
BARGAIN BIN

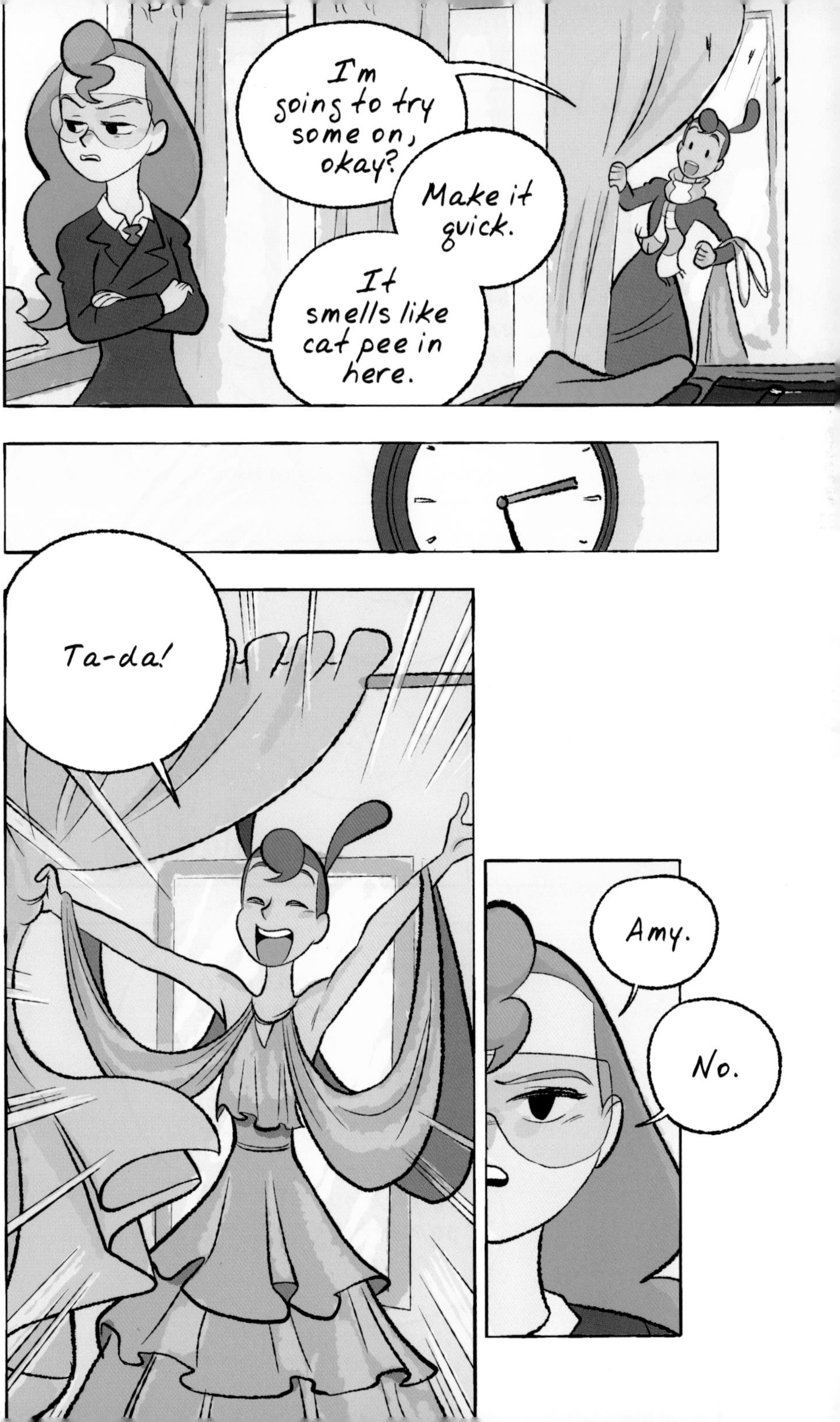
I'm going to try some on, okay?
Make it quick.
It smells like cat pee in here.
Ta-da!
Amy.
No.

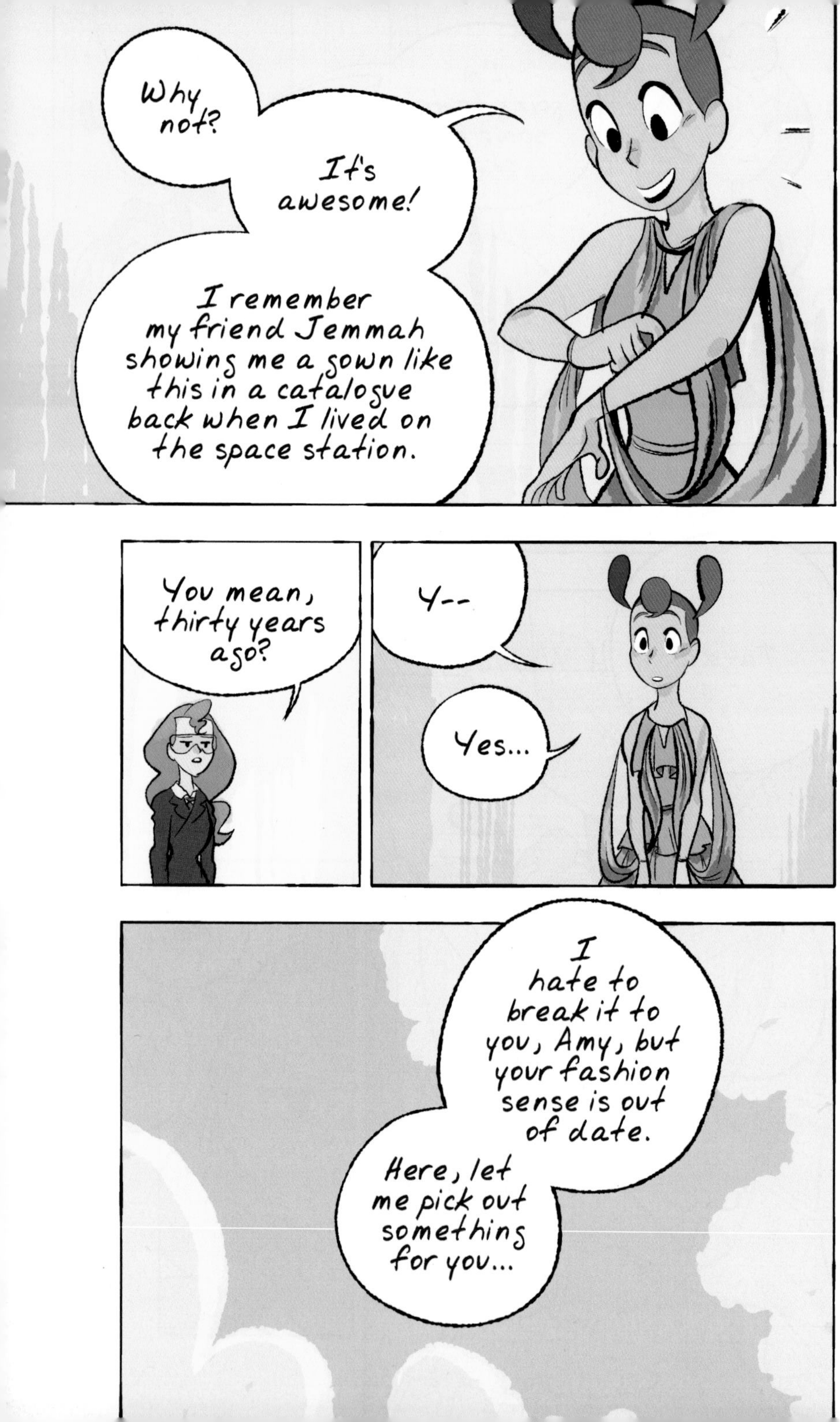
Why not?
It's awesome!
I remember my friend Jemmah showing me a gown like this in a catalogue back when I lived on the space station.
You mean, thirty years ago?
Y--
Yes...
I hate to break it to you, Amy, but your fashion sense is out of date.
Here, let me pick out something for you...

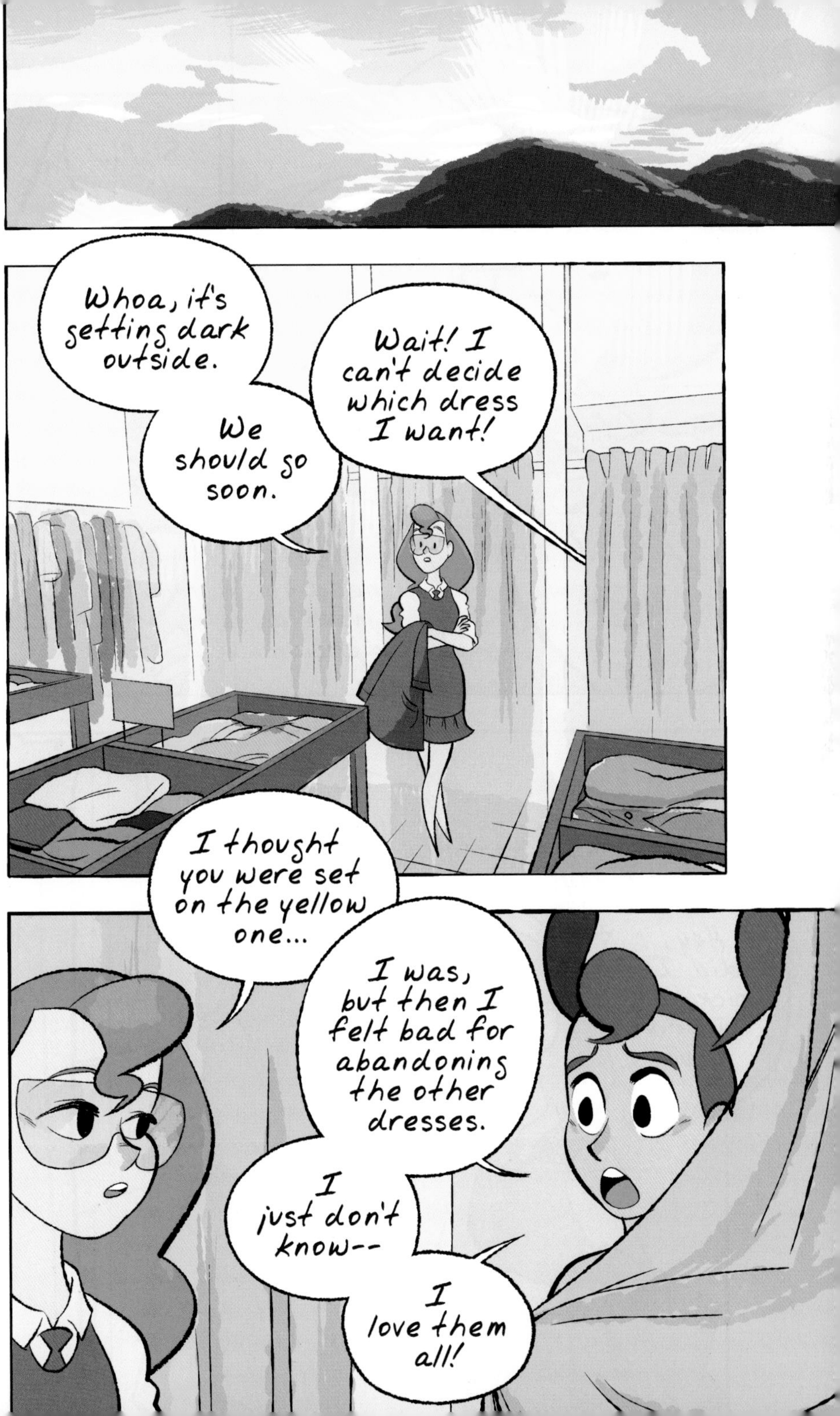
Whoa, it's getting dark outside.
We should go soon.
Wait! I can't decide which dress I want!
I thought you were set on the yellow one...
I was, but then I felt bad for abandoning the other dresses.
I just don't know--
I love them all!

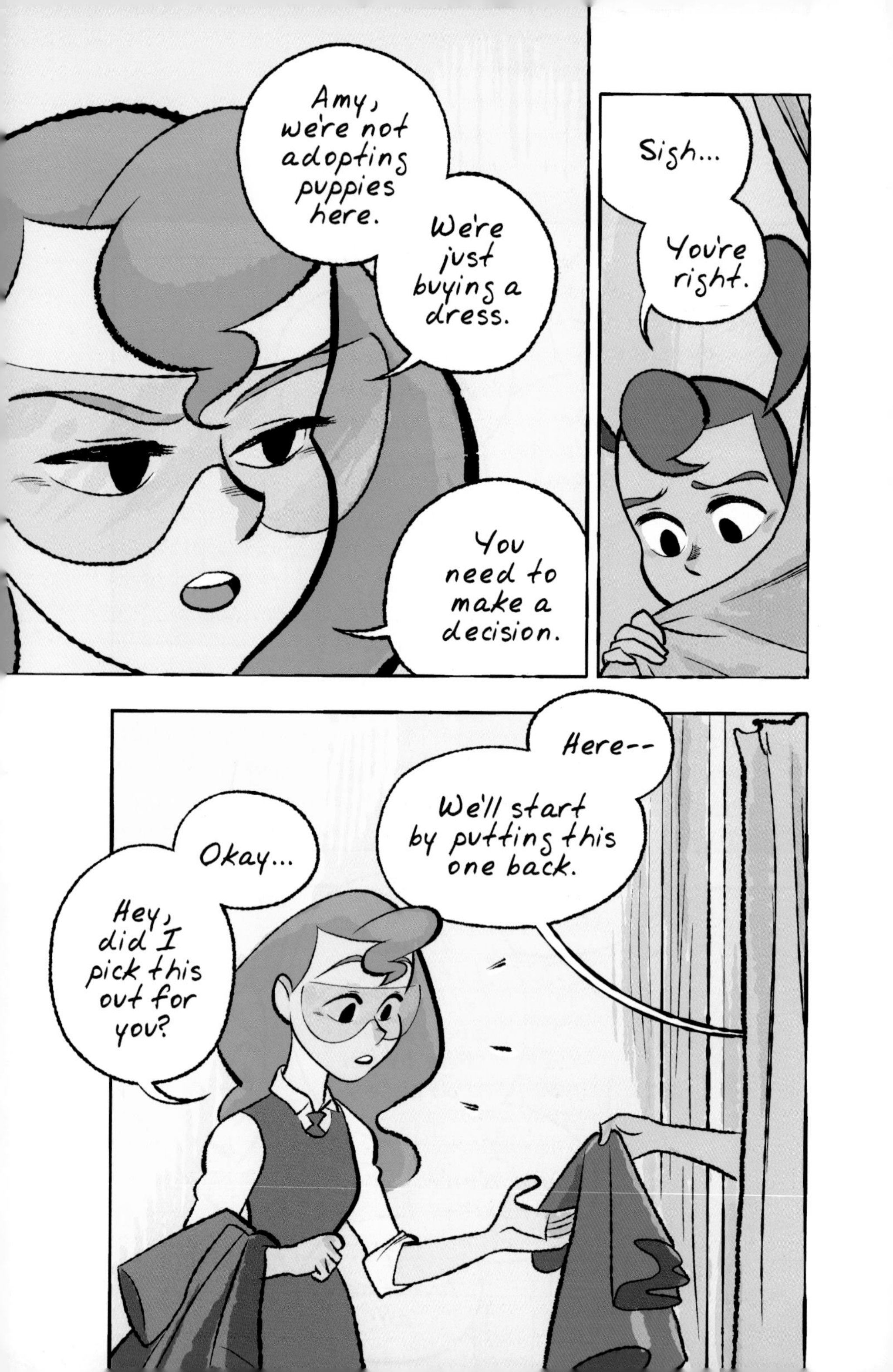
Amy, we're not adopting puppies here.
We're just buying a dress.
You need to make a decision.
Sigh...
You're right.
Here--
We'll start by putting this one back.
Okay...
Hey, did I pick this out for you?

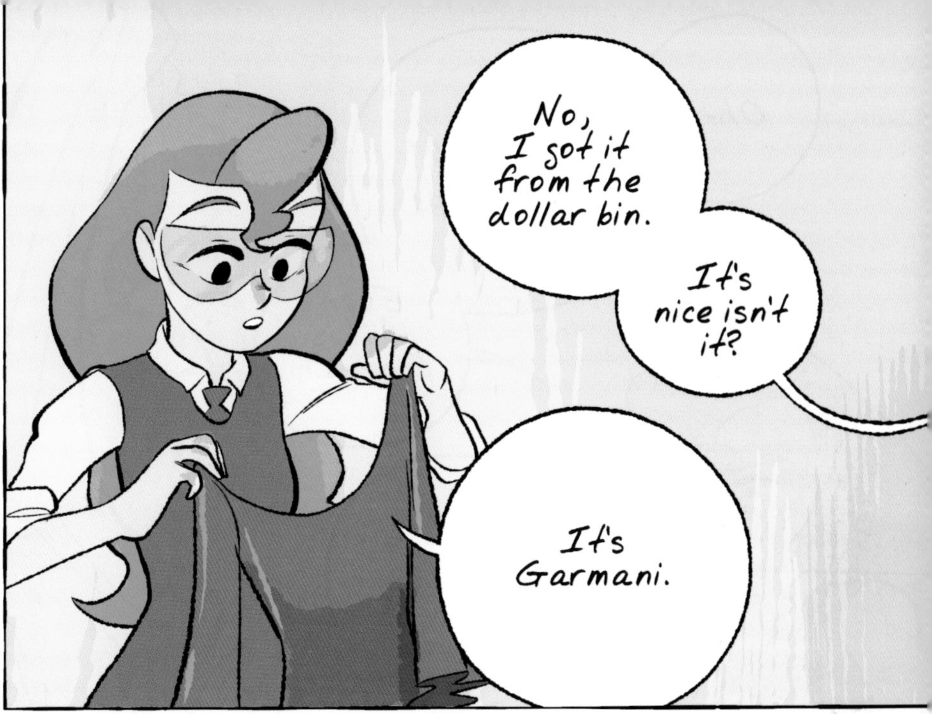
No, I got it from the dollar bin.
It's nice isn't it?
It's Garmani.
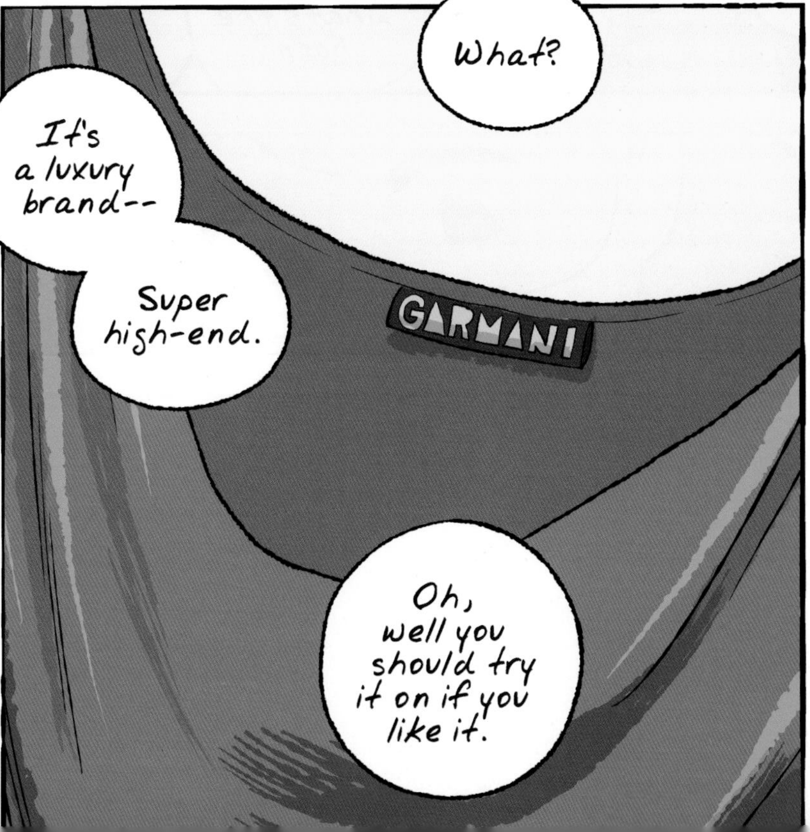
What?
It's a luxury brand--
Super high-end.
GARMANI
Oh, well you should try it on if you like it.

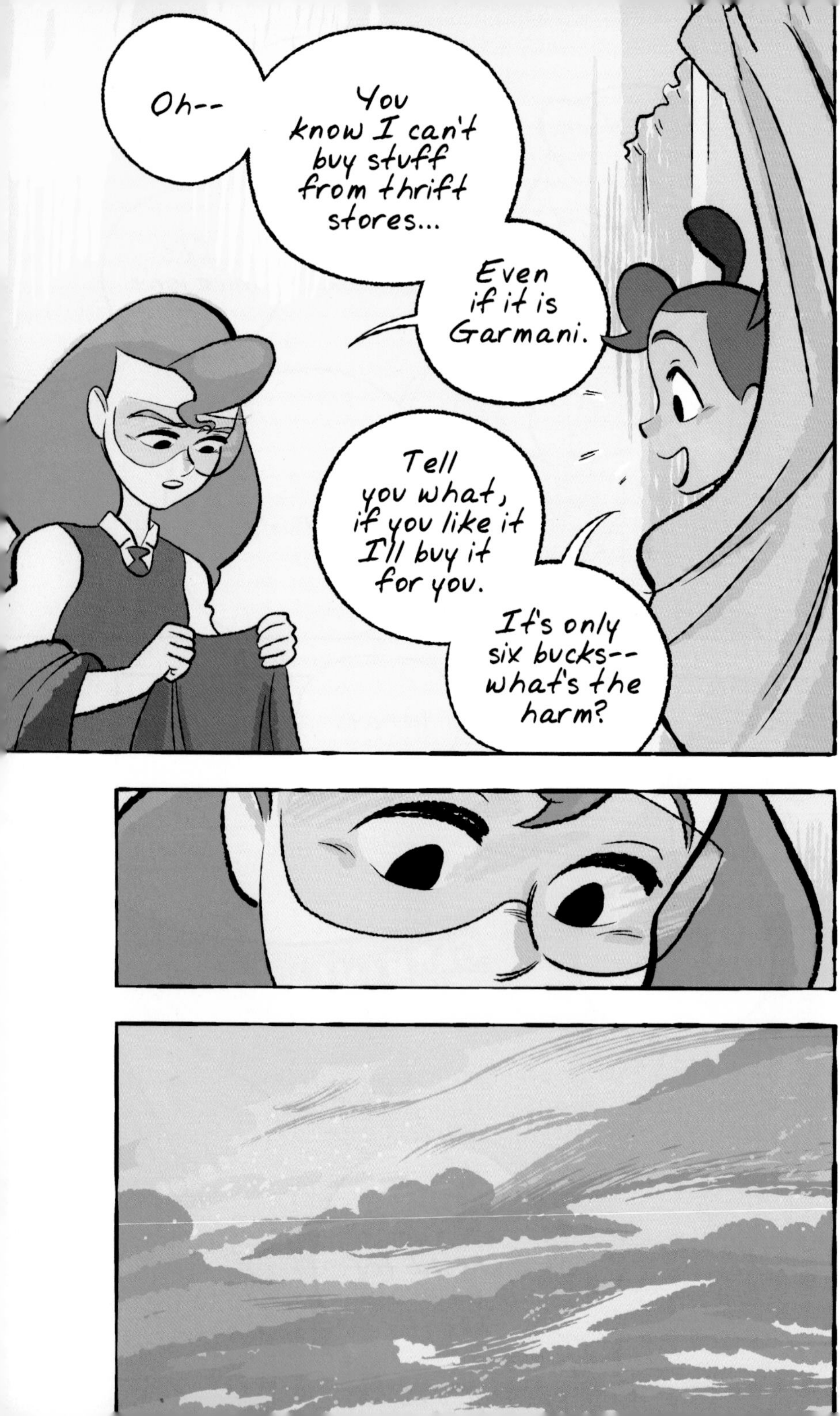
Oh--
You know I can't buy stuff from thrift stores...
Even if it is Garmani.
Tell you what, if you like it I'll buy it for you.
It's only six bucks-- what's the harm?

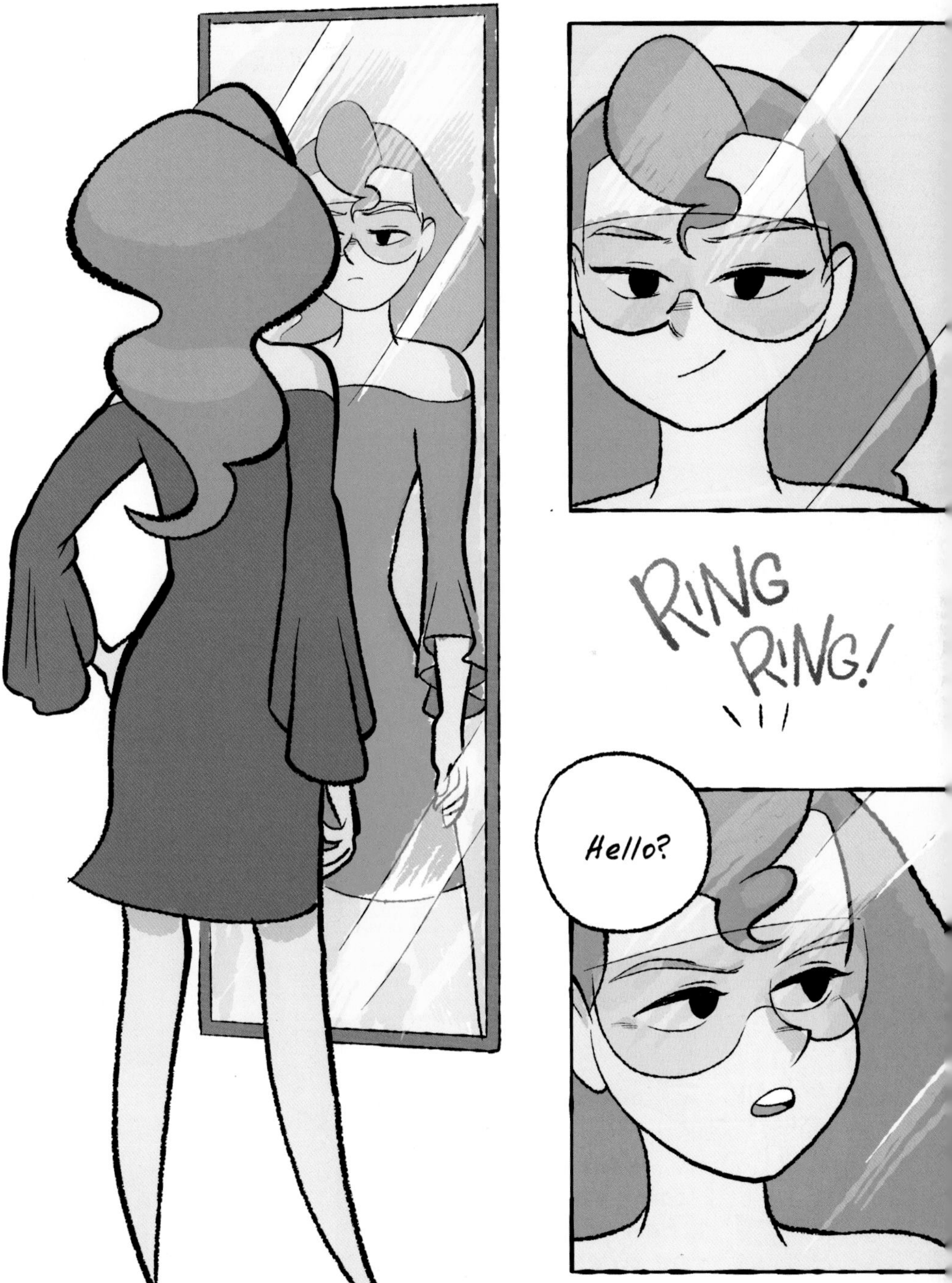
RING RING!
Hello?

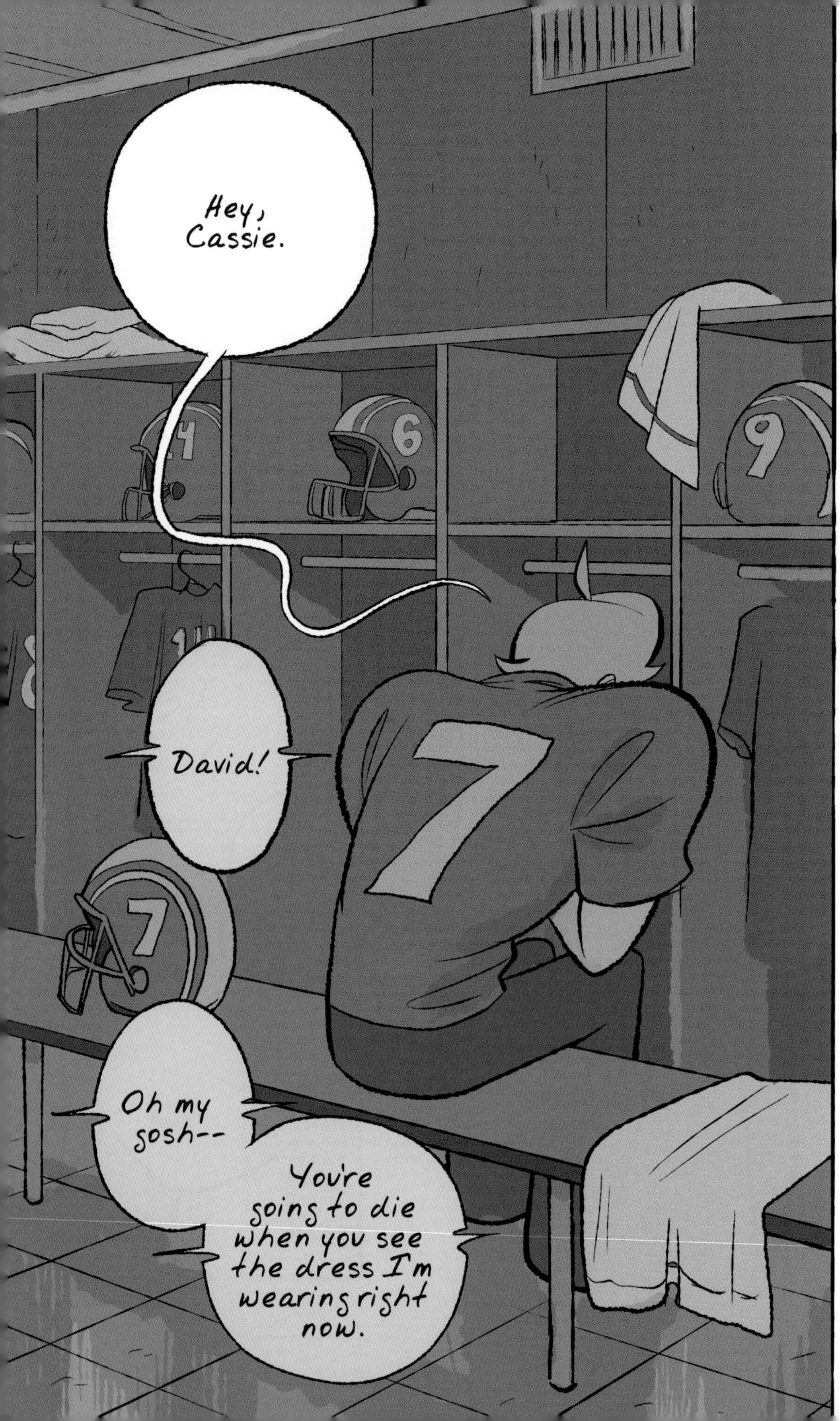
Hey, Cassie.
David!
Oh my gosh--
You're going to die when you see the dress I'm wearing right now.

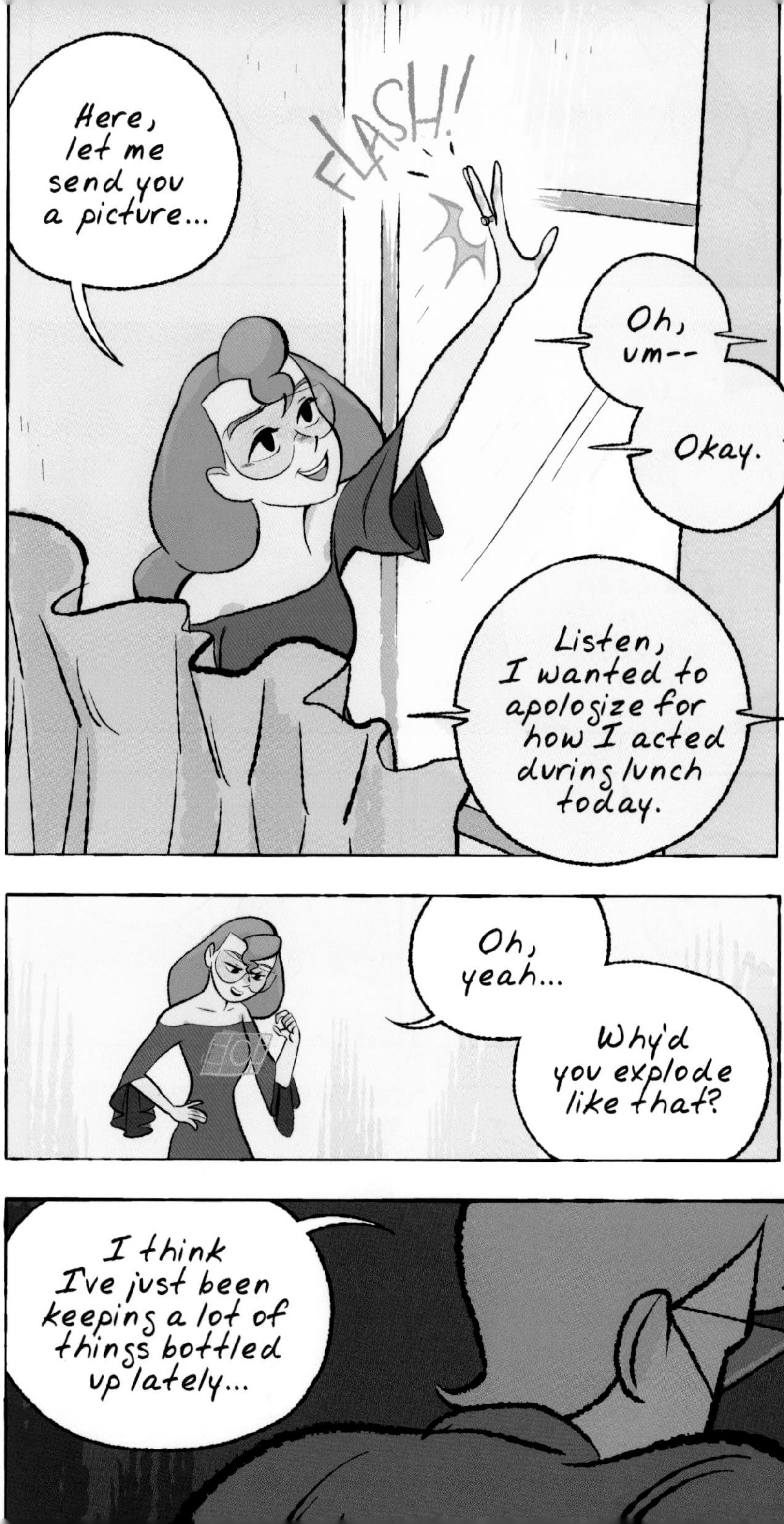
Here, let me send you a picture...
FLASH!
Oh, um--
Okay.
Listen, I wanted to apologize for how I acted durins lunch today.
Oh, yeah...
Why'd you explode like that?
I think I've just been keepins a lot of thinss bottled up lately...

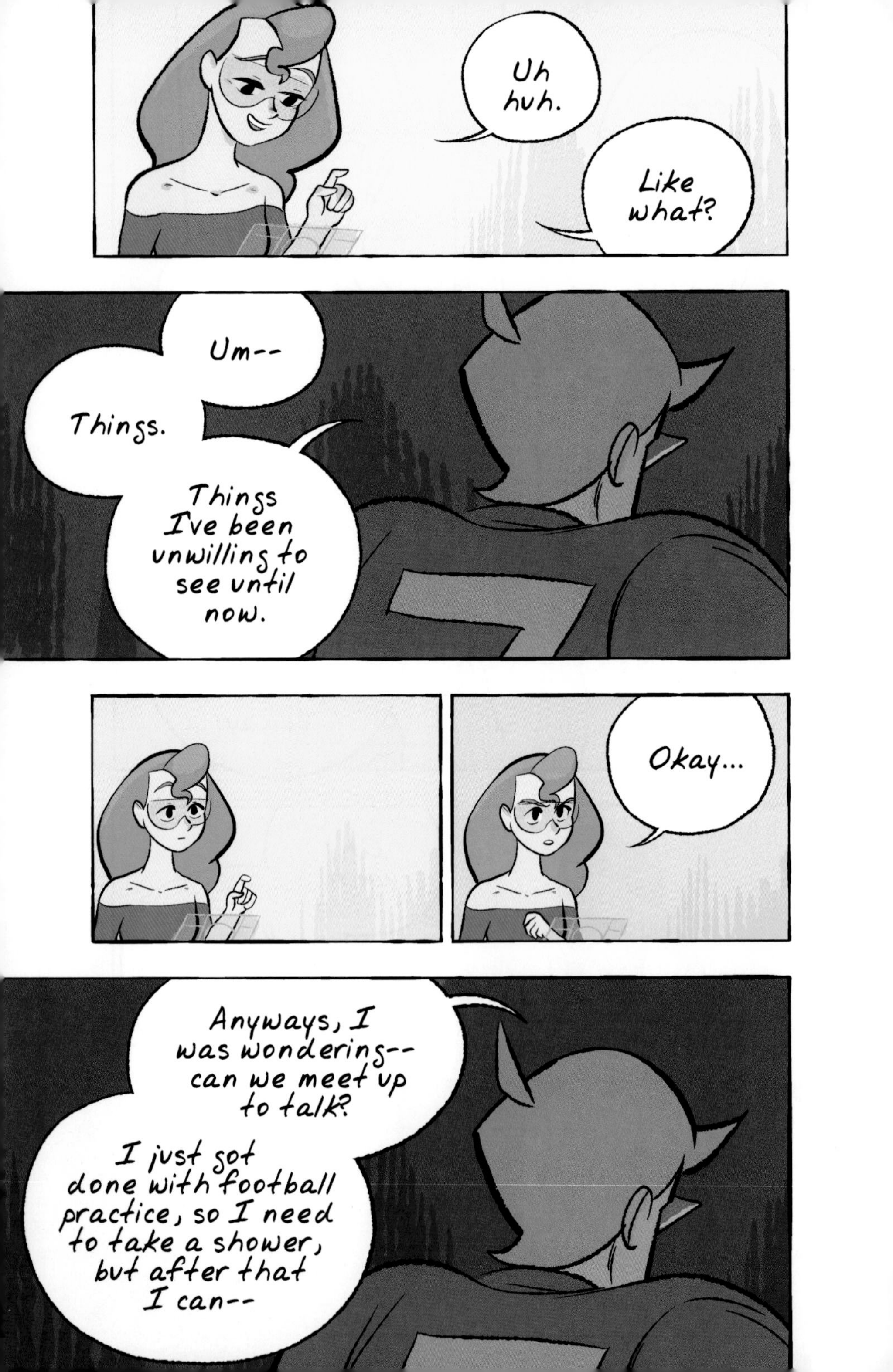
Uh huh.
Like what?
Um--
Things.
Things I've been unwilling to see until now.
Okay...
Anyways, I was wondering-- can we meet up to talk?
I just got done with football practice, so I need to take a shower, but after that I can--

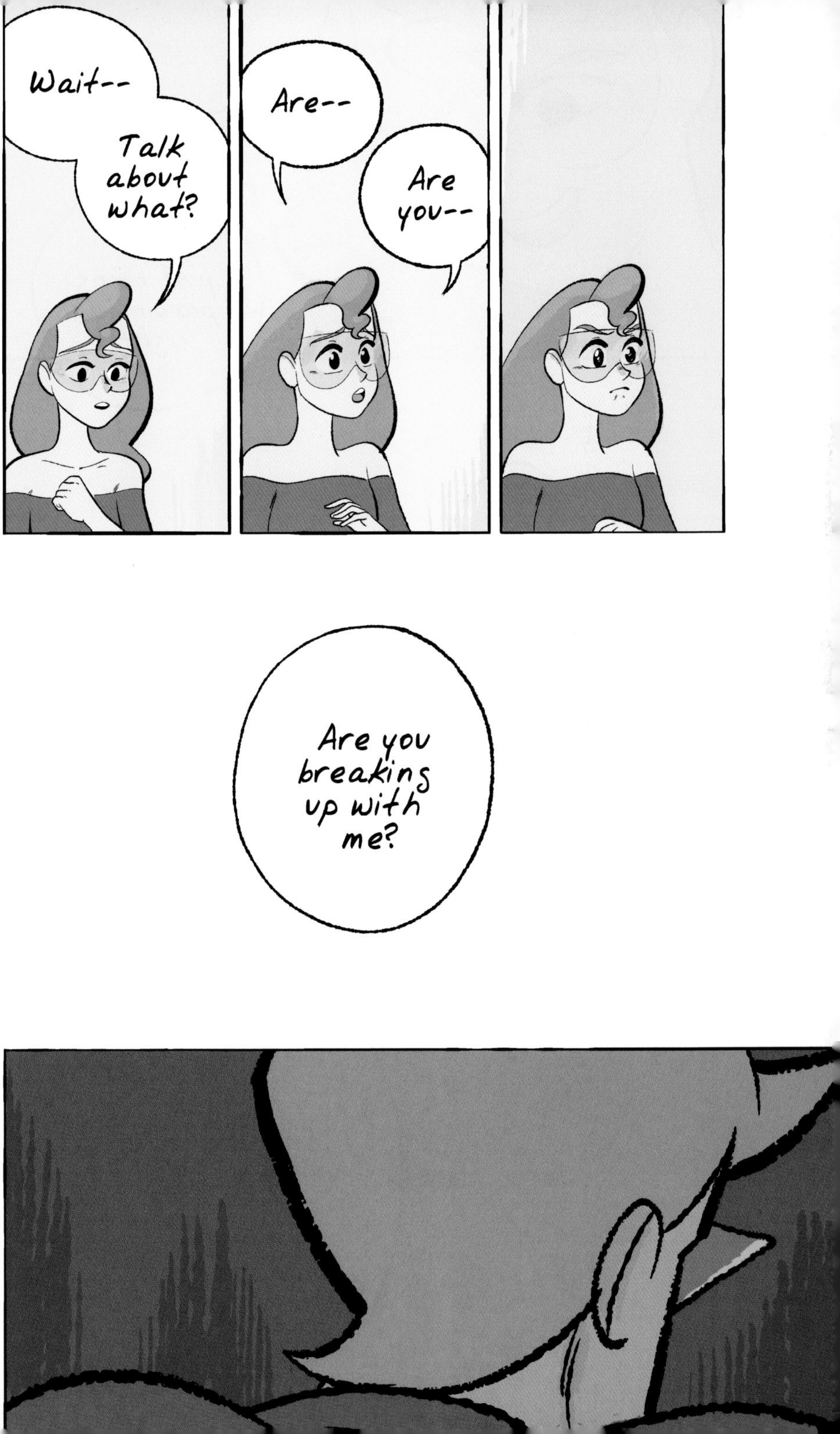
Wait--
Talk about what?
Are--
Are you--
Are you breaking up with me?

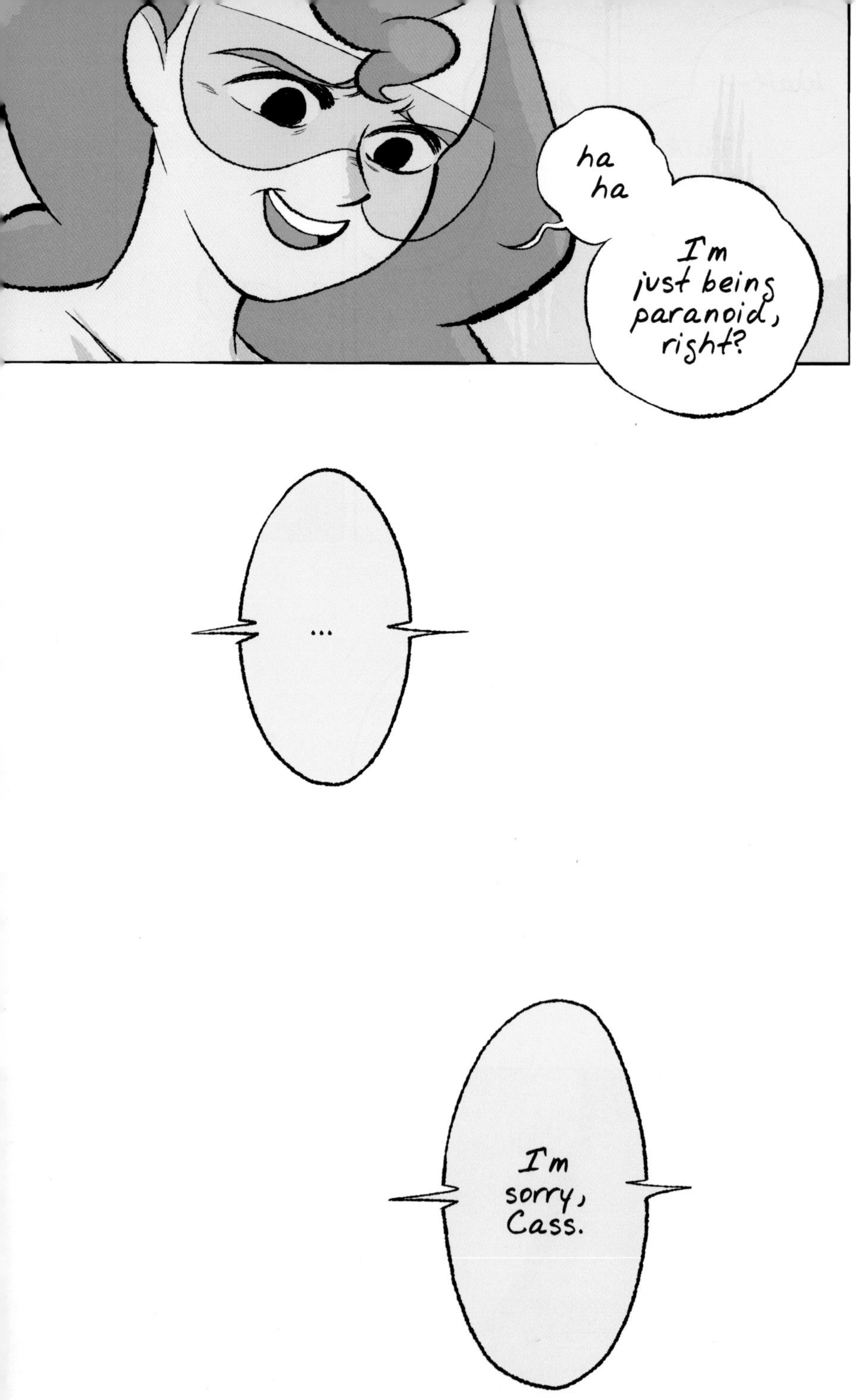
ha ha
I'm just being paranoid, right?
...
I'm sorry, Cass.

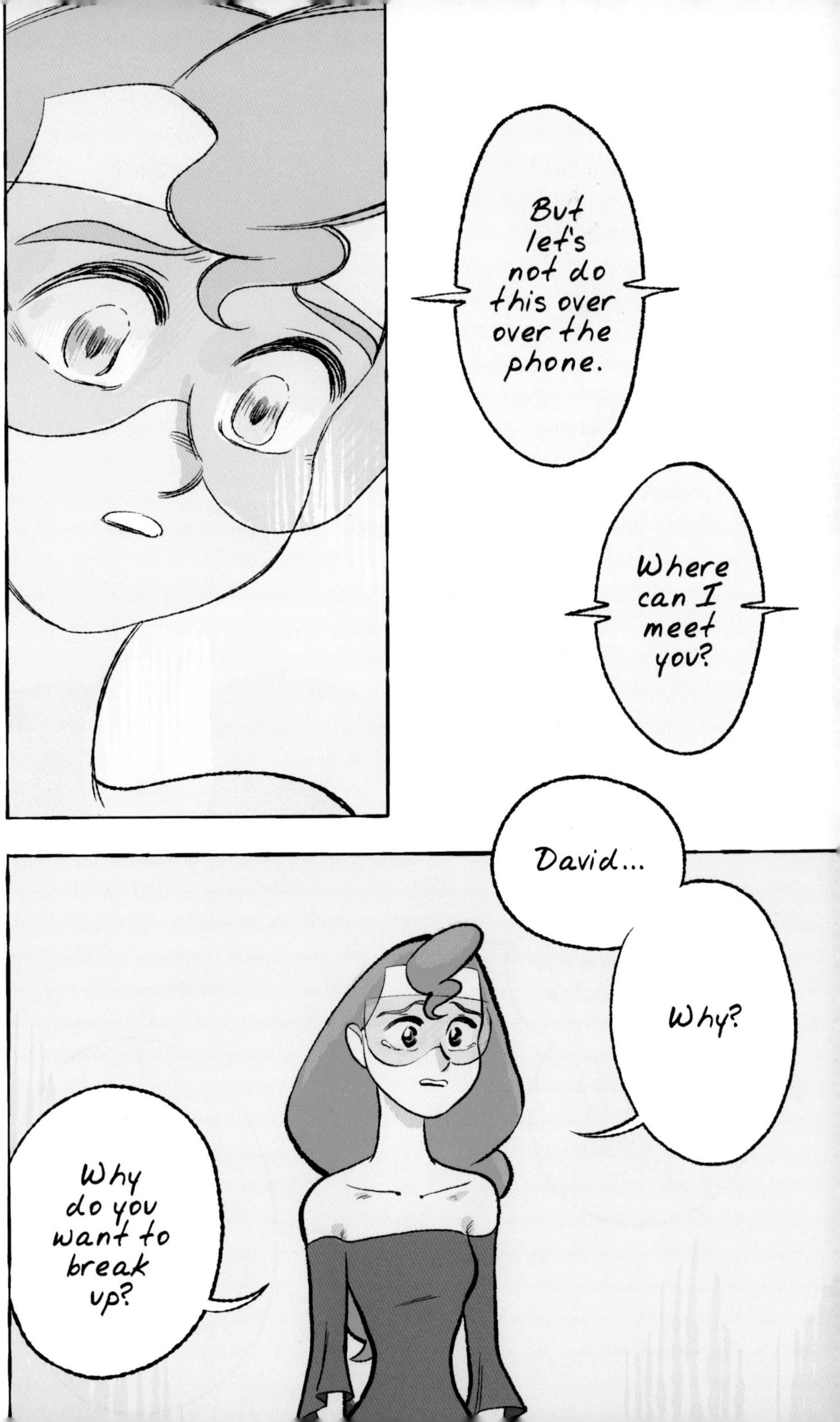
But let's not do this over over the phone.
Where can I meet you?
David...
Why?
Why do you want to break up?

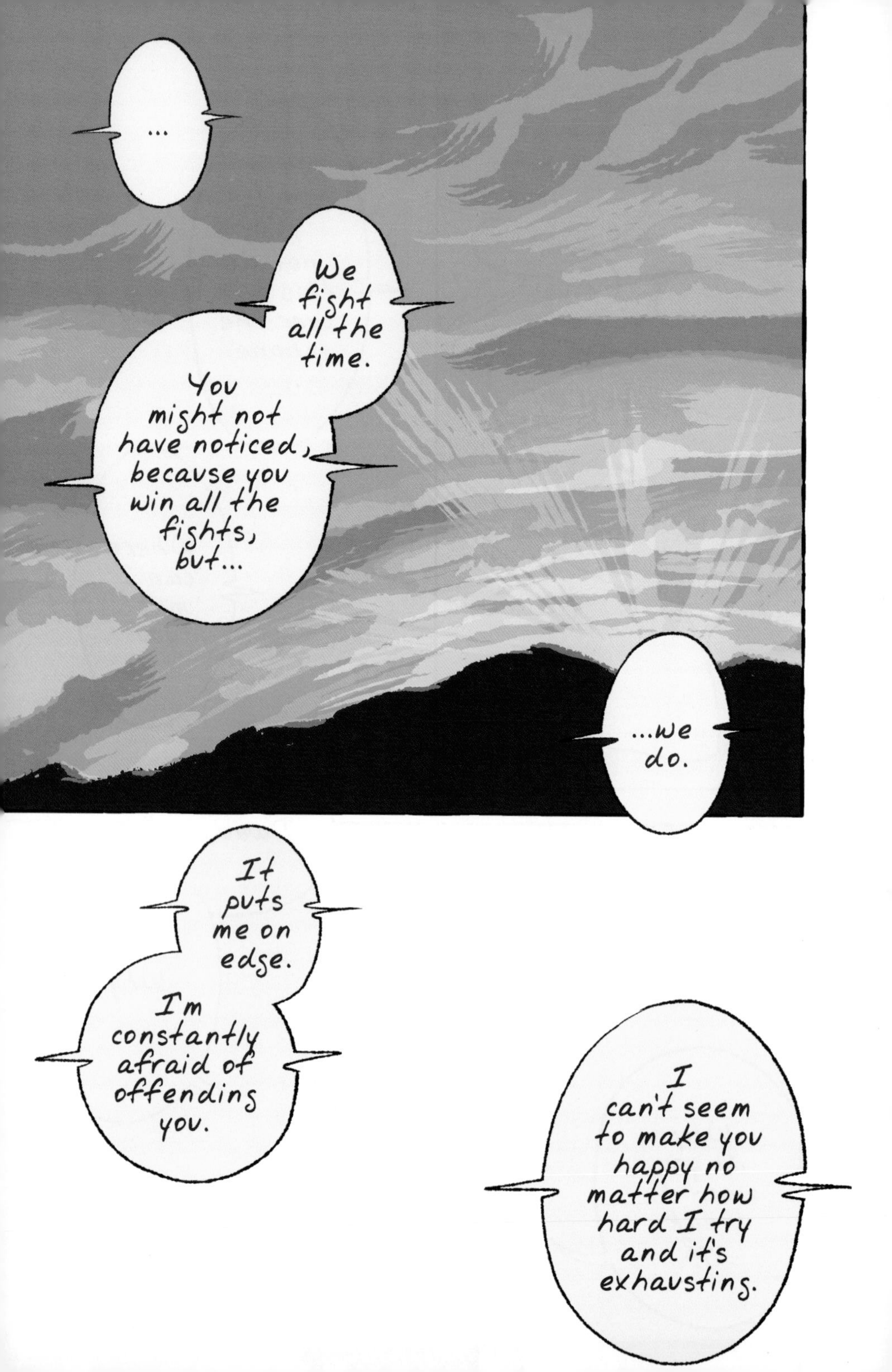
...
We fight all the time.
You might not have noticed, because you win all the fights, but...
...we do.
It puts me on edge.
I'm constantly afraid of offending you.
I can't seem to make you happy no matter how hard I try and it's exhausting.

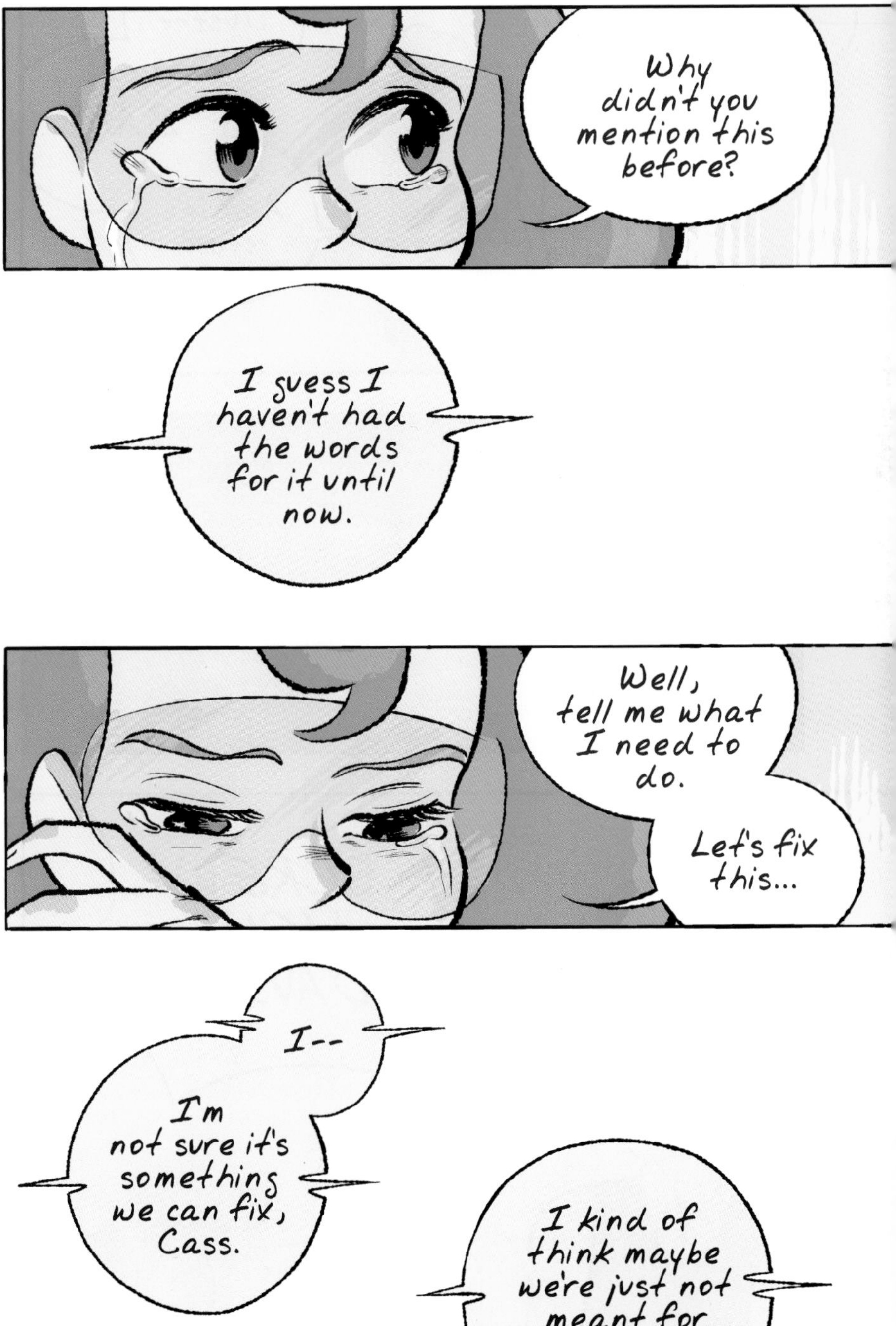
Why didn't you mention this before?
I guess I haven't had the words for it until now.
Well, tell me what I need to do.
Let's fix this...
I--
I'm not sure it's something we can fix, Cass.
I kind of think maybe we're just not meant for each other.

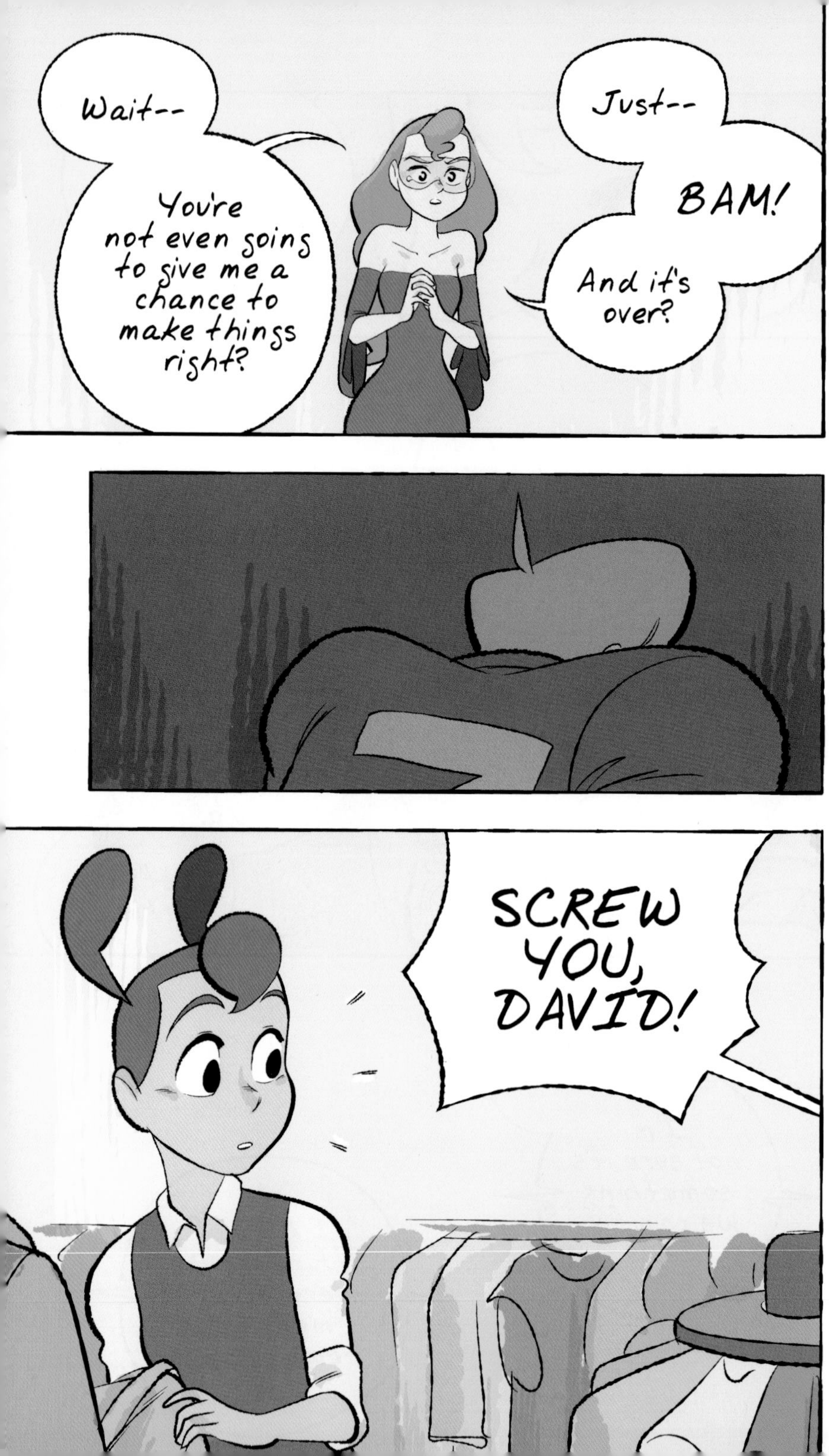
Wait--
You're not even going to give me a chance to make things right?
Just--
BAM!
And it's over?
SCREW YOU, DAVID!

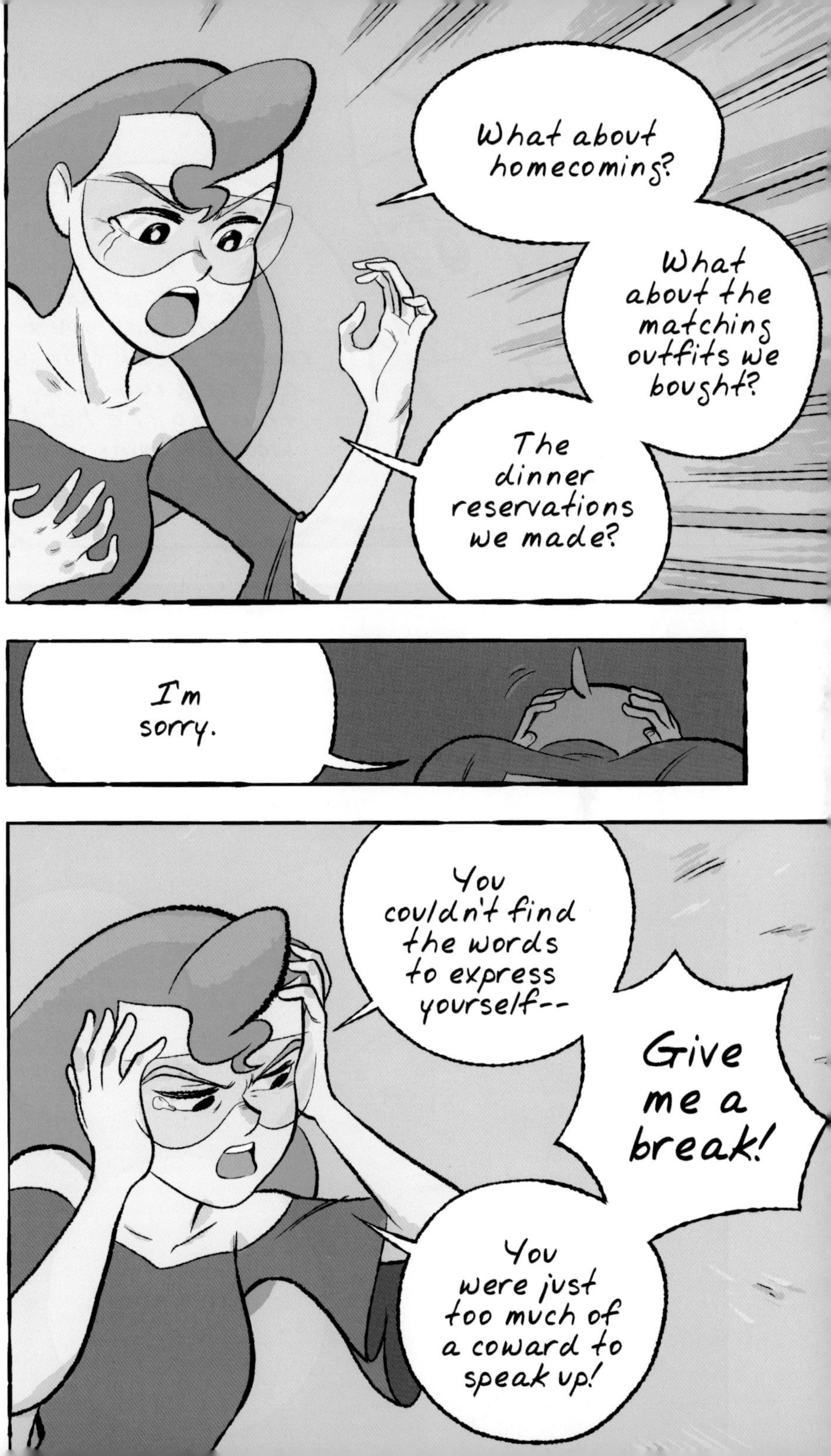
What about homecoming?
What about the matching outfits we bought?
The dinner reservations we made?
I'm sorry.
You couldn't find the words to express yourself--
Give me a break!
You were just too much of a coward to speak up!

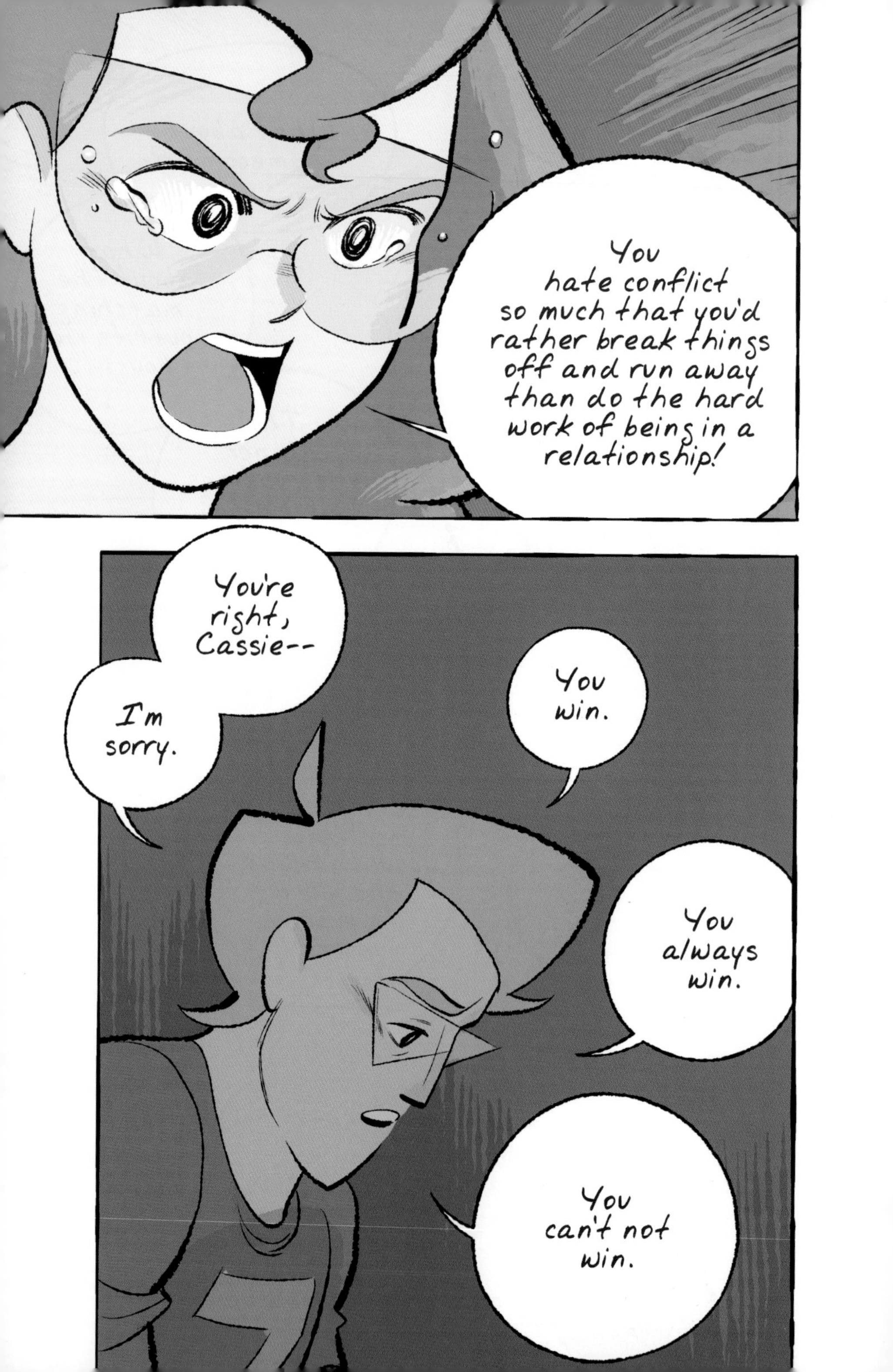
You hate conflict so much that you'd rather break things off and run away than do the hard work of being in a relationship!
You're right, Cassie--
I'm sorry.
You win.
You always win.
You can't not win.

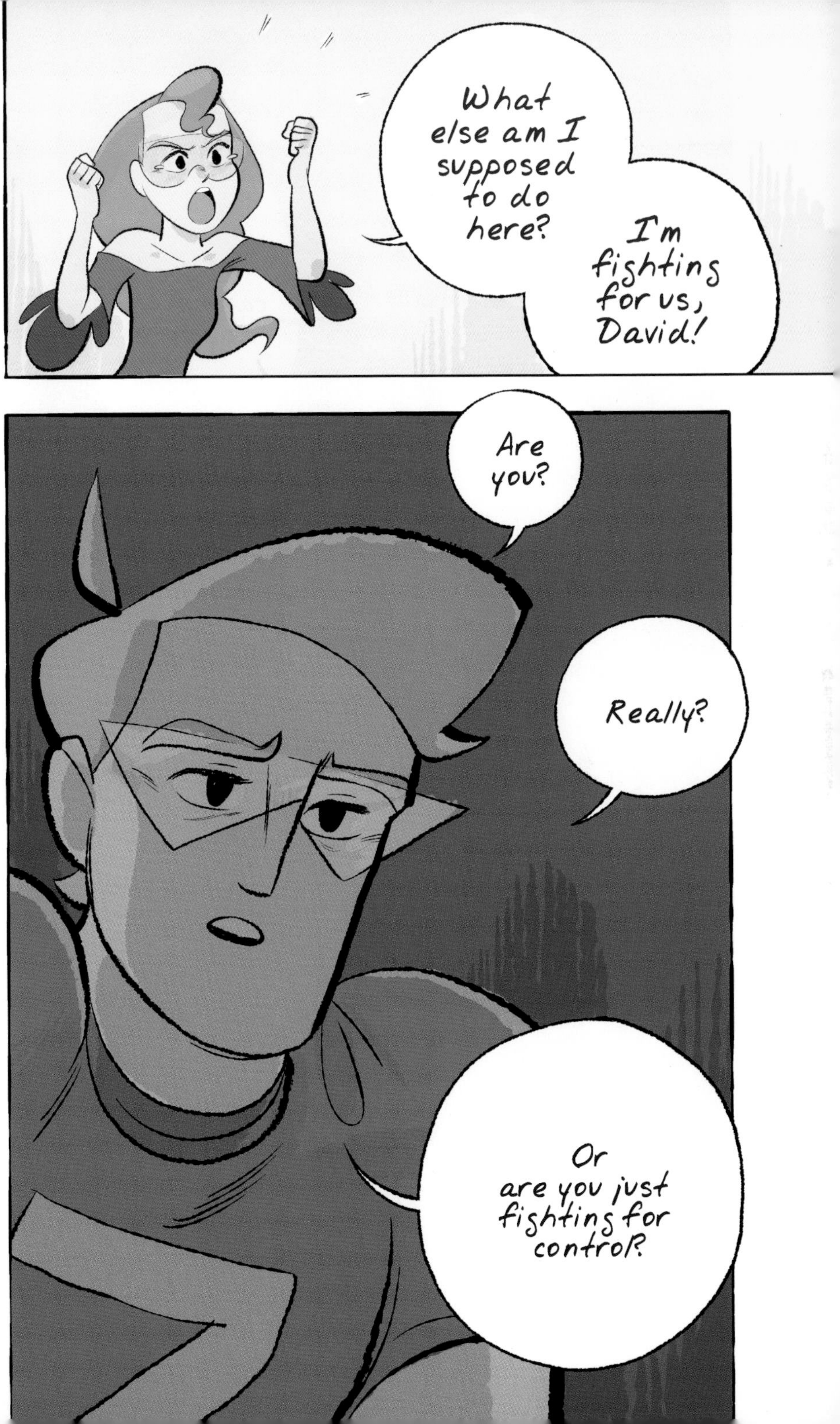
What else am I supposed to do here?
I'm fighting for us, David!
Are you?
Really?
Or are you just fighting for control?

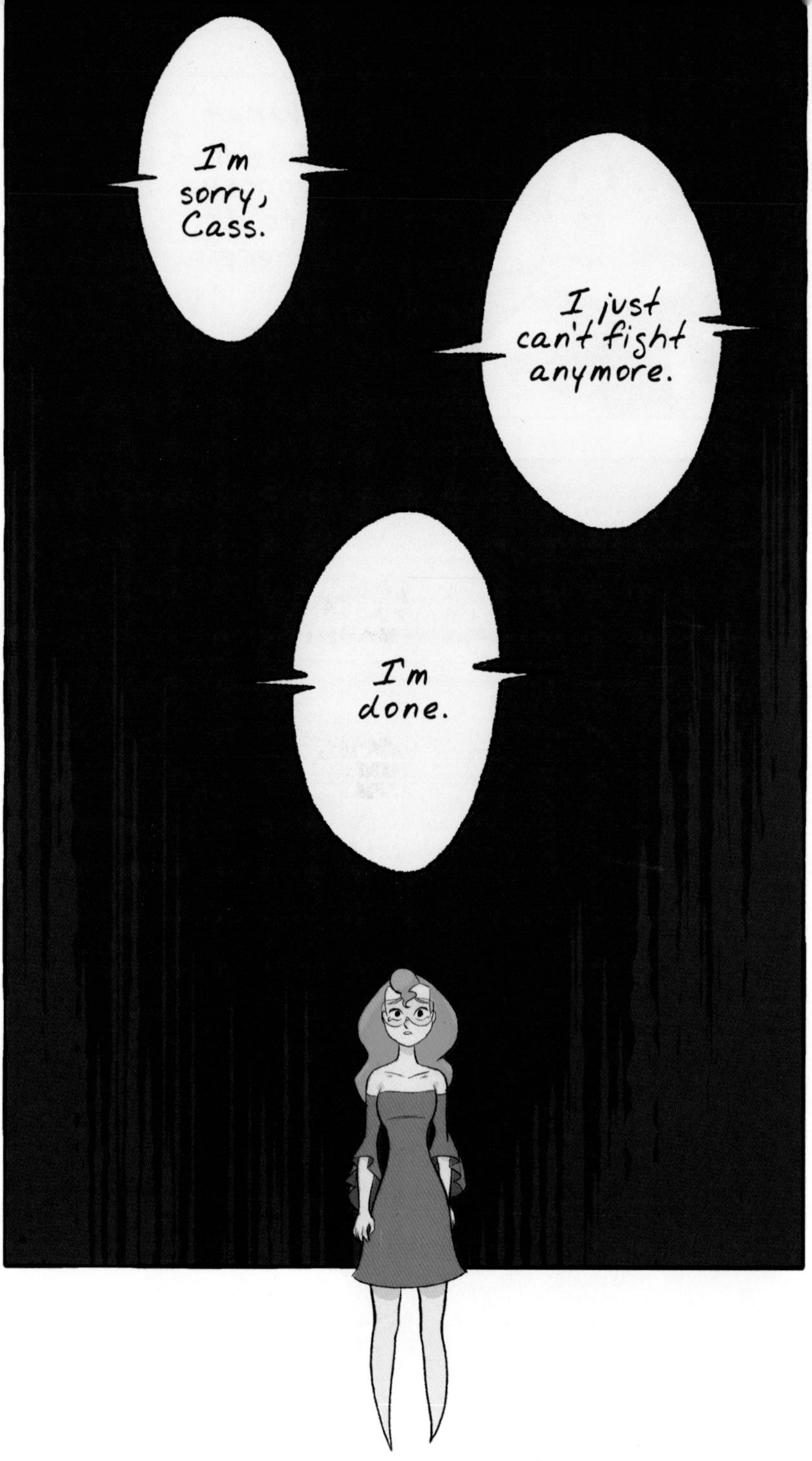
I'm sorry, Cass.
I just can't fight anymore.
I'm done.

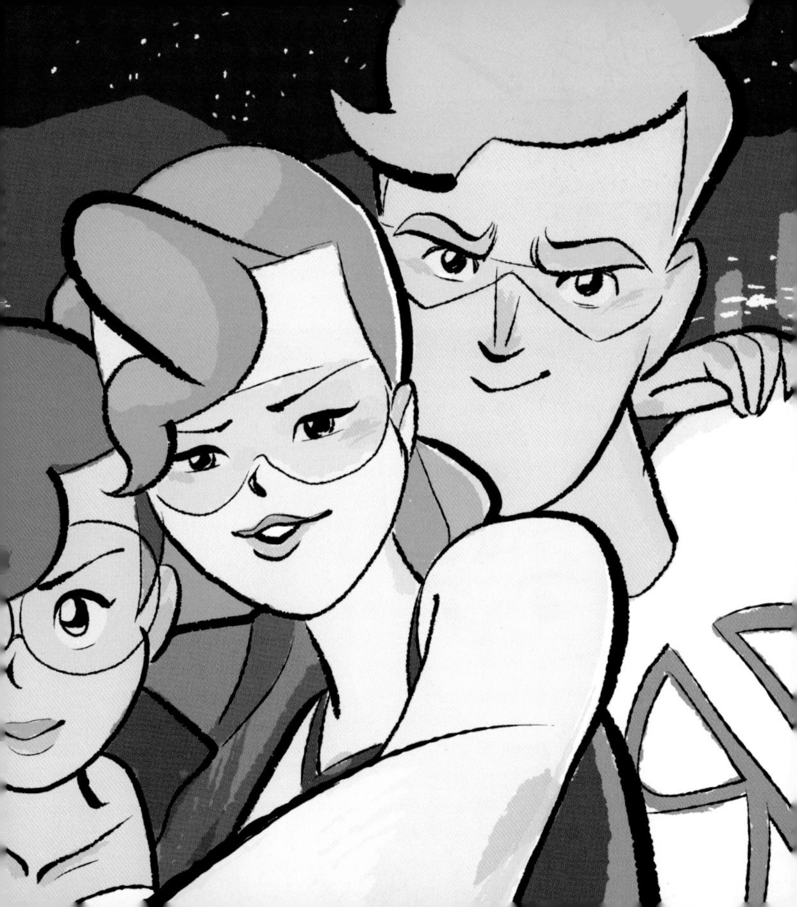

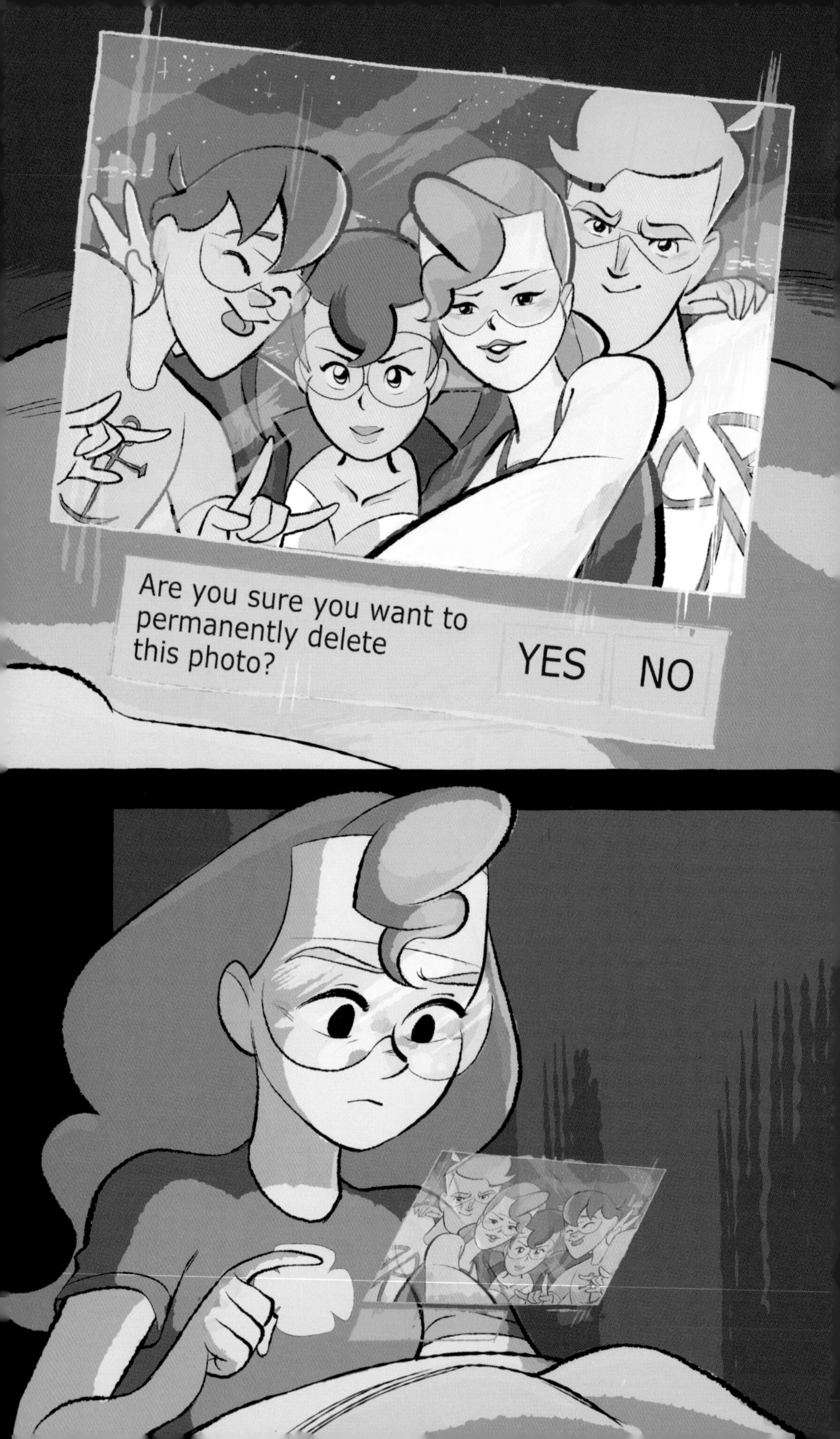

Are you sure you want to permanently delete this photo?
YES
NO

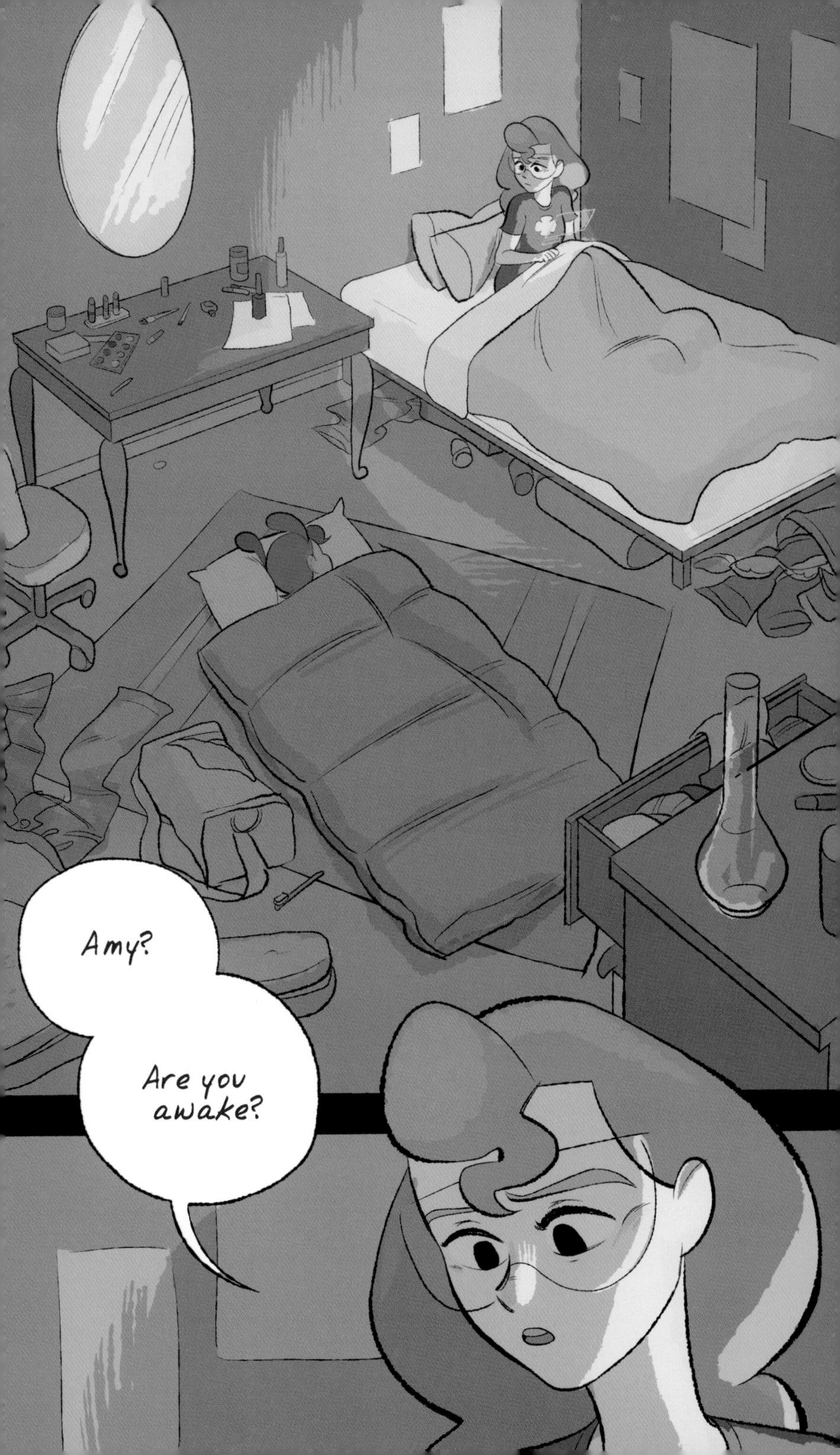
Amy?
Are you awake?

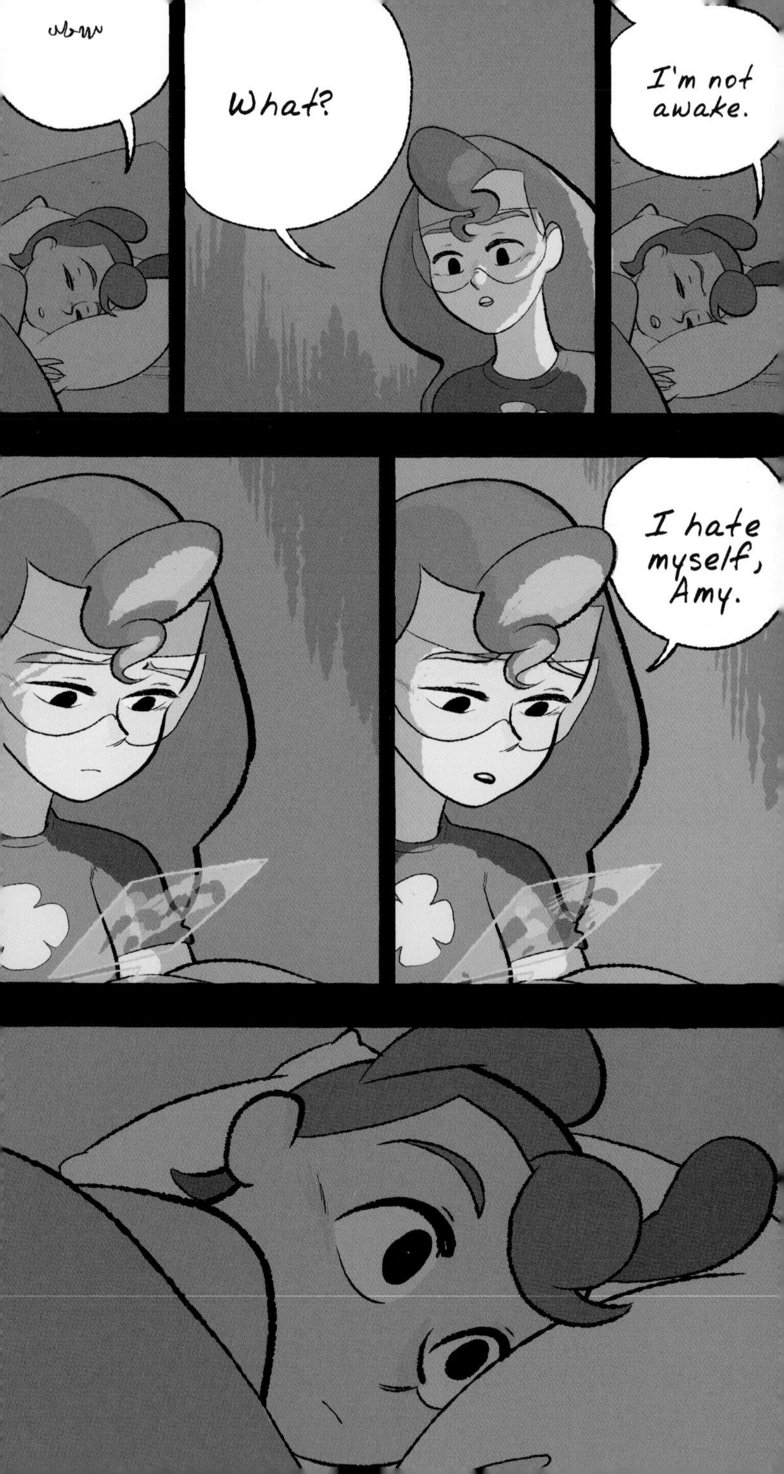
What?
I'm not awake.
I hate myself, Amy.

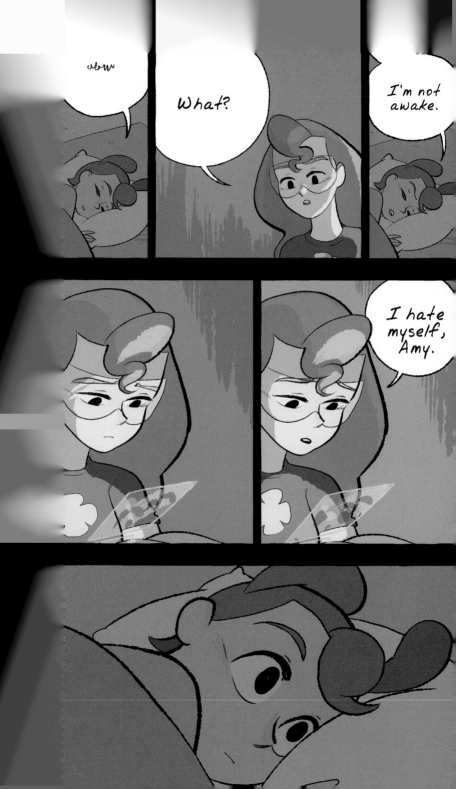

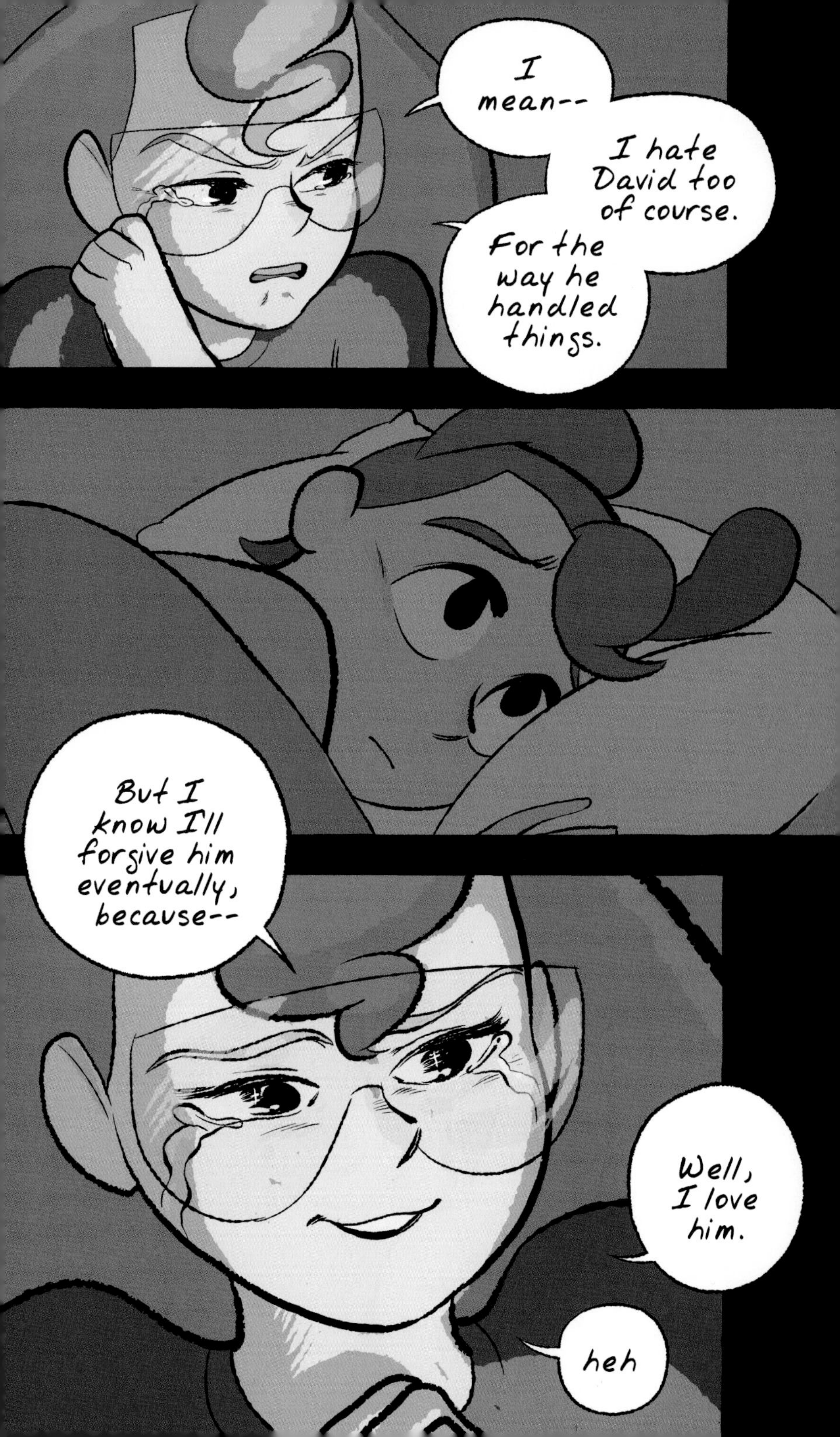
I mean--
I hate David too of course.
For the way he handled things.
But I know I'll forgive him eventually, because--
Well, I love him.
heh

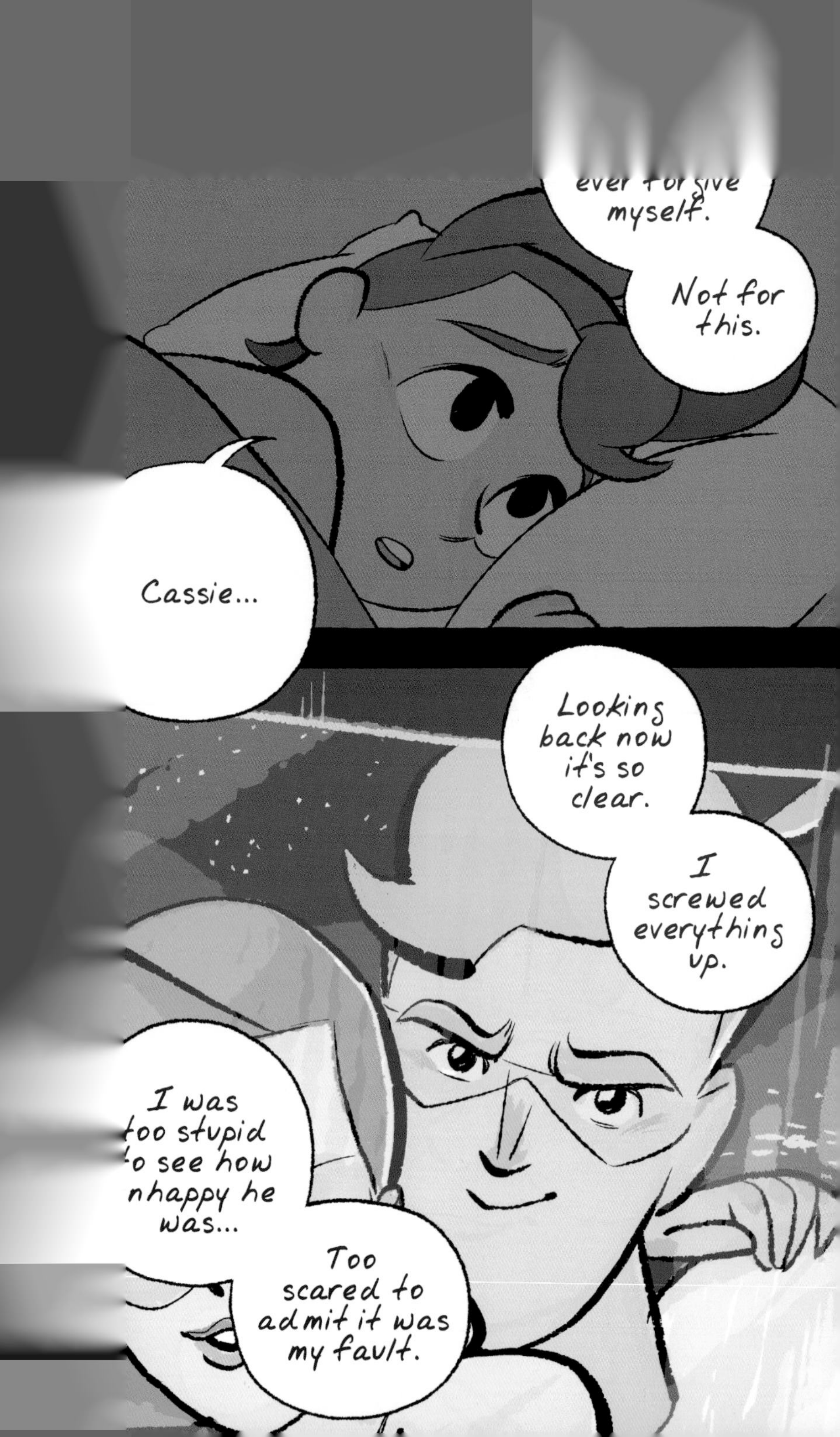

ever forgive myself.
Not for this.
Cassie...
Looking back now it's so clear.
I screwed everything up.
I was too stupid to see how nhappy he was...
Too scared to admit it was my fault.

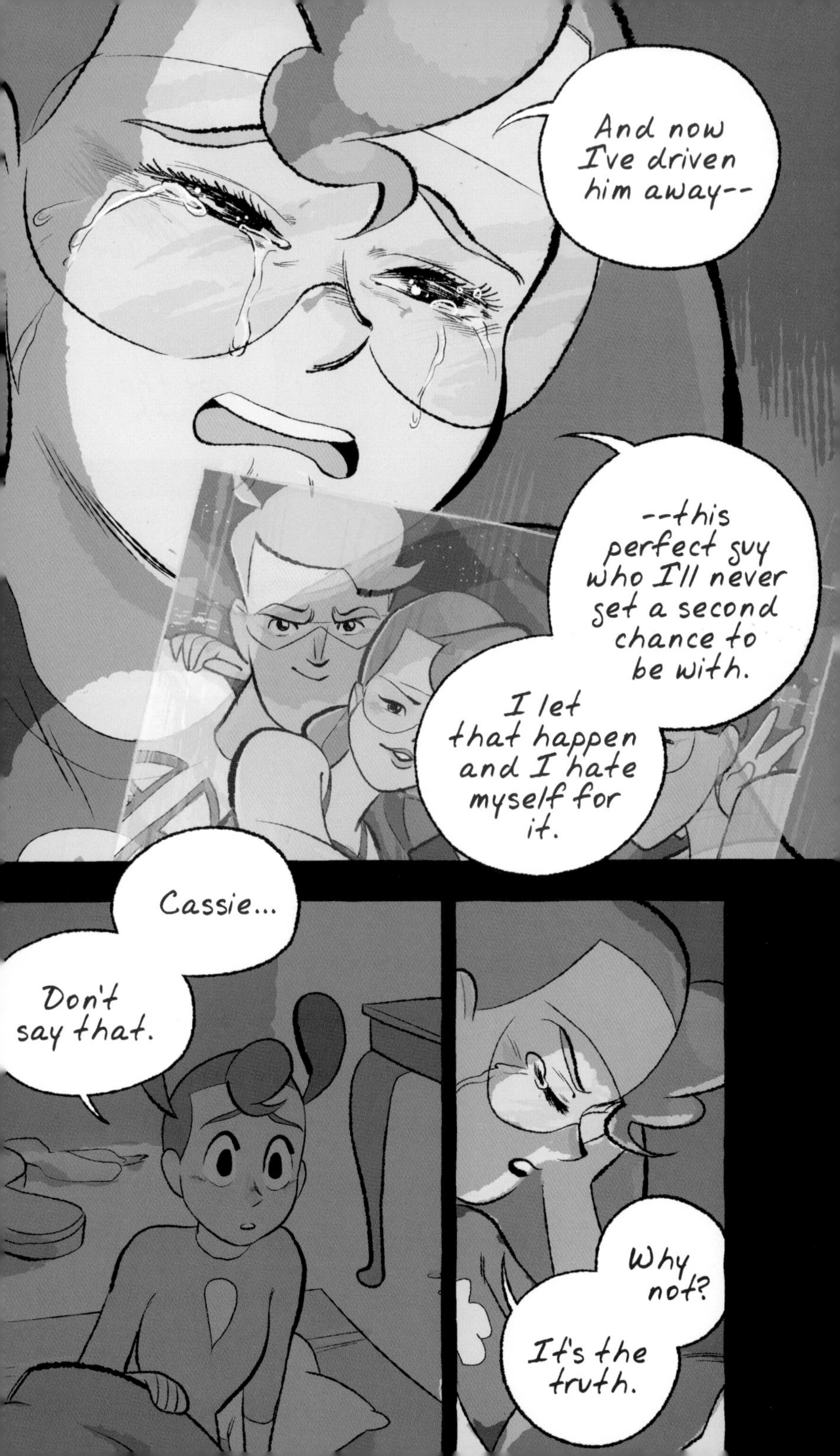
And now I've driven him away--
--this perfect guy who I'll never get a second chance to be with.
I let that happen and I hate myself for it.
Cassie...
Don't say that.
Why not?
It's the truth.

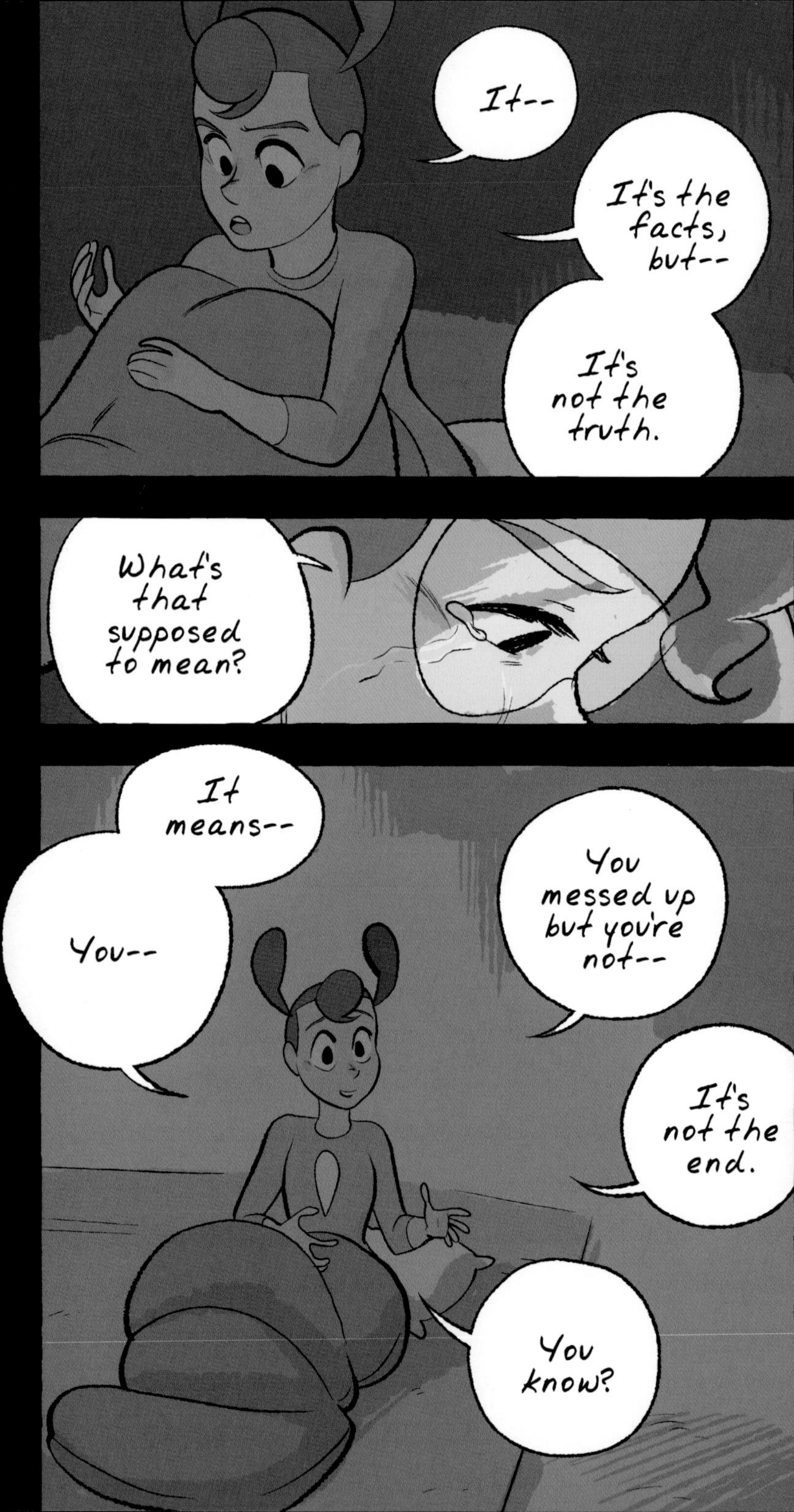
It--
It's the facts, but--
It's not the truth.
What's that supposed to mean?
It means--
You--
You messed up but you're not--
It's not the end.
You know?

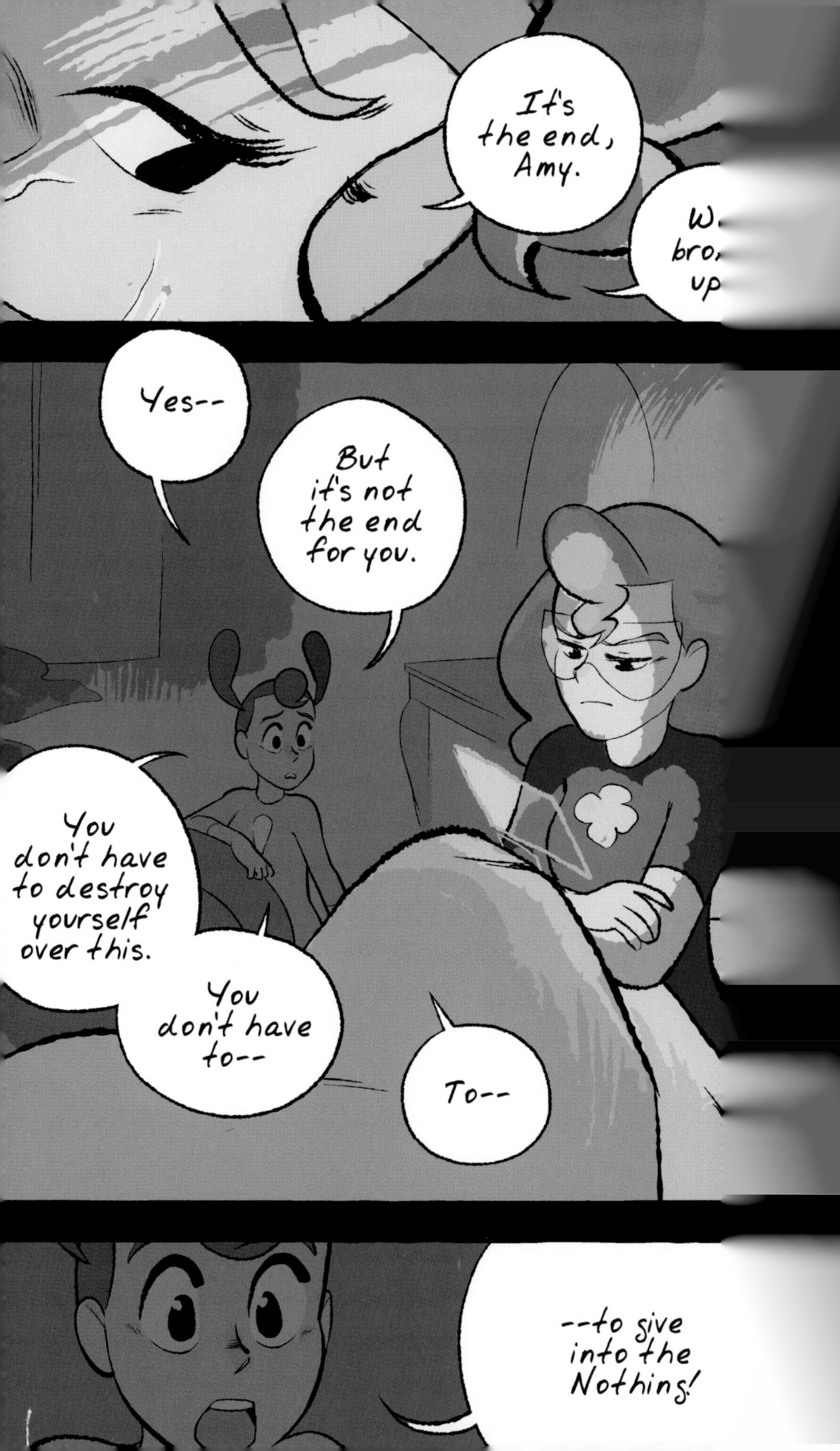
It's the end, Amy.
Yes--
But it's not the end for you.
You don't have to destroy yourself over this.
You don't have to--
To--
--to give into the Nothing!

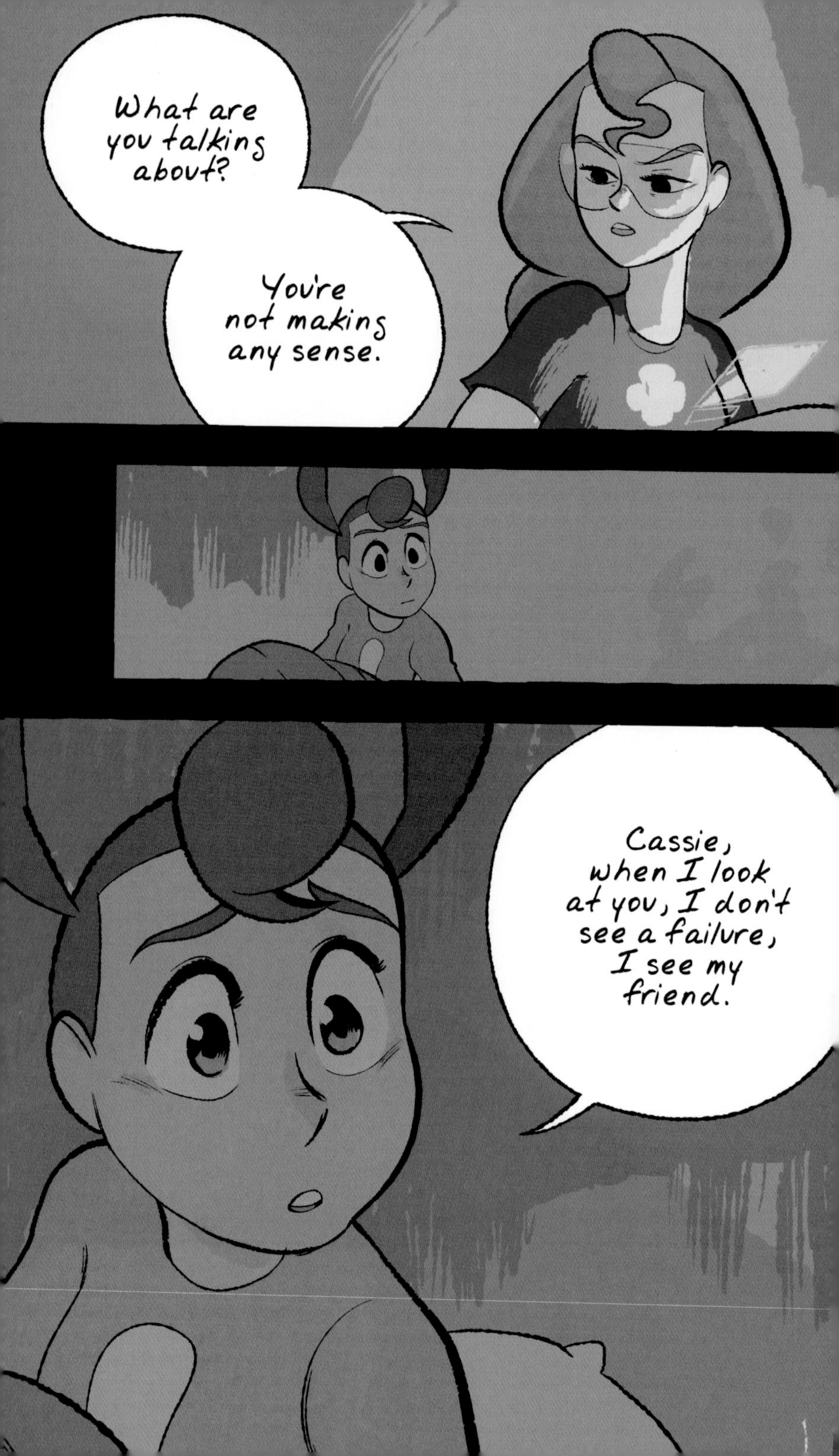
What are you talking about?
You're not making any sense.
Cassie, when I look at you, I don't see a failure, I see my friend.

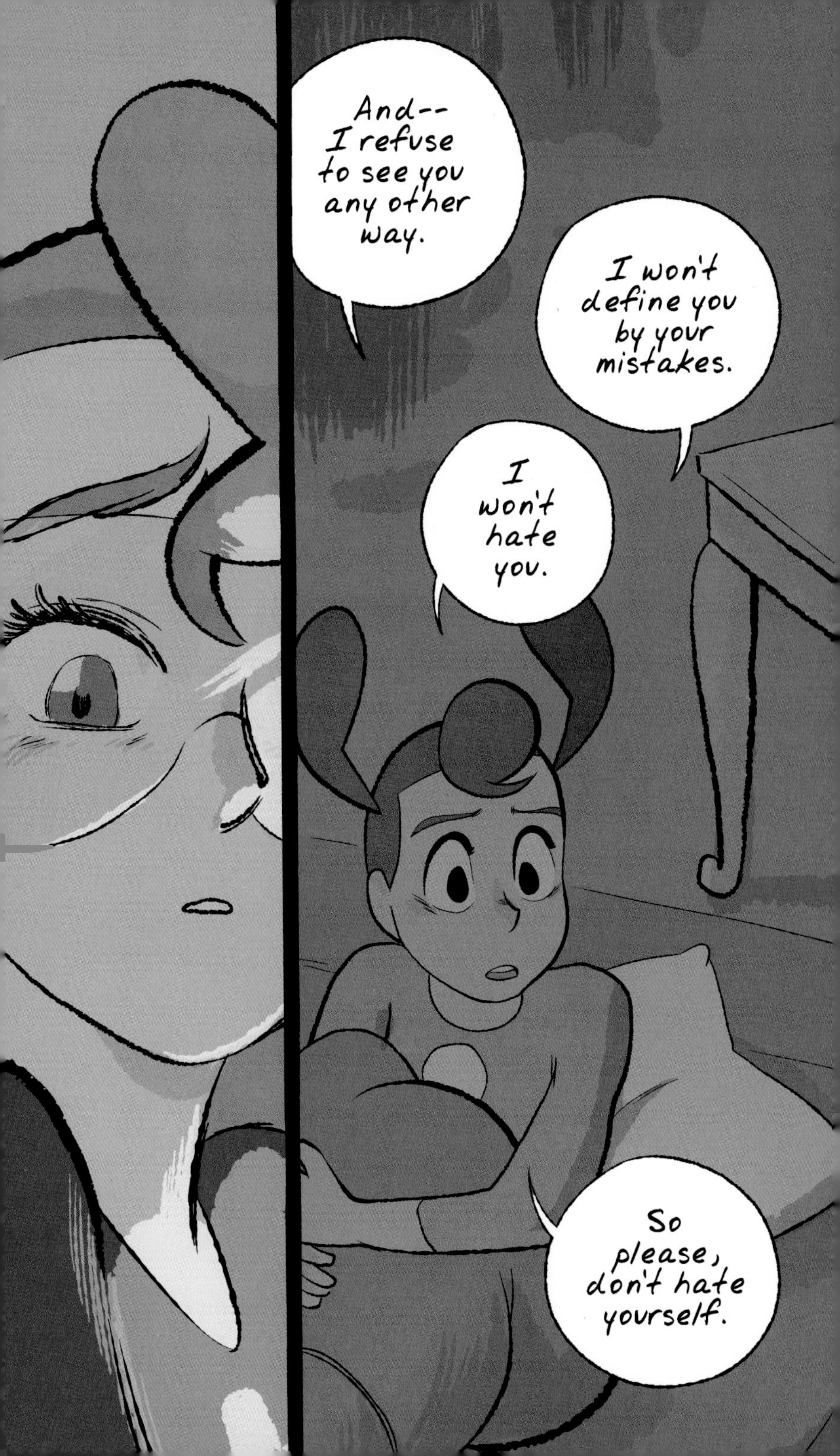
And-- I refuse to see you any other way.
I won't define you by your mistakes.
I won't hate you.
So please, don't hate yourself.

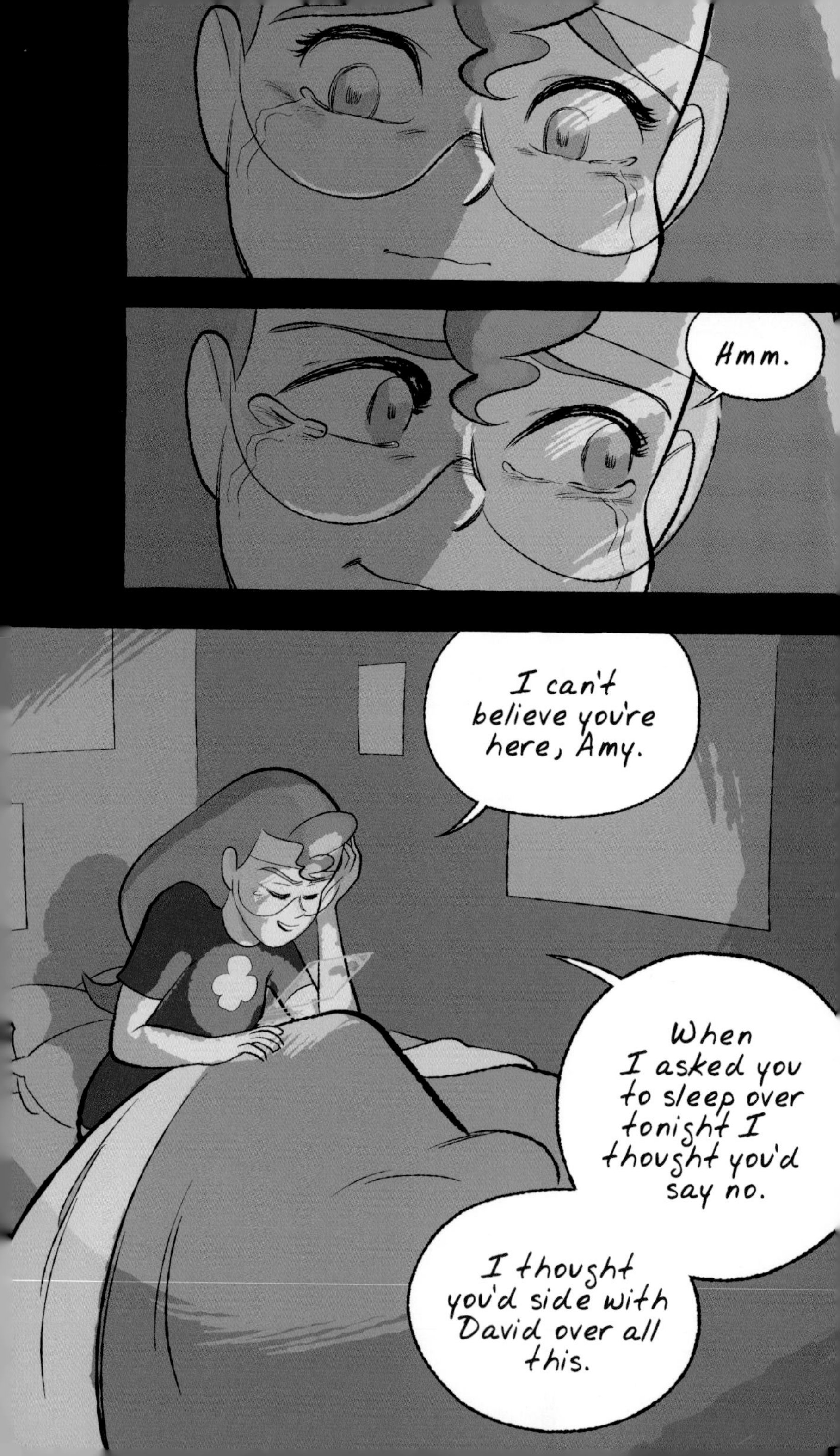
Hmm.
I can't believe you're here, Amy.
When I asked you to sleep over tonight I thought you'd say no.
I thought you'd side with David over all this.

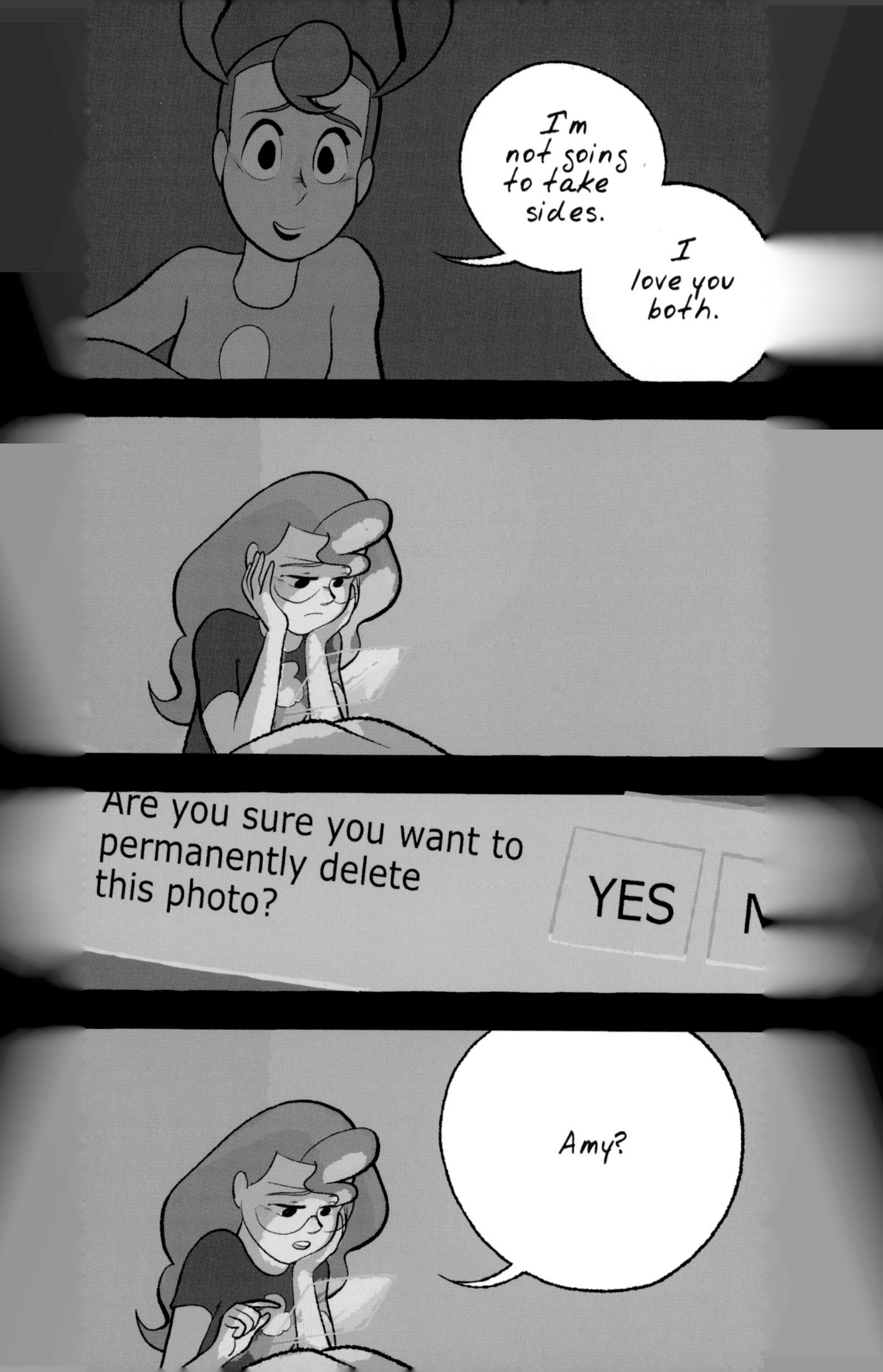
I'm not going to take sides.
I love you both.
Are you sure you want to permanently delete this photo?
YES
Amy?

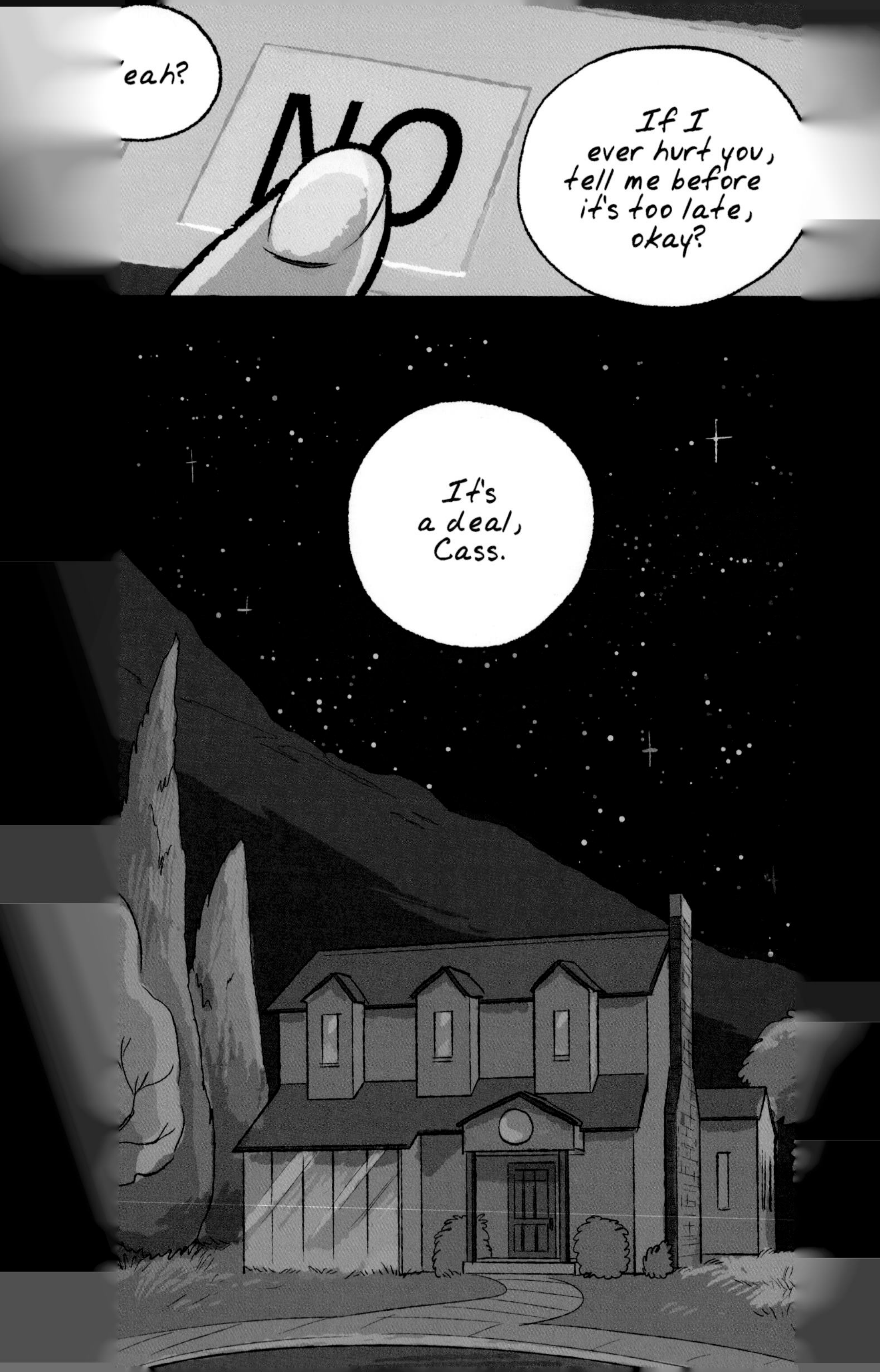

eah?
NO
If I ever hurt you, tell me before it's too late, okay?
It's a deal, Cass.

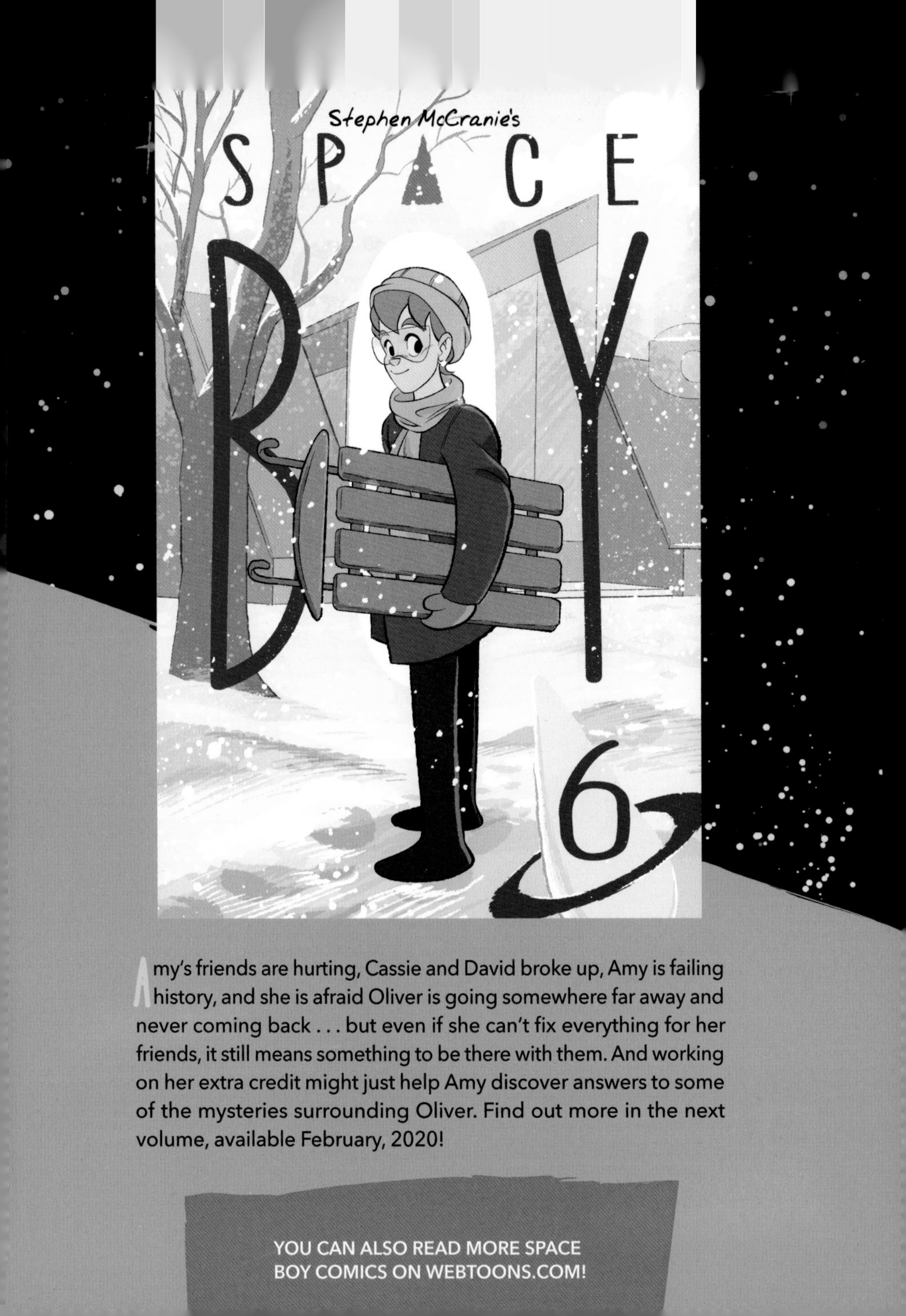
Stephen McCranie's
SPACE
BOY
6

Amy's friends are hurting, Cassie and David broke up, Amy is failing history, and she is afraid Oliver is going somewhere far away and never coming back . . . but even if she can't fix everything for her friends, it still means something to be there with them. And working on her extra credit might just help Amy discover answers to some of the mysteries surrounding Oliver. Find out more in the next volume, available February, 2020!

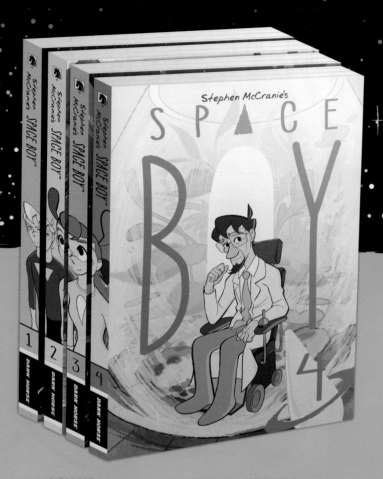